The Orlando File

A MEDICAL CONSPIRACY THRILLER

IAN C.P. IRVINE

ISBN-10: 1484187547
ISBN-13: **978-1484187548**

DEDICATION

To my Mum and Dad.
For all you did for me, and all that I never truly thanked you for.
Thank you.

OTHER BOOKS BY IAN C.P. IRVINE

The Crown of Thorns

London 2012 : What If?

The Sleeping Truth

Haunted From Within

CHAPTER 1
Park Place Apartments
Washington D.C.

"So what?"

It was an incredible quote, and a brilliant way to begin the article. True, it wasn't the most conventional opening line for an important piece of investigative journalism, but who said you couldn't start a story that way?

The CEO of a leading national utility company had been caught with his hand in the till, and when confronted by Kerrin on the phone at his home, he had laughed. Actually laughed.

Perhaps he was drunk, or maybe the CEO was just another of those arrogant bastards that thought he could get away with anything.

Whatever.

Kerrin was going to use the quote, and that was that.

He closed his eyes and imagined the headline of the article in bold print, spread across the top of the page.

"Utility Company Chairman Admits Million Dollar Fraud".

Not bad, but perhaps not good enough. He would fix that later.

First he had to finish the rest of the story.

He focused his concentration back on to the page, his fingers poised lightly on the keyboard and the cursor hanging menacingly above the third line...

There was a shrill, screeching noise in the background, and he bit hard on his lip as he reached for the phone. He hated to be disturbed when he was writing. Since giving up being a cop in Miami and starting from scratch as an investigative journalist at the Washington Post, he spent every day chasing deadlines: and if he didn't get this piece finished in the next five hours, he'd miss Friday's long promised full page spread on Page 3. His best position yet.

"Yes?" he bellowed down the phone.

"Kerrin...is that you?"

"Elizabeth! Sorry, yes, it's me. You just caught me at a bad moment..."

"I'm sorry to disturb you Kerrin, but I need your help. Something...something terrible has happened!"

1

His sister's voice trembled as she spoke the words, and then abruptly she burst into tears.

Kerrin straightened up in his chair, his attention now completely on his sister. "What's the matter? Why are you crying?" In the background Kerrin heard a loudspeaker, announcing the arrival of a flight. "Where are you?"

"I'm at the airport in the Bahamas,… with the kids."

"The Bahamas? What the hell are you all doing there? You're meant to be coming here this weekend…What's going on?"

"I don't know. Martin called me this morning from the office in Orlando, told me not to argue, just to pack as much as I could and catch the first plane to Nassau…He said he'd meet me here this evening. Kerrin, I'm scared…"

"Did he say why?"

"No. There wasn't time to discuss it. We were cut off…but I know it's got something to do with the project he was working on…"

"Which project? He's always working on something that'll 'change the world'."

"Kerrin, don't joke about it. This is serious!…Henry, Tom and Mike are dead! Sam's dead too, and Alex is missing!"

"Dead? What do you mean they're all dead? "

"Exactly that. They're dead!", she shouted back, then started to cry again.

"Elizabeth, take a deep breath. Try to calm down. I'm sure…"

"Kerrin, I'm scared," she continued. "Really scared. According to the police, Tom, Mike, Sam and Henry all committed suicide, or tried to. All in the space of four days of each other."

"That's ridiculous. I was only with Alex and Tom last week when Martin took us out to play golf. They looked a bit stressed, but they definitely weren't suicidal!"

"But now they're dead!… and I think Martin is worried that it might be his turn next. That's why he wants us all out of the country…Kerrin, what do I do? What if he doesn't turn up?"

"Don't worry sis, he will. When's he meant to be arriving?"

"In about two hours. He's flying down in his jet, straight from Orlando."

"Have you spoken to him since?"

"No, nothing…," there was a pause, almost as if his sister was trying to pluck up the courage to say something else. "…But before we were cut off, he insisted that I must get you to come down here as well. He said he needed your help and that it was really important. I know that you don't want to leave Dana alone, but Martin promised that you'd get that big scoop you've always wanted- a front page exclusive. The best story the Washington Post has had for ages! Please come Kerrin…I need you here too…"

CHAPTER 2
The Caribbean Ocean
Day One

The Lear jet flew silently through the cold, dark night. In bright blue fluorescent numbers the digital thermometer indicated that the outside temperature was -40 degrees. Inside the snug, leather lined cabin, Martin held the joystick tightly in his hands and stared out into the sky ahead.

He was flying high above the thin, scattered clouds, the sea far below him. It was fifty minutes since he had taken off from Miami airport, and with the slight headwind, it would be at least another thirty before he landed.

A voice spoke into his earphones, the control tower in Miami handing him over to the air traffic controllers in the Bahamas. He was out of American airspace now.

Martin felt himself relax, his hands slackening their hold on the joystick, the muscles in his arms and wrists losing some of the tension that had gripped his body for the last two months.

No, it was more than stress. Far more than that.

More like fear. Constant fear.

How long could a person live under such tension before having a heart attack? He thought about the other members of his research team, now dead, and his grip on the joystick tightened again.

His eyes scanned the instrumentation panel, registering that everything was okay. The almost full moon drew his attention, and he glanced upwards admiring its beauty.

After the company takeover, the six most important scientists in his team had refused to make the move from Florida to the new corporate headquarters on the West Coast. Not everyone wanted to live in California anymore. Who needed the congested freeways and overpriced real estate? Not to mention the pollution.

No thanks. Florida was just fine.

Until his friends had begun to die.

Or disappear. Like he was doing just now.

A string of 'unfortunate suicides', as the police had officially described them, caused by severe depression brought on from losing their jobs with their company.

From a team of six, in the space of one week, four had become so unhappy that they had all decided to kill themselves?

Not likely.

Martin had known them all. None of them were quitters, and none of them were so unhappy.

Stressed, yes, but for a different reason.

Martin knew exactly why members of his team were dying. They were being silenced, one by one.

Only Alex Swinton and himself were still around from the team that started the Orlando Project and then refused to move to California.

Then this morning Alex had left a message on his private number at work.

"Martin. You'll be next. Get out while you can…"

Was it a threat or a warning? Either way, for Martin it was enough.

It had taken the rest of the day to finalize and assemble the protection he would need for the future. Thankfully, a few days before, he had successfully managed to download all the information he needed about the Orlando Project… just before his network privileges had been revoked…and now he had enough to enable anyone else to repeat the research and the work they had done.

The trip to the airport had been fine. Although he had been on edge all the way from the office to the plane, half expecting to be mugged, or shot, or stopped by someone en route, it had been surprisingly straightforward to load up his plane, fuel it and take off.

He almost wished that he had not taken the last minute precautions: he had been so scared of something happening to him, that he had bundled up the files on the Orlando Project, and put them in a parcel in the post. That way at least, the information would be protected, and if anything happened to him, he would have something to bargain with.

He looked at his Rolex again.

Twenty-eight minutes to go.

It was beginning to look like he had managed to escape safely. Perhaps it would have been better if he had kept the file with him after all.

Park Place Apartments
Washington D.C.

After the phone conversation, Kerrin couldn't concentrate. He had never heard his sister so scared before. She never cried. Never. She was the strong one in the family, the one that was always in control and looking after the other siblings, seldom showing emotion, no matter what trouble they'd all got themselves into. Growing up, she was his rock.

Her words reverberated around his mind, "I need you here…"

He hit the 'save' button on the computer screen, and stored the first three paragraphs of the story. The CEO of Small Holdings had just been granted a last minute reprieve. For now.

Opening up his web browser, Kerrin began to search the internet for flights to the Bahamas. The last flight to Nassau that evening had already left, but according to his favorite travel site, there was another one leaving from JFK at nine the next morning. Kerrin selected a window seat and after putting in his credit card details, he printed off the confirmation and his ticket. He picked up what was left of his rum and coke and walked into the TV room.

Dana, his wife, had nodded off again while watching the Letterman show. He kissed her lightly on the cheek, and she stretched and woke up, throwing Kerrin one of her fantastic smiles.

Just then the phone rang again. Dana spun her wheelchair around and rolled over to the phone table.

"Elizabeth? Is that you? …Yes, Kerrin's right here…"

She held the phone out to Kerrin, covering the mouthpiece as she spoke.

"She's crying her eyes out! Something's wrong…"

He took the phone from her outstretched hand.

It took a while before Kerrin could get his sister to talk calmly. She was babbling almost incoherently.

"…He's dead, Kerrin!…He crashed into the sea!…According to the flight control centre, one minute he was on the radar screen, then the next he wasn't…He just vanished without a trace! Kerrin, they killed him, just like they killed the others! …"

CHAPTER 3
Day Six
Sunny Cove
New Providence Island

The sun rose above a picture postcard sea. Gentle waves slowly lapped long sandy beaches, the calm sea, transparent and turquoise near the shore, transforming abruptly to a vivid deep blue as the coral shelf plunged into the depths further off the island.

It was going to be a beautiful day.

Not so for Kerrin. The past few days had been a living hell. He had arrived at Nassau airport and been greeted by an airport official who had escorted him to a private room, where a female police officer had been comforting his sister. She had spent the night in a hotel, and had been asked to return to the airport the next day to help the police and the airport officials with their enquiries.

Although technically Martin's Lear Jet had not yet entered official Bahamian air space when it vanished, they had been tracking the flight on their radar and had been in voice contact with the pilot. Questions were going to be asked, and if there was going to be an air crash investigation, the trail would start at the air traffic control centre in Nassau.

Elizabeth was in a terrible state. Only after quite a bit of persuasion from Kerrin, had she agreed to take a tranquillizer and go back to the hotel for some sleep. A female police officer had looked after the children for the day, neither of whom had yet been told about the death of their father.

After two days it was becoming clear that there was not really going to be any big investigation. The search for the wreckage and Martin's body had been called off after forty-eight hours. Two helicopters and a light aircraft had scanned the area where the plane had disappeared from the radar, and two ships had criss-crossed the surface of the sea where the plane would have come down. After they had found several pieces of floating fuselage, one with a large letter 'K' written on it, part of the plane's identity number, the search for survivors was abandoned.

It seemed that why the plane had crashed was a mystery that no one would ever be able to explain. It struck Kerrin that since it had happened in international airspace, there was a lack of motivation and accountability for the Bahamian officials to spend any more time or money investigating the cause of the crash.

Four days after the plane accident, Kerrin had taken his sister and her children to the airport and seen her off on an airplane back to the States. She would be met at the airport in Arizona, where she would spend a few weeks with their other sister Jane on their country ranch. Peace and quiet and rest. That's what they needed now.

He stood on the balcony of his hotel room overlooking the bay, watching the holidaymakers and tourists scurrying onto the beach to claim their portion of sun for the day.

It was only 9 a.m. but already most of the beach beds were occupied.

He had always wanted to come to the Bahamas, but had never been able to find the time nor money, and then after his wife had been crippled, overseas travel had become very difficult. Now he was finally here, it was under the worst possible circumstances, and he wasn't in the mood to do any relaxing.

The memory of Elizabeth crying uncontrollably in the small airless office at the airport kicked him hard, and he winced at the thought of the pain she must be going through.

Apart from Dana, he loved his sister more than any other person alive. She and Martin had made a brilliant couple. Sure, they had had their problems, but so did everybody. Martin was a workaholic, never really spent enough time at home with the kids or Elizabeth. At first she had hated playing the patient mistress to his work, but after a few years she came to accept it, taking comfort from the fact that Martin was driven by the will to save lives and was working on something that one day could change the world. Or so he always claimed. Truth was that neither Elizabeth nor Kerrin really understood exactly what it was that Martin did. It was just too complicated.

Kerrin and Dana owed a lot to his sister and her husband. After their accident, they had spent several months at Martin's house in Florida. Their nephew and niece had helped to take their minds off themselves, and Elizabeth had been a tower of strength. Without her, Kerrin didn't know how he would have got through it all.

After the accident Kerrin needed to spend more time with Dana, and it was obvious he couldn't carry on being a cop in Miami: it was too dangerous, the hours were too long, and Dana worried too much. Now she depended upon him, he could no longer take risks with his own life. He needed to be there for her. To look after her. It was Martin who suggested the job at the Washington Post, and he had pulled a few strings on Kerrin's behalf to help get him the interview.

It was tough making the move to Washington, but the job at The Washington Post, in theory, should have been quite interesting. "Being an investigative journalist," he was promised, "is an exciting job. With your background, you'll do great!"

Well, so far, it wasn't working out as exciting as he had hoped for. Too much 'desk' and not enough 'action'.

Still, he owed a lot to Martin and Kerrin was grateful. Unfortunately, he had never really got to know Martin well and now he was dead, Kerrin wished he had made more of an effort to talk to the man his sister had chosen to marry.

Martin was an intellectual. Never really got emotional, or showed that he was upset. A straight talker, independent and strong, he didn't exaggerate, and always called it like it was. If Martin had told Elizabeth that he had needed Kerrin's help, and that 'it was important', then Kerrin knew that it had to be something big.

It was the first time Martin had asked Kerrin for anything, and dead or not, Kerrin still owed it to him to find out what had happened.

He had decided to stay on in Nassau another two days, wanting to spend more time with the authorities and hoping to gain some information, or a few leads to go on.

He had already placed a call to his boss on the newspaper in Washington and had managed to persuade him into financing his trip to the Bahamas. He had been working at the Washington Post for just over five years now, and although he wasn't the best writer or journalist on the newspaper, he was pretty high up there in the ranking of upcoming stars. So far he hadn't come across any Watergate exposés or Iran-Contra affairs, but there had been the Albuquerque Housing Scandal, and the Wright Fund Fraud. They had both been his. It was only a few years, Kerrin reckoned, before he got his own column.

"Listen Paul," he told his boss on the phone earlier. "I can't guarantee anything, but I think I'm onto something. A group of top researchers working for a genetics company, officially lose their jobs and then all commit suicide in the space of one week. And then last night, the last surviving member is trying to escape to the Bahamas, when his plane mysteriously disappears."

"What do you mean 'escape'?" Paul replied. Kerrin could hear the tell-tale sounds of his boss pushing back his chair, and putting his feet up on his office desk. He had taken the bait.

"An inside contact told me he was trying to get abroad as soon as possible before he was found dead just like the others. He didn't want to become another suicide. I was meant to meet him here, then the next thing you know, his plane vanishes."

"Could be coincidence?"

"Could be, but unlikely. With your permission I want to sniff around a bit and see where it takes me?"

There had been a moment's pause. 'Sniff around' invariably meant 'expense account' and things had become tight at the newspaper recently. Sales were down.

"Okay, Kerrin. Okay. But you're not one of the big time front page guys yet, so go easy on the cash. No five star hotels. Call me in a few days and let me know what you get. In the meantime, I'll give your other work to Ed Harper. Any problem with that?"

"None. Ed's a good guy." Kerrin replied, trying to hide his feelings towards the new man on the paper. Ed was hungry just like Kerrin was, and if he was completely truthful, Kerrin was jealous of him.

He closed the balcony window and stepped back into the bedroom, pausing to look at himself in the full-length mirror hanging on the wardrobe door.

The job at The Washington Post didn't really give him the chance for much exercise. In the past three years, he had really begun to put on weight, and now he looked in the mirror he realized just how much it had begun to show.

He was no longer the young man he used to be. He was only thirty eight, but he looked it. He was tall, just short of six foot, broad-shouldered and still quite muscular. Last time he had checked he was 178 pounds. When he had been on the force, he had an amazing six pack, was well toned, fit, and the girls loved him. Kerrin knew that it was his looks that had first attracted Dana to him the night they met at the Police Ball. Unfortunately, now that he was stuck behind a desk at The Post most of the time, the extra pounds had begun to roll themselves too easily into what his English friends would call a 'beer-belly', and what Elizabeth called his 'one-pack'.

Thankfully, it wasn't too late to save his figure. A bit of exercise and Kerrin would be able to get back the body he used to have.

"I need to go to the gym!" he promised himself. "...Just as soon as I finish this story."

He had been promising himself that for the past five years, but had never got round to it. Once he had even paid the membership fees and joined a local health club. Although he never went once, the mere act of joining made him feel better for a month, and he told all of his friends how much healthier he was going to become...then the excuse wore off, and he just never seemed to mention it again.

Luckily, while many of his friends had long ago lost most of their hair, Kerrin still had a full head of brown locks, which were perfectly coordinated with his dark brown eyes.

All in all, in spite of his 'beer' belly, Kerrin was a good looking man. But his best feature was his fantastic smile. When Kerrin smiled at someone, the other person had no choice but to smile back. It was unfair, but people couldn't help but like him. He made them feel happy. A useful skill which helped whenever he was chasing a story and Kerrin was trying to befriend people and encourage them to divulge information.

Hopefully the smile would work its magic in the next few days.

That morning he made no progress in coaxing more information from the airport authorities, so he decided to take a drive up the coast to the north part of the island, and to talk to the captains of the boats that had found the plane wreckage. Maybe there would be a clue there. If nothing else, it would be a pleasant drive, and it would give him the chance to plan what he would do when he returned to the States.

CHAPTER 4
Wharf Tavern
Paradise Island

By the time he hit the road, it was almost eleven o'clock, and already the heat was becoming uncomfortable. How could anyone live without air conditioning? Pulling out of the hotel and heading west, he crossed the bridge that connected New Providence Island to the smaller Paradise Island.

The road to the north side of the tiny Paradise Island ran along the edge of the sea, through many of the resorts where the tourists flocked to from all over the world. Names like 'Paradise Resort', 'Smugglers Haven' and 'Golden Sands Marina' passed by, large pictures of the complexes inside appearing on enormous billboards beside the road. In between the buildings and tall roadside vegetation, once or twice Kerrin got a quick flash of a beach, palm trees swaying gently over snowy white sands, people drinking cocktails and paddling lazily through the inviting turquoise sea.

In spite of the melancholy that he had woken up with, he began to feel slightly better, and by the time he was nearing his destination, he was in a much sunnier mood.

'The Wharf Tavern' was tucked away at the back of the main harbor that serviced the north side of the island. It was here that the police had told him he would be most likely to find either of the two captains from the boats that had found the wreckage of the Lear jet.

'The Sea Dancer' and the 'Highland Glen' were the two ships that had assisted the coast guard in the sea search and, although all the wreckage had been shipped to the main police station in Nassau for closer examination and possible forensics, Kerrin was hoping that chatting to the crew members would throw a little more light on what had happened.

The barmaids were just clearing up from serving lunch when Kerrin walked in the door, finding about twenty people dotted around the interior of the bar.

It took a moment for Kerrin's eyesight to adjust to the dim interior from the bright sunshine outside, and as he stood in the doorway, he could feel the eyes of the locals scanning him up and down, wondering who the new stranger in town was.

It was that sort of bar. Everyone knew each other, and if they didn't know you, you were either trouble, or not worth knowing.

"Hello, what can I get you?" the barman asked, leaning with two heavy hands against the side of the bar, a white towel hanging over his shoulder like some theatrical prop, shirt sleeves rolled up to his elbows and a large colorful tattoo proudly displayed on his right forearm. His big, fluffy grey moustache bristled as he spoke.

"One of your very best cold beers please. And if you have any sandwiches, that would be great too?" Kerrin replied, plopping himself down on one of the tall bar stools running along the edge of the bar.

"New in town?" the barman asked, immediately probing for information. Obviously the local oracle, the man who made everybody's business his own.

"Yeah... I was hoping to find the Captains of the Sea Dancer and the Highland Glen?"

"Ah, anything to do with the airplane that went down the other day?" the barman asked, putting down a large frost covered glass full of blonde beer.

"That's the one. Any idea where I can find them?"

"Sure, about a hundred and fifty miles out on the Dardenal Banks, probably drift netting by now. They left early yesterday."

Kerrin had not reckoned with the fact that they might not be there. It had not occurred to him that the fishermen might actually be out fishing.

"Any idea when they will be back?" he asked, the disappointment showing in his voice.

"Probably sometime next week, depending upon the weather...or their luck, but normally they're away for a week. They're both part of the Dawson Fleet. Big boats. Can stay out for up to a month if they need to."

"Just my luck." Kerrin picked up the large beer, wiping some of the condensation off the side of the cold glass, before taking a long drink. "Ahhh...nothing better on a hot day like this."

The barman left to serve another customer, then returned a few minutes later with a large ham sandwich, garnished with salad and a succulent green pickle.

As Kerrin fought with the sandwich, trying to pick it up with his two hands without the contents spilling out all over the counter, the barman looked him up and down, playing with the edge of his moustache, twirling it back and forth between his fingers, before coming to some sort of decision.

"Of course, you could try talking to Old Ben over there. His ship was out there too. He might be able to tell you something." The barman volunteered, pointing to the far corner of the bar, to a man probably in his early seventies, reading the paper and smoking a pipe.

Kerrin finished his sandwich and ordered two more beers, picking them up and taking them over to the table Old Ben occupied in the corner.

"Mind if I join you?" Kerrin asked, offering the beer to the old mariner. He looked up at Kerrin, his rugged face ridden with lines from years of exposure to the elements and all that the sea could throw at him.

"It's a free world. Do as you please."

Kerrin sat down opposite the man, studying him quickly and noticing that the tips of two fingers on his left hand were missing.

"I hear you were out at sea when the plane went down the other day?"

The old man's eyes brightened slightly, and he reached for the beer in front of him.

"Took your time, didn't you?"

"What do you mean?" Kerrin asked, a little surprised.

"I mean, it's been almost a week since I reported it. That's what I mean!" he said, a slight cockney English accent detectable in his voice, immediately reminding Kerrin of his earlier childhood. Kerrin had been born to a Scottish father and American mother, and after spending his first seven years in Scotland, they had moved to London, England for three years, before Kerrin's parents had finally moved back to the US.

"Reported what?" Kerrin asked.

"The explosion. The cop on the phone said they'd send someone out, but it's taken you a whole week to come and ask me questions! Maybe I've forgotten the details by now. I'm an old man, after all," he replied, before puffing on his pipe and turning to look out the window.

Kerrin was confused. What was the man talking about? The police had only mentioned two boats. Neither of which had reported seeing any explosion.

And if Old Ben had seen something, why had they called off the investigation before they had interviewed him?

"I'm sorry. I'm not with the police. To be quite honest, I'm a relative of the man who died in the plane crash. I'm just trying to find out what really happened. The police don't seem to know anything." Kerrin replied.

The old man turned to look at Kerrin again, appraising him afresh.

"Sorry son. That's different then. It's just that nowadays no one is interested in what Old Ben thinks. No sir. People only ever listen to what the big boys from the Dawson fleet have to say. Well, I can tell you, they didn't see anything. I did!"

"Exactly what did you see Ben?...Would you like another beer?"

Kerrin waved at the barman, who promptly brought over another drink for Old Ben.

"Thanks." The old fisherman took another mouthful of the cold beer, and wiped his forehead with a tattered handkerchief. "See, there I was, out at sea on the Sentinel Reef...the fishing's good out there this time of year...a bit far...but worth it...when we heard this plane flying over, we could even see its tail light flashing..."

"...T'was quite a clear night...only scattered cloud. We were bringing in the nets, but we looked up and watched him fly overhead...it broke up the monotony of the job...been doing the same thing for forty years now...forty years..." The old man started to wander off into his thoughts.

"So what did you see?" Kerrin asked, trying to bring him back from wherever he was going.

"Well...I was watching the plane, see, when suddenly it just blew up. Phuff, bang, and it was gone. A big ball of smoke and fire, and fireworks falling through the air down to the sea. Quite a sight it was. Never forget it, I will. Them pieces of metal started to hit the water hard...one even hit the bloody roof of the boat...cut right through a six inch plank of wood, it did!"

"Have you still got it?"

"Sure have. You can see it if you want...along with the other stuff we picked up!"

"What other stuff?"

"Well, when the sun came up the next day there were bits of flotsam floating on the surface. From the plane like. Wreckage. So we picked it up...'case anybody wanted to see it!"

"Why didn't you hand it over to the police?"

"Tried to. Told them we had stuff, like, but they didn't show any interest. Didn't even come to pick it up! Still got it over at the shed..."

"Are you sure they *knew* you had it?" Kerrin couldn't believe what he was hearing.

"Are you mutton jeff?"

"What?"

"Mutton jeff...deaf! Are you deaf? It's like I told you... I made a full report, told them everything I knew over the phone, even told them about the jet that passed back and forth a few minutes afterwards... just in case it was relevant, like."

"What jet?"

"It was very high, probably nothing related, but about five seconds after the explosion there was a loud roar, and a jet passed overhead in the same direction the plane was heading...then about three minutes later it came back much lower in the opposite direction, before disappearing back towards where it came from. Thought it odd that it came back upon itself, like it did. Maybe it saw the explosion too and came back to have a look-see...thought the police might think that as well..."

None of this was in the official report Kerrin had read.

"Can you show me some of the wreckage you found?" Kerrin asked, getting up from his chair.

"What? Now?" the old man asked.

"Seems like a good time to me. You can bring your beer with you."

The old man's shed was on the other side of the harbor, at the end of one of the slipways that took boats up into dry dock for maintenance and overhauling. Inside the shed, two men were working hard on an old trawler called 'The English Rose', painting the roof, and replacing one of the rails on the starboard side. It was a big boat, but with one look, Kerrin could tell its days were probably numbered.

The building stank of rotting fish, although there were no fish to be seen. Along the edge of the shed, there was a collection of old nets, winches, buoys, empty fish crates, lobster baskets, paint cans and other bits and bobs, and in the corner, a small pile of metal, wooden and plastic objects, which Old Ben pointed to and said was the flotsam which his boat had retrieved from the plane wreckage.

Kerrin bent down and began to sift through it, while Old Ben stood behind him and puffed contentedly on his pipe.

Most of the wreckage was either melted, or burnt, the edges of the metal and the attached charred plastic padding now turned black and green where the fierce heat of a fire had caught it in the flames. Kerrin felt slightly peculiar while touching it, the only trace of what was left of his brother-in-law's plane.

He spent the next hour examining each piece and photographing them meticulously, just in case it might help at some point in the future. But unless they were analyzed in a lab somewhere, Kerrin knew that they would not be able to tell him anything more.

What more did he need to know anyway? There were eye witnesses to an explosion, and the wreckage showed the clear signs of intense heat and flames. It was obvious now that Martin's plane had blown up. What Kerrin would like to know was whether or not the explosion was deliberate or an accident?

On the other hand, the police were clearly not going to follow up on what Old Ben had to say. According to the old fisherman, they definitely knew about this wreckage but had made no effort to come and collect it, and now that the investigation was closed, there was little chance they would do anything else. Had they deliberately lied and kept the old man's sighting out of the police and official air crash investigation, or was it just typical police incompetence? After all, this wasn't America. What could he expect from the Bahamian police?

While driving back to his hotel that night, Kerrin decided that there was probably little point in chasing the officials in Nassau and asking them why they hadn't interviewed Old Ben. They either knew something they weren't going to tell him, or they were just not interested. His time would be better spent elsewhere.

Instead, his thoughts turned to the jet airplane that had passed overhead a few seconds after the explosion. According to the official records there hadn't been any other 'commercial or civilian' aircraft in the area at the time of the explosion. Which only left the military, and they hadn't said anything about a military jet being in the same airspace. If there had been one, then surely the pilot would have seen Martin's plane on its radar... and its instruments would have registered it disappearing off the radar when it exploded? And if so, why didn't the pilot report it? Anyway, Old Ben had said that the plane looked as if it had come around to take a second look. In other words, it must have seen something!

So what Kerrin wanted to know was, had a military jet been following Martin's plane, and if so, where did it come from?

CHAPTER 5
Day Seven
Clifton Beach

Alex Swinton pulled out the factor 35 sun cream and smeared a fresh dollop of the white goo all over his forehead, chest and arms. His sensitive skin didn't tolerate the sun at all, and in spite of years of living in Florida, he had never been able to tan or build up any resistance to the sun's rays. If he didn't watch out he would burn as red as a lobster in less than thirty minutes.

It was hot. Very hot.

He blinked for a second, the sweat streaming off his forehead and over his eyebrows, carrying some of the sun-cream into his eyes.

He wiped them quickly, and rinsed them with some water from his half empty bottle of Evian.

That was better.

He lay back onto the sand, settling his expensive pair of new Ray Bans back onto the bridge of his nose.

This was the life. Sunbathing on one of the most beautiful beaches in the world. It was a far cry from the adrenaline rush of the past few months. He hated to admit that he had thrived on the excitement of the whole thing, particularly as it had resulted in the deaths of several of his colleagues, but Alex was an adrenaline junkie. In some perverted way, he had enjoyed the chase. The thrill was even better now, knowing that he had survived it.

Perhaps what he had done was wrong. Perhaps not. But he had only done what was necessary.

And then he had just disappeared.

No one knew where he had gone.

Here he was just one of thousands of other tourists, inconspicuous in the fact, that like so many others, he was so obviously not from here.

He didn't have any plans, except that for the next few weeks he would lie low. Avoid detection. And in the meantime he would take the time to get some serious windsurfing done. Perhaps at Langebaan, or maybe even along the rugged, lonely coast at Wilderness. The South-Easterlies were really blowing this time of year, and he could get some really good sails if he wanted to.

Being alone out at sea a few k's from the beach, just him versus the wind, would give him the chance to live life at the edge again. Just like he used to do before he got too serious about his work.

Alex's academic career at university had been outstanding. After a year as an undergraduate at the University of Michigan, he had won funding and transferred to a place at MIT. After graduating 'summa cum laude' and head of his year, he had won a fellowship to do a PhD. at Stanford, which had brought him to the attention of David Sonderheim, one of the world's leading geneticists. David was just about to set up a new genetics company based in Florida, which would specialize in the investigation and study of the genetic causes of neuro-degenerative diseases, such as Parkinson's and Alzheimer's. The goal? The holy grail of all the major pharmaceuticals -to find a genetic based cure. A cure which an increasingly ageing population would pay enormous amounts of money for on a regular, extended basis. And the longer they lived, the longer they needed to pay for the treatment.

When Alex had graduated with his PhD. in Genetics and his revolutionary work into the study of ribosomes, he could not turn down the lucrative offer that the new CEO of the Gen8tyx Company had made him. He had packed his wind-surfer and surf boards and driven across America in his beaten-up, red Volkswagen Camper. It had taken him three weeks to make the trip and he had enjoyed every mile of it. As it had turned out, it was the last real freedom he would enjoy for the next six years.

As soon as he had arrived on the campus of the Gen8tyx Company he dived into a brand new project, one so inspired and so radical, that it had the potential to change the world. He had forgotten about the sun, the sea, and the wind and swapped it all for years of long nights in a lab, with a white coat and an electron microscope.

But the results had been extraordinary. As he himself had proved when he had been the first person to test the new treatment they had created.

Then it had all started to go wrong.

After five-and-a-half years of hard work, almost as soon as they knew they were onto something big, something strange started to happen in the background. Suddenly the machinations of corporate finance became more important than the dream they were all trying to fulfill, and as politics and business plans began to take over, David Sonderheim had slowly lost the support of the core team that had made the Gen8tyx Company what it was.

At the same time, one by one new staff were being recruited into the company without the knowledge of the rest of the core team. One day they would come into the lab, and hey presto, there'd be another member of staff, effectively shadowing your work, following you around the lab.

Who were these people? Why were they being recruited?

Then all of a sudden David Sonderheim had made the announcement that the Gen8tyx company had been purchased and was now moving to a bigger facility near San Francisco, California.

Not surprisingly, many of the original core members of the team refused to uproot their families and leave behind their friends.

"You'll be sorely missed. All of you!" was all the beloved Professor Sonderheim had said at the breakfast meeting he had called 'in honor' of a select few. The modern European term 'made redundant' had not hid the fact that effectively they had all been fired, right there on the spot between the orange juice and the toast. Now the purpose of the new recruits had been obvious.

At first the anger had been a blanket which had covered all their reason. Then together they had begun to make their own plans. Plans for their own futures.

He had done his best to protect those plans and he told himself repeatedly that what he had done had only been in the best interest of the group...

That's when the suicides had started to happen. One by one they had been found dead, murder and suicide becoming horrendously confused.

It was time to leave. To disappear.

He had got out just in time and now nobody knew where he was. Not even his sister or brother.

For the near future at least, he was safe.

Sarah Schwartz was an attractive seventeen year old brunette. Five foot seven, a dimple on her left cheek, a fantastic smile, green eyes and very large breasts. Not exactly the typical computer nerd you would expect to find working in the security department of a national bank in New York.

Next year she hoped to go to the local college. If she got good grades in her final exams, perhaps she would even make it to state college and become a math major.

Math was her thing. She felt comfortable with figures, and was easily able to understand and manipulate the notation of mathematics, which others could only see as a foreign language without any meaning. She wasn't a genius. She wasn't gifted. But she was definitely above average. And at $18 dollar an hour, it was probably the best summer job she had ever had.

Brought up with a strict Lutheran background, this was her first time in the Big Apple. She didn't get out much at night time. She didn't have many friends, although recently quite a few strangers had asked if they could meet her for a drink after work. The people in New York seemed to be very friendly. She had been tempted a few times, but she knew her parents in Pennsylvania wouldn't approve. Instead, she stayed at home babysitting for her cousin's daughter, looking out of the window of their apartment on the twelfth floor and watching the flashing lights of the city below.

Today she was on credit watch. It was one of her favorite activities, because it allowed her to study, and get paid for it. For most of the time there was not a lot to do, and for several hours each day she would be able to just sit there and read the latest text book on the list of 'college recommended reading'.

She sat at a large desk in a small dimly lit room at the back of the bank. The room was comfortable apart from the constant hum of air conditioning, which for the first hour of each shift was always incredibly annoying until all of a sudden her brain would somehow adapt to it and manage to filter it out. After that she never noticed it was there, until she stepped outside the room at the end of the shift and was deafened by the silence.

The desk was covered by a large panel of computer monitors, across which a continuous flow of credit card numbers passed in a never ending stream. Each of these numbers represented the number of a credit card which had been stolen or black-listed in the last five days. In the top right corner of each screen there was an empty red box.

Sarah's job was to watch the screens and notice when one of the numbers in the continuously flowing screen suddenly appeared in the little red box. As soon as one did, she was meant to call up that number on another screen and examine the details. The information she would be presented with would confirm that the credit card had just been used again, and would give her the exact details of where and when any transaction had taken place. As soon as that information came up on the screen, she was to hit the 'print' key on her terminal, then carry the report through to Mr Johnson in the other room.

On average, in a six hour shift, about twenty numbers would appear in the little box. The rest of the time her biggest problem was staying awake.

She was halfway through reading the chapter on 'An introduction to Fourier Analysis' when the console beeped at her. She looked up, and there sure enough, was a credit card number flashing in the red box.

As she had done so many times before, she moved to the other keyboard, and called up the details of the flashing number. According to the screen, someone had just used the credit card belonging to a man called Alex Swinton, whose card had been reported missing a few days ago. The record showed that it was a cash withdrawal, about four thousand Rand, a conversion of dollars into the local currency of South Africa. The withdrawal had just been made in a town called Wilderness, at 11 p.m. in the evening, local time.

She waited for the printer to rattle off the details, then swooped them up from the print tray and walked through to Mr Johnson's room. She knocked and waited for the loud 'come in' before entering.

Mr Johnson sat at a large brown desk, peering up from the newspaper he was reading, a fresh cup of coffee steaming in his hand.

"So, what have you got?" he asked from behind his sleek, designer-label, black glasses, his eyes wandering quickly from her face down to her large cleavage, and then to the report in her hand.

"Someone just used a card in South Africa. A few hundred dollars."

She handed the paper over to Mr Johnson and left.

Johnson watched the girl walk out the office, following the wiggle of her bottom and fantasizing for the hundredth time that day just what it would be like. She was good at her job, but that wasn't why he had hired her. They say you make up your mind about someone in the first twenty seconds of an interview. Well, with Sarah, it had only taken three: the amount of time it had taken to see how outstanding her qualifications for the job really were. And since then, coming to work in the morning had been just that little bit more interesting.

He picked up the report she had dropped on his desk and scanned the details. Then reaching inside his jacket pocket, he pulled out his personal diary, flicked it open and found the telephone number he was looking for. He dialed it carefully and when his contact in Miami answered, he spoke quickly.

"We got contact on one of the card numbers you wanted us to trace. Turns out your man Alex Swinton is in South Africa." He read the list of details aloud then hung up.

On his normal bank salary, Mr Johnson would never have been able to afford his active lifestyle. Meeting the woman from Florida in a bar one night had been the best thing to happen to him in years. At five thousand dollars a number, his freelancing activities certainly paid off.

CHAPTER 6
Day Eight
Hooters Bar

Kerrin watched the entrance, keeping an eye out for his old friend. It would be good to see James again. It had been a while.

Old James Callaghan, or IceBreaker as they used to call him, was one of the few people that he still had contact with from his days at the police academy. Over the years he had either lost the numbers of the others in his graduating class, or the phone conversations between them all had just petered out. Only James Callaghan stayed in contact.

He was a hulk of a man, and definitely not the sort of person you wanted to get into a brawl with in a bar. He had earned the nickname 'IceBreaker' during the first week of the academy, by putting ice cubes down on the edge of the bar, and breaking them into pieces with his forehead. A few other people had tried it: one of them almost got concussion, and the other had cut his head open. IceBreaker's skin was so thick that it didn't even leave a mark on him.

Before he had joined the police IceBreaker had spent some time in the U.S. Air Force, until a severe infection had messed up his inner ear so badly that he failed the medical and wasn't allowed to fly again. Being grounded without a pilot's license was not something IceBreaker could stomach, so he had been granted an honorable discharge.

Kerrin had arranged to meet him tonight so that he could tap some of the knowledge from his Air Force days: he wanted to know where the military jet that might have been tailing his brother-in-law could have flown from. IceBreaker knew the skies around the Caribbean, and had been stationed for a while in Florida. Plus, he still owed Kerrin a big favor, for introducing him to the girl that later became his wife.

"Deadeye! How the devil are you?"

His friend stood in the doorway, even more massive than the last time he saw him. Kerrin was shocked to see that he was now almost as wide around the waist as he was around his massive, hulkish arms and biceps. Middle age spread had claimed yet another victim.

Kerrin smiled at the mention of his own nickname. He hadn't heard it for years. So earned, because on their first attempt at shooting handguns on the police firing range, Kerrin had scored a bulls eye. At first they had joked, pulling his leg and saying it was a fluke, but when he had walked off with the academy's 'Top Marksman' award at the end of the course, everyone had stopped ribbing him and given him the name out of genuine respect. Turns out, Kerrin was an excellent shot.

"No one has called me that for years!" He stood up, and wrapped an arm around his friend's shoulders in a quick bear-hug.

They shook hands and while the IceBreaker sat down on the stool beside him, Kerrin caught the attention of the nearest waitress, and ordered two large cold beers.

"So how's the big world of publishing?" James asked.

"Oh you know, never a dull day and all that...not exactly as exciting as the police force, but..."

James knew how much Kerrin had liked the police, and he knew how hard it had been when he had given up the job so that he could spend more time at home looking after his wife. Kerrin had been one of the best officers in his graduation class at the academy. He had just been promoted to Captain when Dana had been crippled. If things had been different and he had stayed in the force, Kerrin would have gone far. He was good at this job and everyone liked him.

"And Dana? How is she?"

"Better, much better..." Kerrin replied.

Over a few beers they caught up on old times, laughing at old memories, and talking about the daily routine of the lives they now both led. Eventually they came round to the question of the evening. It was James who brought it up.

"So young 'Deadeye', what's up? What do you want from me?"

"What makes you think that I want anything?"

"Just call it a cop's instinct. Or maybe it's just that you've paid for all the beers so far...you must want something!"

"Is it that obvious?" Kerrin laughed. "...The thing is, a couple of days ago the paper sent me down to do a routine report on a plane crash in the Bahamas. A wealthy American businessman was flying his jet down to Nassau when it exploded en route. Could be a terrorist attack, or just an accident. I'm trying to find an angle on it, trying to spice it up a little. Interestingly, an eye witness on a fishing boat saw the plane explode and he claims to have seen a military jet flying around the area at the same time the plane exploded. I want to track down the jet, and talk to the pilot to see if he was in radio contact with the businessman before his plane went down, and to find out whether or not he saw anything..."

"What do the airport people in the Bahamas say?"

"Nothing. They spent a few days on it, then closed the case. They didn't mention the jet at all, which was curious in itself. According to them there were no other planes in the area…"

"So what do you want me to do exactly?"

"I was just hoping you might be able to tell me which airbase a military jet flying in that airspace could have come from? Then I can contact the public liaison officer at the airfield, and see if he can help me answer my questions."

"So who was the guy who died? Someone important?"

"Could be, we don't know yet. That's one of the things I'm trying to find out." A small lie, but Kerrin had decided to leave out most of the details. It wasn't necessary to get James involved if there was anything dangerous going on…at least not yet. Maybe later.

"Off the cuff, I would guess that the plane could have come from any one of three or four bases." James said. "Listen, I've still got some contacts. Why don't you leave it with me. I'll make a few phone calls tomorrow, and get back to you. It shouldn't take long."

Day Nine

The next morning Kerrin spoke for an hour with his wife. He hated leaving her alone, but thankfully nowadays she was so much more independent.

Before the accident Dana had been a software designer. Luckily, her old company had given her a new job where she was able to work from home. She only needed to go into the Washington office once or twice a week, for meetings or to discuss her work with her colleagues. At first Kerrin had been too overprotective towards her. It had taken him longer to come to terms with her disability than she had. Then at Dana's suggestion, they had hired a maid who came round each day and helped out around the house. Knowing she also kept a caring eye on Dana, he didn't feel so bad about leaving her alone for a few days at a time. Which was good, because he was going to have to spend a few more days in Florida.

It was only 10.45am, but already the beachfront at Fort Lauderdale was busy, people cruising the beach front in their open top cars, college kids hanging out on the beach, and runners jogging up and down, trying to burn up the calories and lose a few pounds.

He finished his eggs and hash browns at the street side café, and sat back in his chair with a fresh coffee, trying to plan what he should do next. It was important that he try to separate his personal feelings from what was going on. If he was going to get anywhere, he had to be objective, had to distance himself from what had happened. And at the moment there was no real proof that the explosion that killed Martin was not just an accident.

Kerrin had spoken to his sister late last night, and asked for the addresses and phone numbers of Martin's old work colleagues. The next step was to drive up to Miami and visit their families.

He checked out of his hotel, and then drove to the petrol station and filled up with gas. It was a fantastic day, and on impulse Kerrin decided to take the coast road from Fort Lauderdale to Orlando.

The cell phone in his pocket buzzed, and Kerrin whipped it out.

"Hey DeadEye, it's James. Got some news for you!"

"Already? That's fast!"

"What do you expect? Anything for a pal...anyway, I've got to leave in a minute so I'd better make this quick."

"Okay, so what have you got then?" Kerrin asked, pulling over to the side of the road, and taking out his note book and pen.

"I spoke to one of my friends who still flies in Florida, and he agrees with me that a jet would only be able to cover that area from one of four different airbases, Avon or MacDill in Tampa Bay being the most likely. Anyway, being such a nice guy, I called all of them and spoke to the duty public liaison officers...gave them an official police line, about us investigating the mysterious disappearance of a private jet taking off from Miami...did they have any aircraft operational in the area ...and did they see anything on radar at all?"

"And...?"

"Well, it took a while, they all had to make a few checks, but the official line is that none of them had any jets in that area at that time. Nothing. And according to the duty officer at MacDill, there would be no other airfields that would send a jet down there without them knowing about it."

"But, that doesn't make sense...we have an eye witness who saw it!"

"How reliable is the eyewitness? More reliable than Uncle Sam? Officially there was nothing there...Listen, I have to go, is there anything else I can do for you?"

"Actually, now that you ask, there is one more thing..."

Kerrin quickly explained about the suicides he wanted to investigate.

"Woahh, boy. What exactly is going on here? Is there just the slightest possibility that old DeadEye is not telling me everything?"

"Could be. Don't know yet. Anyway, can you get me a copy of the police reports on the suicides...just to look at them?"

"I can't promise anything, but I'll try. I have a friend in the Orlando Homicide department...but you owe me big time, you know that don't you? Anyway, got to rush now boyo. Speak to you later."

It was true. If he could get a look at those files, Kerrin would owe him big time.

Major Anders was a little nervous. The public liaison officer at MacDill Air Force base had just left his office. It seems that things were not as clear cut as he had hoped they were.

Regrettably, he knew he should call his contact in New York. He would have to know.

He poked his head out of his office and told his secretary to hold any calls. Returning to his desk, he sat down heavily in his chair and breathed deeply, trying to control himself. When he felt a little calmer, he dialed the number in Manhattan, and waited for the phone to be picked up. Once again, the phone rang quite a few times before it was eventually answered.

"Major Anders, how pleasant it is to speak to you again so soon..." the man said, obviously surprised that he was calling.

"Thank you, sir. I thought it necessary to inform you that the hole-in-one my golf partner scored in his recent round of golf may have had a witness after all!"

"How exactly do you mean?" the voice asked.

"A police officer has been making enquiries...trying to find out if we had any one out playing golf at the time..."

"And did you?"

"No...officially not. We made that very clear..."

"Good."

There was a moment's silence, then the voice continued.

"Perhaps it would be a good idea if you were to transfer your golf partner. Somewhere far away, just in case he were to brag of the hole-in-one to anyone. We wouldn't want this to go any further, would we?"

"No sir. Absolutely not. I'll see to it right away."

CHAPTER 7
Orlando
Florida

When Kerrin left the outskirts of Miami, he had the beginnings of a rough plan in his mind. As a policeman turned journalist, over the years he had had his fill of conspiracy theories. Modern America was a paranoid nation. It seemed that every second person in the country believed that around every corner, behind every piece of news, or political event, some sinister conspiracy lay lurking in the shadows. Once upon a time, he too had even believed in such things.

But over the years, Kerrin had seen and been through a lot. From his years on the force, his work at the Post, and living through the pain of the car accident, his views on life had matured faster than most. He no longer believed in the 'greater plan', or the corporate monster wishing to devour and control every waking moment of the free individual. Instead he just believed in life. Day to day life. The fight for survival.

Conspiracy theories were the product of a nation gone mad on science fiction or fantasy magazines, a generation that was no longer able to find satisfaction in the day to day routine of everyday life.

People no longer took the initiative to fill their lives with interesting activities. Instead, happiness came from TV, alcohol or drugs, and when something went wrong with their own lives, when more than one or two bad things happened in quick succession, well …conspiracy theory!

Kerrin wasn't one of those people. It would take a lot for him to accept any form of conspiracy theory. On the face of it though, there did seem to be something fishy about the recent events surrounding the Gen8tyx Company, although he didn't yet know whether or not they were related to the explosion in his brother-in-law's plane. However, it struck him as odd that the air force had denied the existence of any military jets in the vicinity of Martin's plane when it had crashed. Normally the public liaison officers of the USAF would have co-operated openly with the sort of police request for information that James had made.

He thought about that a lot during the drive up to Orlando. The only witness to the jet being there was the testimony of the old fisherman.

27

Reporters and policemen alike go a lot on their gut instinct, and Kerrin had no reason to believe that the old man had made it up. His instinct told him he was telling the truth. So why had the air force denied it? There could only be two reasons.

Firstly, the plane had been there on an exercise and the military could not admit it. Which was strange, because if it had been on a secret exercise it would surely have been easy to admit that 'an exercise had taken place but that they could not discuss the matter further'. That was standard procedure.

All things considered, the likelihood was that when they said there had been no exercises taking place at that time, they had told the truth.

Secondly, the other possibility was that the plane had been there, but no records had been kept of its flight. In which case the liaison officer at the base where the jet came from may not have known about it, and he could have been telling the truth. However, the order to authorize a flight and then make it disappear from the records would have had to come from someone very high up. Someone very high up indeed.

He played with his thoughts, mulling them over in his head as he drove, and the more he thought about it, the more he was convinced that Old Ben had not imagined what he saw.

The natural conclusion was that the plane had been there, but the air force had denied it. Which meant, that if he trusted his reasoning, the records of the flight had been deliberately lost: in other words someone had ordered a flight which the US Air Force kept no record of...

"Conspiracy Theory"..."Conspiracy Theory"...the words echoed in his brain. "Shit, this is getting me nowhere...," he swore to himself.

He pulled into a Denny's and ordered himself a salad and some coffee, sitting himself down in the corner away from the rest of the diners. He needed to think.

Okay, so he was suspicious of the events surrounding his brother-in-law's death, but before he would allow himself to make any link to the deaths of Martin's co-workers, all of which could have perfectly natural explanations, he needed to investigate them for himself.

Even if it did turn out that the team had been murdered and they had not committed suicide, who was to say that it had anything to do with the company they had just left? That would be too obvious.

According to what his sister had told him, there had been six members of the original core team that David Sonderheim, the founder of Gen8tyx, had brought together. Five were now confirmed dead. The other one was missing. If in the next few days he also wasn't found dead somewhere, Alex Swinton would become one of Kerrin's main suspects. He was either in hiding and in fear of his life, or he was running away, scared of being caught and probably guilty as sin. Either way, Kerrin would need to talk to him.

For now though, Kerrin needed to speak to the families of those that had died. He needed to find out for himself how they died, and ultimately, why?

The request Kerrin had made to view the police reports of all those who had committed suicide in Orlando, combined with the question about the military jet, intrigued Captain James Callaghan of the Miami police department.

He knew how the mind of a policeman worked, and he knew that reporters didn't ask questions without a reason. So Kerrin, an ex-policeman and now a reporter, would have a very good reason. James would love to know what it was.

When he got back to the station, after dealing with a break-in at a local drugstore, he shut his office door and put in a call to his buddy over in Orlando.

"Hey Andy, how-ya-doing?"

"James, good to hear from you, man. What's up?"

"Oh, you know, just the same things...hey did you hear about that bank robbery down in the Keys last week? What did you make of that?"

"Shit, yeah, a kid of twelve walks into the local bank and holds them up? Shoots the bank manager and leaves?"

"Yeah, but did you hear the latest?"

"Nah,...what?"

"The bank manager was his uncle! They caught the kid...the uncle had been abusing him, and the boy had had enough. In a way, you can't blame him, can you?"

"No. Would have done the same myself...Bloody weirdoes..."

"Talking of weird shit...have you heard anything about four or five guys working for the same company in Orlando, who all committed suicide in the space of a week?"

There was a moment's pause at the other end of the line.

"Yeah, funny business...I had to go and interview one of the families myself. Pretty sad really, the guy lost his job, then injected himself with some drug one night in his old office...He left a note. Clear cut case really. Nothing suspicious... Why do you ask?"

"Oh, somebody from the same company got killed down here, and the wife reckons that somebody was murdering them all. Nothing to do with suicide...Say, mind if I take a look at the files myself?"

"Hell no, anything to help. Listen, I can fed-ex them to you this afternoon. You should have them first thing tomorrow. Is that fast enough?"

"Cheers. Owe you one buddy."

"You sure do."

His friend Andy in the Orlando force was a good man to have in a tight spot. When he had worked in Miami they'd been good friends.

About an hour later, James was sitting at his desk writing up a report from the morning's patrol, when the phone rang.

"Hey James, it's Andy."

"Problem?" James hadn't expected Andy to call back so soon.

"You could say that. Don't know what to make of it either. All the files on those deaths have walked. Disappeared. No E5 forms filled out to say who took them. And on the computer system, the reports have all been given top security Federal access codes. I can't get into them without the passwords, and if I did, it would get flagged up automatically at the FBI offices in Tampa. I can't help you buddy, and I can't chase it without some questions being asked. Say, what's this about, James?"

"I don't know. Best leave it alone I guess."

"Well, I tried. So when are you going to pay us a visit?"

"Soon. Anyway I owe you one. Thanks."

James hung up, and turned to the window, getting up out of his chair and leaning against the window frame. Outside in the street some kid was writing his name on the sidewalk with a piece of chalk. He looked up and saw James watching him, then got up and ran away.

So why were the Feds interested? And where were the files? Files just don't go missing. There were procedures...if somebody borrowed a file, they left a form saying where they were, so others could get access to them too.

Something funny was going on, but unless Kerrin gave him something more to go on, there was little more he could do from this end. He would call Kerrin and give him what he had.

Kerrin already knew that if he needed more help, he only had to ask.

CHAPTER 8
Tom Calvert's House

Mrs. Calvert sat in the chair opposite him, cradling a large cup of coffee between her hands. She sat on the edge of her chair, her eyes studying Kerrin carefully. Kerrin could see that she had been crying before he arrived, and her eyes were still red and puffy from the tears.

She was rather a plain woman, in her mid forties, and quite plump. Her shoulder length brown hair had lost its vitality, and she wore no makeup. Kerrin guessed that looking good was probably the last thing on her mind just now.

"Thank you for seeing me at such short notice. As I explained to you on the phone, I'm a relative of Martin Nicolson, one of Tom's colleagues. Martin was my brother-in-law. I'd met Tom myself once or twice when we all played golf together."

"How is Martin?" the woman asked him.

"Dead. He was killed in a plane accident last week…"

The woman stretched out and placed her cup on the coffee table in front. She rose to her feet and started pacing around the room. Tears began to flow from her eyes.

"Not another one…it's the company. David bloody Sonderheim and his bloody genetic wonder drugs…mark my words, that was no accident…they killed him just like they killed my Tom!"

Kerrin waited a while, letting the emotional wave roll over her. She stood at the end of the sofa, her arms wrapped across her stomach as if trying to comfort herself.

"I'm sorry," she said. "I'll be okay in a minute or two."

She walked out to the kitchen, returning with a fresh handkerchief, dabbing at her eyes.

"I'm fine now…"

"I think I should tell you that by profession I am a reporter with the Washington Post. My sister, Martin's wife, asked me to find out what is going on, and make sure whoever is responsible for these deaths is brought to justice. I promised her I would."

"The Washington Post?" She looked worried..."I've got two children...I don't know..."

"Mrs Calvert, I can assure you that if anything is written about this, then no danger will come to you or your family. At the moment, all I want to do is find out what's going on. And why Martin, ...and Tom...died."

"Okay...Okay...," she agreed nervously.

"Now, what I would like to ask you is this: the police are convinced your husband committed suicide. What makes you think he didn't?"

"Tom...suicide?" she laughed through her tears, coughing a few times as the two emotions collided. "Did the police tell you that Tom was a devout catholic? Catholics aren't allowed to commit suicide. It's against their religion. They believe they will go to hell if they do...Or did they mention, that at college he was on the Anti-Drug Crusade, and that three years ago he started a Big Brother Support Program in a nearby suburb for people trying to kick drugs? *Did they mention that?* So, you can see how absurd it sounds when you're told that your husband just killed himself by taking a drug overdose?" she stood up again, and Kerrin was forced to look up at her as she spoke. She was red in the face, the anger boiling beneath her words.

"Did they tell you that the week before he died he booked a vacation for us all to Europe? A treat for the kids, and an opportunity for him to start a new life with a fresh start. Tom was looking forward to it...Our first trip to Europe together!"

"I hope you don't mind me asking, but did Tom have any financial problems that you were aware of?"

"No. None. Fortunately, that's one problem we've never had to face. Let's just say that he didn't have to work again...And besides, although I don't like to talk about it, I come from a very wealthy family. Money has never been an issue for me...or for Tom...we shared bank accounts. Tom was fiercely independent though, never wanted to touch my money. And recently, even though Tom was completely against the move of the company to California, financially, he did very well from it. What with his severance package, then the sale of his shares in the company. Do you know how much money he made in the past few months from the stock market? A lot!"

"So, if he had no money problems, was he pleased to lose his job and get lots of free time?" Kerrin asked.

"...No. I wouldn't say that. Actually, he was furious about it! Everything he had worked for in the past ten years was gone. Did you know that he was one of the first people that Sonderheim recruited?"

"So why did he lose his job?"

"Because he wouldn't move to California. Same as the rest. Most of the core team refused to go."

"Why didn't he move?"

"...Because we love it here. Life isn't just about money. We've got everything we need right here in Orlando. And the kids love their schools and their friends. Are you a parent Mr Graham?...Because if you were, you'd know that you wouldn't dream of dragging your teenage kids away from their lives and their friends...No, there was no way we were moving to California! No way!" She sat back down in her seat. The outburst seemed to be over for now.

"Do you know what project your husband was working on before he left Gen8tyx?"

"No. Sorry, I can't help you there. None of the scientists at Gen8tyx ever talked about their work outside the lab. They weren't allowed to, and even if they had, I would never have understood it. I could never understand science at college. Languages yes, science no."

"Did he ever bring any notes or work home with him?"

"No, ...nothing. Nobody was ever allowed to take anything out of the office. They were very strict about that."

"In the weeks leading up to his death, did you notice anything at all unusual about his behavior?"

"No. But that's not to say he wasn't stressed out. There was something going on at work, tension between him and Sonderheim, and the whole business about having to leave the company. That got to him, but he never came home and took it out on us. At first he was extremely angry that he was going to have to leave his work, but then after he got used to the idea, he was really looking forward to the opportunities that some time off would give him."

"Can I ask you exactly how your husband died? The police are a bit reluctant to let me see the files." He decided not to tell her that they had all mysteriously disappeared.

"The police found him in his office, sitting at his desk, with a syringe in his hand, and a tourniquet around his arm. He had injected himself with something. Apparently he died of an overdose. The police said he had left a note."

"What did it say?"

"I don't know. They wouldn't let me see it."

"Excuse me? What do you mean they wouldn't let you see it?"

"Just that. Said it was evidence and they couldn't release it."

"You have rights...you're allowed to see it!"

"Apparently not. I spoke to my lawyer, and he said that in cases where these types of drugs were involved, at this stage the new State law gives the police the right to protect any evidence, even withhold it from family and friends!"

It had been five years since Kerrin had left the Miami police. He wasn't up on recent Florida law. Maybe she was right.

"...But they did say it was a classic goodbye note. They did mention one line -it said 'say goodbye to my family...tell them I love them...'." She started to cry again.

"You need to be allowed to see it, at least to be allowed to verify the writing on it!" Kerrin insisted.

"The police said it was a printed letter, written on his computer at work. They knew it was his because he had signed it."

Kerrin thought about what she had just said: unless the police had had the handwriting checked by experts, they couldn't prove it was Tom's signature or rule out the possibility that perhaps someone else had copied it. Kerrin would have to get hold of the letter... Then he realized that now the file had gone missing in the police station, without the letter, he couldn't check the signature and prove it wasn't suicide!

After a few moments, Mrs Calvert spoke again, her voice soft and quiet.

"Mr Graham, you need to know that I loved my husband. We lived together for over twenty years. Twenty years! He was part of me...I knew him inside out...and Tom and I had everything to live for. Everything. As his wife, friend, and lover, I am telling you that my husband, Tom Charles Calvert, did not kill himself!"

Kerrin believed her.

CHAPTER 9
Day Nine
Mike Gilbert's House

In the organizational structure of Gen8tyx, Mike Gilbert had reported to Martin Nicolson. Mike was one of several team members that had been lured to work at Gen8tyx by the honor of working for Professor Martin Nicolson, considered by many to be one of the most outstanding geneticists in the country. Mike was the youngest of the core team. Only twenty eight when they had found him dead on the beach, a hose pipe stuck into the exhaust of his car.

The house was full of photographs of an incredibly active man. Pictures of himself and his friends climbing in Yosemite, skiing in France, and scuba diving in Australia were spread all over the walls, intermingled with portraits of two people very much in love, and enjoying together everything that life could give them.

Mike was single, but it was well known that at the end of the year, he was going to do the honorable thing and marry his long term girlfriend, Isabella. They were expecting their first child, a girl, in January.

Mike had been over the moon when he had found out that Isabella was pregnant. In preparation for the big event, they had moved to a bigger house, and spent the past few months decorating the nursery and shopping together for everything that would make their little girl's life complete. Little teddy bears, dolls and colored rattles littered the nursery, and it seemed like every shelf in the lounge was covered by books on childbirth, "The First Three Years" as well as "How to get your daughter into Yale!"

As Isabella proudly showed him the house that they had been planning to share together, Kerrin couldn't help but get the impression that Mike was a man who was planning to live as long as possible.

His fiancée was beautiful. Her dark hair, brown eyes and Hispanic tanned skin blended with a sexy curvaceous figure to produce a woman that any man would dream of being with. Even with her child so obviously showing she oozed sex appeal and vitality.

Mike had been a man that had had everything. The sort of man that a lot of men would like to be.

"It makes no sense to me," the woman said, leading him through to the lounge. "Did you know he had just had his first book accepted by a publisher? They reckoned he'd get it published in January, about the same time the baby is due..."

"Mike was a writer?"

"Yes...well, he wanted to be...was going to be..."

"Wow..." Kerrin didn't want to admit that he had been trying for years to get a book published, but the fact that Mike was a writer increased his respect for the young man even more.

"What was the book about?"

"It's fantastic! A fictional thriller about Genetics. They always say that you should write about what you know. Well, Mike knew a lot about genetics."

"I'd love to read it...do you have a spare copy?"

"Sorry, it's all on his computer. And I don't know the password to get into his files. It's funny, he changed the password only a few days before he died and didn't tell me the new one."

"I'm pretty good with computers, would you like me to try and hack into it?" Kerrin volunteered. Hacking was one of his specialties. He had been a master at it when he was a kid, then when he joined the police, it had proved to be one of life's true skills.

"I wish you could, but the police came and took the computer away. They said they needed to make sure there was nothing on there that might give them some information on why he killed himself."

"When was this?"

"Just a few days ago. The policeman left me his card. Maybe you can call him if you like. Now the case is closed I'd like to know when I'm going to get the computer back. There doesn't seem to be any good reason why they should keep it any longer, does there?"

She left the room, coming back with a piece of paper with a police Captain's name and telephone number on it. Kerrin would call him later.

"So, Miss Sanchez, if you don't mind, and I know it might be difficult,...but can you tell me in your own words how Mike died?"

"Isabella, call me Isabella please. Would you like a drink? I wish I could have one, but I have to stick to the soft stuff!" She said, patting her belly, as she got up and crossed to the bar in the corner of the room.

"Whisky neat, please." Kerrin replied.

She poured the drinks, handing him his glass.

"They found him in his car, a rubber tube stuck on the back of the exhaust. They said he died quickly. One of the officers tried his best to convince me that he didn't suffer. He insisted it's one of the best ways to go...as the car fills up with the carbon monoxide you get happier and happier, then just fall asleep and die..." She hesitated a second. "When I saw him in the hospital, about half an hour after they'd found him, he looked so happy, so peaceful...It's funny how some things stick in your mind, but I'll never forget how red his lips were!..."

She started to cry quietly. Kerrin gave her a few moments before carrying on.

"Did he leave a note of any kind?"

"Yes...the policeman said he'd found a letter on the passenger seat. In a brown envelope."

"Handwritten?"

"No, typed...that's a funny question...what difference does it make?"

"Was it signed? Did you get a chance to see it?"

"No...wow, I never thought about that before. Maybe he never wrote the letter, maybe somebody else did? Is that what you mean?" A sparkle appeared in Isabella's eyes as she realized where he was going with the question.

"Did you get a chance to see it?" Kerrin repeated the question.

"No...actually I didn't..."

"Do you know what it said?"

"...Oh, apparently it was quite short...'A typical suicide note' was what the policeman had said. But he told me one line from it...it said, 'Tell my Isabella I love her, and that I'm sorry I won't see our daughter.' That struck me as a little bit funny..."

"Why? What was funny about that?"

"...I've not told this to anyone else because some people, my mother mainly, thinks that naming your child before it's born is really bad luck. Thing is, Mike and I had already chosen a name for our baby...Sonia. Whenever we talked about her we called her Sonia. We always mentioned her by name. It just strikes me as weird that in his last words to me he called her 'our daughter' and not Sonia!"

"The more I look at all of this, there are a lot of things that are weird, Isabella," he said, turning over the tape in the little recording machine that he had placed on the table.

"Do you mind if I ask you a few personal questions?"

"No. Go ahead. But I might not answer them all." She smiled, her eyes twinkling, and for a second the haunted look that she had been carrying around with her seemed to lift. She was truly a very attractive woman.

"What about your finances? Any problem there?"

"No...Gen8tyx were very good that way. We got a big package when he left. A lot more than we expected. Two years salary actually!"

"Enemies...any that you knew of?"

"No. None that I'm aware off. He seemed to get on with pretty much everyone."

"And at work? Were there any big arguments, falling out with anyone?"

"Again, apart from the Director David Sonderheim, he got on great with everyone. We used to meet up with the other couples from the lab at weekends, do barbecues together, that sort of thing...actually we were all pretty close."

"What about Sonderheim then? What was the problem?"

"Just that Mike blamed him for destroying the dream. He really enjoyed his job, then Sonderheim ruined it all, and insisted on moving the company to California. Everyone resented that. Hardly anyone wanted to go. "

"Sonderheim seems to be a pretty unpopular guy. Did you like him?"

"Yes. Very charming. But it was only in the last couple of months that people started having a problem with him...it wasn't just Mike...The others fell out with him too."

"Why?"

"Mike said that 'he'd changed', had somehow lost sight of the dream they'd all shared. That he'd become distant from the rest of the group, and wasn't as friendly as before...was constantly shouting at people and pointing out their mistakes...pushing them too hard."

"What was the dream that you keep mentioning?" Kerrin wondered.

"I wish I knew. He often talked about the work they were doing, but in terms which never really gave away any details. All I know was that they were working on something big. Building up to some wonderful achievement. Something imminent. They had possibly even already succeeded. One night, about four months ago, Mike came home from work early. He had bought flowers, and two bottles of champagne ...He was in such a good mood. All he said was that things at the lab were fantastic, better than they had ever been, and that one day soon I'd be very, very proud of him. I'd not seen him so happy in ages, even when I told him about the baby. Something special must have happened that day!"

But what? If only Kerrin knew.

He left Isabella shortly afterwards, politely declining an invitation to the funeral which was going to take place the next week. As he drove back to his hotel in town, he played the tape back to himself, listening for a second time to her answers.

Kerrin was confused. There just didn't seem to be any reason for Mike to kill himself. On the contrary, Mike had everything to live for.

As the man said goodbye to the lady at the door, and turned to walk towards his car, the Nikon MX2, equipped with a large 400mm zoom lens, took twenty or thirty photographs in quick succession. The photographer, a man in his late twenties, wearing a smart, dark brown suit and tie, had been lucky. Sitting in a car on the opposite side of the road, the zoom lens had allowed him to get a clear view from over a hundred yards away. The photographs had caught the man's face clearly.

As soon as he got back to the office, he would run a trace on the car's registration plates. It would be easy to find out who he was, and where he came from. For now though, his orders were to stay put and find out who else was visiting the pretty Miss Sanchez.

CHAPTER 10
Day Nine
Sunshine Meadows
Orlando

The next person Kerrin wanted to see was Henry Robert's widow. When his wife had found him hanging from the tree, Henry had still been alive. Unconscious, but alive. He had been taken to hospital within minutes, but he died two days later, apparently from a massive heart attack. According to Kerrin's sister, Henry Roberts had been the first of the team to die. The others had followed in quick succession.

The Roberts' house lay just outside Orlando, in one of the most exclusive suburbs of the city. As Kerrin drove along the road he watched the house numbers and marveled at the mansions set far back from the road. Large iron gates, and impressive driveways sweeping into the distance, winding their way through immaculately maintained lawns.

Whoever the Roberts were, they certainly knew how to live in style. Or did.

192 Sunshine Meadows was towards the end of the road, set back in the woods, and in one of the best locations of them all.

He stopped the car outside the main gates, and got out, walking up to the intercom on the gatepost. He pressed the button on the wall, and watched how a security camera above the gates swiveled round towards him, the lens zooming out and focusing on him as he waited.

He smiled at the camera, then leant towards the intercom and introduced himself to the voice at the other end.

"Please come in," the woman's voice said monotonically.

When the gates swung open, he drove up the driveway, parking in front of the house. He had only made it halfway up the steps to the front door, when two large Dobermans bounded towards him from the garden, forcing Kerrin to retreat quickly to the safety of his car.

A woman appeared in the doorway, at the top of the small flight of marble steps. She blew a whistle, and the two dogs immediately lay flat on the ground, panting loudly, but still eyeing Kerrin with interest.

"It's okay, they're harmless. They're just playing!" she smiled. "Come inside Mr Graham."

The lady showed him into an impressive study lined with books, with two large green sofas surrounding a long mahogany coffee table in front of an impressive open stone fireplace. As soon as they had sat down, a maid appeared, enquiring what they would like to drink.

"Coffee please. White, no sugar." Kerrin volunteered.

The woman in front of him was in her late fifties, and was dressed in a long, flowing black dress. Although the black showed she was officially in mourning, Kerrin couldn't help but notice the Gucci motif emblazoned on the belt hanging loosely around her waist.

"Well, Mr Graham, I am sorry to hear of your loss. Martin was a kind man. Your sister must be devastated. I'm afraid that when you called I was rather shocked to hear of his death. I had heard that he had disappeared, but had rather hoped he had left the city and was still alive somewhere."

"Thank you Mrs Roberts. And I'm sorry about your husband. Martin spoke very highly of him to my sister."

"Can you tell me please, Mr Graham- how was it that Martin died?"

He explained the details, letting the circumstances of Martin's death sink in, and watching to see her reaction. Her face showed little sign of emotion. If first impressions counted for anything, Kerrin could see that she was a powerful woman, perhaps the driving force behind an obviously very successful man. Henry Roberts had been the Chief Financial Officer of Gen8tyx. According to Kerrin's sister, a shrewd man, quiet, but very clever.

"And do you believe it was an accident Mr Graham, or do you also believe that there was something more sinister behind it all?" the woman probed. Who was questioning whom, Kerrin briefly wondered.

"That's why I'm here. To try and find out what was going on at Gen8tyx. Frankly, Mrs Roberts, I was hoping that I could ask you some questions about your husband..."

"Naturally. Please go ahead. I shall help you in any way I can. But I think that I should tell you straight away that I do not share the paranoia that Mrs Gilbert or Mrs Calvert do. My husband died in tragic and horrible circumstances. He tried to take his own life. But then he died naturally. A massive heart attack. Whatever drove him to such desperate measures, I don't know...," her voice faltered for a second, the slightest trace of emotion rippling through her otherwise placid persona.

"I know this may be hard, Mrs Roberts, but do you have any idea why he may have committed suicide, if it was indeed suicide?"

" None…well, nothing that important. Nothing that should drive a man to such extremes."

Kerrin noticed the hesitation.

"It may not have seemed important to you, however, if your husband was depressed, perhaps…"

"My husband was not depressed, quiet yes, but not depressed. Why is it that everyone automatically assumes that just because a person is quiet that they are sad?"

Kerrin was surprised by how quickly she sprang to defend her husband, particularly as no insult or personal attack was intended. He would have to be more careful in how he chose his words.

"I'm deeply sorry, Mrs Roberts. I did not intend to infer…"

"Oh, no, please, forgive me. It's just that, well…"

"I understand." Kerrin interrupted. "As I said, it's a difficult time for us all."

Thankfully just then the maid arrived with the coffee, politely serving Kerrin first before pouring Mrs Roberts a cup of steaming Earl Grey Tea into a large willow patterned, china cup and saucer.

"Mr Graham, I think I wouldn't be breaking any confidences if I said that something was going on at Gen8tyx that Henry wasn't happy about. It caused him a great deal of stress. I tried to talk to him about it, but he said he couldn't discuss it. He would just come home and lock himself away in his study as soon as dinner was finished, and then speak for hours on the phone."

"Have you any idea who he may have been talking to? It might be relevant…"

"No, I'm sorry. I think a lot of the calls were long distance. They got quite heated sometimes. I even heard him shouting once, and Henry never shouted."

"Did he say anything at all about what was going on?"

"As I said, nothing…," she paused, as if wondering whether or not to mention it. "One night, quite late, about 11 o'clock, Mr Sonderheim came over. He stayed for about three hours, and when he left Henry came into my room and sat on my bed…we normally sleep in different rooms…he sat and looked at me for a while, held my hand, and promised that 'it would soon all be over', that we'd spend more time together, and that 'things would be better'. He said he had got a plan, a way to make sure it would all be okay. But he looked so sad. He kissed me gently, then left. A week later he was dead."

"Had it got something to do with the move to California?"

"I think so. At first we even thought about moving, but then something happened, and Henry said that we were staying put. He was going to retire after all."

"Wasn't Henry the financial genius behind Gen8tyx? I would have thought that they would really miss him?"

"Perhaps, but for some reason, I think Henry discovered that he was not really going to be needed in California after all. I suspect that is why he decided not to move."

Kerrin was beginning to warm towards Mrs Roberts. She was obviously a woman used to high standards and an expensive lifestyle, but in spite of the thick skinned exterior, Kerrin could see that she was suffering inside. He could guess that she was going to miss her husband very much.

"Why don't you think it was murder, like the others?" he asked, referring to Mrs Calvert, and Isabella.

"Of course, I have discussed it with them. Actually, they were both here two days ago for coffee. It was good to talk to somebody else who was grieving too, but Henry never had any enemies. No one would have wanted to kill him...he was so, so sweet! He has...or at least, he used to have high blood pressure. The strain of it all must have killed him."

"Am I correct in understanding that it was you who found Henry after he tried to hang himself?" he asked as delicately as he could.

"Yes. I did." She looked away, staring out of the window. Without looking back she said, "I think I would like another cup of tea. Can I offer you some more coffee, Mr Graham?", she asked, her voice trembling.

Without waiting for an answer she got up and left, not returning until a few minutes later. She had obviously taken a moment to regain her composure. The corners of her eyes were still a little red from the crying.

"I'm sorry, Mr Graham. If I may be honest...this is all rather painful for me. You asked if I found my husband hanging from a tree? Well, yes, I did. How or why he got there I do not understand."

"When was this?"

"Two and a half weeks ago. It was at night, quite late. There had been a phone call. I was in bed already, reading, when Henry popped his head round the door and said he was going back to the office..."

"...An hour or two later, I heard the dogs barking wildly in the garden. They didn't stop. I went to investigate and found them underneath the branch of a tree near the main gate. Daniel, -the maid's husband-, cut him down immediately. Thankfully he was still breathing. The ambulance turned up almost instantly and he was taken to the Mount Royal."

"Did you get a chance to talk to him afterwards,...before he died?"

"No, not at all. I sat beside his bed for two days. I slept in the hospital in a room opposite his, but he was in a coma, and he never came to. He died in his sleep."

"I'm sorry. I know this is hard. But I need to ask these questions...to try and understand what happened and why?"

The maid arrived and re-filled their cups. Kerrin was grateful for the extra coffee. He wanted to stay alert.

"May I ask you one more question, Mrs Roberts. Perhaps a rather personal one?"

"If you must."

"I was wondering if you have any financial problems?"

"To be quite honest, Henry handled all the money, well, you'd expect that wouldn't you, being an accountant! But I can tell you honestly that I am not aware of any financial problems. If there were any, Henry would have told me. Anyway, I'm sure that the money Henry made in his severance from Gen8tyx was sufficient enough to tide us over for quite a while. I got the impression that he'd done rather well out of it all. All else said, Gen8tyx seems to have looked after all of us very well indeed. I know that only last week, rather a substantial amount was deposited in his account."

"May I ask how much?"

"No. I'm afraid you may not. I hope you will understand if I defer from sharing such private details with you, without wanting to seem rude?"

Kerrin took the hint. The interview was coming to an end.

Shortly afterwards, as he drove out of the main gates onto the road, a lady hidden behind the trees lining the street took a photograph of his car.

It was late. The man had been in there for over an hour.

The woman looked at her watch and swore. 9.30 p.m. She should have been relieved thirty minutes ago. She was tired and hungry.

She hated the waiting. It was the worst part of her job.

Her replacement had better get there soon.

She wanted to go home.

CHAPTER 11
Day Nine
See View Heights
Orlando

"Darling, are you okay?" Kerrin asked his wife, genuinely missing her and wishing he was at home. He could do with a hug and a little bit of TLC. The past few days were beginning to get him down. All this talk of death was not his idea of fun.

"Don't worry about me. I'm okay. By the way, Elizabeth called. She said she's been trying to reach you on your cell phone all day. She can't get through. Can you call her when you get a chance?"

"Yes, thanks, I will. My battery is dead, and I forgot to bring my charger with me. I'll stop by a store tomorrow and pick up another one. Listen, are you sure you're fine?"

"Absolutely. I'm not saying it's good when you're away, but I'm getting a lot done. It's fantastic!"

"Nice to know I'm missed. Maybe I should go away more often?"

"Don't be silly darling, you know what I mean. So when are you coming home then? Soon, I hope?"

"Well, I still need to talk to a few more people, then I was wondering if I should fly to Arizona to see Elizabeth again. I might need to ask her some more questions."

"Can't you do it over the phone?"

"Maybe. I'll see. Anyway, after her, I've got to track down some person who seems to have disappeared."

"Why don't you call me tomorrow? It would be nice if you could get home for the weekend."

"I'll try. I'll speak to you tomorrow."

"I love you darling. Look after yourself!"

She hung up and Kerrin felt a tightness at the base of his stomach. He missed her. He would definitely try to be home for the weekend.

It was a hot night. Oppressive and close. Kerrin could feel the static in the air, and could hear the thunderstorm brewing in the background. Infuriatingly, the air conditioning unit in the room had developed an annoying clicking sound. And now he had become aware of it, no matter how hard he tried to ignore it, the tortuous clicking just seemed to get louder and louder.

Swearing aloud, Kerrin jumped out of bed and reached out to the control panel on the wall, sliding the little white button along from "Low" to "Off".

It took him a good forty minutes to fall asleep. Without the air conditioning, the heat on the third floor of the hotel slowly built up in the room, and it wasn't long before he started to toss and turn in his bed, cold sweat drenching his body and the sheets on which he lay.

Restless and uncomfortable, he quickly slipped into the same old repetitive nightmare that he always dreamt when his mind was troubled.

The car he was driving was his labor of love. The fact that it looked almost brand new was the result of all the years he had spent dutifully restoring it back to its former glory. It had been in a terrible state when he inherited it from an uncle, but after five years of hard graft it was once again in pristine condition. Kerrin was immensely proud of his efforts, and he loved to take the Morgan out for a drive in the long tree lined country lanes in the countryside around Dana's parents' farm in Pennsylvania.

The dream was always the same. Every second of it identical.

That afternoon there had been a storm, but now the skies were all clear and the air was clean and fresh.

He would be driving down the country road enjoying the scenery and the sunshine, the warm air coursing over their bodies as they swept around the bends and accelerated along the long, empty roads ahead. The storm had been over quickly. The ozone in the air mixed with the autumn smells from the farmland around, spicing it with the smell of the earth, and the sweet flavors of the wild flowers that grew so abundantly in the hedgerows on either side of the road. Kerrin breathed it deeply into his lungs.

He turned to look at Dana, sitting on the seat beside him, her luxurious long black hair blowing freely in the wind over the back of her shoulders. She smiled back, the late sun sparking in her blue eyes and twinkling back at him. She reached out her hand to Kerrin, and he took his right hand from the steering wheel to hold it.

Her hand was warm. He squeezed it lightly, and she smiled. Dana shuffled over in her seat towards him, pulling the seat belt slack so she could rest her head on Kerrin's shoulder.

He kissed her lightly on the forehead, and wrapped his arm around her before returning his attention to the road ahead.

The tractor was pulling out slowly from a blind entrance to a field. Before he passed through the gates, there was no way the tractor driver could have known whether or not there were any cars on the country road, and if there were, whether or not the car drivers would be paying attention to the road ahead instead of making love to their passengers. It wasn't the tractor driver's fault. This was the countryside, after all.

The brakes on the Morgan were brand new, the tread on the new tires deep and unworn.

Kerrin saw the tractor ahead, his body reacting instantly and his finely trained police driving skills throwing the Morgan into a swerve around the tractor on the opposite side of the road.

Dana screamed.

Kerrin gripped the steering wheel tightly, his eyes meeting briefly with the eyes of the tractor driver as they passed him by, easily clearing the tractor with a foot to spare.

Once past the tractor Kerrin looked on in disbelief as a car rounded the bend ahead, heading straight towards them. He braked hard, spinning the steering wheel quickly to bring the Morgan back onto the right side of the road.

The storm had not been hard, but the dead autumn leaves had thirstily soaked up the rain. As the car turned around the far side of the tractor, the back wheels of the Morgan fought in vain to find traction on the leaf mulch, and started to skid uncontrollably.

The Morgan spun across the road, Kerrin fighting hard to regain control. Then suddenly the tires found resistance on the tarmac, and propelled the car forward. Having over compensated too much, the car now spun around wildly in the opposite direction, its momentum carrying it broadside into the car ahead.

The front of the oncoming car smashed into their passenger side, propelling the Morgan backwards and into the hedge at the side of the road.

Kerrin was thrown violently against the door, away from the oncoming car, and the world went black around him.

Dimly Kerrin began to become aware of steam pouring from the bonnet of the Morgan. He turned his head and saw Dana unconscious in the seat beside him, her twisted body hanging awkwardly over the edge of her seat. The impact had thrown her body sideways, whipping her around violently in her seat, the seatbelt of the Morgan powerless to protect her from the spinning, sideways crash. Blood covered her legs, a shard of bent metal protruding through her thigh and poking out through her torn dress.

That's when he woke up. Screaming, and crying.

Kerrin splashed cold water onto the back of his neck and washed his face. Picking up one of the blue hand-towels from the handrail beside the sink, he wiped his face dry.

He walked back to the bed, switched on the cable T.V. and flicked impatiently through the channels without really paying them any attention.

The dream was always the same, and the nauseating feeling in his stomach when he awoke left him cold and drained. For the first few months after the crash, the guilt had been so bad that he had actually vomited when he awoke from the nightmare, but now, years later, he was able to lie back and ride it out.

He knew the pattern the guilt took. He knew he would never be able to put the accident properly behind him. He knew it wasn't entirely his fault. He even knew that Dana had never blamed him for it.

But it seemed so unfair. Kerrin had been driving. If anyone had been guilty for the crash, it was him. Yet Kerrin walked free with only a few scratches, and Dana had been crippled, the impact forces of the two cars jostling Dana so violently that a few vital nerves in her spinal column had been damaged beyond repair.

Sometimes Kerrin would wake up and lie for hours looking across at Dana. Before the accident he had loved her more than he thought it was physically possible to love any other human being. She was his life.

But now she relied upon him so much, he loved her even more.

Yes, sometimes he felt angry at the world. Anger at himself, and maybe even a little self-hate. But more than anything he felt sad. Sad at the life that had now been denied them. The adventures they had planned so meticulously together, the mountain hikes, and cycling trips and the walks along the beach at sunset. All gone. Dreams they had made, that now belonged to another life, for another couple.

Kerrin would do anything for Dana. There wasn't a thing in the world he wouldn't give if he could just undo those few seconds in Pennsylvania which had stolen so much from them both.

Anything.

Including his own life.

The Gen8tyx Company
Day Ten
Purlington Bay
California

David Sonderheim's office overlooked a scenic bay about ten miles outside of Carmel. His office was massive, a large window sweeping round in a giant curve, affording him an incredible view of the sea and their small harbor below. From here he could watch their guests arriving by boat, or just look at the seals bathing on the rocks beside the quay. In the background he could see the large ships heading in and out of San Francisco.

Light flooded into his office, but whenever he wanted, he could regulate the amount of daylight entering the room by electronically changing the polarization of the glass on the windows. Alternatively, at the flick of a switch, metal shutters could automatically rise and cover the windows, making the room both secure and pitch black.

A small panel on his desk allowed him to control everything about his office. The humidity, the lights, the business facilities, the electronic doors. With the flick of one switch, the far wall would open up, and a large back-lit projection screen would glide into place. From the comfort of his desk he could hold secure encrypted video conference sessions with people all around the globe. In an instant he could view any satellite channel in the world, show company presentations to guests in his office, or divide the screen up into smaller screenlets, so that he could simultaneously monitor the news on CNN, Bloomberg, and Yahoo-Finance.

David Sonderheim loved his new office.

He loved the feeling of power that it gave him. It was obvious to anyone that visited, that the owner of the office was an important man. Successful. Influential.

He crossed the room to the large model of the plant and the clinic, encased within glass and taking pride of place on a raised plinth against one of the walls. He looked down admiringly at the model, and studied the buildings which he had personally helped design and plan. A dream come true.

A dream which had taken a lifetime to realize. It had started long ago in a lower-income family living on the outskirts of Chicago. A young boy with asthma, who had grown up beaten by his father, and taunted and bullied by the other kids at school for his flaming bright red hair, a legacy of his Scottish ancestry.

He had hated his childhood, spending all his spare time in the library, hiding amidst the books and dreading the moment the library would close and he would have to go home. To escape his life, he liked to read stories about other people, people with perfect lives and fantastic families, and he would dream of being someone else.

Someone who could run for miles without running out of breath and struggling for air, and someone who could sleep without worrying about the bedroom door creaking open in the middle of the night and the sound of his father's footsteps coming towards him, drunk and angry.

A weak child, hunted and scared, he dreamt of a day when he would be strong and fit and no one would dare to bully him.

Seeking attention from his teachers, and then later his professors at college, he had studied hard and excelled at everything. He left home as soon as he could and chose a college as far from his father as possible. He soon grew out of being the weak, pathetic child that he was, and turned into a strong, tall and broad shouldered adolescent. His freckled face and flaming red hair helped him stand out from the crowd, and people noticed him wherever he went. And as his confidence grew, he even came to like the attention he received.

As the years past he became fascinated by biology, and then genetics, and slowly his dreams changed.

No longer the scared rabbit, Sonderheim dreamed of power. He saw the promise that genetics offered, the potential to control life, to create life, to change people. He recognized the power that lay behind mastery of the science. The power to take the weak and make them strong. To help the crippled walk, and the ill become well.

And, almost as a side-effect, he saw the opportunity to make money. Vast amounts of money.

Genetics would give him the power he wanted. The power to become a god amongst men.

To do what he wanted, and when he wanted.

And to be able to settle old scores.

Like the one he had settled six years ago, fulfilling one of his childhood dreams.

Since the day he ran away from home to live in dorms at college, he had had nightmares of his father's nocturnal visits. There had been no real reason for the weekly beatings. David had just been an easy target for a weak and pathetic man, who had become embittered with the lot life had given him, and who had not had the courage to do anything about it.

At the time, he had not seen his father for over ten years but his father was a man of habit and he guessed correctly that he probably still drank at the same old watering holes.

So one night they had driven down to the workman's bar, and waited until just after closing time. It was a cold, dark night, it had just rained and steam was rising from the gutters on the edges of the sidewalks. Their large, black limousine looked like an object from another planet, sitting at the end of the road, surrounded by buildings that had long been in need of repair, and with windows broken and boarded up.

Sonderheim sat patiently in the back of the limo, sipping champagne and watching each person as they staggered out of the bar, fifty yards down the road. He had waited a long time for this evening, and now he was in no rush, savoring each moment of anticipation. He was looking forward to the next fifteen minutes very much indeed.

The door of the bar opened, a shaft of light falling onto the sidewalk, and a man staggering forwards into the street. David recognized the figure of the man, stopping momentarily in front of the bar to adjust the cap on his head with both his hands, and reaching into his pockets to take out his cigarettes.

"That's him," David said softly.

The black limo inched slowly forwards, drawing up alongside the man who was walking away from them down the street. Two large men sprang out of the car, and grabbed the drunk man from behind, securing their grip on each of his arms and dragging him into the back of the limo.

Sonderheim's father tried struggling, but as he was pushed down onto the seat in front of David, he stopped resisting and looked up, trying to recognize the face of his son through his drunken haze.

The car drove for a few minutes before turning down a side street and coming to a stop in a dark alleyway surrounded by empty warehouses.

Grabbing the old man, Sonderheim's two henchmen pulled his father out of the car and flung him against the wall, pinning him with both arms and preventing him from moving.

David stepped out of the back door, brushing down his long black woolen coat, and adjusting the black leather gloves on his hands.

He stepped up to his father, who stared at him incredulously without speaking.

The taller of the two henchmen, a black man with a gold filling that sparkled in the orange neon light that dimly illuminated the alley, knocked off the old man's hat and forcibly lifted his face to stare at his son.

"So, father, it's a pleasure to see you again. I won't say that I've missed you, because I believe it's wrong to tell lies, but I will say that I have looked forward to tonight for a long time. A very long time."

"Son, I..." his father tried to speak.

The other henchman, a white man who had spent too long building muscle in the gym, lashed out with his fist. The blow knocked out a tooth and burst the old man's nose, and blood started to pour down his face. Unable to wipe away the blood with both his hands pinned against the wall, his father coughed and spluttered and struggled to breathe.

"No, don't talk when I'm talking to you. That's very rude too." David replied. "You know, it's quite sad really. The number of nights I've spent planning what to say to you tonight, preparing the long speech I was going to give you. But now I'm here, I don't think I'll waste my time. I think I'd rather just get straight to the fun part. Words won't really be necessary. I think you'll get the point...but first, if you don't mind, I'll get myself another glass of champagne. I'm rather thirsty."

David stepped back into the car, and returned a moment later with a fresh flute of sparkling Moët & Chandon. He stood with his back to the car, raised his glass towards his father, and sipped the bubbling, clear liquid. Then he nodded at his men, and watched silently as they began to beat his father to a pulp.

He stood passively, his face expressionless but his eyes alive and full of repressed emotion. He watched each blow and each kick as they rained down on his father, and as the blood flowed and the bones cracked, the memories of those nights in his bedroom came flooding back, a scared child being beaten black and blue for no reason he could understand. He remembered the tears, could once again taste the fear, and worst of all, could clearly smell the mess in his trousers that he often had to clear up quietly in the bathroom afterwards.

It was through a dim haze that David saw his father slide down the wall, bleeding heavily, crumpled and unconscious. David was lost in a world from long ago, erasing the memories of his past. Only slowly did he come back to the present and respond to the question he was being asked.

"Boss...Do you want us to kill him? I don't think he can take anymore."

"No...No, thank you. I think that will be enough."

David drank the rest of the champagne, looked briefly at the glass, then threw it down at the feet of his father before turning and getting back into the warmth of the limousine.

That was the last time David had seen him, but since that night the nightmares had never returned.

The clinic and the building displayed in the glass case had taken just over a year to build. It was set far back from the road, at the end of a small valley and natural inlet from the sea. From the highway, only those with the correct security clearance were allowed to drive down the winding, freshly tarmaced road leading to the bay, and would get to see just how large the new building actually was.

It was a marvel of modern engineering. The design complemented its natural surroundings and simultaneously captured the essence of modernity and ultra style. If it were not for the fact that officially the new Gen8tyx plant did not really exist, David felt sure the architect and the building would definitely win awards for modern architecture. Built from local stone, and the latest in office glass, the building blended in brilliantly to the local fauna and landscape, and although the large and extensive plate glass windows allowed everyone inside to see out, all the windows were one way only: people at Gen8tyx would be able to see clearly what happened in the world outside, but no one outside would ever be able to see inside Gen8tyx.

All the walls and the glass at Gen8tyx were embedded with the latest micromesh technology which prevented stray electromagnetic rays from escaping the building. It also prevented anyone outside scanning the building inside with laser beams, or high frequency radio probes. Even more, should anyone try to penetrate Gen8tyx security, sensors around the outside of the building continually monitored incoming radiation for anything that would indicate that they were being scanned.

Security at Gen8tyx was tight. The best it could get.

However, before they had completed the move to the new building there had been one small problem. There had been a serious breach of security in the weeks leading up to the move, which they had only just discovered. He should have anticipated it, and taken precautions. It was his fault, and he knew it.

The phone rang on his desk, and David walked back to it from the glass encased model.

"David, have you managed to locate the person who downloaded the data yet?"

The man on the other end of the phone was Nigel Small, from the Seattle operation.

"No, not yet. But I have taken precautions. And we'll get the information back soon. I promise you."

"I am sure you will. Please call me as soon as you have it. This is embarrassing me David. You know that in three weeks I'm going to New York, to make my report. I'm sure you will understand me when I say that it would not look good for either of us if I have to report that your security was breached."

"I understand. But please be assured that I have taken precautions. Even if we can't find the files, I can already assure you that no one will be in a position to make them public." David reached up, and wiped his forehead with a fresh handkerchief. In spite of the latest and greatest in air conditioning that money could buy, he had begun to sweat profusely.

"I shall hold you to that, David. Just don't let me find out that I was wrong to welcome you to the table of plenty."

The line went dead. David was surprised to notice that his hand was trembling. For the first time since the move to California he began to wonder if he was perhaps a little out of his depth.

He didn't need anyone in Seattle to remind him about the missing files. He knew the score, and the danger they represented. He was doing everything he could, and they had already recovered all of the copies, bar two. But it wasn't only the files.

Six of the core team had refused to come to California. Six of the best geneticists in the world. Each one of them had become an example of what the Orlando Treatment could achieve.

As long as anyone of them remained alive, the risk of exposure was too high. The progress that had been made through his new found contacts had been brilliant, but one person was still evading their grasp. The Alpha team had been successful in tracking him down to South Africa, but as of yet, Alex Swinton was still free.

David couldn't afford to fail his superiors. He knew only too well that things hadn't gone as smoothly as planned over the past couple of months, but he was determined to rectify that. Nothing would come between him and his dream. Nothing. And no one.

He dialed a number in Miami. It would be about five o'clock there now.

"It's Sonderheim. I want to know exactly what progress you've made. We only have a week left before the shit hits the fan..."

CHAPTER 12
Day Ten
Sam Cohen's House
Orlando

Sam Cohen was the last on Kerrin's list of those who had 'committed suicide'. According to Kerrin's sister Elizabeth, Sam was not married, and he lived with his elderly sister on the outskirts of Burlington, a little seaside town, about fifty miles north of Orlando. Apart from the address, and the telephone number, that was about all Elizabeth could say about him, except that Sam was the quietest of the group, and didn't socialize as much as the others.

First thing in the morning Kerrin drove to the nearest mall, and bought himself a new battery and a cell phone charger. Keeping the receipts so that he could claim it all back on expenses from The Post later, he drove out of town and headed towards Burlington.

En route he stopped at a deli to pick up some breakfast, and made a call to Cohen's sister. Luckily she was at home, and after explaining about Martin and what he was trying to do she agreed to see him.

Once again the weather in Florida was perfect. "Wake up to Another day in Paradise, Welcome to Florida!" he remembered reading somewhere on a car sticker. They weren't far wrong. The place was beautiful.

He missed living in Florida. Deciding that he wasn't in such a rush after all, he took the next exit off the freeway, and found his way back down to the coastal highway. It would only take an extra thirty minutes if he went the scenic route.

The coast road wove in and out of towns clustered around their own little patch of sandy coastline, full of happy people stretched out on the silver sands, playing volleyball and already supping beers. It reminded Kerrin of his times spent on Spring Break down in the Keys, before he had joined the force.

Although not too busy, the route Kerrin had chosen was taking longer than expected, the numerous traffic lights along the way forcing him to continuously stop and start while switching his attention back and forward from the beach to the road ahead.

Just after passing through a little town called Crighton Heights, Kerrin realized almost too late that the light in front had changed color.

Slamming on the brakes, he managed to stop just in time. Anticipating the jarring thud that could come from the car behind slamming into his rear end, he flashed a backward glance in his rear mirror. Luckily, the nearest car to him was quite far behind, a blue Mazda, which had no problem in stopping, and came easily to a halt ten feet behind him. Slightly embarrassed, Kerrin drove on, and learning his lesson, paid less attention to the bikini clad beauties on the beach, and more to the road.

The Cohen household had a fantastic view of the beach. Their private stretch of land ran from the house down across the sand dunes to the silver beachfront, just visible from the road. The house was situated high on a hill at the end of a low lying piece of headland, which commanded an excellent view of the sweeping bay in front.

It had to be said, that the core team of geneticists at Gen8tyx all seemed to be doing very well for themselves. All of them had expensive houses, and the cars parked in the driveways were not exactly cheap.

"It's a beautiful view isn't it? You can understand why my brother loved to live here so much!"

The voice of a woman caught him off guard. He had been so wrapped up in the panorama, that he had not seen her coming out of the house and walking down the path to the roadside.

The three storey house was set back from the road, a large covered porch running around the outside of the building. The sunlight bounced off the bright white walls, and glistened off the beautiful, well-tended, exotic flowers and shrubs that bordered the house and the edge of the path. Everything looked fresh, clean and inviting. The bright green of the grass, obviously irrigated well and often, cut a sharp yet complementary contrast to the bright yellows, reds and blues of the flowers, the white of the house, and the blue of the sky and the sea beyond. It reminded him of a fairly tale house, the sort of house a person always dreamt of owning, but realistically knew he never would.

Except Sam Cohen had realized that dream. Then he had died.

"I'm sorry. I didn't notice you, I was admiring the view of the house and the sea so much. My name is Kerrin Graham...I called you about an hour ago?"

"Yes, yes, I guessed it was you. Welcome to 'Traum Villa'. It would have made Sam happy to know you like the place so much. Come...come, I have tea. Or would you like a cold beer? Sam liked cold beer..."

He followed her into the house, noticing immediately how clean and ordered everything was. The interior was as beautiful as the outside. Golden, bright, almost glowing wooden floors, with white, yellow and cream walls. Luxurious white leather armchairs and sofas, fresh cut flowers. The scent of lemon in the air...In spite of the fact that the place looked too clean, perhaps a little too much like a museum that wasn't lived in for Kerrin's taste, he had to admit to himself that he had fallen in love with the building as soon as he had seen it. He would not have to ask Sam Cohen's sister why he had not gone to live in California. It would be a stupid question.

She took him past several rooms in to the back of the house, to a living room which took up most of the ground floor. The back of the room was dominated by a set of vast, panoramic windows which ran from the floor to the ceiling and captured every ounce of light, letting the vista of the blue bay outside flood into the house and wash over him.

In one corner of the room was a large, white, Steinway grand piano, and immediately Kerrin was seized by the romance of what it would be like to sit at the piano and play, looking out onto such a view.

The room was incredible.

He turned to Ms Cohen, about to say something, but was met by her smile. She had been standing by his side, studying his reaction to the room and the panoramic view, and when he noticed her smile, the pride in her eyes, he knew that words were not necessary. Instead he just smiled back, and for a moment something was shared between the two of them.

"Sam would have liked you Mr. Graham. How can I help you?"

As his sister told the story, Kerrin learned that Sam's story was both a sad and happy one.

In spite of himself, Kerrin began to like the man, and he wished that he had been able to meet him in life, and not in tales of death.

Sam had married once, but after five years of happiness together, his wife and unborn daughter had died in childbirth.

While courting, Sam and his wife-to-be had first found the house together one afternoon, when strolling along the beach. In those days, the house was old and run-down, but in the weeks that followed whenever they walked along the beach, hand in hand, they had looked up at the house and played imaginative games, describing to each other how they would repair and restore it if the house belonged to them. They had dreamt dreams of a life together, and of growing old in the house on the hill.

Then one day, the old woman who lived in the house had died and without his girlfriend knowing, Sam had bought the deeds to the property.

On the night he proposed to her he had taken her to the gate at the bottom of the path that led from the beach to the house, and had gone down on one knee.

She had cried, and when she said 'yes', Sam had given her the keys to the house.

From then on, and for the rest of her life, she had worn the ring that bound the keys of the house together as her engagement ring. Three months later they were married, and together they had started to repair and rebuild the house.

Theirs had been a happy marriage. Two lives, one love. Strong and beautiful.

Sam had never remarried. Had never loved again. Had never fully found how to live again. A life lived in the past.

The house had become a memorial to their love.

The house on the hill.

As Sam's sister had recounted the story to him, Kerrin felt himself strangely moved. The fairytale house with its own little fairytale. It seemed so unfair that tragedy had come back to revisit the same household so cruelly.

"So how did he die, Miss Cohen?"

"The police say he drowned himself. They found the body lying on the beach at the bottom of the garden."

"And did he?"

"Of course not. The part of the story that I haven't told you yet was that Sam and his wife had made a vow to each other, a vow which they had sworn to each other and taken as solemnly as their wedding vows. On the first night they had come here, after Sam had bought the house, they sat in this room and opened a bottle of champagne. They were young, and in love. Their lives were before them, and as they sat in the house with the paper peeling off the wall, the old oak doors rotten with woodworm, and the water dripping through the roof, they made a lover's promise to each other..."

Sam's sister was smiling, but the tears had started to roll from the corners of her eyes.

"...They had promised each other that they would rebuild the house, and turn it into the most beautiful house in the world...a house of dreams…the 'Traum' house. No matter what happened to each other, if one of them died, the other person would make sure it was finished."

"…They were young, they were in love…perhaps a little foolish…neither of them could have foretold her tragic death so soon afterwards. Anyway, Sam never forgot the vow he made. He has spent the past twenty years fixing the house up with his own hands."

"I don't understand…" Kerrin loved the story, but didn't see where she was going with it.

"Come with me…come with me," she urged him, beckoning with her hand.

He followed her out of the large living room and up three flights of stairs, coming out into the attic space beneath the roof. Unlike the rest of the house, which was almost perfect in every way, the attic was a mess. Floorboards were lying piled on top of each other in a corner underneath one of the gables, and the smell of fresh paint still lingered in the air. Electricity cables hung loosely from the ceiling, and some plastic pipes lay in a pile, beside some carpet tiles, which were still in their boxes, untouched and unwrapped.

"Sam had just started working on the attic. It's the last room to be done in the house. He was taking his time with it, but said it would be finished next year sometime. The house was truly a labor of love, in all sense of the words. Sam was heartbroken, yes, but he would never have broken his vow and taken his own life before he had finished this last room…never…"

They were sitting together again downstairs in the large room with the stunning view, drinking coffee and eating some of Miss Cohen's delicious home baked cakes.

"Could it have been an accidental drowning?" Kerrin asked.

"I don't think so. Sam was very strong. He swam in the bay almost every day. He knew all the tides, all the currents. He could swim for a couple of hours with ease. Only three weeks ago I watched with the binoculars as he swam from here right over to the other headland and back. Do you know how many miles that is?"

Kerrin looked out of the window, following the direction the lady was pointing in.

It was a hell of a long way. He must have been an incredibly strong swimmer.

"Did he have any enemies?"

"I don't think so...Sam hardly ever went out. We lived a quiet life here together. Growing vegetables and tending the garden. It's a possibility he did have enemies, but he never mentioned them to me."

"What about work?"

"He was dedicated to it. Apart from the house, it was his main interest in life. Kept on saying that he wanted to be able to help other people, that what he was doing was really important."

"Do you know what he was working on?"

"No. He said that he couldn't discuss it at home. Not that I would have understood a word. It was enough for me that it made him happy."

"Was he under any stress in the last few months?"

"Of course he was! He didn't want to lose his job, Mr Graham. He wanted to keep it. But he wouldn't...couldn't... move to California. His life was here. With this house..." She paused, moving to the piano and stroking the ivory keys, before picking up one of the pictures that sat on top of it.

She stared at it for a while, a look of admiration showing on her face, then she handed it to Kerrin.

"Look...that's Sam in the top corner. They took that about three weeks ago at the bottom of the garden...just over there."

Kerrin took the picture from her. It was a photo of six people standing in a tight group holding beers and wine, and he immediately recognized that it was a picture of all the people whose deaths he was investigating. Everybody was there...he recognized Martin, Alex, Tom, and also Mike and Henry from the pictures he had seen at their widow's houses.

"May I please borrow this for a day or two, and make a copy of it? I'm sure all the other bereaved relatives would love a copy too?"

"That's a nice idea. Please. But take care of it..."

"What was the occasion?"

"I don't know. I think they had a meeting about what was going on...yes, that's it... I remember now. Sam and Tom, that's him there..."she said pointing to the photo..."they were really concerned about the new people that were joining the company. Henry had guessed what was going on, and I think he called the meeting because he wanted to tell everybody something. Henry,...yes, that's him...yes, it was his idea."

"What happened? Did Sam say anything about it later?"

"No. But after the meeting Sam was both angry and excited at the same time. He said, 'they weren't going to take it lying down.' Talked about a Phoenix, and something about them rising from the ashes? Does that make any sense to you Mr Graham?"

"I think it does. I think that Henry Roberts knew what was happening. He had to...he was the financial guru behind Gen8tyx. Perhaps he called a meeting to explain it all to the others? And maybe they decided to stand up for themselves and start their own company!"

"Oh, that would have been nice. Sam always wanted to have his own company...Poor Sam...Mr Graham, do you know why my brother was killed?" she looked at him, a sadness clouding over her eyes.

"No. Not yet, Miss Cohen. But I promise you, I'm going to find out. And when I do, I'm going to make sure that whoever is responsible will pay for it."

As Kerrin left the house, closing the garden gate behind him, he noticed the blue Mazda sitting on the opposite side of the road, about a hundred yards further up the hill. As he glanced in its direction, there was a flash of light from something inside the car on the driver's side, almost like the reflection of sunlight off a mirror.

He climbed into his car, switched on the ignition, and drove slowly down the hill towards the sea. With one eye on his rear-view mirror, he noticed the Mazda pull away from the sidewalk and start to drive after him.

The same blue Mazda that had nearly crashed into him at the traffic lights only hours before.

The man in the blue Mazda, dropped the newspaper and picked up the camera. His target was just coming out of the house.

"Damn, the sunlight!" the man swore as he tried to take a quick picture. The sunlight was streaming straight into the lens and it made taking any photographs impossible.

He picked up his cell phone from the seat beside him, speaking without introducing himself to the woman at the other end.

"He's just leaving the Cohen woman. What do you want me to do?"

"Nothing yet. Just follow him, and find out where he's staying..."

"Okay. Will do. Have you heard anything from New York?"

"Not yet. In the meantime, don't lose him. We need to know what he's going to do next."

CHAPTER 13

Try as he might, Kerrin could not shake off the Mazda. It wasn't as easy as it looked in the films and the last time he had been in a car chase, he was the one doing the chasing. He tried stopping and letting the car behind him pull past, but a few minutes later the car was there again, back on his tail. He pulled into a gas station. The car waited outside.

He doubled back on himself. The Mazda followed.

He tried everything he could. It didn't help.

Whoever the person in the Mazda was, they were pretty good. The sort of 'good' that only came from being a professional.

"Come on...you used to be a professional too...Think boy, think!"

The car had been tailing him for almost an hour. He was passing through the outskirts of Miami now, his heart racing at over one hundred and twenty beats a minute, even though he was sitting still and the car was doing the driving.

He frantically absorbed his surroundings as he drove, mentally noting all the alleyways and shops on either side of the road.

"How can I lose him? How?"

He was looking for somewhere to hide. Somewhere to disappear.

It was almost dark now. That at least would help him.

The Mazda was about five cars back. Good, that was giving a little distance between them.

Suddenly on the left hand side Kerrin spotted a garage. A car was just driving out of the attached car wash, and there was no queue behind it. When he looked back to the road he realised he was just coming up to a changing light, and on instinct he gunned it, pushing down hard on the pedal and shooting across the junction.

The cars behind him stopped, trapping the Mazda behind them.

Kerrin accelerated, heading towards the next junction as fast as he could. He reached it just as the lights were changing, and as he pulled through it he immediately hung a left. As he shot off into the street ahead, he glanced sideways, noticing the Mazda just clearing the first set of lights.

The street he had entered was quite clear, and using every ounce of skill he could remember from his police driving courses, he threw his car into a one-hundred-and-eighty-degree hand-break turn and headed back to the junction he had just come from, his high beams on full. As soon as the lights changed, he turned right on the inside lane, a row of moving cars flanking his left hand side.

As he made the corner he noticed the Mazda passing him in the other direction, turning left into the street now behind him.

Kerrin accelerated again, this time easily making the light ahead before it turned to red. Without slowing down he pulled into the garage twenty yards past the lights, and drove straight into the covered car wash.

He jumped out of the car, and walked to the edge of the covered exit, poking his head round the corner just enough to see the road. He waited.

About fifteen seconds later the blue Mazda accelerated past him, heading back down the road towards the edge of the city.

He walked across the forecourt into the shop.

"What's the slowest wash?"

"Wash, wax and dry. Six dollars."

"Fine. Give me four!"

"Four?"

"My car's very dirty."

The man flicked him four blue tokens and change from thirty dollars and Kerrin walked back to the car, popping the first token into the slot. As the machinery around him whirred into action, and the water poured down over the car, he slid back into his seat and started to relax.

Twenty minutes later, he pulled out of the car wash. The blue Mazda was nowhere to be seen.

Two blocks away he found a Hertz rental agency. He took the car in, and swapped it for something a different colour and a little faster. But not so clean.

As soon as Kerrin got back to the hotel room he paid the bill and checked out. Keeping a careful eye out for any suspicious looking cars, he drove about ten blocks away and checked into a motel, where sixty dollars a night got him air conditioning, a T.V. and a room with no view. For now, Kerrin wanted to disappear.

Who had been following him? And why?

He needed to think. To pull together what little he knew, sift through it all and see if there was anything solid that he could go on.

Using the pillows, he propped himself up on his bed against the wall, kicked off his shoes and settled down to do some work. Changing the batteries in his tape-recorder, he pulled out his notebook and listened to each of his interviews once again. This time he made notes, picking up a few new things, some important, some not, that he hadn't caught the first time around.

It was ten o'clock when he had finished, and as he scanned his notes, he satisfied himself that something interesting was beginning to emerge.

He wandered through to the bathroom and ran himself a bath. As he lay back in the warm water, he emptied his mind. His heart was pounding and his mind was racing, and only then did he realise just how wound up and excited he was. Trailing round the relatives of the those who had died, asking questions and trying to unravel the puzzle that was beginning to appear before him, then the car chase... It reminded him of the old days when he had been in the force. He hated to admit it, but even though he shouldn't be given the circumstances of the investigation, he was beginning to enjoy himself.

He took a breath then sank down under the water, trying to relax. But try as he might, he couldn't. Questions kept popping into his mind, new questions, good questions, questions which needed to be answered.

Who were the owners of Gen8tyx?

Henry Roberts had been planning to go to California, but had changed his mind. Why? His widow had guessed that perhaps he had found out that he wouldn't be needed after all.

How could that be? Why would Gen8tyx want to replace their Chief Financial Officer, at a time when he should be needed more than ever?

And what were all those late night long distance phone conversations about? And why had Henry gone to the office so late at night on the evening he had hung himself?

Did he actually make it to the office?

What was it that Henry knew about the business that the others didn't?

Questions. Questions. And more questions.

He got out the bath and towelled himself down, returning to his bed. He decided to go with the flow, and started making more notes as the questions continued to flow into his mind.

His thoughts returned to the suicides...

What amazed him was just how quickly the police had closed the files on their deaths. It was obvious to Kerrin, after just three days of investigating, that none of the deaths were clear cut suicides. The circumstances of their deaths were highly suspicious, and everywhere you started to scratch at the surface you uncovered more questions.

Coupled with the fact that those who had died had all worked for one of the most advanced Genetics companies in the world, on a secret project that none of them could talk about. A project, that according to Mike's fiancée was just about to, or possibly already had, just come to some fantastic conclusion, before they were all fired!

And then again, why had David Sonderheim brought new people into the company months in advance of the move to California? Thankfully, that question at least, was probably easily answered.

Sonderheim had obviously been planning the move for a while, and had perhaps known that the core team wouldn't go. So he had planned it in advance, bringing new people on board, all master scientists in their own right, to slowly take over the work from the original team members.

The question that deserved to be asked though, was 'Why did Sonderheim want to move the company in the first place?' Why was he prepared to lose the experience and enthusiasm of the founding core staff and run the risk of hindering the ongoing development of the company?

The more you thought about it, the more suspicious it became.

"Conspiracy theory. Conspiracy theory…"

The words rattled round inside his head. He quickly shut them out, refusing to let his imagination run wild. He had to look at it all objectively.

But the more objectively he looked at it, the worse it got.

Why had the files in the police station disappeared?

Why were the files on the computer classified by the FBI?

And then, in the midst of all these questions, he remembered Martin's jet blowing up miles above the Atlantic Ocean. He had already concluded that a military jet had been in the same airspace when the explosion had taken place, but that its flight plan had possibly been covered up.

But who had the authority to make a military flight take off, then erase the records as if it had never happened?

"Conspiracy theory. Conspiracy theory…"

Kerrin got up and walked to the fridge. He took out a cold can of coke, and popped the lid, drinking it slowly as he sat back down on the edge of the bed.

"Military jet…explosion…cover up…" His mind was racing. Then suddenly a new thought entered his mind.

"Did the military jet deliberately shoot down Martin's plane?"

The thought filled his head, and for a few minutes Kerrin sat there in silence, staring into space.

Slowly he became aware of a regular, annoying, dripping sound. He got up and went to the sink in the bathroom, turning the tap off tight. He leant on the hand-basin with both hands, staring at himself in the mirror. His face was tired and drawn. Beads of sweat were beginning to appear on his forehead, and his pupils were tiny pinpricks in the centre of his eyes.

The face looking back at him was of someone he did not recognise. It belonged to someone who had just begun to experience the sensation of fear. Kerrin was scared.

"Hey, James, what are you doing?"

"Just got off my shift, heading home! It's been a long day. Two homicides and an armed hold-up. Why, what are you up to?"

"I'm buying you a beer. I need to talk to someone...and I need your help again."

Thirty minutes later the girl behind the bar at Hooters plonked two large cold Budweisers in front of them, pulled a pen from behind her ear, and made two marks on their coasters.

James picked up his beer, studying the bubbles bursting from the bottom of the glass and racing towards the surface.

"So, what's up? I thought you'd be back in Washington by now. Not that it ain't nice having you around. It makes a break from watching re-runs of Friends on cable!"

"Would you believe I just like the weather so much that I don't want to leave again?"

"Nope. You've already told me you need my help. So being the great detective that I am, and using all my powers of deduction, would you be surprised if I guessed that it had something to do with the Orlando Suicides?"

"Wow. I'm impressed. Truly impressed."

"I'm a man of wonders. So what's the deal...what did you find out?"

"Not enough. I've now got more questions than I started with. But one thing's certain. They didn't commit suicide. They were killed," Kerrin said, watching for James's reaction.

"Are you sure? Why don't you run it by me from the top?" James turned to Kerrin, making himself a little more comfortable in his seat at the bar.

Kerrin looked around him quickly. Satisfied that the other people wouldn't be able to overhear them, he started off from when they had last met. James listened attentively, stopping him every now and again to ask a few questions, but on the whole listening to everything Kerrin had to say. When he got to the part about the blue Mazda, his eyes lit up. At the end of it all James whistled aloud. Then he went silent for a while, and Kerrin decided to take a convenience break, leaving his old friend to absorb what he had just heard. He returned a few minutes later.

"So what do you want me to do, good buddy?" James asked him.

"First of all, I want your opinion. Your gut reaction."

"Okay, gut reaction? Catch the first stage out of town, and don't look back. Something funny is going down. And without your badge, you're in way over your head."

"I'd reached that conclusion myself. But I'm glad you agree."

"Second..." James turned to his old friend, resting his hand on his shoulder..."We both know that you're not going to walk away from this, so you're going to need help. And since I'm the only other fool in town, I suppose that means me. "

"Bingo. That's the other conclusion I had reached too. But that's as far as I got...what do I...we?...do next?"

"I'd say your next step is to try and track down the guy Alex Swinton. Either he's dead in a ditch somewhere, or he's the only person alive that might know what's going on around here..."

"But how do I find out where he is?"

"That's where I come in. Leave that bit to me."

"What about the obvious?"

"And what's that?" James asked, annoyed that he might have missed something.

"What about going straight to this guy David Sonderheim?"

"Why? What can he tell us just now? If he's the guilty one, and you start sniffing around asking him questions, he'll just get defensive, and you'll lose any element of surprise you may have. No, you can't talk to him unless you know a bit more about what's going on. Anyway, these deaths might have nothing to do with him."

"You're right. But can you get me some information on him?"

"Like what?"

"Anything. Something's better than nothing. Like, for example, where is he now?"

"I'll see what I can do."

"What about the police files on the suicides? Are you sure you can't get access to the files?"

"No. As I said before, it's not easy. They need Federal access codes. I would have to get somebody else to do it for me...pull a few favours...but the Feds would soon know we were messing around. What's the point anyway? If you know already they were killed, you won't get any new information that way."

"Okay. Okay..." Kerrin agreed. Perhaps seeing the files would give them nothing new.

"What about the hospital? Would they have done an autopsy on Henry Roberts?"

"Maybe."

"Something happened the night Henry Roberts died. There was a phone call late at night and after he took it, he told his wife he had to go back to the office. It would be good to know if he actually made it there."

"Who's to say he was going to the office? He could have been going anywhere. What would really help you, is to know where the call came from, and also where all those long distance calls you mentioned were coming from? Why don't you ask me to get copies of the phone bills?"

"Could you?"

"For you? Sure. No problem."

"Great! The thing is, I was wondering if Mr Roberts had met somebody that night. Somebody who wanted to kill him. Maybe they tried to make it look like suicide by hanging him from a tree, but forgot about the dogs patrolling the grounds. Then they got chased off before they could make sure the job was done properly."

"Feasible..."

"Then luckily for them, ..."

"...Whoever 'they' are..." James interrupted.

"Exactly, then luckily for them, he goes into a coma. But what would happen if he woke up, and told everyone what had happened?..." Kerrin waited to see if James could see where he was going.

"...So they had to make sure he didn't wake up?" James suggested, beginning to enjoy the train of thought.

"...The police told his wife it was a heart attack. Are there any drugs that can kill a man quickly but would make it look like a heart attack?"

"Quite a few, but you wouldn't know they had been used unless you thought the death was suspicious and you were looking for them. When's the funeral?"

"I don't know. "

"Well, if it hasn't happened yet there's still a chance I could have a word with the coroner and ask him to run some basic tests for me."

"Okay. Can you get on to that tomorrow?"

"No problem. Is there anything else?" James asked cheekily.

"Don't think so."

"So what are you going to do next?" James asked him.

"I'll head back to Washington tomorrow. Spend a few days with Dana. Then as soon as you get any information on the whereabouts of Alex Swinton, I'll go after him. In the meantime, I want to find out a bit more about Gen8tyx. I've got some friends in Washington who can help me with that."

"Boy, what would you do without friends?"

"That, my friend, is one question I hope I never have to answer."

CHAPTER 14
Day Eleven
The Gen8tyx Company
Purlington Bay
California

The long, black limousine pulled up in front of the reception to the Gen8tyx Company and Trevor Simons opened the door, and stepped out slowly. He steadied himself against the side of the car, then stood up tall and smoothed down his expensive Versace suit, before adjusting the position of the Rolex on his wrist. He watched in mild amusement as the group awaiting his arrival scurried out from the protection of the air-conditioned reception hall into the thirty-five degree heat of the Californian afternoon.

His aide stepped up beside him, carrying his attaché case and walking stick, and Trevor took them both.

"Thank you Daniel. Please arrange for my luggage to be taken directly to my room."

"Certainly, sir."

The first of the reception committee walked up to him, reaching out his hand and welcoming him. He recognized him immediately as David Sonderheim, CEO and founder of the Gen8tyx Company. The file he had just finished reading on him was quite comprehensive: an impressive man, intelligent, charismatic and rich, but one whom he should not be foolish enough to trust. Sonderheim was a man of some caliber, but he had not got to where he was today without demonstrating the characteristics of many of the world's great leaders: greed, loyalty only to one's self and one's own personal cause, and the ability to lie proficiently.

Yet every man had a weakness, and Trevor made it his business to find them. Trevor had smiled knowingly to himself when he read the report on Sonderheims' Achilles' heel and weakness. Women. The same, simple Achilles' heel of almost all powerful men, and one with which Trevor would easily be able to manipulate Sonderheim in the future, should the necessity arise.

The others who came scurrying out behind him would be of no importance. Minions of no strategic value. Looking through and behind them, he noticed that Colonel Packard had not ventured outside into the heat. Instead, he was waiting patiently just inside the glass doors, within the confines of the cool, dry air and out of reach of the direct sunlight. Trevor respected that. He was not a pawn like the others, to be played as and when was required. Colonel Packard was a powerful man indeed. The title of course was false, and betrayed his true position in the military. Who he really was, Trevor may never know. Like himself, Colonel Packard had no file.

"Mr Simons, welcome to Gen8tyx. I trust you had a pleasant journey."

"Thank you I did. It is a pleasure to meet you Mr Sonderheim. I am looking forward to learning about the Orlando Treatment first hand. Your reports have been most interesting. And if I may say so, your photographs do not do you justice. I did not realize you were so young..."

The direct personal touch caught Sonderheim off balance for a second, and while Trevor scanned the man's eyes for a reaction, he held onto his hand in a long, prolonged handshake which immediately made Sonderheim feel uncomfortable. The first battle of charisma and power had been won. Sonderheim would be no match for Trevor Simons.

"Have the others arrived?" Trevor asked.

"Yes. Everyone is here."

"Excellent. Then let us proceed."

Miami
Day Eleven
Florida

The next flight to Washington that day would be at 1 p.m. That gave Kerrin several hours to tie up a few loose ends.

Foremost of these was to try and get a look at Mike's computer. Ideally, Kerrin would like to have a look at the hard-drive for himself.

Just before falling asleep last night he had remembered that Mike's fiancée had given him the telephone number of the policeman who had taken the computer away for inspection. The telephone number was a local Miami number. Not knowing exactly what he was going to say, he dialed the number. Kerrin always thought on his feet. He would bluff his way along.

A woman's voice answered.

"Hello, Miami Police Department. How may I direct your call?"

"Hello. May I speak to Officer Trevelli of the Miami Police Computer Investigation Department, please?"

"Could you spell it for me please?"

"Officer T-r-e-v-e-l-l-i."

"I'm sorry sir, but Officer Trevelli is no longer with the police department. Can I direct you to anyone else?"

"That's surprising, I was just given his card last week by a man who claimed to be him. Can you please put me through to someone who might know where I may be able to find him?"

"I'm sorry, but you say you were just given his card? Can you hold please, I will transfer you to one of his colleagues."

The sound of an orchestra playing "Don't Cry for Me Argentina" took over from the voice of the operator, and Kerrin had just begun to enjoy the music when a brusque, male voice boomed down the phone.

"Hello? This is Captain Weiss. I understand that you were recently given the card of Officer Trevelli, and that you claim to have spoken to him? May I ask in connection with what?"

"He was working on a suicide investigation and he took away the computer of a friend of mine for investigation and analysis. The case is now closed, and we wanted to have the computer back."

"Can you describe to me what this man looked like?"

Kerrin was surprised by the questions being asked. Something was obviously wrong.

"Excuse me Captain. Is there a problem?"

"Yes, you could say that. Captain Trevelli was murdered ten days ago. I was wondering, could you please come down to the station to make a statement for us...?"

Kerrin hung up.

"Hello, Mrs Roberts, this is Kerrin Graham. We met a few days ago when I came to your house to talk about Henry?"

"Oh yes. How are you? Do you want to ask me some more questions?"

"Just one. I know your husband worked from home a lot. I was wondering if there was a possibility that your husband might have had some information on his computer that could help me in understanding why he died."

"You may be right. Unfortunately if you want to look at the computer you will have to talk to the police department. About a week ago, one of their officers came and took away the PC and the laptop he used to take with him on business trips."

"Can you remember the name of the police officer, or can you tell me how I may get in contact with him?"

"Certainly, the officer was very polite, and he left me his card. I'll just go and get it..."

Mrs Roberts returned two minutes later.

"Captain Trevelli. That was his name. Would you like his number?"

"No. Thank you Mrs Roberts. That won't be necessary. I already have it."

Fifteen minutes and two more phone calls was all it took to find out that Captain Trevelli had also paid a visit to the widow of Tom Calvert and the sister of Sam Cohen. The annoying thing was that Trevelli, whoever he really was, had only just visited Ms Cohen last night. That meant that the computer had still been there when Kerrin had been talking to his sister! If he hadn't been so caught up in the tales of Sam's love life, he might have had the presence of mind to ask the question yesterday, not the next day when it was too late.

The description that Sam's sister had given of the Captain was too generic to be of any use. A police captain dressed in uniform. Polite. Dark hair. Italian looking. It could be any one of a thousand police officers in Miami.

Kerrin could kick himself. From now on he had to stay focused. This was no longer a game. People were dying all around him.

Kerrin had to find Alex Swinton fast. Before Captain Trevelli's namesake did.

Of course there was one other widow that 'Captain Trevelli' would not yet have had the opportunity to visit: his sister. She had not returned home after her husband's accident.

He glanced at his watch. It was 11.45 a.m. It was probably already too late to make the flight to Washington. He would have to put it off for another day.

He had better call his wife, to stop her driving out to the airport to pick him up.

He dialed her number.

The phone rang. There was no answer.

He redialed the number. She should be home. He had already called her first thing that morning and when he had spoken to her, she'd had no plans to go out.

Still no answer. He hung up.

What should he do? What if something had happened? He suddenly remembered the vision of the blue Mazda tailing him in his car's rear-view mirror, and a surge of panic passed through him. Had Captain Trevelli's friends got to his wife?

He dialed the number again, doing a quick calculation in his mind to see if he would still have time to get to the airport to get the Washington flight home. Yes, he might just make it if he really hurried.

"Hello darling. Did you just call me a minute ago? Sorry, I was outside in the garden..."

"Thank God!" Kerrin made no attempt at hiding his relief.

"Why? What's the matter?"

"Nothing…nothing. It's okay. Just overreacting. Listen, I'm sorry. I'm not going to make the 1 o'clock flight after all. I think I need to go over to Elizabeth's house."

"Okay, that's fine. But please try to make it home tomorrow…you know we're meant to be going to dinner with the Petersons tomorrow? Oh, by the way, Elizabeth called this morning. Wanted to know what you were up to and if you'd made any progress. She sounded a lot better…"

"I'll call her now. Are you okay?"

"Yes. Fine,…don't worry about me. But just make sure you're back tomorrow!"

Kerrin knew that his sister was trying to reach him. His cell phone told him she had called him three times so far, while he was on the phone to the others but he had not yet got round to calling her back. He dialed her cell-phone number.

"Hey Sis! How are things going?"

"Oh…as good as can be expected I suppose. The weather here in Arizona is fantastic. And there is so much to do here on the ranch. It's keeping us all occupied. But the children have taken it very hard. I try my best to console them, but I don't think they understand yet…I don't think I do either. We all miss Martin. Anyway,…how's everything going with your investigation?" Elizabeth asked.

"Interesting. Very interesting."

"Listen Kerrin, don't do anything stupid, will you? Promise me? I've already lost Martin…I couldn't bear to lose you too!"

"Don't worry. I'm a big boy now. Elizabeth, I would like to go round to your house and have a look at Martin's computer. Would you mind?"

"No. Not at all. Do you still have your keys?"

"Yes."

"Okay, but I'll need to tell you the security code so you can disable the alarm on the way in the door. Don't forget…otherwise you'll have half the Orlando police force on your back."

"Did Martin have a safe-place where he might keep any private files or personal CD's, …or back-up hard-drives or memory sticks for his computer?"

"Yes. In his office he had a book on the bookshelf that looked as if it was leather bound, but was really hollow on the inside with a metal box hidden inside the cover. It's on the third shelf up beside the window."

"What's the book called?"

" 'A Golden Collection of Shakespearean Tragedies.' It's quite thick with a red cover. And the spare key to Martin's study will be with the others in the usual place." Kerrin knew where that was. It was inside the large green vase beside the television. That's also where they kept the spare car keys.

They chatted for a while, Kerrin took a note of the security code to disable the house alarm, and then said goodbye. He promised to call her again later that night.

It was a long drive back up to Orlando. This was the third time he had made the trip in as many days. The sunny mood that he'd been in a few days ago had evaporated, and he had lost interest in sightseeing along the coastal route. He took I-95, the Interstate freeway, hoping to get there as soon as possible.

Martin and Elizabeth's house was in the small suburb of Angelsea, south of the city. A large house, impressive yet not over the top. Since they had moved to Washington, Kerrin and Dana had spent many happy days there, visiting his sister's family as often as they could. It would be strange going there by himself this time, the first member of his family to go into the house since Martin had died.

He wasn't looking forward to it.

Kerrin kept both of Elizabeth's house keys on his key fob. He let himself in through the front door, and hurried into the hallway, quickly typing in the six digit security code into the alarm's control panel. Thankfully he had got it right, and the flashing light turned a constant green. He turned round and gently closed the door behind him, putting the pile of mail he had brought up from the mailbox onto the table in the lobby.

Unlike the other times Kerrin had been visiting, when the sound of screaming children, conversation and loud music had filled the house with life, this time it was uncomfortably quiet.

Walking through the rooms, stopping to reach down inside the long dried willow grass and pick up the study key from inside the green vase, he could feel the presence of his brother-in-law all around him. Martin had been a good, strong man, and an excellent father. His sister had been lucky to find him.

Martin's study was at the back of the house, facing the indoor swimming pool. He used to sit there at his computer, watching his children and wife swimming in the pool through an internal window he had had especially knocked through the wall.

The water in the pool looked inviting as Kerrin slipped past it into the study. Perhaps he would take a dip afterwards.

He stopped in his tracks.

The door to the study was wide open, having been visibly forced. He reached for the gun in the holster underneath his arm. Perhaps the intruder could still be inside the room! He couldn't take any chances.

He quietly kicked off his shoes so that his footsteps wouldn't give him away on the marble surrounds to the swimming pool, and stepped slowly forward.

He reached the door to the study, and with a single deep breath, he stepped swiftly into the room, his gun outstretched and searching, looking for a target.

Thankfully, there was none to be found. The room was empty.

Empty as in 'no intruder', but also empty as in 'no computer.'

Somebody had beaten him to it.

He looked around at the bookshelf beside the window. None of the other books had been disturbed but on the third shelf there was a gap in the tightly packed row where a single book was missing. A gap where until recently Kerrin knew there would probably have been a copy of Shakespearean tragedies.

Kerrin felt a chill run down his spine. Whoever had got into the house had known both the security codes for the house alarm, and where Martin had kept his secret box. It had to be either a very close friend of the family, or someone who must have intercepted the phone conversation between Kerrin and his sister that morning!

Whoever it was, they had also known where Martin and his sister had lived. They must have come and gone very recently, probably within the past few hours. He checked the rest of the house, making sure all the other doors were still closed and the windows locked. Everything was fine.

As far as he could see, nothing else had been taken and the rest of the house looked completely untouched. That meant that the person who'd let themselves into the house had been a true professional. He or she hadn't been tempted by the obvious valuables lying around the house, only in completing a specific task: taking the computer and the computer disks.

He sat down in one of the large chairs in the living room. What should he do now?

He debated going to the police to report the theft, but then wondered what help that would bring. The police must know by now that the suicides had been murders, but in spite of that, they had closed the investigations, and mislaid the files. Whoever had persuaded the police to ignore the suicides, would make sure this got a similar treatment.

As he lay back on the sofa going over everything in his mind and wondering what his next move should be, a blanket of exhaustion overtook him, and he fell into a deep sleep.

He was woken a few hours later, the loud ringing of a telephone very close to his head ripping him out of his dreams and thrusting him back into the world of questions that had become his life in the past week. He struggled to open his eyes, for a second not remembering where he was or how he had got there.

The phone stopped ringing and the answering machine kicked in. It was Martin's voice.

"Hi! We're not in just now. Could you leave a message please and either Elizabeth or myself will get back to you! Bye."

Kerrin could hear the person at the other end of the phone hesitate for a few seconds, obviously wondering whether or not to leave a message.

"...Hi, Martin, it's Alex...I was just wondering if you're okay..."

Kerrin lunged for the phone, knocking the phone off the table as he did so, then fighting with it on the floor, and trying to grasp the handset and untangle it from the cable.

"Hi... Hi Alex,...DON'T HANG UP! It's Kerrin! Martin's brother-in-law! You know me! We met a few weeks ago!"

The voice on the other end of the line stopped talking in mid sentence.

"Don't hang up," Kerrin shouted. "Martin's dead and I need to talk to you!"

Silence.

"Alex, I hope you're listening to me. I'm a friend. I know you are scared and probably don't want to talk to anyone, but I need to talk to you... We can't speak on this line. It's probably bugged...but don't hang up. I have an idea. Follow my instructions... I want you to think of the place we met a few weeks ago. Remember the name of the place...Take the first part of the name and remember it. Now I want you to go into an internet café and create yourself a hotmail email account and sign onto the messenger service, so that we can chat online. Make your username the same as the first part of the name of the place we went to...i.e. first-name-of-place@hotmail.com. Got it? I'll get to an internet café too. In one hour from now, I'll send an email to you at that account name, and then we'll chat using the hotmail Messenger Service. We'll take it from there? Do you understand...just say yes if you do, then hang up."

The line at the other end had not yet gone dead...Kerrin knew there was somebody listening to him. He prayed that person would acknowledge him with a 'yes'. The few seconds seemed like an age, but eventually the man at the other end grunted a 'yes', then hung up. So far so good.

Now all Kerrin had to do was find an internet café within the next hour.

Actually, it wasn't as difficult as he first thought it was going to be. As he drove down I-95, he passed a big mall, which he guessed would be quite a good place to look for one. He pulled into the parking lot, and walked inside. Sure enough, on the second floor, just opposite Gap for Kids there was a little trendy café that sold a million different types of coffee and internet connection by the minute.

Within a few minutes Kerrin had created himself his own new email identity, 'QuestionsMan@hotmail.com', and had sent an email to Alex, wherever he was. He just hoped that Alex had been able to remember that the name of the golf club where they had played only a few weeks ago under such different circumstances was called Duddingston Gardens Golf Club. Just in case, he sent emails to three different addresses:*Duddingston@hotmail.com*, *DuddingstonGardens@hotmail.com* and *DuddingstonGardensGolfClub@hotmail.com.*

Hopefully, if Alex had really understood his instructions, at least one of the emails would get to him.

Kerrin then signed onto the Messenger service offered by Hotmail and MSN, and created three buddy aliases under the three email ids *Duddingston, DuddingstonGardens; and DuddingstonGardensGolfClub*. If Alex was online and had signed onto Messenger under any of these id's he would be able to see him.

He only had to wait ten minutes. A little message popped up into one of the MSN messenger boxes to tell him that his 'buddy' was online.

Kerrin immediately sent him a message back.

"Alex, Hi! It's Kerrin. Please prove your identity. Who won the day we first met?"

Two seconds later a message box popped up on his own screen.

"Hi Kerrin. Martin did. What happened to him? And why were you in his house?"

From that point a barrage of short messages flowed back and forth across the internet between them.

"I was there to pick something up. Martin tried to escape from America. His Lear Jet blew up in mid-air en route to the Bahamas. Do you think it was suicide like the rest?"

"Like hell it was. None of them were…"

"Where are you, Alex?"

"How can I trust you?"

"You can't. But who says I can trust you either. You're the only one left alive? Did you kill the others?"

"Fair point. And no I didn't. Forgive the precautions, but if you are who you say you are, then you can ask your sister's son a question. Ask her to tell you where I went on vacation last year! Her son kept the postcard. The postcard comes from the town where I am now…find the postcard…find the town…and find the entrance to the place mentioned on the postcard. I will meet you there at 2 p.m. in five days from now. Come alone."

"Okay…"

Kerrin waited for a response but there was none. A message popped up on his Buddy List saying that Duddingston had signed off.

He paid the spotty teenager behind the bar for his thirty minutes of online time, then walked through the mall, trying to find a shop that sold pre-paid cell phones. The phone he already had was obviously bugged, and he had to stop using it.

He found a shop near the entrance, paid for a phone in cash, and left the mall. Inside his car he called the business office at his sister's ranch, and asked the office manager to transfer him to Elizabeth, who was a guest in the main house. When she eventually came on the phone, he apologized for the skullduggery, and explained that her cell phone may be bugged. Then he asked her about the postcard.

"Yeah, Danny loved it. It was from South Africa, some windsurfing place…hang on a second I'll get him…"

There was a few minutes silence, then the next voice that spoke was Martin's son. His voice had lost the excitement it normally had. There was no joy there. Only sorrow.

"Uncle Kerrin? Hi…"

"Hi Danny. How are you?" Stupid question.

He could hear the boy fighting back the tears.

"Can I ask you something Danny…it's important. Last year, one of your dad's friends sent you a postcard…from South Africa?"

"Uncle Alex? Yes…it's an ace card…" The little boy's voice had livened up a bit.

"That's the one. Do you still have it… I need to take a look at it…it's important."

"Yes, I do…Why do you want to see it? "

"I can't tell you…but it'll help me find out why your father died."

The boy at the other end thought for a moment.

"Okay, but it's in my secret place…with my secret stuff. If I tell you, you have to promise not to tell anyone else, and you have to promise…make me a double promise that you won't look at anything else there, and that you won't read my diary…? Promise?"

"Absolutely. I double promise you Danny. And I won't tell anyone about where your special place is. Especially your sister. Okay?"

"…Okay. Do you know where…" And Danny told Kerrin where all his childhood secrets were kept.

Twenty minutes later, Kerrin slipped the postcard out of a cardboard box hidden underneath a loose floorboard in Danny's bedroom. Before he put the lid back on the box, he dropped three twenty dollar bills into the box and smiled. Danny was a good kid.

The postcard was split into two separate photographs juxtapositioned against each other. In the bottom left picture was a long, sandy bay, with rolling surf crashing onto the beach. Two windsurfers were in the photo, one surfing a wave on a board with a tall yellow sail, and the other flying upside down above the surf, caught by the camera in the middle of doing a jump.

The other picture showed a long, blue stretch of water covered by Windsurfers.

Along the bottom of the picture were the words, 'Langebaan Bay, South Africa.'

CHAPTER 15
Day Twelve
New York

His office on the sixty-third floor of the Rohloff Tower building looked out over the water towards Staten Island. The view, as Rupert Rohloff had once described it to his mistress, was 'truly exceptional.' And it was. Rupert never failed to lose interest in the view of the world outside. From here he could see the merchant ships arriving in the harbor, bringing their goods to America from every corner of the globe; tourists flocking to the Statue of Liberty on the pleasure craft that brought them to see the greatest symbol of freedom in the world, and the ocean liners arriving and disgorging their cargos of rich playboys, excited about arriving in the best city in the world.

Rupert Rohloff loved America. Only in the United States could he have arrived as a poor student thirty years ago, armed only with a degree in Electronic Engineering and a will to succeed, and turned his dream into a reality that spanned every state of the country, and overflowed into Europe and beyond. Rohloff Enterprises Worldwide was one of the most powerful conglomerates on the planet. The companies hidden under the banner of Rohloff Enterprises had interests which spanned electronics, computers, networking, telecommunications, semi-conductors, health-physics, bio-medicine, genetics, and most recently bio-science. In the past three years during the collapse of the stock market which accompanied the dot.com technology crisis, an aggressive campaign of acquisitions had brought many household names under the control of his holding-companies. Yet, he preferred to keep the extent of his wealth and power a well-protected secret.

Rupert Rohloff was not a vain man. It mattered not to him that people did not understand the true scope of his power. Politically, it was often more prudent that way. Economically, it made things much easier.

Rohloff Enterprises Worldwide was a private company. There were very few shareholders. Rupert Rohloff himself owned 78% of the stock. That made him the undisputed owner, CEO and boss of over three hundred thousand people in the world.

Yet, if you asked the average man on the street, hardly anybody had ever heard of his name. Although, those who had, never forgot it.

Rupert Rohloff was not what you could realistically call a good looking man. He was only five foot six tall, what most women would describe as small, and he was almost completely bald. Only a few patches of brown hair still clung to the sides of his head above his ears, but they too were beginning to disappear. Rupert's brown eyes were a little too close together, and this sometimes made people a bit uncomfortable when they looked at him. His nose, broken in a fight when he was a child, had never been professionally reset and now the bridge angled down obliquely to a bent and flattened tip. His round and extended belly protruded a few inches over the edge of his trouser belt. Rupert knew that he looked a little odd, and to compensate he spent a fortune on clothes. His expensive designer suits went some way to making up for his lack of stature and good looks, but not far enough to attract woman on their own. What attracted the women was his money.

It was unfortunate for them that Rupert had little interest in women. True, he had a mistress, but he saw her only once every few weeks, and shared little or no real emotion with her. Rupert was an insular man, not able to make friends easily, and not able to establish any real bond of affection with anyone apart from his dog, Sam, a small Scottie that he took with him everywhere.

He had little time for sex or friendships. His life was his work, his goal to extend the scope and success of his company, REW, from strength to strength and to make it the largest single company within the matrix of the Chymera Corporation. His mistress was money, his aphrodisiac was power.

The green phone buzzed, and when Rupert leant across his desk and pressed the speak button, his secretary's voice came across the loudspeaker.

"I've got that call for you that you wanted, Rupert. Can you take it now?"

"Yes, put him through...and could you rustle me up some fresh coffee? Cuban? Thanks..."

There was an electronic beep, and Rupert was through.

"Nigel, it's Rupert. How are you?"

"I'm fine. What can I do for you?"

Rupert had been trying to get hold of Nigel Small for over two days. He had either been very busy, or had been evading his calls. The Phase Two trials should have just started, and Rupert wanted to know exactly how things were going.

Since the day of its incorporation, the board of Chymera had run the company more like an army than a profit making organization. Responsibility and power within the Corporation was divided up in two ways. Firstly, according to the economic might and assets controlled by each of the board members, and secondly, according to geographical area. The territory around the globe across which the Corporation wielded power and had investments in was divided into twelve main sectors. North America, one of the main sectors, was itself further sub-divided into four cells: The Northern States and Canada, The Southern States and Mexico, and The Western and The Eastern Seaboards. That meant that in the divisional structure of the Chymera Corporation, the Gen8tyx Company based in California now came under the auspices of the Western Seaboard Cell, which was Nigel Small's authority. Rupert held overall responsibility for all four of the cells making up North America, and as such, Nigel reported directly to Rupert.

Rupert had been invited to present on the Orlando Project at the next board meeting of the Chymera Corporation in three weeks time. Before he walked into the board meeting Rupert needed to be fully briefed by Nigel, and convinced that he had no surprises up his sleeves.

"I want to know how the trial is coming along with Gen8tyx, and how the integration into Chymera is progressing. I don't want any surprises."

"I know Rupert. Please be assured that..."

"Thank you. I accept. I will be assured...and I want you in New York in two weeks time. I will expect you in my office on Wednesday 28th. At that time I will give you the whole morning, and you can 'assure me' then."

"I'll be there."

"I know you will."

Nigel Small was fuming. Why was Rupert Rohloff calling and chasing him up? Had someone gone above him and said something they shouldn't have? The Phase Two trials had already started and were going excellently.

Problems? Yes, there were a few, but none that he couldn't deal with. He hated relying on other people. Sonderheim had the responsibility of sorting this mess out, but he was dragging it out too long and getting nowhere. Nigel couldn't rely on him to wrap it up, and if he didn't sort it out quickly, it would look bad on him. It would be better if he took the initiative and took a few precautions of his own. After all, if there was one thing he had learned in business it was never to put all your eggs in one basket.

Nigel was CEO of Small Holdings, a utilities company and an oil distributor which was headquartered in Seattle. Their business dealt mainly with energy and water in the US, and exporting and importing oil to and from Asia. Last year his organization had turned over $5 billion dollars. Perhaps he was still small fry in comparison to some of the others in the Chymera's Western Seaboard Cell, but he had plans. He knew where he was going. And nobody, especially Sonderheim and his mistakes, was going to hold him back.

It was time to call in a favor.

The phone rang in the office of Cheng Wung in the CIA's new southern headquarters in Tampa. Cheng saw the code flash up on the LCD display and realized that he wanted to take this call.

"Excuse me gentleman, could you please wait outside, I'm afraid I have to take this. Grab yourselves a fresh coffee...be back in five?" He explained politely to the section heads in his office. They were in the middle of a briefing for an up-and-coming sting on a huge heroin trafficking ring which had been newly uncovered in the Keys.

"Mr Small? It's good to hear from you again...it was a pleasure doing business with you before. Is this just a courtesy call, or can I be of some assistance to you again?"

"Mr Wung, I have no doubt that it was a pleasure for you the last time we did business. I'm sure that such 'assistance' is always most beneficial to you." Nigel was sarcastically referring to the $2m it had cost him, the last time he had asked for the honorable Mr Wung to indulge in a little bit of freelancing and use his government backed resources to help him out.

"Mr Small, I will not deny that your patronage is appreciated. I trust that you appreciate my help in return, otherwise you would not ask me to assist you again."

"Enough of this bullshit double entendre. When did you last have this line swept? Can we talk freely?"

"If my lines are not secure, then none are. "

Cheng Wung was head of the Southern Section of the CIA. He reported personally to the Director in Washington.

"Okay... I have another job for you..."

Every man has a price. Cheng's was higher than most, but since the resources at his disposal were unique, he believed his price to be fair value.

Cheng called the other section heads back into his room. While they carried on with the presentation, detailing the planning and time-scales for the sting, Cheng paid little attention to what they said and in his mind he began to plan the next extra-curricular project he would soon be carrying out with the help of Uncle Sam.

Sonderheim was nervous. Normally he wasn't a particularly nervous man, but he knew that this time there was more at stake than ever before.

"So what is the state of play just now?" He was talking to two other men and a woman on a conference call. "Adam, you go first."

"In the weeks before their deaths, we discovered that all of those who died had downloaded copies of the Orlando File, the main database of information which contains all the information necessary to recreate the Orlando Project."

It turns out that each of them had downloaded copies of the Orlando File onto their hard drives, just as you had suspected. It goes without saying that if we're to keep the lid on this thing, we have to recover all six copies of the Orlando File before their contents are made public. "

"And, what is the progress so far?"

"Good. Very good. At this point we're pretty confident that we've now recovered all the computers, including all the personal home computers, from all six suspects. The last two to be recovered were from Alex Swinton and Martin Nicolson. We originally believed that Martin was carrying the Orlando File with him out of the country on his Lear, and hence the necessity to ensure we intercepted his flight. But to complete the operation and secure all the copies of the Orlando File in Nicolson's possession, yesterday afternoon we visited his home and removed his home PC and all his storage disks."

"And Swinton?"

"Yesterday we finally managed to find where Alex Swinton had been staying before he disappeared and we recovered a computer from the apartment. It's just arrived back at the lab this morning. And we have recovered the Orlando File from the hard-drives of all the other computers we secured."

"Good job Adam. Your section has done well. Laura, have you been able to track down the location of Alex Swinton yet?"

"Not yet. We know he was in South Africa a week ago. Our men are in South Africa now. He must be moving around. We haven't been able to find him yet, but we think he's still in the country…We're working on something at the moment. Hopefully we will have something for you soon."

"Let me know the moment anything develops."

Laura was part of the same cell as Adam, but her forte was dealing with the security agencies. Information gathering was her specialty. It helped that she worked for the FBI.

"John, what have you to offer?"

The last person on the call had remained silent throughout. The cell he led was based in the North East.

"My team is on standby. As soon as we get the authority, we are ready to go, but I believe that at this stage it would be wrong to initiate any action so close to home. As Laura pointed out on our last call, the man who had been doing the rounds of the widows is Kerrin Graham. Formerly a police officer in Miami, and now a reporter for the Washington Post. Until we know what he knows, and whom he has told it to, we cannot and should not, do anything. A reporter for one of the most powerful newspapers in the world is not someone we should underestimate…"

"Thanks John. Your point is taken. Which is why for now, we all have to leave Graham alone. But make sure your men are ready to go, as soon as I give the word!"

"However, there could be a new problem to take care of..." Laura interrupted.

"And what is that?" David asked.

"...It seems that there is a policeman in Miami asking lots of questions...I don't know why yet, but I have started my investigations."

"Okay Laura. It could be nothing...there were a number of deaths after all...or it could be something...in which case I want you to deal with it. I will trust your judgment."

Laura understood exactly what he meant.

F.B.I. Offices
Day Twelve
Miami
Florida

As soon as the call finished, Laura left the conference centre, and took the elevator to the 3rd Level of the underground bunker. As she stepped out of the elevator, she showed her badge to the armed security guard behind the desk, and then stepped towards the bullet proof glass doors.

She pressed her hand against the palm and finger scanner, then bent forward so that the retinal scanner could examine the back of her eyeball.

The light above the security gate flashed green, and she stepped through the doors, which opened with a characteristic 'swoosh', which always reminded her of the sound made by the elevator doors opening in the old Star Trek films.

She stepped lightly through the air-conditioned computing complex, knowing full well that through the glass partitions many male heads would be turning as she walked past. It was no accident that her white blouse opened just a little lower than it should, deliberately but somewhat erotically exposing the top of her white bra and the curves of her ample cleavage, or that she wore a smart Gucci suit that hugged her figure and showed off her incredible stocking clad legs.

She knew the power of female sexuality. She had never understood the term 'female exploitation.' She only believed in 'male exploitation.' She oozed sexuality from every pore. She made sure she did. Not surprisingly promotion had come quickly to Laura over the years. She knew what she wanted and she got it. Yet still she was bored. To satisfy her hunger for risk and adventure, she got her kicks by combining lucrative extra-curricular activities with her FBI work. They were a marriage of convenience, and a relationship which had the blessing of both her bank manager and her stockbroker.

As she entered one of the many secure surveillance rooms, one of the young computer nerds at the back of the room looked up, smiled and took the walkman off his head.

"Agent Samuels? How are you today?" the young man asked, sitting up straight, and swiveling his chair round towards her.

"Excellent Agent Rodriguez, just excellent, and you?"

Laura put her hands on a waist high filing cabinet beside the young man, and eased herself backwards up onto it, sitting down and crossing her legs slowly but carefully so that her skirt rode up and exposed a fraction too much of her thighs.

"Getting better every moment! You know, Agent Samuels, how the hell are any of us meant to get any work done, when you keep coming round...?" He asked her, his eyes quickly scanning her body so that she understood exactly what he was referring to. He may be young, and a nerd, but the young man knew how to flirt with the best of them.

"Sorry, I didn't know I had that effect on you..." Laura smiled. " So, do you think you will be able to do it or not?"

"I've done it."

"Already?"

"Sure...it wasn't exactly hard..."

"Good, I don't want to make things too hard for you..."

"...Well, you may be too late for that...," the young nerd replied, smiling back at her without blushing.

Laura ignored him. She wasn't about to be upstaged by a twenty two-year old.

"What have you got then, and how did you get it...", she said nodding her head towards the computer, indicating that he should show her.

"Okay...let's get down to business..." he said, turning to the computer screen. He minimized the application he was in, and brought up four new screens, toggling between them as he went.

"Okay, it was you who did the hard part really, Agent Samuels. Once you gave me the registration number of his car, the rest was easy. All I did was dial into the Hertz system. Hertz are really friendly, they co-operate with us on almost anything we want to do. It only took a few minutes to get his details. Look, here's the rental agreement...and here's his driving license, complete with picture."

Laura bent forward towards the screen, the curvature of her breasts coming very close to Agent Rodriguez's head. He could smell the faint musk rising from her cleavage. Laura realized why the young man was smiling, and slapped him playfully on his head.

"Naughty boy. Show me what else you've got..."

"I will if you will...The problem was that two days ago he took his car back and swapped it for another one. That fooled me for a little bit. It was only yesterday morning, when I checked the Hertz system again that I realized what he had done. This is the new rental agreement...Okay, what I did next was put the new registration number into the main Computer Automated Vehicle Visual Recognition System, ...we call it CARS for short...anyway, as you may know, every time a vehicle passes a CARS camera on the freeway or on a street, the camera photographs the number plate, digitises it and then compares the registration with the CARS database...if there a match it sends us a message telling us where the vehicle was sighted..."

Laura was beginning to be impressed. The boy knew his stuff.

"We started tracking the new rental car he was driving in the Orlando area. After it left the address you gave me yesterday it was picked up by five different CARS cameras in the next two hours..."

Agent Rodriguez switched to another screen and a map came up.

"...Here you can see the places he was spotted..." he said, pointing to the screen.

"The interesting thing is that between the sighting here, and the sighting there, an hour had elapsed. Which means that he probably stopped the car and did something somewhere along the way.

Rodriguez closed down the map, and brought up another screen. It was a analogue tracing of a speech pattern. At the bottom of the screen there was a play button, a fast forward and rewind, and a stop button. A series of numbers at the top of the screen indicated that it was a recording of a phone conversation taken from a telephone number in one of the Orlando suburbs.

"What's this?"

"All telephone and email conversations in the US are automatically recorded. This is the telephone number of the house at the address you gave me. I took the liberty of looking at the calls that were made to and from that number yesterday. There were no outgoing calls all day...maybe the people are away on holiday or something...or at least I thought so until in the afternoon one of the incoming phone calls was answered. This is the conversation..."

He hit the play button, and Laura could hear the conversation that had taken place the day before between Kerrin and Alex Swinton, the suspect they were looking for.

"Okay, so you'll notice he said that he would email him in an hour from then? Right? Okay, so if you look back at the map, you'll see that he was somewhere between here and there during that time...right...now he could have been dialing into the internet from a laptop with a cell phone, or from a smartphone or tablet with wireless, ...or from an Internet Café. I monitored his cell phone number, there were no more calls, so it wasn't a laptop or a handheld. Just out of interest, I took the zip code of that part of town, and cross-referenced it against the business directory for Orlando...Bingo...Three internet cafés in that area."

Laura smiled.

"So, using this little piece of code..." Rodriguez flicked to another screen,"...I entered the details and the Calling Line Identities of the internet cafés into my network probes and sniffers...sorry, am I going too fast?...The CLI is basically the telephone number from where the dial-up modems call when dialing into the internet, and probes are just complicated devices that listen to all the internet traffic and break it down into its component data packets...they can identify things like destination and source email addresses, and source and destination telephone numbers where the dial-up or broadband DSL modems are connected to...okay?...good. Well, the probes help us keep records of all the internet messages and emails that are sent...And through a combination of looking at the signals stored on the probes, sniffers, and the large database which stores all the internet traffic going to and from the US for the past month, what we shall see next are all the messages and emails that were sent during the next two hours coming from the three internet cafés we looked at..."

A screen came up showing three separate boxes, each containing a list of the titles of the emails and messages that were sent from those internet cafés.

"The next thing was to run a little program to look at the text of the messages from the three cafes, to try and identify any source words we cared to include. I chose the names of the people we were looking for...'Alex'...'Swinton'...'Kerrin'...'Graham'...and other words like 'Gen8tyx' and 'Genetics' etc..."

'And this is what we got...' Agent Rodriguez proudly displayed a new list of messages and emails, all coming from the same, single, internet café.

"What you can see here is internet chat...these are the messages that were sent back and forward between Graham and Swinton. These guys are quite clued up...refusing to talk on the phone and using the internet instead was a really smart move...there's no way we would have been able to eavesdrop on them if we hadn't got a good idea which CLI numbers Graham was using."

Laura wasn't listening to him. She was more interested in the messages displayed on the screen. The last one was of particular interest:

"Fair point. And no I didn't. Forgive the precautions, but if you are who you say you are, then you can ask your sister's son a question. Ask her to tell you where I went on vacation last year? Her son kept the postcard. The postcard comes from the town where I am now...find the postcard...find the town...and find the entrance to the place mentioned on the postcard...I will meet you there at 2 p.m. in five days from now. Come alone."

When she had read it, she pointed to the screen and asked Rodriguez,

"Can you identify where Alex sent the message from?"

"Sure can..." he replied, while bringing the image of another map onto the screen.

"Alex is using Messenger to communicate with Kerrin across the Internet, but he's logged onto the Internet using a dial-up connection. I've tracked the CLI number of the call to an internet café near Langebaan. It's a windsurfer's paradise in South Africa, near Cape Town. They're still using a dial-up connection and don't have broadband yet. It's probably somewhere in the middle of nowhere."

It made sense. The last place they had been able to track Alex to was the town of Wilderness, a windsurfers hangout too. Alex Swinton must be a keen windsurfer.

She turned to Agent Rodriguez..

"Can you print the email messages out for me, and give me a copy of the map. Also, keep an eye-out to see if Alex sends any more emails from that café. The moment you get anything, let me know. Can you put all of this into a proper report format, and send it to me later today?"

"Sure thing."

"Thanks. You've done great!"

She stood up, and leant forward, kissing him playfully on top of his head, then she ruffled his hair with her right hand, smiled and left.

Agent Rodriguez watched Laura as she walked down the corridor, following the sexy to and fro of her hips, and thinking the same thoughts as all the other men whose gaze followed after her.

Perhaps one day...just perhaps...

As Laura rode the elevator back up to her office she quickly calculated her next move. Alex Swinton was in South Africa. He would be meeting Kerrin Graham somewhere in Langebaan in four days time. They had to get to him before Graham, i.e. the Washington Post, managed to talk to him first.

In other words, they had four days to get down there, find him, and kill him.

CHAPTER 16
Day Twelve
Miami

"So why are you calling me from a payphone? Have you lost your cell phone?...And why are you still in Miami? Are we never going to be able to get rid of you?" James 'IceBreaker' Callaghan asked, jokingly.

"My cell phone is being tapped. Probably the people who were following me in the blue Mazda. I'm flying back to Washington tomorrow morning. I was wondering if you'd had any luck in your investigations?"

"Yes. We need to talk...How about Hooters in half an hour? I'm just getting off work, and I could do with a large cold one."

Hooters was heaving. Friday night, and the weekend had begun. When Kerrin got there, James was already at the back of the bar, a large pitcher of beer sitting in front of him, two large glasses already poured.

"So what have you got then?" Kerrin asked, shaking James hand. It was good to see a friendly face.

"You're not going to like it...it's interesting though. First of all, you'll find some information in here on your guy David Sonderheim, including a copy of his driving license. Next, here are all the telephone numbers of all the calls dialed and received from Henry Robert's house. There's a lot of Washington and Californian numbers there. And there are a few from New York."

James slid a clear see-through plastic folder across the table. Kerrin pulled out the contents and started to scan the list of numbers on the paper.

"His wife told you that the night he died, Henry had received a call from the office asking him to come in? Well, according to the phone records, no he didn't. Old Henry was telling porkies."

"So who called him then?"

"At 9.30 p.m. that night a call was picked up at the house, maybe by Henry or his wife. But the call came from the private home number of David Sonderheim."

"That doesn't surprise me..."

"...But shortly afterwards another call came in...from the private cell phone number of Alex Swinton...the only one in your group who is maybe still alive now, right?"

Kerrin looked up. That was even more interesting.

"So who did Henry go to visit? Was it Alex or David? If either of them..."

"I don't know. But whoever it was, they probably killed him. It makes you think though...maybe Alex is the man we're looking for. He killed the rest of the team, and then took off!"

"It's something we can't discount. You said 'killed', did you speak to the coroner?"

"Yes, and this is the thing, the new tests the coroner ran show that Henry was definitely murdered. It wasn't suicide. Shit, Kerrin, this is heavy stuff...what are we getting ourselves into here?"

"We're not getting ourselves 'into' anything. We're already in it. Tell me what happened with the coroner?"

"Okay, so I call the guy up, naturally telling him it's on police business. I ask him if an autopsy was carried out on the Robert's body, and if it was still in the morgue. Yes, and yes. But the coroner says it was clearly a heart attack. I ask if there was any possibility that the heart attack could have been induced. He says that that could happen...that there was a whole number of ways that it could be done."

"...I ask him if he could run some basic toxicology tests to see if there are any signs of poison in his system. He said it would normally take a while, but since there was a shortage of bodies for him to cut up, he could start straight away: apparently the department was going through a bit of a quiet spell at just then!...What sort of man gets his kicks out of cutting somebody else up? Never could figure these guys out..."

"...Anyway, he called me back about three hours ago...says he got something on the very first run..."

"What was it?" Kerrin asked.

"I can't remember...I wrote it down somewhere...he's sending the file over to me tomorrow. But basically he said it was some type of muscle relaxant...he found an injection mark between his toes. where someone had pumped him full of the stuff. The guy's body stopped responding to his brain commands...he stops breathing, and dies...at first glance it looks just like a heart-attack."

"So what do we do now?"

"Not much. I can't really do anything without the Feds starting to ask questions about what I'm doing. And I can't tell my boss what I've done, or he'll want to know why I'm running around the place playing games with you. Looks like that information has to remain between the two of us for now."

"Okay..." Kerrin agreed.

"Fact is Kerrin, these guys are serious, whoever they are. It takes a lot of nerve to walk into a hospital and kill someone in cold blood. They knew what they were doing...they've got to be professionals...Someone with a lot of clout has got to be behind this. Someone with connections in the FBI, and who can get files to disappear in police stations...someone who can manipulate the police to their own end. Who else could get the police to close an investigation into what is so obviously a series of murders, and cover them up as being suicides? No, there's some weird shit going down here. And we've got to start watching our backs..."

Laura sat in her car outside the bar. One of her men had tailed Captain Callaghan to 'Hooters'. Not one of her FBI men, but one of the external secret team she had built up over the years to help carry out her extra-curricular activities.

She had done some investigating and found out that the man they were trailing was working independently which was the best news she'd had all day. The questions he had been asking were not part of any authorized official police investigation and the new autopsy on Henry Robert's body at the hospital had not been authorized either.

Her group hadn't been involved in the Orlando murders. That had been down to John's group from the North East Sector. He had flown down a couple of his men to do the job. They had fucked up, not her. If it had been down to her, the man Alex Swinton would never have escaped in the first place.

Exactly why David Sonderheim wanted all these people dead, she did not know. All she knew was that Sonderheim was part of Chymera, and that she was part of the Security Division at Chymera. In effect, they were work colleagues.

Chymera had recruited her over three years ago, and since then it had proved to be a very fruitful relationship indeed. The kind of fruitful that had put $1m dollars in her account. But it wasn't all about the money...She enjoyed being part of something big, part of the bigger picture.

Her cell phone buzzed, and she picked it up from the passenger seat beside her.

"They're leaving. What do you want us to do?"

It was one of her men parked in the van nearest the entrance to the bar.

"Hold tight for just now. We'll see what they do next."

As she watched, the policeman came out of the club with the other man, whom she now knew to be Kerrin Graham. She had watched him go into the club a few hours ago, and it had immediately put the other piece in the jigsaw puzzle. Captain Callaghan was somehow working with Kerrin Graham.

The temptation was to get rid of both of them then and there. Otherwise Laura might just bump into Graham in South Africa in a few days time. Unfortunately, she couldn't. Sonderheim's orders had been quite specific. They had to leave him alone, until they could find out what he knew, and if he was working alone or in a team.

At the bottom of the steps in front of the entrance to the bar, the two men shook hands, separated, then walked towards their own cars.

She picked up the cell phone.

"Let them go. We'll proceed as planned. It'll be better that way."

Day Thirteen

The next morning James and his partner were driving round the suburbs of Miami as they did every normal day. They made a few circuits of the neighborhood, stopping to talk to some characters they knew, and checking with the locals what was going on in the vicinity. Then they stopped to pick up some strong fresh coffee at the local deli, just as they did every time they went out on patrol.

As they were driving around the block from the deli, the radio buzzed, and James responded.

"Car 282, over. "

"Robbery going down at Daniels Pawn Shop on 28th Street. Please attend."

"Roger. We're only one block away."

Two minutes later, sirens blaring and lights flashing, they pulled up in front of the Pawn Shop.

Covering each other, they quickly entered the premises. It was dark inside, and it took a few minutes for their eyes to adjust to the lack of light. Regrettably, if they had been able to see straight away they would have realized that the pawnbroker was already dead, his body lying behind the counter where he had fallen.

They would also have seen the two men with black hoods and black overalls, standing just inside the door, shotguns raised and pointing straight at them.

The impact of the shotguns at such short range blew both of the policemen back out of the door and into the street. Both were dead before they hit the sidewalk.

The two men in the black overalls ran out after them, deliberately spilling most of their stolen money over the bodies, and leaving it lying scattered in the street. A red car swept around the corner, screeching to a halt in front of them. The two men jumped in, and the car accelerated away.

In a second they were gone, leaving behind them two bodies sprawled across the sidewalk, their blood forming a pool which spilled over the edge of the curb and began to run down the gutter into the nearest drain.

CHAPTER 17
Day Thirteen
The Gen8tyx Company
Purlington Bay
California

The hospital wing attached to the back of the main section of the building offered the most advanced modern medical facilities available. No expense had been spared on providing whatever Sonderheim and his medical team had needed.

The sixty individual hospital rooms were more like luxury apartments, providing the ultimate in comfort for those who would be attending the clinic. Sonderheim and his team of doctors and nurses would be paying host to some of the most influential people in America, and it was going to be their duty to provide the best medical care available. In fact, the 'Orlando Clinic', as he had christened the hospital, was the only place this treatment was going to be available.

Phase Two of the trials of the Orlando Treatment had just begun and they were now three days into the schedule. Already there were some signs that the patients were beginning to respond, something which they had not anticipated so soon.

Unfortunately, there had been one death, but it had been unavoidable. The patient in question was already in the final stages of lung cancer when he had arrived at the clinic, and he could hardly breathe: it had only been a matter of time. Unfortunately the treatment had been too late to save him.

Trevor Simons and Colonel Packard, the two most important patients to be treated in Phase Two, were thankfully also amongst those who were being the most responsive to the treatment. Both were important executive directors in the Chymera Corporation, and strategically it was important that both experienced impressive results from the trials.

Their rooms were on the third floor of the clinic, with the best views overlooking the bay. Sonderheim had personally made sure that everything about their treatment received the best attention and focus.

In spite of the personal animosity that he had immediately felt towards Trevor Simons, Sonderheim could not help but marvel at his determination and bravery, and at the progress he was making. It had taken a lot of courage for Simons to abandon the conventional treatment he had been undergoing in Los Angeles, and agree to participate in the program. Sonderheim knew that the man was a gambler, and had taken enormous risks throughout his life. Well, it looked like this was one gamble that was going to pay off.

When Simons had first arrived at the clinic, they had put him through a number of physical and medical examinations, to ensure they could chart his progress at every stage of the procedure. The journey down to Purlington Bay had taken a lot more out of him than Simons had admitted. It was typical of the man not to tell anyone that he was in the final stages of leukemia. His T-cell blood count could drop through the floor at any moment, and he could be dead within twenty four hours. Regardless of the risk, Simons had come to Sonderheim's clinic in the hope of demonstrating some sort of cure.

David Sonderheim had explained at length to Nigel Small, the director of the Western Seaboard Cell, who would possibly benefit from the Orlando Treatment. They knew that the Orlando Treatment worked. The only question they had, was how well?

He had explained clearly that leukemia was not one of the conditions that the treatment had been designed to treat. That said, he had also confessed that there was a good possibility that the disease could respond to their new procedure...but, in reality, he just didn't know.

The fact was that the effects of the Orlando Treatment went far beyond everything they had initially predicted. Just how far, they didn't know. And that was exactly why these trials were so important.

They needed to know. They needed to find out.

Day Thirteen
Washington D.C.

She waved at him excitedly as he walked through into the Arrivals Hall at the airport. As soon as she spotted him she spun her wheelchair around and rolled it towards him.

"Dana...Hi!" Kerrin bent down towards her, wrapping his arms around her shoulders and hugging his wife passionately. "I told you not to bother...I said I'd catch a taxi!"

"Sshhh...I missed you..." And she threw him one of her fantastic smiles. He couldn't bring himself to be angry with her. Truth was, he loved it that she had made all that effort to come to meet him.

He kissed her once more, and putting his small suitcase across the lap of her wheelchair, he pushed her out to the parking lot. Kerrin helped her into the passenger side of the car, and then switched over the especially designed controls to 'normal' driving. The disabled controls on the car had been a godsend for Dana, enabling her to drive the automatic car safely, and just as well as any other person.

"Darling...you look stressed. And you've lost some weight! Tell me what's going on?" Dana asked Kerrin as they drove back from the airport to the suburb where they lived, on the outskirts of Washington D.C.

He wanted to tell her everything, but he wondered if he should. He didn't want to worry her unduly, and until he knew more about what was going on, perhaps he should keep it to himself.

But how was he going to tell her that now he had just got back, that he would be leaving to go to South Africa the very next day? He would leave that one for a few hours. It would be best to choose the right moment...if there was one for something like that.

He knew she would be disappointed. South Africa was the place that they had always planned to visit together. It was their dream destination. Dana loved animals, and she had spent most of her adult life planning to go on safari, 'hunting' the Big Five with a camera and a pair of binoculars, and sleeping out under the stars on warm, summer nights.

Then Dana's accident had temporarily put a halt to their dream. Afterwards they had promised themselves that they would still go together, but somehow, although they knew they would be able to cope, they just never got round to booking the trip. The wheelchair had taken away the spontaneity which had once made life so much fun for them.

"Oh, by the way, your big friendly boss called. Wants you to check in with him as soon as you get back. Told me to tell you that you still worked for him,...just in case you forgot! Oh...and he wants to know who's paying for your tickets to Cape Town tomorrow,...and why you're going?"

"Oops..."

"Exactly. Care to explain, Mr Husband-of-mine?"

"Where do I begin?"

"The beginning?...It's usually the best place."

"Can you remember Alex Swinton? A friend and work colleague of Martin's?"

"Vaguely..."

"Well, out of all of the core team that Martin worked with, Alex is the only one left alive. He's in South Africa. I need to get to him and tell him about the others...and to warn him that whoever killed the others will be after him too. Dana, I need to speak to him: he could be the only person alive who knows why Martin and the others died!"

"But South Africa is our special place......" Dana choked for a second, and Kerrin noticed her visibly fighting to regain her composure. "No...forget that...that's just being childish. Okay, so I can see why you have to go, but if he's the only person left alive from that group, has it not occurred to you and that little brain of yours that perhaps he's the one that killed the others, and that's maybe why he's in hiding?"

Kerrin looked at his wife, taking his eyes off the road ahead for just a second.

"You're the second person to say that in twenty four hours. Maybe you're right...but I've got no choice. I'm pretty sure he didn't do it though. Elizabeth said he and Martin were good friends,...I don't believe that Alex could have killed him."

"Aha! So you're pretty sure that Martin was killed then, and that it wasn't just an accident?"

His wife didn't miss a trick. It was obvious, that despite his misgivings, the easiest thing was going to be to tell her everything. Otherwise it would probably all just come out in dribs-and-drabs anyway. So he started to tell her exactly what had happened over the past week. They were just pulling up into their driveway when he finished. Dana had remained pretty silent throughout, but as Kerrin switched off the car and turned to face her, she whistled.

"Wow...are you sure you're not just making this all up? Because if you're not, this would make a brilliant book. Maybe when it's all done, you could write a bestseller, and we can retire! If you're still alive, that is." A tear grew in the corner of her eye and started to roll down her cheek.

"Kerrin, I'm scared. Promise me you'll be careful?"

"Yes, I promise."

He leant over to her, and gently kissed her cheek, catching her salty tear on the edge of his lips.

"And when it's all over...I promise I'll take you to South Africa, just as we've always planned."

Dana had a point though. The whole thing was just beginning to sound like the plot to a best-selling thriller. If only he could just flick to the last chapter and find out who'd done it. Instead, he was going to jump on a plane and fly half way round the world to meet someone who could very well be the killer who had just murdered all his work-colleagues and could somehow be responsible for the death of Kerrin's own brother-in-law. In which case, Kerrin could end up just as dead as the others, and Dana would become just another widow with a nice house.

It didn't bear thinking about it.

"So what's the deal, pal? I hear South Africa is beautiful this time of the year? Should I come too, or would I just be intruding on your holidays?" Paul, Kerrin's boss bellowed down the phone. It was seven o'clock in the evening, and Kerrin was half hoping that by the time he called, his boss would have gone home and he would have been able to just leave a voice message. No such luck.

"Sure. If you want to. And if you don't mind a little bit of danger. I could do with a man of your great experience, and girth, to act as a body shield from any stray bullets that may come my way."

Kerrin knew that although his boss was a tiger in the newspaper office, in spite of his harsh words and aggressive business style, in the world outside his office door he was really a closet coward.

"Perhaps not then...Can't leave the office and all that! But seriously pal, what the hell is going on? Vicki brought in a pile of invoices to sign, and top of the list is a business class flight down to Cape Town! Is there any particular reason why you're going to South Africa?"

"Paul, suffice it to say there are several. But, and I'm not kidding when I say this...I can't talk to you over the phone...I think it's bugged." He said, half in truth, and half as an excuse not to talk to him just now.

"Well, how about stopping by the office tomorrow morning and explaining to me why I should pay for all of this?"

"Sorry boss, no-can-do. First flight out and all that...just no time...Trust me on this one. Something strange is going down...I'll make it worth your while!"

"Trust you? You're a newspaper man. I can't trust you! Okay kiddo, enjoy yourself in Nelson-Mandela-land, but go easy on the champagne...and it would be nice to see some decent copy from this one day. For what this is costing me, it had better be front page stuff!"

"How's Ed Harper doing with my work?" Kerrin asked, but immediately wished he hadn't.

"Brilliantly. The guy's good. He could be a little competition for you. If I were you I'd make sure this thing you're working on is great stuff...just in case..."

"I'm glad he's doing so well. The paper needs good people."

"Like you, I suppose?"

"Exactly. And while we're talking about good people Paul, can you pop your head round your door and see if Fiona is still there? I need her to do some stuff for me."

Fiona was one of the researchers at the paper, who had helped Kerrin out in the past by chasing down material for some of his articles. There was a few moments silence before his boss returned to the phone.

"She's still here. I'll transfer you. Take it easy, Kerrin, And if there is anything dangerous happening down there, just make sure you get back in one piece...I can't afford any insurance or liability claims, okay?"

"...And for a second I thought you cared," Kerrin replied, smiling.

There was the sound of electronic pulses down the line, as Paul redialed and transferred his call to Fiona.

"Kerrin? Long time no see. How's tricks?" Fiona bubbled. She was one of the liveliest people in the office.

"Excellent. Listen, I need you to do a few things for me over the next few days. I'll be out of the office till next week, but it would be great if you could give me some of your time to help track down some information?"

"Sure thing. What sort of stuff are you after?" Kerrin could already hear her gearing up for the challenge of the search. She seemed to thrive in finding out information about the most obscure things. The people in the office had nicknamed her the 'Wunderkind' because she could seemingly work miracles and find information that no one else could.

"I want you to check out a company called Gen8tyx. Until last month it was based in Orlando in Florida, but it's moved to somewhere in California now. I want anything you can get on it. They're a genetics company. Try to find out what they were doing, if they have printed any white papers or scientific articles..."

"Okay, anything else?"

"Yes, can you talk to your friends in Wall Street, and find out what the buzz is on the Gen8tyx stock? Although, it could be a private company, so maybe it's not listed...And can you check the company records to see who the directors are? And if it is public, then look at their internal share dealings, the sales and purchases of the directors etc?"

"No problem, I've got that...anything more?"

Kerrin could hear her champing at the bit, rearing and ready to gallop off into the archives to find out everything there was to be found.

"That's all for now...but use your initiative...anything that strikes you as odd, check it out. Okay?"

"Like I said...'no problemo'. I'll get right down to it!"

As Kerrin thanked her and hung up, he was already beginning to wonder what the wunderkind would dig up on Gen8tyx. Whatever she found, he was sure it would be good.

CHAPTER 18
Day Thirteen
Purlington Bay
California

Colonel Packard opened his eyes. The anesthetic was beginning to wear off. A wave of nausea rolled over him and he groaned. He felt the room wobble and distort.

The light was bright. Slowly, the silhouette of a woman came into focus beside him.

It was Nurse Peterson. She was leaning over him, mopping his brow and smiling.

He smiled back.

"Colonel Packard...Welcome back. How do you feel?" Nurse Peterson asked softly.

"Like a train just hit me...but I'll survive."

"You'll feel a little strange for about an hour, but after that you'll start to feel a lot better. If you don't mind, we'd like to do some tests then?"

"No problem..." The Colonel closed his eyes again. The room span, and he gripped the edge of the bed with his hands, riding out the nausea. Thankfully it passed quickly.

When he opened his eyes again, he felt well enough to look around the room.

He focused on the view of the sea, and the blue sky above. It was a beautiful day outside. A fantastic day.

And if the Orlando Treatment worked, he hoped to spend many more just like it with his wife and grandchildren.

That was the reason he was doing this.

That and the fact that if the Orlando Treatment worked, he would be able to walk again for the first time in thirty years.

Miami
Florida

Laura sat at her desk, puzzled. She wasn't often puzzled, but there was something in the file in front of her that she didn't quite understand. At least, it wasn't immediately obvious.

It had taken a little bit of leg-work and persuading, a few smiles and sexy looks at hideously ugly men who she would never consider dating in a million years, but it had worked.

She picked up the phone and dialed a number in New York.

"John, it's Laura. Sorry to bother you again so soon, but I have a little question for you."

She didn't like dealing with John. He was a shady character at best. Laura had always suspected that although he was employed by Chymera, he was really working for the government. Almost like her, but in reverse.

"Are we secure?"

"Yes. With the latest 1024 bit key voice encryption."

"Okay, so what's your question?"

"I've just received a copy of a report from the Coroner's office here in Miami. The Coroner was persuaded by someone in the police department to do another autopsy on Henry Roberts. It makes interesting reading. It confirms again that he suffered severe trauma from a suicide attempt, by hanging himself, but it then goes on to say that he didn't have a heart attack as was first believed by the doctors...I was just wondering if your guys had any more involvement with him, after they botched up the initial attempt to kill him?" Her words were pointed. She enjoyed pointing out other people's mistakes.

The man at the other end of the phone seemed relatively unfazed by the blatant dig at his professionalism.

"No. When David Sonderheim called us, we picked Roberts up from Sonderheim's home as requested. Then we took Roberts back to his house, and dangled him from the tree. But not before we got the rest of the information from him that we needed. Anyway, he'd already divulged most of what we needed to know directly to Sonderheim quite willingly on the phone, before we arrived. Seems he'd had a falling out with the rest of the group. They didn't see eye-to-eye on everything...Anyway, after we got the rest of the information we needed from him, we carried out the order to kill him ..."

"Well almost, but after your men botched up the fake suicide, did they finish the job in the hospital?"

"No. We knew he was in a coma and not likely to come out of it. I had a man waiting outside the hospital round the clock, just to make sure that if he did wake up, then we could silence him properly before he could talk...but with all that hospital security, it just seemed madness to risk sending someone inside, especially when he was already in a coma, and not expected to pull through. And I resent your reference to a 'botched job'. Please do not refer to it again. If you had provided us with better information, if we had known about the dogs...we would have killed him somewhere else."

"Let's not start throwing blame around like a couple of kids. All I am trying to establish here is whether or not your group were responsible for murdering dear old Henry. According to the coroner's report, someone gave him a lethal injection of a muscle-relaxant, which induced paralysis and death...and made it look like a heart attack."

"That's very interesting...but it wasn't us." John replied, an element of surprise almost breaking through his incredibly boring, monotone voice.

"Are you telling me that someone else beat you to it?"

"Looks that way, doesn't it!"

"If it wasn't you, who the hell was it then?"

There was no direct flight from Miami to Cape Town, so she would have to fly to Washington first, spend the night in George Town, and then catch the South African Airways flight the next day. It was going to be a long trip.

It was a thirty minute drive to the airport from her apartment by the beach. She hit a button on the dash board, and the roof of her Audi coupé import slid back silently into its awning at the back of the car. She reached up and pulled the pin from her hair, shaking it out and letting it flow freely in the warm air as she sped down the outside lane of the freeway.

With one hand on the steering wheel, she ran her spare hand through her long, auburn curls. The question went round and round her brain, and it was beginning to bug Laura.

"If we didn't kill Henry Roberts, who did?"

Until this afternoon Laura hadn't quite made up her mind if she would handle this personally or not. She had a few FBI contacts in South Africa who could do the job for her, but this business was beginning to intrigue her.

And besides, after she had ribbed John and his team for messing up the Henry Roberts killing, she had to make sure that there were no mistakes in getting rid of Alex Swinton. If her team messed up, she would be no better than he was.

No, this one definitely called for the personal touch. She would direct the operation herself.

CHAPTER 19
Day Fourteen
Washington Airport

Even though it meant setting the alarm clock for 4. 30 a.m., Dana had insisted on taking Kerrin to the airport.

They arrived early, giving them the chance to check in then grab a coffee together in Starbucks. He didn't want to admit it, but Kerrin was a little nervous. He was a good reporter. He enjoyed his work, but it had been years since he had been a policeman, and he had grown accustomed to a relatively quiet life. Although he was enjoying the thrill of the chase, it was a sudden jolt to the system to be thrown back into the stress of living on the edge. What had started out as a few visits to some mourning widows had now turned into an adventure which at every turn thrust him closer to an unknown danger. A danger which seemed to lurk in the shadows, becoming more menacing the closer he came to revealing the hidden face of the person lying in wait around the next corner, the person who was responsible for the deaths of his brother-in-law and the others he worked with, and the person whose identity Kerrin had vowed to uncover.

He couldn't admit to Dana that she could be right. Perhaps he was flying to South Africa only to come face to face with the man who had murdered his work colleagues in cold blood. Yet, he had to know. Like a moth drawn to a burning flame, Kerrin could not avoid the task before him. He had to find and meet with Alex Swinton.

When the loudspeakers announced his flight, he gave Dana a hug, kissed her passionately in a public display of affection that surprised even himself, and walked through the departure gates.

When he got to gate nineteen, he found the flight was not yet boarding, so he walked back to the nearest shop and picked up a selection of magazines to read en route. Checking on the gate again, he found that the flight was still not boarding, so he walked across to the bar and sat down. Time for another coffee. As he waited for the waitress to come to his table, he noticed a paper lying on the seat opposite him, recognizing it immediately as the Miami Chronicle. He leant across and scooped it up, checking the date to see how old it was. It was yesterday's, the late edition. A passenger from Florida must have brought it up on a flight last night.

His coffee arrived and as he lifted the cup to drink from it, he spread the broad-sheet out on the table in front of him. His eyes were immediately drawn to the main story of the local paper: "Two Miami Policemen die in Bungled Raid".

Immediately below the by-line were two pictures of the policemen who had died.

The one on the left was his friend James 'IceBreaker' Callaghan.

The picture had been taken some years ago, probably just after he had graduated from the academy and before he had started to put on the extra weight, but Kerrin recognized the picture of his friend immediately.

He scanned the story quickly, sat back in his chair and took a few deep breaths, then leant forward across the table and read the story again slowly. The article only took up a third of the front page, but it took Kerrin several minutes to take it all in and digest it properly.

He couldn't believe that James was dead. When he came to the end of the article for the third time, he realized that his hands were shaking and that his heart was beating fast. He had even broken out into a sweat. He stood up slowly, slightly unsteady on his feet, and made his way to the restroom where he splashed his face with cold water, dabbed it down with some paper towels, then found a cubicle and closed the door behind him and sat down.

He unfurled the paper and reread the article again for the fifth or sixth time. One of the sentences stuck in his mind.

"...obviously disturbed in the middle of the raid, the gunmen shot their way out of the shop, dropping most of the stolen money behind them as they ran. Relatives of the deceased shopkeeper estimated that they only managed to escape with about $200..."

$200! Was that all a life was worth nowadays?

He read the article again.

Now that he had begun to calm down, something about the article began to trouble him. Memories of his days as a policeman on the beat came rushing back to him. His instinct, once finely tuned from years of patrolling the crime ridden streets of America, was telling him that something was wrong.

Then he spotted it. It was really a combination of two things:

'...The two police officers responded promptly to the alarm, and arrived within ten minutes of the gunmen entering the premises...'

and

'... the gunmen shot their way out of the shop, dropping most of the stolen money behind them as they ran.'

What had the gunmen been doing in the shop for over ten minutes? In Kerrin's experience, the gunmen got in there, grabbed the takings and got out immediately. Four to five minutes tops. But ten?

And then they left all their money behind?

It seemed too much of a coincidence to Kerrin that James had died just as he had started to help him investigate the Orlando Suicides.

And then suddenly it all made sense.

It hadn't been a robbery. It had been an execution designed to look like one. The robbers hadn't really intended to steal the money. They had only wanted to lure the policemen to the shop so that they could kill James... to stop him from asking too many questions...and then make it look like a bungled robbery!

Grabbing his stuff, he left the toilet and ran to the nearest phone. He dialed Dana's cell phone, swearing to himself, and urging her to answer it. It took a few minutes for her to pick it up.

"Dana? Where are you?"

"Almost home...I'll be there in about ten minutes? Why?"

"Listen to me. Please, please don't argue with me, or ask too many questions. Can you remember how I told you about my friend James in Florida, and how he helped me over the past few days?"

"You mean 'the IceBreaker?' "

"Yes! ...James...He was killed yesterday. Shot. Dana, James is dead..." he paused for a moment, trying to grab his breath. "Dana, I want you to pack some things, and go and stay with a friend. Just get out of the house. Don't stay there...Call my boss Paul from a payphone and tell him where you are. I'll come to you when I get back!"

"Kerrin? Do you think they'll try to kill you next? And me? ...*I'm scared.*"

"So am I honey. So am I. I don't know, maybe they don't know about me yet, but I think they do. I told you that I think someone must have tapped my phone? Maybe I'm just being over cautious, even a little paranoid, but I don't think so....Listen, I have to go to South Africa and find this guy Alex Swinton. If he's behind this, I'll catch him and that'll be the end of it...and if he's not, then maybe he'll know who is...I have to go...but I can't go if I know you're in the house alone!" Kerrin almost shouted down the phone, the words spilling out of his mouth and unable to hide the fear in his voice. "Will you go to a friend's...please...as soon as possible?"

There was a moment's pause, then the answer he needed to hear.

"Yes. Okay. And I'll leave the number with Paul."

Behind him Kerrin could make out the voice on the P.A. system urgently requesting the last remaining passengers of Flight 203 to make their way quickly to gate nineteen, where the flight was now closing.

"Dana, I have to go. My flight's just leaving...go to your friends...Today! *Now!*"

He dropped the phone onto the cradle, grabbed his papers and ran to the gate, the last person to board the plane.

As he walked onto the flight, searching for his seat in the fifth row in Business Class, an attractive young lady looked up from an aisle seat in the second row as he passed her by. She looked away again quickly, burying her head in the magazine she was reading. She had recognized him immediately. The question was, had Kerrin recognized Agent Laura Samuels?

CHAPTER 20
Day Fourteen
The Gen8tyx Company
Purlington Bay
California

When Trevor Simons had arrived at the clinic he was exhausted. Even so, when he entered the complex he had refused the wheelchair that had been offered to him. He despised weakness, and he despised it even more so in himself.

He was fighting the illness, the monster within him, trying to destroy it with every ounce of willpower that he had left. Yet sometimes, the monster seemed just too powerful, and recently he had felt fear for the first time in his life. Fear that he might not win the battle. Fear that he may die.

Whenever the fear came, he had locked himself away in his office or his house, and refused to let anyone else see him. Sometimes sleep overcame him, and when he awoke he felt better. At other times he would sit in a chair, or lie on the floor or on his bed, until the strength returned to his tired bones and muscles, and he was able to carry on.

He was not a stupid man. He knew the prognosis was ultimately fatal. It had been a risk stopping the other treatment that could potentially have prolonged his life and coming to Purlington Bay. His doctors had advised him against it. Of course, he had not told them what he knew about the Orlando Treatment...the hope that it offered...but he knew that if he didn't take the risk and join the new Phase Two Trials now, then he may not be around for the time when Phase Three started. It was all or nothing. A last minute gamble. A final role of the dice.

His memory of the past two days was obscure. A dream that shifted from reality to fantasy to reality and back again, until the dreams and the reality blurred and became indecipherable. Visions of people, doctors, nurses, beautiful women dressed in white...or were they angels come to collect him? No, that they certainly weren't. The day he died, he knew there would be nothing angelic waiting on the other side to meet him. Where he was going, it was going to be very hot indeed.

In his dreams he could remember big machines, tunnels in rotating domes, injections, tubes hanging out of every limb, blood transfusions,…and smiles, laughter, followed by exhaustion, and dreams within dreams. Had he really cried at the pain of it all? Had he been delirious? Was it all a dream, and how much of it had been true?

All he knew was that he couldn't remember what had happened to him. As soon as he had entered his room on the first day he had collapsed into a deep sleep. He had awoken to the voice of a beautiful nurse, and then there had been a doctor…and then…?

Then there was now.

And now?

He lifted his head off the pillow and noticed for the first time the blue sky outside his bedroom window. He could see the sea birds soaring on the thermals, rising and falling with the wind and the hot air blowing inland across the bay, and he felt strangely moved. How lucky they were to be so mobile, so free.

He turned his head back to the room, half expecting the movement to be accompanied by a wave of pain or exhaustion. But there was nothing.

His eyes scanned his living quarters and he realized how comfortable and bright they actually were. It occurred to him then, that for the first time in months he was noticing 'detail'.

In the past, 'detail' had been his thing. It was his attention to detail that had helped him get to where he was now: one of the richest and most powerful men in America. With interests spanning munitions, heavy machinery and transport, Simons Holdings was one of America's greatest companies. A company which Trevor himself had built up from nothing. From nothing to a vast fortune, all in forty years. All created by his attention to detail.

He smiled to himself and decided to try and get out of bed. He swung his legs over the edge of the mattress and tried to sit up, and found himself doing it with surprising agility.

He stood up, and strolled towards the window.

His footsteps were solid and strong. The muscles in his legs tight and powerful. He reached the window expecting to have to steady himself against the window frame but felt no need to do so. He turned and walked back towards the mirror, a slight spring in his step. He stood before the man whose reflection looked back at him, and was surprised to see how healthy the stranger in front of him seemed.

The bags under his eyes were no longer as dark and pronounced as before, and the haggard look which had haunted him for months had been replaced by a peaceful mask which contorted his face into something almost acceptable…someone he hardly recognized.

It was then that he realized that he felt great. Really great. Not tired. Not sad.

Just great.

In the room next door Colonel Packard awoke from his dreams. He had dreamt that he had been running in a football match, straight down the outside of the field, just about to pluck the ball from the air and score the winning points in the game.

As his eyelids flickered open he realized there was something troubling him. Something unusual which he took a while to recognize and identify.

It was an odd sensation. Almost as if...no, it couldn't be...but it was!

Packard sat up in his bed and bent forward. Stretching his hand out as far as it would go, he scratched his foot.

"Oh...," he thought to himself ."That felt good!"

He rubbed and massaged it, then scratched it again. Then he cried.

For the first time since a Viet Cong bullet had sliced through the edge of his spine in Vietnam, Colonel Packard was able to feel a sensation in his foot. It was itching.

Business Class
33,000 ft above the Atlantic Ocean

Kerrin was a nervous wreck. He couldn't stop thinking about James, and his death. The more he thought about it, the more convinced he became that James had been professionally executed. They had been clever. Very clever. What sort of people had gone to all that trouble, instead of just shooting him dead in the street? Someone, somewhere, had gone to great lengths to silence James without drawing any more attention to the questions he had been asking.

Kerrin was scared. He was worried for Dana.

But as he thought about it a transition began to take place in Kerrin. A metamorphosis.

A change, which took place so slowly that he himself didn't realize it was occurring.

This was becoming personal.

Very personal.

Whoever was behind the Orlando Suicides had killed two people that Kerrin had liked, even loved. They had ruined the lives of his sister and nephews, and taken a father from their children. And now there was the possibility that the very core of his existence, his wife Dana, could also be in danger.

Slowly the fear within Kerrin grew, turned itself inside out, and changed into hate. His hands that for the past few hours had been trembling nervously with fear, now shook with anger.

Kerrin swore to himself that he would track down whoever had done this to his family and his friends. He would find those people and destroy them. And if need be, he would kill them.

For the first time, he knew with absolute clarity that it was now them or him. He would make sure it was them.

The loudspeaker announced that the cabin crew were going to dim the lights.

Kerrin felt much calmer now, but he could do with a stiff drink. Perhaps he would read a little to further calm himself down. Reading always relaxed him. It took his mind off his own problems and allowed his mind to soar, to live life through the eyes of the authors, and to experience worlds far beyond his own.

He reached into his bag and pulled out a copy of 'RAGE', a novel he had started reading over two years before but had never got round to finishing. It was a book about South Africa, and he had grabbed it from his study just as they had left the house. Maybe he would get the chance to finish it before he landed.

He picked himself up and made his way to the small bar on the upper deck of the aircraft, ordering a double malt whisky and taking residence on a pew beside the small counter.

At first Laura couldn't quite believe the coincidence, but on further reflection she realized that it was not so strange after all. Kerrin had to be in Langebaan in two days time to meet Alex Swinton, and there were only a limited number of flights to Cape Town, so there was always a fairly high chance that they would end up sharing the same transportation.

In actual fact, there was very little for her to be worried about. Whereas she now knew a lot about Kerrin, there was little if any chance at all that Kerrin knew anything about her. Why should he? There was no connection from her to him. As far as he was concerned, she was just another passenger en route to Cape Town.

The big question was: 'how could she turn this accident of fate to her own advantage?' She decided that the best thing to do would be to somehow introduce herself. If she could make friends with him, then perhaps she would be able to find out a little bit more about his movements and intentions in South Africa. And maybe she would be able to have a little fun in the process.

She pulled out her compact and while pretending to examine something on her face, she looked at the reflection of Kerrin in the small mirror. He was sitting about four rows back in an aisle seat, skimming through a glossy magazine.

Laura's taste in men was quite varied. Kerrin was slightly overweight, but not at all unattractive. He easily came within the realm of 'acceptable'.

The plane was not too crowded, and only half the seats in business class were occupied. On this flight down there was no real distinction between First Class and Business Class, and both groups of passengers were invited to use the small bar on the top floor of the airplane.

About two hours in, just after the in-flight entertainment episode of 'Friends' had finished, Laura took her headset off and flashed a glance back down the aisle. Kerrin's seat was empty. She hadn't noticed him make his way past her to the toilets at the front of the aircraft so she guessed that he might have gone up to the bar.

She flicked the release catch and slipped out of her seatbelt, straightening herself up and smoothing down her skirt. She stretched, smiled at the woman sitting beside her, and made her way to the stairs going up to the top deck.

As she emerged into the small area above, she found three people sitting at the small bar: two business men who looked like they were talking shop, and Kerrin who was sitting by himself sipping a whisky and reading a book.

She took the seat beside him, catching the attention of the flight attendant and asking for a Martini. Taking the cocktail stick out of the glass and sucking the alcohol off the green olive, perhaps a little too erotically, she turned to Kerrin.

"Good book?"

He looked up, smiled at her, and closed the novel, placing it on the bar counter beside his drink.

"Wilbur Smith. Perhaps the best author on the planet. Thought I'd read something topical."

She looked at the title. A single word, 'Rage', ran across the front of the book, the author's name written in gold underneath. It was one she had already read and she had loved it.

"Rage? What's it all about...sounds a bit 'angry' and violent." she smiled innocently back at him.

"Not really. It's a novel set in the years running up to the abolition of apartheid in South Africa...sort of gives you an idea of the cultural events leading up to Mandela being elected.

"Would you recommend it?" she asked, smiling at him, her eyes twinkling in the light from the bar lamp.

"Absolutely...actually, I've only got about eighty pages left to read. If I finish it before we land, I can give it to you, if you would like?"

"Oh...I would like that very much. Thank you..."

Kerrin adjusted his position in his seat. Was the lady coming on to him? He picked his whisky up and took a sip, his eyes appraising her quickly over the edge of the glass. Kerrin reckoned she was about twenty-eight years old. She was smartly dressed, a pearl necklace complementing an elegant pink cardigan and a chic blue skirt. Her eyes were emerald green, her long auburn hair, cascading over her shoulders and disappearing down her back. The only thing wrong with her, as far as Kerrin was concerned, was that her breasts were slightly too large for his taste. Kerrin was more a leg person. Still, if he had been a single man, and maybe just a few years younger, he would have been quite attracted to her.

Laura followed his eyes as he scanned her body, and was pleased when he smiled back at her when the assimilation had been completed. Why were men so obvious? Yet she had to admit that she found Kerrin quite attractive too. He seemed to be very laid-back, quite cool and self confident, and he had an incredible smile. Laura could normally make up her mind about someone in the first few seconds of meeting them, and with Kerrin she realized two things.

Firstly, she liked him. And perhaps she was even interested in him.

Secondly, she immediately recognized that Kerrin was not the sort of person that fell off his chair every time a gorgeous woman walked past. He was not the type to be easily led by looks, but belonged to that rare subset of the male species that actually looked behind the external appearance and saw what was inside the person. There would be no point in carrying on flirting so overtly with him. That approach would just turn him off. No, if she wanted to have this man, she would have to flirt with his mind and not what was in his trousers.

The idea excited her. She knew she was playing with fire, perhaps dancing a little too close to the flame, but this was something she had never done before. This was new. Seducing the man who, sometime in the near future, she may be asked to kill.

"So will this be your first time in South Africa?" she asked.

"Yes...and you?"

"Me too...but I'm afraid that for me, this will be more business than pleasure. Not enough time to play..."

"But you're lucky that your work takes you to such nice places. Just think of all those people who never get the chance to travel abroad at all."

"Oh, I suppose you're right. It's just that I hate these long trips abroad by myself. No, don't get me wrong, I find them exciting...but sometimes you get a little tired of being away from home so much. You get so lonely..." She replied, turning towards him.

"May I ask what's taking you down there then? Who do you work for?" he asked. He seemed genuinely interested.

"Oh...I don't actually work for anyone really. I have my own business. I work in the travel industry. I'm just coming down to check out a new idea I've had."

"Sounds interesting. Is it a secret or can you tell me what it is?"

"I suppose so. You can be my market research. Tell me what you think of my idea...I'm thinking of running specialist adventure holidays for Americans in South Africa. I'm going to start off with Specialist Windsurfing holidays, and I'm going to spend the next few weeks checking out the hot windsurfing destinations."

"It sounds a great idea. I love windsurfing, and that's the reason I'm flying down too...I'm a journalist, and I want to write something about windsurfing in the Cape."

"Wow, that's a coincidence." She smiled back, and they both laughed nervously.

"Can I introduce myself? My names Kerrin. May I ask you what your name is?"

"Carol. You can call me Carol..."

"Well Carol, can I get you another drink?" Kerrin asked her, signaling politely to the stewardess for some attention.

"Please. That would be nice."

The conversation flowed easily between them. At first Laura tried to manipulate it, attempting to extract some valuable information from him, but after a while she just relaxed and started to enjoy the conversation for what it was.

Kerrin was an interesting man. Although he revealed little about his personal life or his work, he willingly shared his ideas and views with her about politics, religion and the arts. Laura found herself enjoying his company.

She definitely was dancing too close to the flame.

She was surprised by how much she was warming to this man. How much her body was becoming attracted to him. How much she wanted him...Perhaps, this had not been such a good idea after all.

"Kerrin...It's been wonderful talking to you, but I'm going to be really selfish and leave you to finish your book, so that you can give it to me tomorrow morning." She stood up and stretched out her arm to shake his hand.

As Kerrin shifted the glass from his right to his left hand she noticed the flash of gold on the wedding finger. She was even surprised at her own reaction to it.

She was disappointed.

As Laura walked back down the stairs Kerrin smiled to himself. He may be old and fat, but it was true that some women were still attracted to him.

He hadn't lost it after all. He couldn't wait to tell Dana that he had been hit upon, and to tease her about it when he called her the next day!

CHAPTER 21
Day Fifteen
Cape Town
South Africa

Kerrin hated long-haul overnight flights. He hated the jetlag that hit a few hours after he stepped off the airplane and usually accompanied his every move for the following week.

Over the years he had developed his own theory on how to survive the ravages of international travel. His rules were simple:-

1: Don't sleep on overnight flights.

2: When arriving, do your best to adapt immediately to the local time zone by staying awake until the normal time of the day that you would consider going to sleep.

3: Drink lots of water on the flight.

Staying awake the whole night was the hardest part to do. If he slept, he knew he would feel terrible the next day. If he didn't sleep, he would just feel very tired. Either way, he would be exhausted.

Tonight though, keeping awake had not been a problem. Although his conversation with the attractive woman in the bar had taken his mind off things a little, he couldn't help but think more about James's death.

It wasn't every day that you found out one of your best friends had been murdered. And it was probably because of Kerrin: if Kerrin had not got him involved, James would still be alive now!

When the cabin crew switched the lights back on, and did their best to wake the sleeping business men and women in as polite and charming a way as possible, he stretched over the empty seat beside him, and lifted the shade on the window, allowing himself to see out and give himself his first glimpse of the African continent.

They were flying parallel to the mainland, several miles out to sea. As Kerrin watched, a golden sun rose, signifying the start of a wonderful cloud free day ahead.

A smiling stewardess brought him a tray with fresh coffee, orange juice and what did its best to look like freshly made scrambled eggs with bacon and tomatoes. Starving, Kerrin wolfed down the contents of the breakfast, and catching the attention of the stewardess asked if there were any possibility of a second helping. She smiled back, returning shortly with a second tray.

Thirty minutes later, the 747 jet flew over Robben Island, the island prison of Nelson Mandela, then turned back towards the mainland, circling the mountain range and massive plateau that is Table Mountain. As he looked out across the cityscape of Cape Town, sprawling across the base of the mountain range, Kerrin couldn't help but feel excitement in his chest. An excitement which was swiftly accompanied by a twang of guilt.

Guilt that he would be exploring Cape Town by himself, without Dana by his side.

And guilt because he could feel such positive emotions, when only a few days before his friend James had been murdered.

A short while later the plane disembarked, the business passengers leaving the aircraft first. As he reached into the overhead locker, Laura made her way past him to the exit. Surprisingly, in spite of the overnight flight, she looked remarkably fresh.

"Good morning, I hope you slept well?" she smiled at him.

"Oh no, I never sleep on overnight flights...and besides I had a lot of reading to catch up with...which reminds me, would you like the book we talked about?" he reached into his bag and offered his copy of "RAGE" to the attractive lady.

She took it gratefully, and flashed him a wide smile, her green eyes twinkling in the bright cabin lights.

"Thanks...I'll look forward to reading it."

As she moved past him, she turned and looked at him once more.

"I hope you have a pleasant stay...you never know, since we're both here for related reasons...maybe we'll bump into each other again?"

"That would be nice, but in case we don't, I hope that you have a fruitful stay." Kerrin replied.

"Thanks, I'm sure I will. I fully intend to. "

Laura smiled at the man one last time. She liked him. More than she should. Sadly though, next time they met, she would probably have to kill him.

It was almost ten o'clock in the morning before Kerrin had loaded his luggage into the trunk of his white Toyota Corolla at the airport in Cape Town. Instead of taking a cheaper local rental company, he had opted for the more expensive Hertz option, feeling more comfortable in the knowledge that should he break down anywhere in the expansive countryside outside Cape Town, Hertz could arrange for his car to be picked up without any hassle. He didn't like the idea of driving several hundred miles away from Cape Town into the Karoo desert, or breaking down in the mountains, and then finding out it was his responsibility to fix the car and return it to Cape Town. No, for peace of mind he would pay the few extra dollars it cost.

From the airport he took the N2 motorway into Cape Town, already grateful for the air conditioning he had insisted upon there being in the car. Outside the sun was blazing from a cloudless sky and the temperature was creeping up into the thirties. Thankfully a light breeze was blowing in from the east, which would make it more bearable when outside the car.

He was heading into the town centre. On the plane he'd had a chance to read a section from the "Lonely Planet Guide to South Africa", and following its suggestion he had decided to have lunch in the wharf area of Cape Town harbor. He would give himself a few hours to do a spot of sightseeing, then in the afternoon he was going to head out along the coast road to Langebaan. According to the map it was about three hours drive from Cape Town, and hopefully he would get there about six o'clock, giving him enough time to find a hotel somewhere.

He had agreed to meet Alex Swinton in two days time, but Kerrin was going to do his best to find him either later that night or the next day. He wanted to try and reach him as soon as possible.

The N2 petered out, and scanning the overhead motorway signs, Kerrin managed to follow the roads down to the back of the harbor.

The car-park bordered the wharf area, which consisted of a large modern shopping complex and a number of old boathouses which had been converted into shops, bars and restaurants. Walking through the shopping mall, Kerrin came out onto the quayside, where directly in front of him a large number of fishing boats, pleasure craft and tourist ferries huddled and rocked together in the water of a large harbor.

On the right hand side the skyline was dominated by the awesome and magnificent panorama of Table Mountain. The mountain rose steeply from the bay beneath, sheer cliffs a thousand feet tall rising to a plateau, which looked as flat as the top of a kitchen table. From where he stood he could see a cable car making its way up the side of the cliff.

The mountain range of which Table Mountain was a part, ran along Kerrin's right hand side, stretching along the coastline as far as he could see.

To his left, large cargo ships blocked the view of the ocean, but the smell of the sea beyond filled his nostrils. Squawking seagulls chased the fishing boats returning from a day at sea, and some seals swam amongst the boats in the harbor and basked on one of the harbor walls.

The air was filled with the sound of people laughing and having fun, and the water was alive with the reflections of the boats and the colorful marine buildings bordering the harbor.

His senses thrilled to it all, and Kerrin was lost in the moment. What a place!

All thoughts of the reason he was here were momentarily forgotten, and for a few minutes Kerrin was a tourist, seeing a beautiful new city through the eyes of a traveler. If only his wife Dana had been here to share the experience with him. It was incredible.

He walked along the edge of the quayside, admiring the boats in the harbor, and sharing the excitement of the tourists milling around the dock. He had wandered for an hour before he realized how hungry he was, and then he followed the smell of pizza to one of the many pavement restaurants overlooking the harbor. He ordered a large cold 'Castle' lager, and a Four Seasons pizza, and settled down in his seat in the sunshine, studying the view of the mountain above.

This was the life.

The drive to Langebaan was interesting, although almost disappointingly the massive mountains that formed such a dramatic backdrop to Cape Town slowly began to drop behind him and diminish in size. Soon he was just driving through flat, featureless countryside devoid of houses or farms.

The tarmac road ran on for miles straight ahead, green and brown bushes, called 'fynbos' by the locals, covering the otherwise barren ground on either side. Occasionally Kerrin got a glimpse of the sea, and every now and again he could see seagulls swooping down low to pick up scraps from the road.

About three hours after he had left Cape Town he drove through a small group of buildings which formed the town of Langebaan. After passing through the town Kerrin circled round and drove back into the centre of the main street, stopping in front of what was obviously the only hotel in town.

He parked, and stepped out of the car. A wall of heat hit him broadside and he suddenly understood why the main street was deserted. Everyone with any sense was hiding inside the air conditioned buildings. He stretched, walked round to the back of the car and pulled out his suitcase and hand luggage.

From outside, the hotel didn't appear to be anything special, but walking through the door into the air-conditioned reception area, he was pleasantly surprised by the tasteful interior. The hotel had a homely feel to it, with a distinct Dutch influence immediately apparent in the choice of décor. There was a bar, and a restaurant on the left which spilled out on to an open veranda overlooking the main street, and on the right there was a spacious lounge. From the hall, a sweeping staircase led up to the three floors above. Before entering, the hotel had appeared deceptively small and cramped, yet once inside, it was spacious and relaxed. Kerrin realized that several of the buildings on either side of the original façade must have been absorbed into the hotel. The biggest building in town, Kerrin guessed that this place was probably the hub of the community, the bar beside the restaurant probably the only one in town.

"Good day, may I help you sir?"

A young lady asked, stepping out from the restaurant to behind the reception desk at the base of the staircase. Kerrin was struck by her beautiful blue eyes and her long blonde hair. He guessed she was about twenty three years of age.

"Yes, I hope so. I was wondering if you have a room for a couple of days?"

"I believe we do. You're lucky though, at this time of the year we are normally quite full."

She smiled at Kerrin and typed a few things on a computer keyboard, scanning the screen as if making the choice of a room.

"Is it just for yourself? Would a single room be okay? No smoking? Okay, and for how many nights would that be sir?"

"Two nights for now, please."

"May I see your passport for a moment please sir?" she asked politely, taking it from Kerrin's outstretched hand and typing the passport number into the computer.

"There you are, sir..." she said, pulling down a key from the board behind her. "Room 348. Breakfast is included in the price, and is served between 8 a.m. and 10 a.m. in the restaurant... would there be anything else I can help you with sir?" she smiled again.

Kerrin hesitated, then bent down and unzipped the sports bag he had used as his hand luggage on the plane. He reached inside and pulled out the postcard from Alex Swinton from an inside pocket. He straightened up and showed the woman behind the desk the picture on the front of the card.

"Actually, I'm a journalist from America, I've come here to do a story on windsurfing in the Cape. I'm meant to be meeting one of my friends here, at the entrance to this park...can you tell me where it is?"

The woman looked at the card and smiled.

"It's not far from here. You just keep going out of town, and after about four miles, on the left you will come to a tarmaced road which will take you down a dirt track to the entrance gate of the park...it's about ten minutes tops."

"Thanks." Then just as he was turning to go up to his room, Kerrin added as an afterthought. "My friend is called Alex Swinton...I don't suppose he's staying in this hotel is he?"

Since this was the only hotel in town, perhaps Kerrin would be lucky.

A moment later the woman looked up from the computer.

"No, I'm sorry...there's no one here by that name, but if he's in town for the surfing, I would suggest you try Old Ronnie's down by the beach. In about an hour's time the light will start to go, and the surfers will come off the waves, change and head for a beer…maybe you'll find him there."

"Could you tell me where it is?" Kerrin asked.

"Sure…let me draw you a little map…"

Kerrin felt refreshed. The shower in his room was powerful, and cool, and the water had invigorated him and washed away the fatigue of travelling half way round the world. His poor, confused body clock, struggling to adjust to the new time zone, was quickly filled with a flood of unexpected energy. Although the evening was coming on fast, he felt like it was only the beginning of the afternoon.

His stomach on the other hand was completely lost. It didn't know if it was breakfast, lunch or dinnertime. In the end it had just shut down, and now Kerrin didn't feel the slightest bit hungry.

He followed the map the receptionist had given him until he came to the spot where the smooth tarmac stopped and where a sign pointed to the 'Langebaan National Reserve', where he turned and drove his rental car through an open, unattended entrance gate and down a sandy, dirt-track road towards the beach. The road wound around a number of small sand dunes, then dipped down and came out into a small parking area surrounded by large bushes. As he stepped out of the car, he could hear the sound of surf crashing onto the beach, and following the sound he came out onto a wide, clean, white beach that ran in both directions as far as the eye could see. Beyond the line of surf the sea was calm and still. The sun was beginning to set, and its orange reflection stretched out across the surface of the sea from the edge of the surf line towards the horizon.

A few, wet-suit clad youngsters were just emerging from the waves, carrying their sails and boards from the surf. A few yards away a group of excited people sat around on rough wooden benches in front of a buzzing beach bar, the tops of their wetsuits rolled down to their waists. The sand around them was dotted with windsurfing equipment and a row of tall, colorful sails stood in a rack in the lee of the wooden building. Some of the people threw Kerrin a cursory glance, but quickly got back to their conversations, excitedly discussing the day's windsurfing.

Kerrin slipped off his shoes, letting his toes dig deep into the sand, and stood silently in awe of the sunset. He breathed the salt air deeply into his lungs and exhaled slowly.

It was a far cry from Miami and Washington, and the deaths he had come here to investigate.

A far cry indeed.

"Kerrin? …Is that you?"

A man stood up on the far side of the beach bar crowd, and walked towards him, beer in hand. At first Kerrin didn't recognize him. His hair was bedraggled and still wet, his blue wetsuit gathered round his waist exposing a muscular, hairy chest. The man came towards him with his hand stretched out, and as Kerrin took it in his, the stranger wrapped him into a powerful bear hug.

"Kerrin…it's good to see you man! How did you find me?"

Kerrin was taken aback by the sudden show of affection from the stranger, and stepping back quickly, he looked him in the face. About five-foot-six, a squat-muscular frame, and thick biceps, his hair had been dyed blonde, and he had shaved off his beard. But now he was closer up, Kerrin recognized him.

He had found Alex Swinton.

It was an incredible view. The vista that stretched out before them took her breath away. It was a beautiful day and from the top of Table Mountain, Laura could see for miles. She was leaning over the wall just outside the top cable car station, and from where she stood she could see right over the edge of the cliff.

The cliffs of the mountain fell vertically beneath her for a thousand feet, before it hit the sloping ground, which then rolled down towards the bay of Cape Town at an angle of about forty-five degrees.

As she looked over the edge she felt a strange and sudden twinge in the pit of her stomach: the height and the sheer cliffs repulsed her from the edge, and yet simultaneously drew her towards it, and for a second she experienced a bizarre urge to climb on top of the wall and jump over the edge.

She pushed back with her arms from the top of the wall, and took her eyes from the dizzy fall beneath her.

Cape Town, or Kap Stadt as the locals called it, lay stretched out in the bay beneath her. The city fitted into a natural amphitheatre, a curved bowl surrounded by a wall of stone and mountain, the harbor area being where the stage should be.

On the left as she looked out to sea, the city was bordered by a large hill rising to a sharp point, called the Lion's Head. Beyond the foothills of Table Mountain on the right, the vista was a stark contrast, with flat land stretching out as far as the eye could see, bordered by a broad silver line of sand running along the edge of the coastline.

Turning to look behind her, she could see that Table Mountain ran flat for several miles before it started to rise and fall in a line of mountains which eventually petered out into the sea in the famous Cape Point, the most southern part of the African Continent.

On her left beyond the Lion's Head, her eyes followed a range of hills, which her map told her were called the 'Twelve Apostles' and led to a famous fishing village called 'Hout Bay'. Beyond that lay another peninsula and miles of golden sands.

The sea extended around her on three sides, the land only continuing to the North on her right.

The man beside her pointed to the flat land in the distance.

"That's where we're going next. Langebaan is about three hours drive over there..."

At first she had found his South African accent quite hard to understand, but after fifteen minutes she had begun to understand him a bit easier. Dirk Van Der Waal was an impressive man. Reliable, strong, intelligent and deadly. He was the leader of the in-country team that she had been using to track down Alex Swinton. She had never met him before, but when she stepped out of the cable car at the top of the mountain, she spotted him instantly beside the look-out point opposite the exit, their prearranged meeting point.

She had studied his file several times before she had flown out, and she knew he could be counted on should the situation get ugly. His team were mainly made up of South African ex-army or air force. Before being recruited as an FBI Overseas Agent, Dirk had spent several years in Namibia, Angola and Zimbabwe. He had served for two years in the South African equivalent of the UK's Special Air Services and his file showed that he had led many interesting and dangerous covert expeditions in the days leading up to the end of Apartheid in South Africa. Impressive was not the word.

In real life, he was even more handsome than the large photographs in his file. When Laura shook hands with him for the first time, she felt irresistibly drawn to the man before her. Over six foot tall, blonde and blue eyed, Laura could easily make out his powerful muscular body beneath his loose fitting T-shirt and long, green trousers. He oozed sex appeal, and Laura knew that his looks were just another of the many weapons that Dirk had mastered over the years.

"Make no mistake about it Laura," she told herself. "This man's a killer. He would eat you up and spit you out before breakfast!"

She found the idea strangely appealing.

"Did you bring the weapons?"

"Yes, as requested. They're in the van. Don't worry. Johan is guarding them."

"Excellent. Let's get going then. It's important that we get to Langebaan as soon as we can. Kerrin Graham came in on the same flight as me. He's not meant to meet Alex Swinton for another two days, but I'll bet your bottom dollar that he's headed straight out there now, hoping to find Swinton as soon as possible. We have to get there first. We've already wasted six hours by meeting up here. We should have met there."

"I'm sorry, Agent Samuels, but we didn't know until last night that you were coming, and we couldn't take the risk of meeting in town..."

"Don't call me 'Agent'. Call me Laura, and I'll call you Dirk."

"As you wish. Okay, then let's go. I took the liberty of sending my colleague Marieke ahead of us to Langebaan. She'll be there now, trying to locate Swinton before we get there. If he's there at all. Most likely he won't turn up for another two days..."

"No Dirk, that's where you're wrong. My gut instinct tells me the guy's there now. I'll bet you that even as we speak he's out there windsurfing in the sea. I hope he enjoys it, because with any luck today will be his last time. Our orders are to terminate him. Officially this is a Code Green Operation. Once it's over, it never happened. Do you understand?"

"Yes, Laura. I understand."

As Laura looked at Dirk, she saw that he was smiling, and she recognized the look in his eyes. Laura had never admitted it to anyone before, but she got a thrill, almost sexual, whenever she pulled the trigger on a gun and ended someone's life. From the way Dirk's eyes suddenly glistened at the mention of their mission, it would seem that he and she were the same. They both enjoyed to kill.

CHAPTER 22
Langebaan Bay
South Africa

The past couple of days had been fantastic. For the first time in months Alex Swinton had been able to put the dreadful happenings at Gen8tyx behind him. He had lost himself in a world of adventure, danger, sun, sea, and sex. Meeting Angelique had been the best thing that had happened to him in years.

Their attraction to each other had been instant. That they both shared the same passion for windsurfing was the icing on the cake. They had spent the past five days windsurfing together for most of the daylight hours, before collapsing exhausted in Angelique's bed at the end of the day, where they exhausted themselves even more through an insatiable union of their bodies.

Angelique had been the catalyst that had helped him forget the life he had fled, and through her the guilt had been lessened. Although it had only been two days, he knew now with absolute certainty that they had a future together. She was his new start, someone with whom to build a new life.

He had never intended to go back to America. Now he had a reason to stay in South Africa.

But first, he had to meet with Kerrin.

He was hoping that Kerrin would give him closure on the Gen8tyx affair. The guilt had been building up for the past few weeks, and before Angelique had arrived on the scene, he was scared that it would tip him over the edge. If Kerrin knew what he had done and had come to face him about it, he would confess.

There were no extradition agreements between South Africa and America. Even if he did confess, he would be safe here. He could go on to build a new life, and a new company to rival Gen8tyx right here in this new land. South Africa was a land waiting to be born. It had a vast ocean of talent just waiting to be tapped. Alex Swinton would tap that potential, and through him the dreams of their group in Gen8tyx would finally be recognized.

Yes, Alex had been looking forward to meeting up with Kerrin. For Alex, it was going to be the start of his new life.

"Alex, wow...sorry, I didn't recognize you there for a moment! You look so different from when Martin introduced us on the golf course. I'm glad you recognized me, because if you hadn't I would never have spotted you!" Kerrin blurted out. Smiling, and with a new hair style, the relaxed and tanned man standing before him now looked at least five years younger than the man he had met several weeks before. The clean South African air and the windsurfing were obviously doing him a power of good.

"...And I wasn't expecting to see you for another two days...but hey, it's good to see you. I've been looking forward to your visit. We need to talk," he patted Kerrin roughly on the side of his shoulder. "...But what brings you down so early?" he asked, his blonde eyebrows lifting up questioningly as he spoke, worried that Kerrin already knew what he had done.

Kerrin threw the others in the beach bar a quick glance.

"Sorry, I don't think it's a good idea to talk here...Can we go somewhere else?"

"Sure...listen, where are you staying? I could do with some food. I'm starving."

"I'm staying at the Langebaan Hilton." Kerrin joked in reply.

"Oh...you mean 'The Constantia Gardens Hotel'? Don't knock it pal, it's not only the best hotel in town..."

"..It's the only hotel in town!" Kerrin finished the sentence for him.

Alex laughed.

"Kerrin, give me a second or two. I've just got to say goodbye to a friend."

Kerrin watched Alex walk back across to where he had been sitting. A very pretty woman looked up, and smiled at him. Alex bent over her, whispered something in her ear. She laughed aloud and then looked across at Kerrin, waving a hand at him. She said something back to Alex, who looked at his watch, replied, and then kissed her again on the lips.

"She's lovely," Kerrin said as Alex returned.

"You're telling me...She's the best thing that's ever happened to me."

"So where are you staying then? Not at the hotel?"

"No. That would be a little too obvious. I'm trying to lie low at the moment...I was sleeping on the beach, but now I'm sleeping with Angelique at her place. Couldn't have worked out better."

"When did you meet her?"

"Just last week,...a few days after I got down here."

As they walked back to the car and drove back into town, Alex told Kerrin the story about how they had met.

"Can you drop me off just here? That'll be fine. I'll grab a shower, change and then meet you in the bar at the hotel in thirty minutes? How does that sound?" Alex asked.

"Sounds like a plan. See you then." Kerrin agreed.

When Alex walked into the bar thirty minutes later, he was a changed man. He certainly spruced up well. He wore a green shirt, and a pair of thin, cream, cotton trousers which were ideal for this hot climate. His Vans shoes were sensible but stylish with it, the tell-tale brilliant white along the edges showing that they were still almost new. With a pair of new Ray Ban sunglasses perched on top of his head, and a thin gold chain hanging tastefully around his neck, Kerrin couldn't help but admire the way the man looked. Alex strode purposely across the bar towards him, and took his hand firmly in his own.

It was obvious to Kerrin that this was not a man who seemed as if he was about to commit suicide. Like the others, he seemed to be enjoying life to the full. Someone who had everything to live for. The better question to ask was, had he killed the others?

"Beer?" Kerrin asked.

"Yes, but not one of those Castle lagers you're drinking...they're worse than American beers, if that's possible. I'll have one of those German imports please...a bottle of Becks!"

"Coming right up. Do you fancy sitting outside for dinner? The restaurant has some tables overlooking the street. There's a nice breeze, and we can see the sea from there."

"Okay. Sounds good."

Alex followed Kerrin outside, taking a seat on the veranda at a table overlooking the street.

"Cheers!" Kerrin lifted up his glass and toasted Alex.

"Cheers to you...and thanks for coming, although I still don't know exactly why you're here." Alex lifted the cold beer to his lips and drank half the bottle in his first sip. "Aah...that's better. I've been looking forward to that."

"Alex," Kerrin began."Let's get straight to the point. I'm here to warn you. To try and save your life and to find out what the hell happened at Gen8tyx. I want to know *who* killed my brother-in-law and his and your friends, and *why* they were all killed?"

Alex's face became very serious. The smile disappeared, and a haunted look took its place. In the space of a few seconds Alex seemed to have grown older and very tired. For a while neither of them said anything, and they sat in silence, Kerrin waiting for Alex to open up. When he did, it was almost in a whisper.

"I tried to warn Martin...I told him to get out...I'm sorry he didn't make it. He is...was, a good man." Alex said somberly, his voice suddenly deeper and almost monotone.

"What happened Alex? Who killed him, and why?"

Alex put the bottle down on the table, and turned his face away from Kerrin. He looked out to sea, his mind cast back to the events in America.

It was dark now, the sun had gone, and in the heat of the African night, the rhythmic pulsing of crickets provided a natural musical backdrop to their conversation.

"What do you know about Gen8tyx?" Alex asked Kerrin, turning back to face him.

"Not much…"

"Do you know what we had achieved?"

"No…"

"Okay, I'll tell you. I'll tell you everything…but first, tell me how Martin died."

"He was trying to escape America. He'd told his wife and kids to fly to the Bahamas by themselves, and he had taken his private Lear Jet and flown it out to meet them there. Only he never made it. His plane blew up in mid-air. The official investigation didn't come up with anything. I've been digging around and it looks to me like it was shot down by a US military jet. Of course, the US Air Force deny it, and say they have no record of any flight intercepting Martin's plane."

He left it a moment, watching how Alex took the news. He said nothing.

"Alex, I know about the meeting that took place at Sam Cohen's house. I know that Henry Roberts called the meeting, and I know that you all planned to launch your own company. I suspect that's why everyone started to die…" Kerrin hesitated. " I also know that you called Henry Roberts at his home and had an argument with him the night he died…"

"What else do you know?"

"Not much…but Alex, it looks bad for you. You're the only one left alive. Everyone else is dead. I don't think you did…but…"

"…But you're wondering if I killed the others?"

"…Basically…Yes. It could look like that!"

"And what do the police think?"

"Well, when I left last week, officially the police had closed their files, but…"

"So, why don't you leave it at that? You don't know what you're messing with."

"I was about to mention that the police have just started looking at all the deaths again, starting with Henry Roberts." Kerrin lied. What he was saying was not strictly true, but he needed to provoke a reaction from Alex.

"And?"

"…And they found out that Henry Roberts was murdered. Injected with a muscle relaxant. Something to make him look like he'd had a heart attack. Someone obviously didn't want him to wake up from his coma…"

Alex looked away again, his face turning up to the sky for a second before he swallowed hard and faced Kerrin.

"You don't know the potential of what we discovered. If you did, well, then you'd understand..."

"Try to help me understand. Tell me what the hell was going on at Gen8tyx!"

"First of all, you have to believe me when I tell you that I didn't kill Sam, or Tom or Mike. I had nothing to do with Martin either...It was the Company...they knew what we were up to, and they were trying to stop us from going public with our results. Trying to stop us from setting up our own company, one which would make the new treatment available to everyone, to the whole of mankind..."

Kerrin noticed that Alex had not mentioned Henry's name. Why not? Had he accidentally left it out, or was it deliberate?

"And Henry Roberts? Did you kill him?"

"Kerrin, you've got to understand. If you did, you would have done exactly the same."

"Done what?"

"Tried to stop him!"

"Who? Henry Roberts?"

"Yes...it was him or us...I tried to save the others...I tried to save Henry too..."

"How?"

"When we met at Sam's place, Henry had got us all together to tell us what he thought was happening. He had fallen out with Gen8tyx's founder, David Sonderheim. He brought us together to warn us in advance that the company was going to move to California...that Gen8tyx was going to be going through big changes...and that those who didn't move with the company would be kicked out ..."

"And nobody else knew anything about this beforehand?"

"We knew something was up, but we didn't know exactly what. Sonderheim had been recruiting new scientists into the company without consulting us. We all thought it was something to do with natural expansion, preparing for future growth. We were just about to issue a press release about our discoveries...just about to share our findings with the world. Then all of a sudden, two days before the big press conference, ...wham!...everything was cancelled. No explanation, nothing. Just that it wasn't going to happen. A week later Henry called the meeting at Sam's..."

"And what happened at the meeting?"

"Henry knew that we wouldn't move to California...he thought we were getting a rough deal...you've got to understand that we'd all been together practically from the beginning. Gen8tyx was as much our baby as it was Sonderheim's!"

"And so?"

"...And so we decided to form our own company in Florida...Fuck, if Sonderheim was going to steal our futures from us, we were going to steal the company back from him! We weren't about to take it lying down."

"So what happened...?"

"...So, we planned to steal that which was rightfully ours anyway, and to download all the files onto our own computers and servers, and to copy all the information, data, and results that we needed to start again from scratch!"

"Isn't that totally illegal? Sounds like industrial espionage to me..."

"Technically maybe it is, but we really felt that it was Sonderheim that was stealing the information from us. It was our research. We did the work. In the past few years Sonderheim had become nothing more than a figurehead...he was more of a politician than a scientist!"

"So what went wrong?"

"Nothing...well, not immediately. We all succeeded in getting the information we wanted, and storing it off-line, on our own home computers... Put it this way, we got what we needed. And we proved the process worked...The Phase One trials were a success!"

"And what were they?"

"We all took the Orlando Treatment...We became walking examples of what it could achieve. The results were almost immediate, and everyday it becomes more apparent ...better...more effective...Kerrin, it's incredible!"

"Then what went wrong? Why did everyone start dying?"

"Because Roberts sold us out. Shit...I knew that Roberts knew more than he was telling us...something else was going down that we didn't know about...I started to do my own research...Do you know that I owned 5% of the Gen8tyx shares? I still do. Well, Sonderheim tried to force me to sell them, and then it all started to make sense. Suddenly I knew what this was all about...and how much danger we were all in. Then Henry chickened out. He knew what was happening too. I knew he did! He came round to see me one evening. He told me he'd had a change of heart...we had a big argument...He said it was unethical what we were going to do, argued that it was wrong, truth of the matter was he was just shit scared... Like I was..."

"Why? What was happening? What was Roberts going to do?"

"Henry threatened to tell Sonderheim about what we had done, and what we were going to do...The fool...I told him that if he did that he'd put all our lives at risk...By that time we knew that Sonderheim was messing around with some pretty heavy people. And they weren't exactly likely to put up with us doing our own thing. If Sonderheim wanted to stop us, he'd have no choice but to kill us all! I told him...I bloody warned him...but he wouldn't listen!"

Alex was getting emotional. His face was becoming red, and his hands were gripping the beer bottle so tightly that the whites of his knuckles were showing.

"Who were these people Alex? And why would they kill you? Why?"

"Don't you see? They couldn't afford to let us live, knowing that we would make the whole Orlando Project public, knowing that we were all walking examples of what could be possible,... knowing that we knew enough to start our own company... Do you really think that a billion dollar company would simply make their best employees redundant...'Here, Mr Chief Scientist...here's a golden handshake...have a nice life...oh, and please...would you mind awfully if you don't use your expert knowledge and compete with us in the future?' Do you really believe that? For fuck's sake...They're not about to give you a golden handshake...they're going to give you the golden bullet...give each person a golden bullet in the head. Personally delivered with 'the Company's' gratitude! Kerrin, the days of redundancy are gone...in the future, if you're redundant, you're dead!"

It was a startling concept: the idea that a corporation would actually have key members of its own staff executed, rather than risking them going over to the competition or building a business to compete with their own!

Kerrin was silent. He sensed that Alex was just about to tell him something important. Alex was looking down at the table, his head bowed, his voice low, speaking almost in a whisper again.

"I had to do it. There was no choice..."

"What did you do Alex?"

"Henry was determined to tell Sonderheim, and I believed he would. The man had become a fool. He just couldn't see it! So,... I drove round to his house, to try and talk to him one more time, but as I got there I saw an ambulance leaving... I followed it to the hospital, but it wasn't till the next day that I found out that he'd tried to kill himself...Mrs Roberts was a mess... According to the hospital, Henry was in a coma...Fuck, things were getting way too intense..." Alex paused for a second, shook his head, then lifted his beer and took a long drink.

"I don't really know what happened...or why he tried to kill himself...but all I could think about was that if he came out of the coma, if he hadn't already told Sonderheim what was going on, then he would do just as soon as he could speak...I knew that I had to make sure that he didn't talk to anyone...What would you do? It was like a golden opportunity had been given to me!" He looked at Kerrin, almost pathetically, his eyes searching Kerrin's for approval.

"So what did you do Alex?"

"I went to the lab, got some TertraZyamide 236,...a commercial muscle relaxant we use routinely in lab experiments,...and I just walked into the hospital dressed in my lab gear...no one stopped me...it was too easy...Henry wouldn't even have felt it...he died in his sleep...and no one would ever suspect anything was wrong...Kerrin, it was him or us!"

"Are you telling me that you killed Henry Roberts? It was you?" Kerrin couldn't believe what he was hearing.

Alex looked him straight in the eyes.

"This is completely off the record...you'll never be able to prove anything...and I'm not coming back to the States. I'm staying here. Henry would have died anyway. I was just making sure. Making sure that he wouldn't get the rest of us killed!"

"Did you kill him, Alex?"

"Yes...Yes, I did."

Kerrin was stunned. Of course, it would be impossible for Kerrin to prove anything against Alex...even if he wanted to. And yet, from what he was saying, he could understand why he had done it. He even believed that Alex had genuinely acted in self-defense, in an attempt to save the lives of his friends.

"..Then Sam died..." Alex said, looking straight into Kerrin's eyes. "...then Mike ...and I realized that I'd been too late. Henry had already told Sonderheim before he died. After that, I knew I had to get out quickly, otherwise they'd kill me too. So I disappeared. But knowing that from now on that I'll have to live, day in and day out, with the guilt that I've taken another human life for no reason..."

He was silent for a while. Then he continued.

"...You know, I thought about it afterwards and figured out that maybe Henry had tried to kill himself because he realized too late that he'd put the death sentence out on the others and he couldn't live with the guilt...Or maybe Sonderheim had tried to kill him too. The first 'suicide'...In which case, Henry was a dead man anyway. If I hadn't killed him, Sonderheim would have finished him off later."

This all didn't bear thinking about. Kerrin looked away from Alex, gazing down the street, and staring at the moon without really seeing it.

A car drove down the road, heading out of town in the opposite direction from Cape Town. The noise brought Kerrin back, and he turned to face Alex again. That so many people had died to protect the secret of the work they had done at Gen8tyx...Whatever they had been working on had to be special. Very special indeed.

"Alex, I need you to tell me about the Orlando Project. What was it that you developed or discovered that was so valuable that Gen8tyx was willing to kill its employees to protect its secret getting out?"

"Perhaps if I tell you Kerrin, perhaps then you will understand me more. You won't judge me so harshly for what I did? Maybe then you'll understand that I didn't just kill Henry for ourselves, to save our own lives. I did it to save humanity!..." Alex drunk the rest of the beer, and pushed the empty bottle to the side of the table.

"Gen8tyx was a brilliant company to work for at the beginning. Fantastic. David Sonderheim was one of the most outstanding Geneticists in his field...and when he asked me to come and work for him, it was literally an offer I couldn't turn down. The rest of the team were brilliant too. Each one was handpicked by Sonderheim. The best of the best... And Sonderheim really enthused us all. Right from the start everyone knew that what we were doing could really make a difference...could save lives...could even maybe one day change the world..."

"...We started off looking at how genetics could help us find a cure for Alzheimer's and Parkinson's disease, but then when Sam Cohen joined us we started a new field, looking at stem-cell technologies. It was a really exciting time...we all gave up our social lives, started practically living in the labs. For four years we pushed back the boundaries of science. Soon we believed we knew how to cure Alzheimer's, and had found a way how to rid the world of Parkinson's, and then,...*then* came the chance discovery that changed everything!"

"You found a cure to Alzheimer's?" Kerrin interrupted Alex, incredulous of what he was hearing. His own father had been diagnosed with Alzheimer's, and although he had lived with it for five years, for the last two years of his life, his father hadn't known who he was or who his relatives were. The disease had killed his father long before his body had finally stopped functioning.

"Yes...but that's trivial in comparison to what we discovered next! Mike Gilbert was the one who noticed it. He's the one who should get the credit. It may even go down as the single most important discovery in the field of genetics and medicine ever. You see, one day, while looking at..."

A car drove down the middle of the street. It slowed down as it approached the veranda outside the hotel where Kerrin and Alex were sitting. Kerrin was too engrossed in listening to Alex to notice a figure leaning out of the back near-side passenger window. He was too mesmerized by Alex's revelation to hear the loud click of metal as the person in the car flicked the safety catch off the Ingram Sub-machine Pistol, and depressed the trigger.

Alex Swinton was lifted off his seat and thrown against the wall of the hotel, his head bursting open and his face disappearing in a cloud of red and grey.

His legs caught the underside of the table, flicking it up and into Kerrin, knocking him backwards onto the wooden floorboards of the veranda, a spray of bullets passing over his head as he fell. He lay on the ground, stunned and dazed, but as his brain picked up the sound of a car engine braking, he glanced at the road and saw the car swinging round and heading back up the road towards them.

Too slow to react or move for cover, he watched helplessly as the car came closer, a gun protruding from the other passenger window.

A full view of the car was obscured by one of the wooden beams which ran alongside the outside of the veranda, forming a fence bordering the restaurant, but peering between the bottom rung and the wooden floor Kerrin could make out the faces of two people in the car as it drove past. Both faces were looking out the window anxiously, checking to make sure their victims had been killed.

Kerrin didn't recognize the man in the front of the car behind the wheel. As he drove past his face was in the shade, and aside from his blonde hair, he couldn't distinguish any real detail. But the woman on the near side holding the gun was familiar. Very familiar indeed.

It was the lady who had flirted with him in Business Class the night before.

As the car drove toward the restaurant Laura breathed deeply, trying to control her racing heart.

The thought of the impending kill excited her. She felt strangely aroused.

As they drove through town for the first time, she had noticed Kerrin talking to Alex on the veranda of the restaurant. That Kerrin had already hooked up with Alex was something she hadn't reckoned with.

She had to think quickly...What had Swinton already told Graham? How long had they been together? Was it too late? Their mission was to find Swinton, interrogate him and then dispose of him, but they had to stop him talking to Graham at all costs. They couldn't waste a minute more.

"Turn round. We have to kill Swinton now!" she ordered Dirk.

"Are you mad? We could be seen!"

"We have no choice. Swinton is talking to Graham as we speak. We have to kill him before he tells him too much."

Dirk swung the car around on the open highway a few minutes past the last house in the main street, pulling over to the side of the dusty road facing in the direction of town. He got out and walked round to the trunk of the car, lifting up a false bottom and opening up a hidden compartment beneath the spare tire. They had transferred the weapons from the van to the car before leaving Cape Town, choosing to travel with the faster car rather than the larger van.

Dirk slipped a magazine into the Ingram, and took a bundle of extra ammunition clips out of a box in the secret compartment. He closed the trunk, and tossed the extra magazine to Laura.

"Have you used a Ingram before?" he asked almost patronizingly.

"Yes." She took it off him, examining the deadly weapon in her hands, before climbing back into the back seat of the car. "Let's go...but slow up as you get to the restaurant...We'll hit them on the way past, then turn and drive back to make sure he's dead."

Dirk put the manual into gear and drove off.

As the restaurant came up on their left side, Laura wound down the window and leant out, arms outstretched and ready to absorb the recoil from the rapid fire. Apart from Alex Swinton and Kerrin Graham, there was no one else on the veranda, and Swinton was on the side of the table nearest them as they approached. She took aim, flicked the safety catch off, and depressed the trigger.

A hail of death erupted from the muzzle of the gun, and despite trying to anticipate the recoil, the kickback from the weapon pushed her backwards onto the rear passenger seat.

Dirk turned and laughed at her.

"Quick, turn around...NOW!" Laura shouted, pulling herself up. "Did I get him?"

"Yes. Lifted him clean off his feet and spread him against the restaurant wall."

The car skidded, and spun around in the road, the squealing of the brakes echoing loudly off the sides of the buildings in the main street. Laura struggled back up into a sitting position, the muzzle of the gun protruding once more from the window. The car shifted forwards again and pulled up slowly beside the restaurant. Alex was dead, his head blown clean off and his torso lying quivering on the floor against the far wall. Laura turned her attention to Kerrin.

"Shit...You've shot Kerrin too! You were ordered to leave him alone!" Dirk shouted.

Laura looked quickly at the body of Kerrin on the floor, the dining table lying on top of his chest and his legs. It was a brief look, but in those few milliseconds their eyes met and Kerrin was looking directly back at her.

"No. No. He's okay...He's alive, I don't think I hit him...Quick, get us out of here. This place will be swarming in a few minutes..."

Without any further bidding, Dirk put his foot down hard on the accelerator, the wheels spinning for a second before they eventually found traction and propelled the car out of town. As soon as they were underway, Dirk pulled the cell phone out of his pocket, and dialed a number.

"Marieke? Mission complete. Call the chopper in... NOW...to the second agreed rendezvous point! We'll be there in ten minutes...TEN MINUTES...Do you understand?..."

Minutes later, they swung over onto a dirt track, and headed towards the ocean. When they got to the beach, Dirk and Laura jumped out just as a helicopter came in from the sea, and hovered just above the sand.

Laura and Dirk ran around the car, quickly emptying a couple of cans of gasoline over it. Grabbing their bags and the other weapons from the trunk, they ran to the waiting helicopter and jumped aboard.

"Okay...go!" Dirk ordered to the pilot sitting in the cockpit.

As the helicopter began to rise above the ground, Dirk broke open the first aid kit inside the cabin, and leaning forward out of the open helicopter door, he fired a distress flare at the abandoned car.

There was a rush of flame, and a flash of heat as a fireball burst from the car, dark smoke billowing into the sky above.

"Take me directly to the airport," Laura shouted above the din of the rotating blades. "There's still time to make the last flight to Jo'burg, and from there I'll take the first flight to Washington tomorrow morning."

Fifteen minutes later, they landed beside an obscure hanger on the outskirts of the airport. Grabbing her bag, Laura dashed across the tarmac and made her way into the main hall. Luckily, the gate for the last flight to Johannesburg was still open, and she managed to get herself a ticket with some time to spare.

She looked at her watch, and then finding a seat far enough from everyone else in the departure lounge so as not to be overheard, she dialed an international number on her cell phone. It would be about two o'clock at home. Hopefully she would be lucky and catch him at his desk.

The phone picked up on the second ring.

"Hello, Rodriguez!" the man answered.

"Agent Rodriguez. Hi! It's your favorite flirt Agent Samuels here. I need you to do a favor for me!"

"Anything for you darling...anything..."

"Good, but I need this done *NOW*, okay?"

"Okay, what do you want done?"

"Last night I flew down to Cape Town in South Africa. I took the overnight flight from Washington D.C. with South African Airways. I sat in Business Class, seat 2B. I want you to hack into the South African Airways reservation system, find the flight details, and the passenger list and erase my name. Make it like I was never there. Okay? "

"Okay..."

"Yes, but can you do it in the next half hour? I need to know..."

"Maybe...if you promise me a reward..."

"Stop fooling around Agent Rodriguez...Can you do it or not?"

"Yes Agent Samuels. I can. It won't be a problem. But what about border control? Did they make you fill in a visa form and leave it with immigration control?"

"Shit, yes, you're right..."

"No problem...leave that to me too...I'm good...Very good..."

"Then please get on with it...and maybe, just maybe...one day..."

CHAPTER 23
Day Fifteen
Langebaan Bay
South Africa

He watched the car speeding out of town but could do nothing but stare after them helplessly. Lifting the table with his arms, Kerrin rolled over onto his side and pulled himself up into a sitting position.

He turned to Alex.

His body lay crumpled against the wall of the restaurant. His head had been blown off, and the side of his torso had been cut open by the bullets, the white of his exposed ribs gleaming in the light of the restaurant lamps. A large pool of blood had formed on the floor of the veranda, which was already spilling over and disappearing down the cracks between the wooden floorboards. The wall of the restaurant was splattered with blood and flesh and grey material which Kerrin realized with horror was all that was left of Alex's brain.

A wave of nausea swept over Kerrin, and he retched violently, the contents of his stomach mixing with the blood on the floor and adding to the disgusting horror of the scene.

Dimly Kerrin realized that someone was screaming, and he turned as if in a dream to see the waitress standing in the doorway to the restaurant. She had dropped her tray on the floor, and was standing with her hands on her head, screaming for all she was worth. Almost as an added bizarre detail to the whole scene, Kerrin noticed that a stream of urine had started to make its way down the waitress's legs and was gathering in a pool at her feet.

Kerrin was in shock too. Things he would see in the future would trigger memories of the scene around him now, and in vivid detail he would instantly recall the entire scene and the horror of it all. A yellow flower would remind him of the vase which had fallen from the table, the bright yellow sunflowers which it used to hold now lying on the ground, the yellow petals dipped in the bright red of Alex's blood, the colors contrasting vividly with each other.

The smell of wood would trigger memories of him lying on the wooden floor of the veranda, his nose pressed to the floorboards, unavoidably sniffing the scent from the South African pine.

And loud firecrackers would forever startle him and trigger the sensation of him falling backwards, the smell of cordite in the air, conjuring up an overpowering sense of doom and tragedy.

The associations between colors, smell and sound that had been set up in the past few seconds would never leave Kerrin. It was a moment captured in horrific detail that would haunt him for the rest of his life.

Yet, through the horror of it all Kerrin realized one thing.

He was still alive.

The sound of the high velocity bullets passing so close to his head was deafening. Concussive waves of sound had assaulted his eardrums, and now they rang violently in the aftermath of the event.

Kerrin staggered to his feet, steadying himself against the wall between the gruesome sight on the ground and the screaming waitress. Wrapping his arms around her shoulders, he turned her gently and walked her back into the building and away from the murder scene.

People were running out of the bar, and when Kerrin recognized the manageress hurrying down the staircase, taking two steps at a time, he handed the screaming waitress into the arms of the barman and pulled the manageress into her office.

"Call the police...and an ambulance!"

He reached up to the side of his head. He felt something warm on his neck, and he realized that his ears were bleeding, the blood dark and dull.

Then the world spun around him, and the floor came up quickly to meet his unconscious falling body.

While two of the policemen took statements from the guests, now rounded up and confined to the bar, the inspector and his colleague tried to ask Kerrin questions in the manageress's office. As they spoke, the paramedics put the final touches to a bandage around Kerrin's head.

Outside on the veranda the police photographer had set up a tripod and was in the process of trying to take some photographs of the crime scene. He had already taken numerous photographs of the rubber tire marks the breaking and accelerating car had left behind on the tarmac of the street.

Suddenly a woman ran from the road and onto the veranda of the restaurant. Her face showed no emotion, her breath coming to her in short bursts. One of the policemen tried to prevent her from entering the crime scene, but she screamed at him, protesting that the dead man had been her boyfriend.

At first not knowing how to handle her, he let her slip past the cameraman to the limp body, lying against the wall. She knelt beside him in the blood, collapsing in tears on top of the shattered torso.

The policeman looked at the camera-man and winced. This was the part of the job he hated most.

Distracted, he didn't see the woman slip her hand quickly inside the dead man's pocket, and pull out a set of keys.

After a few seconds the policeman stepped forward and touched the woman gently on the shoulders. "Ma'am...it's best not to touch the body...we mustn't disturb the crime scene...we have to photograph it all first."

He held her tightly by the shoulders and lifted her back up, her knees now covered in dark red congealing blood. The woman turned to the policeman, as if about to say something, but then thought better of it and ran from the restaurant back down the street and into the night.

The phone rang in Cheng Wung's office, and when the Divisional Director of the CIA picked up the phone in his office in Tampa, Florida, he quickly agreed with his PA that he would take the long distance call from South Africa.

"Miss Weinbaum, it is good to hear from you again so soon. What news do you have?"

At the other end of the line, the woman paced the bedroom in her apartment, pulling back the curtains from the window and looking out into the street as she spoke.

"Mr Wung. I have bad news. My assigned contact has just been killed. Seemingly assassinated by an unknown third party."

The news was both good and bad. The good news was that Alex Swinton was now dead. The bad news was that it was not his agency that had fulfilled the brief. Another party had completed the assignment before him.

"Did you succeed in making contact prior to his death?"

"Yes...I did. As directed by yourself. I spent the last few days in close proximity with the target. I'm afraid I learned very little from him. He would not speak about the Orlando File and he never mentioned the hard-disk, no matter how hard I tried to coax him, without breaking my cover or making my questioning too obvious. However, I've just had the opportunity to go through his possessions with a fine-tooth comb and although he was not carrying any files or computer disks, I did find a locker key."

"And...?"

"I've only just found it, and haven't had a chance to identify it yet, but I would guess it comes from a left-luggage locker in the airport or the train station. I will get onto it straight away, and will report back to you as soon as we have something."

"Good. Is there anything else?" Cheng asked, irritated that the woman had let Swinton be killed before they had located the hard-disk from his computer. His sources had told him that when the fools in the FBI had raided Swinton's home and brought his computer in, it had been a whole day before they had noticed that someone had already removed the hard-disk. And now everyone was panicking that a copy of the Orlando File was still missing. It had to be recovered, at all costs.

"Yes. I have to report that Alex was meeting with someone this evening when he was killed by machine gun fire from a passing car. Does the name Kerrin Graham mean anything to you sir?"

"Unfortunately it does." Cheng was angry now. He had not been informed that Kerrin Graham had already entered South Africa. "Do you know how much Alex told him?"

"I'm afraid not sir. I have no way of knowing. I was not invited to be with them during their meeting this evening. I can only assume that the third party who killed Swinton was also trying to prevent the conversation taking place".

"Conjecture. Stick to the facts Agent Weinbaum. Where is the Graham man now?"

"The police are interrogating him as we speak."

"The police. No, that is not good. We don't want anyone asking questions they shouldn't be. We need to make the body and the incident go away." Cheng paused for a second.

"What would you like me to do sir?" the agent asked her superior.

"Locate the locker and retrieve the contents, and then contact me as soon as you have something…Oh, and Miss Weinbaum…?"

"Yes, sir?"

"…What is your first name please?"

"Angelique, sir. Agent Angelique Weinbaum."

"Angelique, you are doing a good job! Thank you for your help."

In her small, newly rented apartment in Langebaan South Africa, Angelique smiled. She liked to be appreciated.

Kerrin was getting tired. The police interrogation was beginning to annoy him. For the past five hours two officers had taken it in turn to ask him questions, questioning him over and over again about the most trivial things he said or mentioned.

Kerrin knew how to play the game. He had seen this same scene acted out in an interrogation room in Miami a thousand times before. He was only too aware of the pattern the investigation was taking, and the roles the two interrogators were playing: one of them was endeavoring to become Kerrin's friend and was trying to protect him from his colleague, who was bad tempered, demanding and probably quite violent.

"Just give us the answers to the questions we ask you!" The angry one shouted.

"Kerrin, we want to help you, but you have to help us first..." The friendly one implored.

'Well,' thought Kerrin. 'You can all just piss off.'

"So, Mr Swinton. You still say that you are a journalist from the Washington Post here to do a story on windsurfing in South Africa?"

"Yes... as I've told you before...I was down on the beach...heard a friendly American accent and got talking to the man who was killed. I was just interviewing him over dinner. How many times do I have to tell you?"

"So where are your notes?"

Kerrin pointed with his index finger to his head.

"In here. I'm good at what I do. I don't need notes."

"Mr Graham, I have no doubt you are good at what you are doing...all I'm trying to do is establish what it is that you really do? Why you are really here?"

A cell phone went off somewhere in the room, and the friendly-interrogator reached inside his trouser pocket and pulled out a small phone. He looked at the display, flicked it open, and spoke to the person at the other end.

"Excuse me please..." He said, as much to Kerrin as to his colleague, and he stepped out of the room. On the other side of the door there was the sound of raised voices, although Kerrin couldn't make out what was being said.

A second later the 'friendly' police officer came back in, whispering something briefly into the ear of the other officer, who swore loudly and stormed out of the room.

The friendly officer turned to Kerrin, all traces of amicability in his voice gone. Instead his tone was harsh and cold, his South African accent thicker than before.

"Mr Graham, or whoever you really are. You must have friends in high places. You are free to go. We are sorry to have taken up your time..." The man turned towards the door, but as he reached it he turned back and added.

"There is a flight to Washington tomorrow afternoon. Make sure you're on it."

Kerrin stood up, not exactly sure what had just happened. He walked out of the manageress's office and out into the street, just in time to see several police cars disappearing along the road back towards Cape Town.

He turned towards the spot where he had just been sitting with Alex only six hours before, and was shocked to see that already there were two people sitting drinking beer, at a table with a fresh table-cloth and a new blue vase full of bright red flowers. The two men stopped their conversation and looked up at him, almost questioningly. Kerrin stared back.

Alex's body had disappeared and the crime scene had been deliberately sanitized. The wall had been scrubbed clean of blood and torn flesh, and bleach on the floor had already begun to stain the woodwork white where the blood had been. All signs of the calamity that had occurred there only hours before had been systematically removed.

It was almost as if it had never happened.

CHAPTER 24
Day Seventeen
Washington D.C.

The return trip to Washington from South Africa was a long and boring one. The flight was busy, and all the seats were taken. Kerrin ended up sitting beside the 'nightmare passenger from hell'. Incredibly overweight, bulging out of his wide business class seat and into most of Kerrin's, the man sweated profusely throughout the flight and snored loudly. Even the video head-phones sitting on top of Kerrin's ear-plugs couldn't drown out the sound of the man beside him, snorting and almost choking in his sleep. He tried asking the stewardess if he could be moved to another seat, even one in economy class, but was told most apologetically that the plane was full.

After a few hours Kerrin resigned himself to the discomfort and did his best to focus on his own problems. He needed to think.

At first he had been overjoyed to be released by the South African police, but afterwards when he had attempted to catch a few hours sleep in the hotel room, it dawned on him that perhaps it was not the blessing he had first taken it for. In fact, it even occurred to him that it may have been safer to spend the night in jail. Now he had been released, he was once again at the mercy of the assassins who had killed Alex.

It was already obvious to Kerrin that the murder was never going to be investigated. There had been no further questioning of the hotel staff, and from the mute reactions of the hotel's employees the next day, it looked as if they had been warned not to talk to him.

He tried to recall in as vivid detail as possible the faces of the people he had seen in the assassin's car. The woman's face was indelibly etched on his memory, but the man behind the steering wheel had not been so visible. Kerrin knew that the first thing he had to do when he got back to the US was to try and find out from the airline who the lady in row 2B really was. He was confident he would be able to get the name from the passenger listing of the flight from Washington to Cape Town.

One last question troubled Kerrin concerning the whole affair.

Why had they not killed him?

Perhaps they had just missed him on the first attempt...but the car had driven past a second time, and the woman had seen his eyes...knew that he was still alive...and still she had not tried to shoot him again. Why?

They had already managed to kill his friend James Callaghan in the States, so why had they not tried to kill him?

So many questions. So few answers.

Alex Swinton was dead. Kerrin hadn't got all the answers that he would have liked, but he had made some progress. As he thought about it all, he realized that there was still one person alive who would still know what had happened, and why everyone had died.

One person.

Perhaps it was time to pay David Sonderheim a visit in California.

The plane landed ahead of schedule, and Kerrin was relieved to at last escape the body heat and stale sweat of the passenger beside him. He headed straight to the executive lounge where he showered and shaved, standing in the shower with the powerful jet of steaming water pounding his neck. Refreshed and once again alert, he made his way quickly through customs. Although he knew his wife would not be here to meet him this time, it did not lessen the disappointment as he watched others being met by loved ones.

By now it was only 7.30 a.m. He would still have to wait another thirty minutes before his boss, Paul, would arrive at his desk at the Washington Post. He had told his wife to tell Paul where she was, and he wanted to see her before he did anything else.

During the flight Kerrin had realized that he couldn't return to his own home. Not until this whole affair was over. People with the resources and power that they obviously had, would surely know by now who he was and where he lived. Worst of all, maybe they were waiting for him now?

Wandering around the shops at the airport, he stopped to pick up a newspaper and found a free seat inside Starbucks where he read the latest Washington Post and slowly savored a decent Colombian Café Late. As he turned to page three he swore loudly as he lost his concentration for a second and accidentally poured hot coffee over the edge of his hand. The spilt coffee didn't bother him. What bothered him was the large article spread across the whole page.

"Utility Company Chairman Admits Million Dollar Fraud". Underneath the headline was the name and photograph of the journalist: Ed Harper.

"Ed Harper? How come he gets the credit? That was my baby...I did most of the work on that!" Kerrin fumed. For a moment he forgot about everything else, and a combination of anger and jealousy swept over him. He glanced at his watch, simultaneously wiping the coffee of his hand with a napkin. It was almost 8 a.m. Paul should be there by now.

He let his boss's phone ring about twenty times before it was eventually picked up.

"Yes...Paul Cooper here!" His boss bellowed in his ear.

"Paul? What the hell's going on? Ed Harper's got my page three spread on the Utility Company Fraud!"

"Good article, huh? The boy's got talent!..."

"But that was my baby! My work! Where does it mention my name?...I'll tell you where...bloody NOWHERE!"

"Calm down Kerrin. The article was going stale. I found out that one of the firm's accountants was going to go public, and we'd lose the scoop...I didn't want your work to go to waste. And you haven't been in the office for over two weeks..."

"Okay...but I did ninety percent of the work, and practically wrote the whole bloody thing and my name isn't mentioned once!"

"Sorry about that. I'll have a word with Ed...but you've got to admit he finished it up well?"

Congratulating Ed Harper was the last thing on Kerrin's mind just now, although he had to agree that the boy had done an excellent job. Almost as good as Kerrin would have done.

"So, I gather you're back then...or did you get someone to deliver a copy of The Post to you in South Africa?" His boss tried to change the subject.

"Nope. I'm back. Listen Paul, we'll park this one for now, but I'm not going to forget it. We'll discuss it again later. But for now I've more important things to deal with. Have you heard from Dana?"

"Yes, she's..."

"No...Don't say anything! I think your phone could be bugged. I need to meet you. I can be in the centre in an hour. Paul, can you remember where I took that photograph a few years ago, and fooled you into believing I'd been in NASA?"

"...Yes. I'll never forgive you for that one buddy, I really..."

"Okay. Meet me there in one hour...and try to make sure you're not followed."

The entrance to the IMAX-Cinema in the Smithsonian National Air and Space Museum in the centre of Washington D.C. was already crowded with people queuing for the first performance of the latest 3D-IMAX film. When Kerrin had first become friends with his boss Paul and started to socialize with him outside of work, he had once pulled a childish prank on him. IMAX, the world's largest cinema screen complex, had been showing a rerun of the old film "The Dream is Alive" in 3D.

The film had been shot from the space shuttle orbiting the earth, and the sequences had been so real, that when Kerrin had secretly taken a camera into the cinema with him and taken photographs of the film being projected on the screen, he had later been able to show his friends the photographs and convince them that he had personally taken the snaps of the distant earth while he was a 'guest journalist' orbiting inside the space shuttle itself.

At first Paul hadn't believed it, but then not seeing any other possible way that Kerrin could have taken the photographs, he had eventually fallen for it and believed that Kerrin had somehow been aboard the shuttle.

Since then, Paul and Kerrin had played a constant series of childish pranks on each other, each one sillier than the last.

Kerrin spotted Paul first, and walking across from the entrance to the cinema, he grabbed him lightly by the arm and redirected him quickly onto the escalator and back into the sunshine on the street outside.

"What's with all the James Bond stuff, Kerrin?" Paul asked straight away.

"Just taking precautions. I'm in way over my head. Now I'm just trying to survive."

"You're hot property, mate. People...and I mean big people...important official people, if you get my drift...are looking for you. Did you know that we've had two visits from funny looking people in suits in the past two days? Asking questions about you...demanding copies of your files?"

"What? What did you tell them? Did you give them the files?"

"I had no choice pal. They flashed a couple of serious official looking passes at me, and gave me a copy of a court order."

"Who were they? Where did they come from?" Kerrin asked, sitting down on one of the benches in the park opposite the museum.

"The first visit was from the FBI. The second was the CIA. But you should have seen the faces on the guys from the CIA when I told them that the Feds had beaten them to it?"

"So, what did you tell them?"

"Just that you were out of the country...weren't expected back for a week or two...I told them that you were heading up a team of people investigating a seemingly suspicious group of suicides that had taken place in Orlando. They wanted to ask a lot more questions, but I told them they would have to speak to you directly. They asked how many other people were working on the story, and when it would be published. I guessed they had to be asking for a reason, so I took the liberty of embellishing the story a bit. I thought it might help you a little, if it sounded as if you were onto something really big! So I told them that it was going to be a big story, that three other people were working on it under your supervision. They wanted to know the names of the others, and I told them to fuck off. They didn't like that. Not a bit. But I did. I enjoyed that part a lot. Last thing they asked was when it would be published. I told them that as far as I was concerned, the sooner the better, but it was up to you to decide. I advised them to leave you alone, unless they wanted to become part of the story. They got a bit nervous at that, especially when I reminded them about how well our boys did in the Watergate scandal. They weren't too happy with that either. I thought the one in charge was going to threaten me for a minute, but he managed to control himself. In the end, he waved some sort of court order in my face, and cleared your desk ...took stuff from your drawers. Sorry, pal. I couldn't stop them."

"Thanks for that. You did good. Did they take my mail?"

"They would have...but you can thank the Wunderkind for that. She's been looking after it for you. She's hidden it all in her desk drawer. But she's beginning to complain, says that you got way too much...oh, and by the way she asked me to give you this..." Paul handed a large brown folder over to Kerrin. "Told me to tell you that you should call her to talk about it...I told her you might not want to talk to anybody in the office, so she gave me her home phone number. You can call her there this evening between eight and ten pm." He handed Kerrin a piece of paper with a number scrawled on it in blue ink.

"Now Mr Graham, would you mind telling me what this is all about? What happened in South Africa?"

"A lot. Listen Paul, you're not just my boss, you're a great friend of mine...you've got family...two teenage kids...just believe me when I tell you that, for the moment, the less you know the better. The guy I went to see in Cape Town had his head blown off right in front of me. I still can't figure out if I'm alive by accident or because they think they can't kill me. Maybe they think I know something I don't...shit that's it...they're scared the Washington Post might have a story...and that's why they're asking you questions about what I'm working on! They're fishing! They're trying to find out exactly what we know, and until they know just exactly how much we do, they have to let me live. They don't dare kill me, in case we already have enough to incriminate them...But it's only a matter of time before they realize we have nothing...Which means I probably only have a matter of days to find out what it is that they think I might already know!" Kerrin stood up, adrenaline shooting through his system.

"So what do you want me to do?" Paul asked.

"Just be vague...make them think that the paper is onto something. Make them think we've got more cards than we have, and in the meantime I'll put the rest of the pack together."

"No problem, pal...but where's this going to end? Shouldn't you report this to someone?"

"And who would you suggest? The Feds? The CIA? They're both looking for me already! Why? How? What for? I don't know! Five suicides...five murders and just because I investigate them I suddenly become public enemy number one. There's something funny going on here, and it must go right to the top...I don't know where it ends, but I've got no choice but to keep going."

Kerrin got up to go.

"Paul, can you tell me where Dana is then?"

"Yes..She told me to give you this address."

"Paul..."

"I know...don't even ask. I've already forgotten the address. I won't tell anyone, no matter who asks."

Paul got up beside Kerrin, and resting one hand on each shoulder, he looked him directly in the eyes.

"Kerrin, the Washington Post has a proud history behind it. You're not the first person to have his life threatened while working on a case. Sometimes...well sometimes, it takes a brave man to root out the truth against all the odds. I don't know exactly what you're onto, but I know you, and I know your work. You're a good man. And maybe one day you'll be one of the best, right up there with the likes of those who went before you on Watergate and the Iran-Contra deal. The Washington Post is behind you my boy. And we'll help you in any way we can...just say it and it's yours."

He held out his hand.

"Stay safe...and just in case...you might need this..."

He handed Kerrin a gold credit card.

"All you have to do is sign it. The paper pays the bill directly...just don't go overboard okay? Excuse the name, but I had to make up something."

Kerrin looked at the name on the front of the card.

Mark Twain.

Kerrin had just been given a new name.

CHAPTER 25
Day Seventeen
Newark
Delaware

It was a two hour drive across to Newark, Delaware. He laughed when he read the address on the paper Paul had given him. Dana had gone to stay with her friend, Sandy, who had landed a job in academia and now taught in the Physics Department at the University of Delaware. It was an in-joke between Kerrin and Dana. Kerrin had always found it funny that very few people had ever heard of the state of Delaware, and he was constantly amazed that people who lived even less than an hour away from the first state to be founded in 'the United States' did not even know where the place was. The fact that she had gone to hide there was a stroke of genius. The joke was that the average person wouldn't be able to find the whole state, let alone a single person in it!

Kerrin had been pleased to see that Dana had only given Paul the name of her friend, and where to find her.

Kerrin parked his car in a quiet parking lot just off Main Street, and walked down a flight of stairs leading from the road to a large long broad strip of grass, bordered by tall trees and impressive University buildings on either side. Professor Sandy Williams taught Condensed Matter Physics and had an office in Sharpe Lab, the large and beautiful looking laboratory with a Georgian facade in the middle of the beautiful tree-lined Mall.

He crossed the Mall, walking amongst the students who were eating their lunches, throwing Frisbee or simply lying with their backs against the trees, studying their books.

The entrance to Sharpe Lab was at the top of a flight of marble steps, on which the physics grad students were sprawled out drinking coffee and talking shop. As he made his way up the steps, he caught snippets of unintelligible conversations discussing 'quantum strings', 'Hamiltonian equations' and someone discussing the 'wave function Phi' in a loud, deep voice.

Physicists, Kerrin believed, were related to aliens. They lived on another planet all of their own.

He found Sandy's office on the first floor, having been directed to it by a lovely old lady in the main office, who Kerrin guessed was the departmental secretary and probably the only person in the whole building who truly lived on planet Earth.

He knocked once, and walked in.

"Professor Williams? I'm Kerrin, Dana's husband. We spoke on the phone about an hour ago?"

The lady behind the desk stood up quickly. Her face started to pale before Kerrin's eyes, and in less than a second she had turned almost white.

"Kerrin...? But...?...but...I...?"

"What? What's the matter?"

"You can't be Kerrin Graham! The real Kerrin Graham was here only ten minutes ago...and I gave him Dana's address already!"

"You did what?" Kerrin almost shouted, a feeling of sudden panic beginning to rise within him.

"...I told him where Dana is. He looked just like the description Dana gave me of him...Anyway, how do I know that you are Dana's husband?"

"You don't. We've never met before, except I know a lot about you. What about the time you gave Dana chickenpox at your fourth birthday party...that's where Dana got the spots on the side of her cheek from...from you!...and what about when she had the accident. You sent her irises, her favorite flowers. They lasted for over a week, and she loved them...and ...and you couldn't come to the wedding because you were on sabbatical in France..."

"Okay. Okay. I believe you..."

Sandy sat down hard in the wooden chair behind her desk, her hands covering her face.

" Oh no, what have I done?"

"Tell me. Exactly how long ago was the man here? What did he say to you?"

She looked quickly at the clock on the wall.

"He was here about twelve minutes ago...he said the same as you...that he was Dana's husband, that I was expecting him...He was wearing similar clothes...Dana told me what you liked to wear...he was the same size, same age..."

"They must have listened to a phone conversation between Dana and my boss...shit...they're after Dana. How far is your house from here?"

"It's about thirty minutes. I live on the outskirts of Wilmington."

"Does Dana have access to a phone? Your home phone? Did you give the phone number to the other man?..."

"No...no...Dana won't answer my home phone...and I only gave the man her address. I called her about ten minutes ago to tell her to expect you."

"You called her...how? You said she wouldn't answer your phone?"

"I gave her my cell phone, so she wouldn't have to exert herself too much..."

"Quick. Call her now! I need to speak to her!" said Kerrin, grabbing the phone on her desk and thrusting the receiver towards Dana's friend. She recoiled slightly away from him, but then took the phone gingerly and dialed the cell phone number, before handing it back to Kerrin.

The phone was ringing at the other end.

"Pick up, damn it...pick up!!" he whispered aloud.

Suddenly there was a voice at the other end. Thankfully it was hers.

"Hullo..."

"Dana! It's me! Listen, are you alone?"

"Yes...why...I thought you were coming..."

"Listen to me... I love you...Please don't argue with me now. Just do as I say. In about five minutes a man is coming to Sandy's house to come and get you...He's one of them...You must leave the house now. Immediately. Just go...Get out of there! Take the cell phone with you...Call me in ten minutes on my cell phone number to let me know you're safe. Let it ring three times and then hang up...I'm coming to meet you now. Drive to the train station in Wilmington and I'll meet you at the ticket booths...now GO!"

Kerrin hung up.

"Quick!" Kerrin almost shouted at Sandy, leaning over the table and grabbing her by the hand. "You're coming with me."

Together they raced along the corridor past rooms full of students just about to start their afternoon classes, and down the stairs at the end of the building, before pushing open one of the fire exits and emerging out onto the mall.

When they got to the car, they jumped in and Kerrin reversed out of the parking lot onto Main Street, and headed off past the State Theatre cinema and the Deer Park Tavern.

At the end of Main Street they turned left and within minutes they were on the road to Wilmington. Kerrin drove, beads of sweat appearing on his forehead and running down over his eyelashes into his eyes.

He drove as fast as he could, ignoring the speed limit and shooting across two lights just as they were turning to red. A car ahead of them pulled over sharply onto the side of the road, letting them career past at twice the speed limit, the driver of the other car shouting and waving wildly at them as they overtook.

Kerrin's world was turning upside down before him. Thoughts rushed through his head, fears and nightmares forming and disappearing, visions of Dana being dragged out screaming to a waiting car, and disappearing from his life.

He pulled his cell phone out of his pocket and put it on the dashboard, willing it to ring three times and to let him know that Dana was safe.

When after ten minutes the phone still hadn't rung, Kerrin picked up the cell phone and looked at it.

"Shit, the battery's dead!" He swore aloud, realizing he hadn't charged it since he got back from South Africa.

"How far is the train station from your house?" he asked Sandy loudly.

"About five minutes...it's not far...she should easily get there before us, if she made it out of the house before they arrived."

A chill ran down Kerrin's spine. If she hadn't managed to escape in time, Kerrin would be powerless to help her.

Dana put the cell phone into the pocket in her dress, and wheeled herself across to the window. She pulled back the curtain and looked out into the street. There was no one outside. Her keys...she needed her car keys. She spun her wheelchair around and wheeled herself through the living room to the kitchen, where she had left her jacket draped over the edge of a chair. She rifled quickly through the pockets of her short leather jacket, and pulled out her key fob.

She turned towards the door again, and wheeled herself back through the living room, but as she came to the other side of the room, she heard the sound of a car engine outside.

She reached across the radiator on the wall and cautiously pulled back the curtain a few inches. Outside, a large grey van was parking in the street. She hadn't seen the van before, and this was a small and closely knit neighborhood. If it didn't belong to a neighbor then it was most likely the man that Kerrin had warned her about.

"Shit..." she whispered under her breath. There was no time to make it out the front of the house to her car.

She spun the wheelchair around again, and propelled herself back into the kitchen. When she got to the backdoor of the house, she opened the door, and gripping the edge of the worktop running around the edge of the kitchen, she pulled herself quickly up on to her feet. Snatching her two crutches from where she had left them leaning against the kitchen door, she put them under her armpits and let them take her full weight.

Standing now, she unclipped several catches on the wheelchair, quickly collapsing and sliding it under the kitchen table.

There was a knock at the front door. Then another.

She froze.

Someone was trying the door-handle.

Without waiting any longer, she turned herself around, closed the kitchen door gently behind her, and maneuvered herself carefully down the five concrete steps from the kitchen door into the garden.

IAN C.P. IRVINE

She could hear the doorbell ringing, and the door being pushed rather hard against its hinges. Someone was calling her name through the letterbox.

By now she was outside. The grass was long and overgrown: what was once a lawn, but now more like wild field, led back about a hundred and fifty feet to some trees at the bottom of the garden. About half way down there was a red shed, dirty and falling apart. The grass reached up about two feet high, flowering weeds giving the effect of a wild summer meadow in the hills.

When Dana had first seen the garden she had considered it a mess. But now, she hoped it could be her friend and salvation. Using all her strength, she swung herself through the long, clinging grass, her crutches finding support on the hard stony ground underneath.

Within seconds she had made it to the garden hut, where she swung herself around to the far side and dived into the long, tall grass, lying as flat as possible. She pulled the metal crutches under her stomach, and gasping for breath, tried to rearrange the long grass so that it once again stood tall and proud above her prone body, hiding her from view.

Although from this side of the hut she couldn't see the house, she correctly interpreted the sound of a man jumping over the garden wall, having walked around the side of the building to the wall that separated the front garden from the back.

She held her breath, not moving an inch.

She could hear the man walking up the stairs to the kitchen, and trying the door. It opened, and she heard his footsteps go inside.

Then there were the sounds of a second person landing on the concrete, having followed the other one over the wall.

"Pete?" she heard the man call.

"Yeah?" answered the voice of the first man re-emerging from the house. "There's no one inside...she must have scarpered just in time."

"Too bad...listen, that was Control on the cell phone...they said they just intercepted a call between her and her husband. He was warning her that we were on our way. He told her to get out as soon as possible, and to meet him in Wilmington at the ticket booths at the train station. That was about five minutes ago. She'll be well on her way by now..."

"Yeah, so what do we do?"

Dana couldn't see anything, but the voice of the man called Pete sounded as if it came from a big man. She imagined him to be powerful, and deadly.

The other man sounded smaller, less powerful, but probably just as deadly.

"They said, if she's gone, to leave it. Not to follow up or pursue them in a public place. We'll have to pick her up at another time...C'mon. Let's get out of here."

Dana could hear them clambering over the wall, and in the distance she could make out the sound of the van engine starting and driving off. She

154

breathed out, took a sharp intake of breath and let her face fall onto the ground.

Only now did she begin to shake and to cry softly to herself, whimpering without sound, not trusting herself to stand up or make a move just in case they were conning her and were actually waiting for her to emerge from the undergrowth or wherever else she was hiding.

After five minutes she slowly pulled the cell phone out her pocket and dialed Kerrin's number. There was no answer. His phone was switched off.

Dana lay there in the grass, crying louder now, the tears streaming down her cheek and disappearing into the dirt under her face. She had never felt so alone. Unmoving, she lay hidden in the grass for Kerrin to come and rescue her, to take away the fear and make it all go away.

They drove up to the entrance to the train station, making no attempt to park properly. With the engine still running, and the key still in the ignition, Kerrin jumped out of the car.

"Stay here...Don't move..." Kerrin shouted through the open door at Sandy.

Kerrin raced into the arrivals hall at the station, turning his head from side to side as he ran, dodging the busy commuters milling around inside the station. Where were the ticket booths?

There...over in the far corner.

He bumped into a large black lady, knocking two large hat boxes from her hands. Apologizing profusely, he backed away from her towards the far corner of the hall, leaving her to pick up the boxes by herself.

Commuters were streaming from one of the arrival gates, just having arrived on a local train from Philadelphia. He fought his way through them, but arriving at the ticket booths, he found no trace of Dana. Two lines stood in front of the three service points in the wall. The third booth was closed, a large arrow on a white board on the counter pointing to the window beside it.

Kerrin turned around, scanning the busy hall. Dana was nowhere to be seen. There was a café in the middle of the station, and Kerrin ran over to it. He ran inside, but only found two couples and an old man reading a paper.

He checked at the ticket booths once again, then ran back outside.

A police officer was standing beside his car, arguing with Sandy and pointing at the sign on the wall, which made it clear that this was a no parking zone.

Ignoring the police officer, Kerrin jumped back into the driving seat and spun the car around, driving back out of the station.

"Five minutes from your house? It's taken us fifteen minutes to get here...she's not here! She must have been caught...or if she's putting up a struggle, they might still be at your house. We've got to get there fast!"

"Okay, but follow my instructions. We'll take a short cut...Take the first road right." Sandy replied.

Following her every instruction Kerrin made it to her house in four minutes. Jumping out the car as soon as it stopped moving, they raced up the stairs. Kerrin pushed on the front door. It was closed. He rang the doorbell, and while Sandy inserted her house key into the lock, Kerrin looked through the window from the front garden into the living room.

It was empty.

"Let me go first..." Kerrin said, gently pushing Sandy aside and easing his way ahead of her.

Inside the house Kerrin quickly made his way from room to room, opening the cupboard doors and checking inside. The ground floor was empty. He raced upstairs, taking the steps two at a time and pulling himself up with his hand on the banister. No luck upstairs either. The house was empty. Dana was gone.

"Kerrin...down here quickly!" Sandy shouted.

Kerrin found her in the kitchen, pulling Dana's wheelchair out from underneath the table.

"That's odd...why's it folded up?"

He looked up and noticing that the kitchen door was slightly ajar, he stepped past Sandy and emerged out into the garden. Apart from the long overgrown grass and rusty, falling down shed, it was empty. Dana was nowhere to be seen.

"Shit!!!" Kerrin swore aloud. "We're too late...they must have taken her!"

Kerrin sunk to his knees, throwing his head backwards and screaming at the sky.

"Sandy...I'll fucking kill them...I swear it...when I catch them...if they've harmed one hair on her head..."

Suddenly there was a voice in front of him.

"Kerrin?...KERRIN?"

He looked up and he saw Dana emerging on crutches from the long grass behind the shed.

Her hair was tussled and her dress was muddy and crumpled, but when Kerrin saw her he realized she had never looked more beautiful in all her life.

She was safe.

CHAPTER 26
Day Seventeen
Philadelphia

"Are you sure she'll be okay?" Dana asked Kerrin for the tenth time.

"Of course she will. They'll never go back to Sandy's house. They were looking for you, not for her. And besides, from what you told me about what they said on the cell phone to their superiors, they are not looking for any unnecessary publicity. I'm beginning to get a feel for how they work now...no, Sandy will be okay."

Of course, Kerrin was lying. There was no way that he could guarantee that Sandy would be safe in her own home. And he had no idea how 'they' operated. He didn't even know who 'they' were. But what could Kerrin do, apart from telling Sandy to leave town for a few days, which she'd reluctantly agreed to do.

Kerrin and Dana had gathered up Dana's things as fast as possible, then waited for Sandy to pack some clothes into a case, before driving her back to the University and dropping her off at her car. After a quick hug and a few tears from Dana, Kerrin and Dana had headed north.

They had driven for over an hour, almost randomly, talking and crying, connecting and catching up again. Kerrin told her everything that had happened in South Africa, and about the visits that had been paid to his office by the FBI and the CIA. He made Dana tell him again exactly what had happened to her that afternoon, getting her to repeat the exact words the intruders had said to each other and to the person who had given the orders to them on the phone.

"They said they had intercepted my call from Sandy's office to her cell phone? How the hell could they do that? Who are these people?"

"Kerrin, it's been an urban legend for years that the NSA could listen to every single phone conversation that takes place in the States. Maybe it's no legend..."

"No, it's true, but they tape millions of calls every day. To be able to identify and monitor our calls so quickly and to filter them out from all the rest, shit, that takes some doing! These people have got to be really well connected to be able to do it."

"Who do you think they are?"

"I don't know...if not the CIA, then maybe the FBI, or some other secret government organization...but from now on we have to lie low, and not call anyone we know...or if we do...we can't reveal anything to them about where we are..."

"What do we do now?"

Kerrin looked around him. They were driving through the suburb of Cherry Hill, New Jersey.

"We'll find a motel, and check in. I'm dead beat. I didn't sleep at all on the plane last night. I've been running on adrenaline for the past few hours, but now I'm calming down a bit, I'm exhausted. We need to get some food, and some rest."

"And then?"

"Tomorrow, we start getting smart. Until now, I've just been asking questions, but today they made it personal...so tomorrow, instead of them looking for us, we're going to go after them! And when I find the people responsible for Martin's death, I promise you, I'll kill the bastards."

Dana put her hand on his, and smiled sympathetically. She didn't know what else to do. She had never seen Kerrin so angry before. He wasn't a violent man. He wasn't a killer. She prayed it wouldn't come to that.

The Sunshine Villa's motel complex was quite new, the rooms clean, bright and smart. Each room had its own computer and internet connection, and although it was quite expensive, it was just what Kerrin was looking for. He pulled out his credit card, and signed the invoice using his new name, Mark Twain.

Dinner consisted of take-away pizza and a few beers. While Dana soaked in a hot bath, Kerrin started to look through the information Paul had brought to him from the Wunderkind. While he was scanning the contents of the file, he suddenly remembered the other information that James had given to him when he had last seen him alive in Miami. He reached into the bottom of the travel bag he had taken to South Africa with him and pulled out the transparent folder containing the details of the phone calls made to and from the Roberts' house on the night of his death. Inside the folder he found a small brown envelope.

He emptied it on the bed, picking up and studying the contents. David Sonderheim's face stared back at him from a color photocopy of his driving license. Kerrin walked through to the bathroom and sat down on the edge of the bath.

"Look...this is the man who knows all the answers. " He held out his hand, holding the photocopy of the driving license in front of her face. She studied it carefully, her eyes squinting as she focused on the man in the photograph with the red hair.

"David Sonderheim. Founder of the Gen8tyx Company. From what Alex told me before he was killed, he's the number one suspect behind all the murders. If we can find him, then we'll be one step closer to getting to the bottom of all this."

Dana slipped backwards underneath the water, wiping the soapy water out of her eyes and smoothing her wet hair out across the top of her head with the palms of her hands. Pulling herself up with her hands on the side of the bath, she emerged from the water again and looked up at Kerrin, cocking her head to one side.

"Leave Mr David Sonderheim until tomorrow." She reached out and pulled his hand gently towards her..."Get in!...That's an order. I think you need a wash..."

Sometimes Kerrin knew better than to argue with his wife. The Gen8tyx Company could wait until another day. Kerrin slid the driving licence back into the file on the bed, took off his clothes and on his way back to the bathroom he grabbed another two bottles of cold beer from the fridge.

"How come I always get the end with the taps?" he complained, as he slid into the water beside her.

"Shut up, Kerrin Graham. If you don't like your end, stop complaining and come here and give me a kiss."

New York
Day Seventeen
1 p.m. that afternoon.

Rupert Rohloff stared out at the Statue of Liberty from his executive office in the Rohloff Tower. He had just taken a call from Washington.

The view across the water was magnificent at this time of day. He stood beside the window, his hands clasped behind his back, his mind pondering the conversation he had just had with his superior. The board meeting of the Chymera Corporation was taking place in just over a week. From the latest reports he had reviewed only this morning, the Phase Two trials of the Orlando Treatment were yielding results. Remarkable results. He was confident they would have a lot to report, and that his boss would be pleased with their progress.

The intercom on his desk buzzed, and without moving from his position, Rupert simply said 'Speak', and the office speech recognition system switched on the loudspeaker.

"Rupert, Mr Small is here to see you. Shall I show him in?"

It was fortunate that Rupert had moved his meeting with Nigel Small up a week. Rupert had correctly anticipated that in light of the recent events, the board meeting would be brought forward. He prided himself on always being ahead of the game. In business, it was the only way to maintain the strategic advantage, and in business, holding the strategic advantage, whatever the cost, was the key to success.

Recent events in Iraq, the destruction of one of the world's largest oilfields, and the subsequent change of relations with Iran would significantly impact the Chymera strategy to the Middle East. Some hard decisions had to be made. Would Chymera endorse and permit OPEC's new pricing, or would they decide to move to the next phase of oil production in Antarctica? Of course, no one knew of Chymera's secret drilling operation in Antarctica. That they had been able to keep the operation secret from the world was in itself an indication of the power they now held, and the influence which they could yield across international politics and commerce.

But the most interesting item on the agenda would surely be the results of the Orlando Project Phase Two trials. Rupert knew that there were those on the board who were looking forward to Phase Three as much as he was. Indeed, he knew of at least two people who without Phase Three, would be forced to step down from the board, in light of the fact that their future would probably be very short indeed.

Rupert considered making Nigel Small wait a little longer, but glancing at the clock on the wall above his desk, he saw that it was already later than he would like. He had a lot to do today, but he wanted to make sure he gave as much time to the Gen8tyx affair as it required. He was actually looking forward to Small's report.

"Deborah, please send him in."

Nigel Small, contrary to the image his name may project, was a giant of a man. According to his file, he had played pro-football for three years, making himself millions of dollars in the process. He was as shrewd a man as he was large. When a broken leg had forced early retirement, he had invested his money wisely, and had built a powerful business. His achievements were not to be compared with those of Rupert's, but for any other man, they were admirable.

Rupert had always suspected that there was more to Nigel than there seemed. In recent years, his business empire had grown considerably, perhaps faster than would ordinarily have been expected from any normal, successful entrepreneur. Rupert's contacts had fed him some useful information on Nigel's interesting business strategy. If his contacts were right, Rupert would be best advised not to underestimate the man. He could be dangerous.

"Nigel, thank you for coming. Please sit, make yourself comfortable. Can I offer you tea, coffee, perhaps something stronger?"

Rupert was a gracious host. Even if the hospitality was an act, those who were invited to meet the man always commented on his manners. Few realized that behind the warm welcome, was a calculated effort to allow Rupert to exert his power over his guests, to put them off guard, and to dominate their presence.

Nigel Small was not a stupid man however. He recognized the cold calculating eyes behind the famous Rohloff smile, and although he played along, he never let himself be fooled or lulled into a false sense of security or cordiality. Every meeting between these two men was a game of poker. A game which Nigel was honest enough to admit he seldom won. One day, he promised himself, that would change.

"So...I am looking forward to hearing your report on the Phase Two trials. Very much. But before you do, please update me on the situation in Miami and Orlando. In particular, I would also like to understand why I was not informed of the incident in South Africa?"

Rupert's opening card immediately threw Nigel off balance. How had he known about Alex Swinton's execution so quickly? It had only been two days ago?

"I apologize. There was no intention of not informing you. I just wanted to update you face-to-face. And to give you the good news personally."

Nigel reached inside his attaché case and pulled out a small black electronic device, which he placed upon the table in front of Rupert.

"The missing hard disk. It was recovered from Alex Swinton in South Africa, as I promised it would be, hidden in a left-luggage locker at the airport."

"Has it been analyzed?"

"Of course. It contains the last remaining rogue copy of the Orlando File. The data has been downloaded, and I have left a copy with your secretary. With your permission, I will arrange for this to be returned to Sonderheim in Purlington Bay."

"Good...I knew I could rely upon you. However, I am still a little concerned about our friends at the Washington Post? I hear that Kerrin Graham has disappeared?"

Nigel went slightly red. It was not his fault that those who worked for him were incapable of completing their missions successfully. However, since he was in charge, it was he who took the blame.

"...It is true that at present we have not been able to locate him for over twenty four hours, but I am confident he will soon be found. We are also confident that he does not know as much as we had previously thought. Now we have recovered the last outstanding copy of the Orlando File, there is little chance he will find out much more about the Orlando Project."

"Are you confident, Nigel, or are you sure?" Rupert asked quietly. "There is a difference, after all..."

"At this stage we are only confident, but..."

"Then I expect you to take no action against him until you are 'sure'. The power of the press must not be underestimated. The Washington Post remains one of the biggest thorns in our side, and despite all attempts, our influence over them remains negligible."

"I understand. However, I believe that this matter will be resolved sooner rather than later."

"Make sure it is. You have seven days to do so. It will look very bad for you if you have not concluded the affair before the board meeting. Now, let's move on to other matters. Tell me how it is going in Purlington Bay!"

Purlington Bay
Day Eighteen

Trevor Simons felt wonderful. He was standing outside on his balcony overlooking the bay, admiring the view and breathing in the fresh salty air. He had just eaten breakfast and it had been delicious. For the first time in months he could taste the fantastic flavor of the fresh coriander leaves he always had served on top of his eggs. That he would regain the full function of his taste buds was not something he had expected, and the sensation had pleasured him almost as much as the spontaneous sex he had enjoyed with his attractive nurse the night before.

He felt strong and powerful. His legs and arms pulsed with energy, and the confines of the room, no matter how pleasant they were, had begun to irritate him. It had only been four days since he had woken from the long induced sleep, but the changes he was noticing in his body on a daily basis both amazed and scared him.

What if the changes were only temporary?

To be shown a vision of how his body used to be, to experience such vitality again, only for his body to fail once more? That would be something he couldn't cope with. Over the years he had forgotten what it was like, but now the memories had been refreshed, to know and feel the life force within him again so strongly, to be able to make love twice in one evening, and feel aroused once again the next morning...to hear the birds singing clearly, and to see with the eyesight of a twenty year old...

Having tasted the fruit of the vine once again, he would settle for nothing less. No, if this was not permanent, Trevor would kill himself while the memory was still fresh.

In the meantime he was going to savor every single second of this energy. Every moment of the day would be a treasure, and every ounce of life would be lived to the full.

The doctors had taken samples of his blood every eight hours since he had arrived in the clinic. Today he would meet them and be informed of the results.

He glanced at his watch. 10.30am. The meeting was less than an hour away.

He showered and shaved, taking great pleasure in removing the strong stubble from his chin with the edge of his razor. It had grown in fast and dark, with no signs of the usual grey. He was almost tempted to leave it and let it develop into a beard.

His eyes were bright and the red blood vessels were gone. He looked great. He felt great. He prayed that the doctors would tell him he was great.

When he had put on his favorite pale brown slacks, and a thin blue cotton shirt, he opened the door to his room and strolled down the corridor of the clinic. As he walked past the other closed, white doors, each with its own two digit number on the front, he wondered if the other patients were responding to their treatment as well as he was to his. He hoped they were.

At the end of the corridor he came face to face with a pressing new dilemma. Should he take the elevator or the stairs down to the level below? He flexed his legs, bending down and almost touching his toes. He lifted one leg off the floor, bending it at the knee.

He was fit enough to take the stairs.

At the bottom of the steps he turned right and continued along the next corridor, following the sound of voices.

It was a long corridor, and as he made his way down it, the end seemed to get further and further away. His heart began to pound in his chest, and he suddenly felt exhausted and light headed. He needed to sit down.

The voices were just ahead of him now. He turned another corner and entered a communal area where several groups of people were sitting around tables, or lounging on soft, red sofas, drinking water or juices, reading, talking or simply watching the others around them.

Trevor found a seat and sat down. He bowed his head slightly trying to catch his breath. His heart was beating fast, and his legs were tired. As he acknowledged the symptoms he felt the fear surge within him. Fear that the treatment had not worked after all, fear that his body was not as strong as he had hoped. Fear that he was still going to die.

He felt a warm hand on his own, and he looked up to see his beautiful nurse kneeling in front of him, and looking caringly into his eyes.

"Trevor, are you okay?" she asked. "Did I not tell you to wait for me? You shouldn't be walking around by yourself."

"I feel terrible...tired...so tired...I don't think the treatment has worked!"

The nurse smiled back.

"No, that's not necessarily true. You must understand that you've been lying in your bed for a week, and apart from last night, you've not exercised at all during that time. It goes without saying that you will have some muscle atrophy, and that you need to start to exercising again, slowly... Being tired just now is normal. Don't worry, it's honestly to be expected. But you'll still have to take things easy for a while." She said reassuringly.

"Wait here, I'll get a wheelchair, and then I'll take you into the doctors. They're waiting for you with your results."

The nurse stood up and walked away, and as she did Trevor felt the panic within him subside.

'...Being tired just now is normal. Don't worry...' She had said.

He looked around him. There were about twenty other people in the room with him. Some old, some young. He noticed one or two familiar faces. Public faces, people of power and influence. One in particular caught his attention. He was in the far corner playing table tennis and his face was disturbingly familiar.

Just then the nurse returned pushing a wheelchair.

"Trevor, taxi's here... jump in!" she smiled.

"Rebecca, do you know who that man is over there? The one facing us playing table tennis?"

"I'm not really allowed to disclose details of any of the clients. Confidentiality is key here."

"He looks like old Sam Novak, the Senator for Texas. Is it his son?"

"Sam Novak's son is not a client at this clinic. However, if you are able to recognize Sam Novak yourself, I am not disclosing any confidential information to you, am I?" she winked.

Trevor looked at her, then glanced quickly back at the man, then back at Rebecca.

"That's Sam Novak? It can't be. Sam Novak was forced to retire five years ago due to ill health, Parkinson's I think it was, and he was significantly older than that man is..."

"I'm sorry, Trevor. I couldn't possibly comment." She said turning his wheelchair and pushing it towards the doctor's office. "Anyway, once you're done with the doctor, if you wish I could bring you back to talk to him...maybe you would like to play a game of table tennis together. I hear that Sam likes a good game with the newcomers, but I must warn you, he's as quick witted and sarcastic as they come, and nowadays his memory is as sharp as a pin. If you ever crossed him in the past, he'll remember you for it, and he's certain to exact a cruel revenge from you over the table tennis table."

Trevor tried to turn around, straining to look at the table tennis player as Rebecca pushed him away. It seemed hard to believe that the old man was still alive, let alone playing table tennis, and with the agility and looks of someone almost twenty years younger than the eighty years of age he should be.

If the Orlando Treatment can do that for Sam Novak, it would only be a matter of time before Trevor Simons would be back out fishing for sharks on his deep sea fishing boat. Suddenly Trevor no longer felt tired.

Yep, he felt great again. Just great.

Washington D.C.
Day Eighteen
6.45 a.m. E.S.T.

Buz Trueman was a hard man. Ex-marine, ex-senator, and more recently ex-husband, his divorce had just come through, he had few friends, and he really didn't care. He lived for power. And he had a lot of that.

Built like a tank, heavy and tall, regulation army hair-cut with large biceps and a big-barreled chest, if he hadn't been a shrewd and intelligent businessman, he would have done well as boxer or a professional wrestler. The survivor of a street education in the Italian district of New York, he had first broken his nose in a fight at the tender age of seven. Buz had lost the fight, and he had never forgotten the shame he felt when he had limped home, blood pouring from between the fingers of his hand as he tried to stop the blood and hold his face together. His mother had hidden him from his father, a butcher who had arrived in New York from Italy just after the war, and when he had eventually asked his son about how it came to be broken, Buz had lied and said he had fallen over.

His father had laughed, and told them that the whole neighborhood knew that his son had been beaten up in a fight, and that he had cried and run away. Buz senior had called his son a wimp, and had laughed some more.

After that Buz had deliberately sought out fights, often starting them himself, determined to prove himself and make his father proud of him. He lost twelve straight fights in a row before one day he almost killed a boy two years older than himself. When his father had picked his son up from the police station, he was smiling. On the way home, he took his son to the cinema, and bought him some ice-cream. His father hadn't stopped smiling for days.

After that, Buz never lost a fight again.

As he grew older, Buz's business acumen came to the fore. After a rather unspectacular stint in the marines, he went back to New York and opened a stall selling electrical goods. Soon he had a proper shop, then a chain, which grew from one city to another. New York, Chicago, San Francisco, one by one his electrical business opened outlets in all the major cities across America.

As the years passed by and the money began to roll in, he swapped the street brawling for the corporate boardroom, although it was well known but never proven that occasionally he would resort to the tactics of his youth to sort out a wayward business rival.

With a personal fortune estimated well in excess of $13billion dollars, he had everything he needed, apart from everything which he didn't have. And he wanted that too. When Buz Trueman decided that he wanted something, no matter what it was, he got it.

Nowadays, there were few people on the American continent, or anywhere else for that matter, that would knowingly go up against him. Buz Trueman didn't take prisoners, and he seldom lost. He had built his empire through hard work, ruthless business practices, and more than anyone's normal fair share of luck.

But giving credit where credit is due, when Buz Trueman needed some luck and there wasn't any around, he went out and made his own. Or he would buy it.

To put it mildly, Buz Trueman was well-connected. Although officially he was not a politician, the number of Congressmen, Senators and even Presidents that were or had at one time or another been in his pay book, gave him more political clout than most of the Senators sitting in Washington.

His tentacles reached deep into the military, the FBI and CIA, and even controlled many of the upper echelons of the NSA. His information and security network was one of the most advanced in the U.S. and little of any importance slipped unnoticed past his network of spies, advisors and information gatherers.

Buz Trueman was indeed a well informed, powerful, and even dangerous man.

The ideal person to be in charge of Security Operations for the Chymera Corporation.

Buz closed the door and walked quickly towards his desk. He reached the red phone just before it stopped ringing.

"Buz, I'm glad I caught you in. I wanted to discuss something with you. Something that concerns me."

Buz had just arrived in his Washington office, and hadn't even had time to hang up his coat on the old-fashioned mahogany coat stand in the corner of his palatial penthouse suite. The sun was only just rising over his stunning panoramic view of the city, and already his boss was calling him about work.

"Kendrick, good to speak to you. How can I help?"

"Buz, rumors are circulating amongst some of the Vice-Presidents of the Corporation about the Washington Post. What's it all about?"

Buz cursed under his breath. It was the Orlando affair again.

"Don't worry. It was a problem, but I'm hopeful that it should soon be sorted. The fact is David Sonderheim, the head of Gen8tyx made a complete balls up of the transition of power from Gen8tyx to Chymera. He had six of the former Gen8tyx executives killed, and now a relative of one of the deceased, who is incidentally a reporter for the Washington Post, has got hold of the story. Since then Sonderheim has authorized a series of badly concocted attempts to silence the man. I've discussed it with Rupert already. He was supervising the affair from afar, but now he has handed it over to me. We want it resolved, and fast."

"Why don't you just kill him?"

"We have reason to fear that the Washington Post may already be in a position to publish something..."

"Shit! The Phase Three trials are about to start! Listen Buz, can you take care of it before the next board meeting? Next week?"

"That's our goal. It doesn't help that your guys have never been able to silence the Washington Post. They're a bloody pain in the neck. Sonderheim's latest attempt alerted the reporter, a Mr Kerrin Graham, and he's gone underground. As soon as we locate him, we'll bring him in and find out what he knows. We'll take it from there. No more messing around. I'm only sorry that Sonderheim was allowed to run wild with this one for so long. He's a bloody scientist, not a politician."

"Agreed. Do your best, that's all I'm asking. Hey, is your name not down for Phase Three?"

"Sure is. You too, as far as I know?"

"Exactly. Neither of us can afford for anything to go wrong. See to it."

The phone connection went dead, and Buz dropped the receiver onto its cradle from the other side of his desk. He walked across to his coat-stand and carefully hung up his jacket, smoothing a few creases out as he did so. He placed his hat on top of the stand and returned to his desk.

"Jane", he said into the intercom connecting him to his PA outside his office. "Cancel my appointments for this morning, and get me the Director of the FBI on the phone, ...and bring me a fresh pot of coffee."

CHAPTER 27
Day Eighteen
Sunshine Villas
Cherry Hill, New Jersey
11 a.m. E.S.T.

"I could kiss her!" Kerrin shouted loudly so that Dana could hear him from the bathroom.

"Who?"

"Fiona...you know...the Wunderkind! She's done it again...hurry up in there and come and see this."

There was the sound of a flushing toilet, and the bathroom door opened. Dana rolled over to Kerrin, hoisting herself from the wheelchair onto the bed beside him.

"Okay, amaze me then. What has she found?"

"Look, I asked her to look into the Gen8tyx Company and get me information on the directors, the company founders, its stock movement, and to speak to her friends in Wall Street...she knows everybody...and to try and find out what the buzz on the street about Gen8tyx was. Well, look at this!"

Kerrin held up the pile of documents, articles, newspaper cuttings and photographs that Paul had passed on to him from her.

"There's so much here it'll take a while to digest properly, but what do you make of this?"

Kerrin held up a document on the headed paper of the Slateman, Jones and Burney office from New York, one of the largest stockbrokers on the east coast of America. It was a report on the share dealings in Gen8tyx over the past six months. It included several charts graphically outlining the trading volumes in the stock, and the spot price of the shares at the end of each day's trading.

"Looks interesting, but what does it tell us?" Dana asked, holding the document in her hands and scanning through the pages.

"Turn to page four. Okay...that's a list of all the substantial purchases of Gen8tyx stock in the past six months. Look, you can see that five companies had been consistently buying the stock. REW, Purlington Venture Holdings, Small Holdings, Philadelphia Pharma, and Sabre Genetics Inc. Recognize anything? They've all been actively buying into Gen8tyx. Look, here on page four, you can see that about three months ago, the combination of those four companies owned stock which came to about seventy-two percent of the total shares of the company, the rest belonging to the staff and directors. Look, David Sonderheim had started off with thirty percent, but then he sold sixteen percent of his holdings to Small Holdings. According to this he made over sixty million dollars!"

"And he's still working? What for?"

"With these guys, I don't think the money counts. They're motivated to achieve something far beyond any monetary value. Let's see if Martin and his friends sold any of their stock. I got the impression that most of them did very well from stock sales over the past couple of months. Here, you look through these..."

Kerrin handed over a few pages of the document to Dana. They were looking now at a listing of all the major stock movements in the Gen8tyx Company by the directors and senior management. Details of numbers of shares bought and sold, by whom, to whom, and when.

"What about this? Mike Gilbert...$10 million dollars...and here Sam Cohen, sold stock for $7m."

"...And here, look, Henry Roberts made $22m for his share. ...Hang on, look at that...all the shares were sold and bought on the same day...two weeks before they started to die..."

"...But, not to the same company. Mike sold to REW, and Sam to Philadelphia Pharma..." Dana interjected.

"...And Henry Roberts to Purlington Venture Holdings. Strange that it all happened the same day though. Did Martin make any money, or sell any stock? See if you can find anything."

It was on the last of the pages that Kerrin had given Dana.

"I know Martin was rich anyway from share options in the last company he used to work for, but according to this, he just made another $15m from Gen8tyx! " Dana exclaimed aloud.

"When?"

"The same day as the others sold theirs."

"Strange, Elizabeth never mentioned it. I wonder if she even knows."

"Maybe Martin didn't tell her?"

"Maybe. Hang on a second...I want to add them up."

Kerrin started jotting down the amounts of shares that had been sold from each person and made a few calculations.

"Yes...that makes sense...the only person who didn't sell his shares was Alex Swinton. He told me he had five percent of the stock and that he refused to sell. I wonder what happens to them now? Would that have been a reason to kill him in itself, I wonder?"

They were both silent for a moment, looking through the rest of the papers. Suddenly Dana spoke.

"Kerrin, I think you'd better take a look at this..."

She handed him the last piece of paper she was looking at, pointing to the transactions in the middle of the page. It was one which gave the details of Martin's dealings.

"REW, Philadelphia Pharma, Small Holdings...they all sold the Gen8tyx stock they had purchased to another company on Thursday 8th!"

"And then the next day Sabre Genetics and Purlington Venture Holdings all did the same...all selling out to exactly the same company!" Dana pointed to the bottom of the page.

"...And look, the next day, even David Sonderheim sold out his remaining stock...and made another $50m...a better price per share than for the first tranche. That guy's loaded!" Kerrin exclaimed, reading the last line on the page.

"The question is who bought them? Some company called 'C.C.' ...What do the initials 'C.C.' stand for?...Okay, help me look through the rest of the stuff Fiona gave me. We want to find out anything we can about 'C.C.' " Kerrin said, handing over half the remaining bundle of documents lying on the pile beside him on the bed.

"That makes C.C. the majority owner of Gen8tyx, with ninety five percent of the stock." Kerrin said, while flicking through the other pages. "It makes sense now. Maybe that's what Henry Roberts knew...he would have to know that they were being swallowed up by this other company, 'C.C', and maybe that's why he changed his mind about going to California..."

"Or maybe Sonderheim changed it for him. Maybe the new company didn't need him after all?"

"Possibly...and then he called the meeting to tell the others, because he was so pissed off?"

"Could be. But why move the whole company to California?"

"Maybe the C.C. company, whoever it is, has its headquarters there?"

Another thought occurred to Kerrin.

"There's something else that makes sense too...the C.C. company and Sonderheim and Roberts must have been talking...a takeover just doesn't happen like that. One of the things that had puzzled me was why Sonderheim started to hire lots of new people...okay, Alex Swinton told me that he had guessed that it was because the move to California had long been anticipated, so Sonderheim was bringing in new staff and training them up before the move was announced. He knew the core team wouldn't go. What if Sonderheim didn't want the core team to go? Maybe he wanted them out of the company, right from the start!"

"And what if the new company, the C.C. company, had started to put its own people into Gen8tyx ahead of the acquisition...do you think that

Sonderheim and the C.C. guys were in cahoots, bringing in C.C. people ahead of the game?" Dana suggested excitedly. She was enjoying all this.

"It would make sense...I wonder if it's illegal though..."

"What?"

"All this talking, corporate discussions ahead of the actual deal, without the other shareholders knowing? You know, Martin and Alex and the rest?..."

"Maybe...but I'm beginning to get the impression that these guys don't really care about what's legal or not. If anything, they seem to be able to manipulate the law to their own advantage." Dana reached forward and touched Kerrin on the arm, suddenly quite serious. "Kerrin...this is scary stuff...maybe we're not meant to know all this?"

"I think it's too late to worry about that. These guys are already after us. We just have to get them first."

"How can we do that? I mean, realistically. I don't know if you've noticed or not, but there's only two of us...and these guys are everywhere. Look at the money that's being thrown around here! It's enough to buy a small country. How are we meant to win against people with that much wealth?"

"Have you ever heard the expression 'Information is power'. We need to find out everything we can about these guys, we need to find out what it was that Gen8tyx discovered that made them so valuable, and we need to establish just what 'C.C.' stands for, what they do and who they are..."

"...and then?"

Kerrin was silent for a moment.

"That's a good question, ...but if we get that far, then I'm sure we'll be able to think of something. One step at a time, okay?"

He leaned forward and kissed her, then wrapping his arms around her, he hugged her tight.

"Okay..." She whispered in reply over his shoulder, a small tear running down her cheek.

CHAPTER 28
Day Eighteen

Fiona sat at her desk in the Washington Post, her eyes rapidly trying to digest the latest information she had been able to dig up on the Gen8tyx Company. She looked at the phone. She was nervous. Her cousin in the State Department should have called her back by now. Hopefully she would have been able to find out something for her on who 'C.C.' were. It seemed that no one else in the world had ever heard of them. It was almost as if they didn't exist. Calling her cousin was a last ditch attempt at trying to find something out. She knew she couldn't hassle her too much, or it would place her cousin at risk. But Sheryl owed her one, and Fiona needed a favor.

She hadn't heard from Kerrin yet, but she knew, just knew that the first question he would ask when he eventually called her would be, 'Who are the "C.C" company that bought Gen8tyx? Can you find something out on them?' She could almost hear his voice in her head.

She munched on another chocolate chip cookie, and washed it down with some more Coke. For all the junk food she ate, it was amazing she wasn't fatter than she was. Still, at 78kg, she knew that she was far too overweight for her height of only five foot six inches. She would have to do something about it soon.

She looked at the clock on the wall again, and then took off her black glasses and polished the thick round lenses. She breathed on the lenses and held them up to the light, checking that she hadn't missed any dust. Placing them back on the bridge of her nose, she reached up to her hair and took off one of the hair bands that held her hair in two pigtails on either side of her head. She smoothed the hair together again and rewound the band around the hair, so that it was tighter and more secure.

The combination of the pigtails and the heavy black glasses made Fiona look a little odd, maybe even geeky, but what she lacked in beauty she more than made up for in natural exuberance and vitality.

Fiona bubbled with energy, was always full of jokes, and laughed louder than anyone else in the office. Most important of all, people liked her, and in the past two years she had been working at the office, she had become a key part of the office life. Without her, her department would just not be the same.

She had just begun to start thinking of going home and maybe going jogging for an hour, when the phone saved her and begun to ring. She picked it up.

"Fiona, hi it's Sheryl. I've got something for you…it's not much, but it's all there is. Ready?"

"Go for it…what have you got?"

" 'C.C.' stands for the Chymera Corporation. There are no files on it, nothing. No list of directors, no annual reports, nothing, nada…zip. But there are a few rumors about it. Best I can make out, the company is registered in Buenos Aires. The company funds some of the government officers down there, and basically, they can get away with murder…the whole company is shrouded in secrecy, operates as a law unto themselves…It doesn't post results, or record their interests. The government there doesn't challenge them. I bet they don't even pay any tax. I can't find out anything about what they do, or who runs it. Total information shut-down. It's very weird."

"Well, that's a lot more than we knew before."

"There is one thing though. I heard that about a year ago a reporter across at The Post was trying to run an article on the Chymera Corporation. Apparently he died before the article was finished…There was even some speculation that maybe his death wasn't a coincidence…"

"Who did you hear that from?"

"Sorry, Fiona. I can't say. I shouldn't even have told you what I did…" There was a pause at the other end of the line…"Anyway, does that help? I have to go now…"

"Yes, it does. What can I say, except that you're a star! I owe you one …see you at Thanksgiving. "

There was a pause at the other end of the line.

"Fiona, I think it would be better if you don't mention this to anyone. And you never heard this from me, okay?"

"No problems. I protect my sources too…"

Fiona stood up, and walked across to Katie O'Connel's office, head of Human Resources for the Washington Post. The Washington Post was a pretty informal place to work. Hectic, high-pressured, but informal. She loved working there. As she walked through the throng of people working late, she wondered so many people like her were willing to work so many long hours for such poor wages. What was it about the newspaper industry?

She smiled to herself knowingly.

Once bitten by the newspaper bug, few people could give it up.

"Katie?" Fiona stuck her head round the HR Manager's office door, knocking lightly as she did.

"Fiona isn't it? Sure come in...I'm just about to leave, but I've got a minute. How can I help?"

"You've been with the paper a few years now, haven't you?"

"Too many to mention. Why?"

"I'm just trying to research an article. Someone told me that there was a reporter at the paper last year who might have been working on something similar to my current project, but apparently he died before he finished the story. Can you think who that might be? Maybe his notes are still around, and they could help me. "

Katie sat back in her swivel chair, her hands in her lap.

"Wow...that's a good one...let me think. As far as I can remember, there were two deaths last year...no, three, counting old Willie...but that was after he retired...I would guess it would either be Rob Daines or Mat O'Brian. Can this wait until tomorrow or..."

"Probably more of the 'or'...it's important." Fiona replied, the corner's of her mouth turning up at the edges and her eyebrows lifting, pleadingly.

"Okay, give me ten minutes. Take a seat. I'll go get their files."

Fiona sat down and looked around the office, playing with the executive toy on Katie's desk. One day Fiona would have a room this big, with her own executive toys to play with, and her name on the door just like Katie.

Five minutes passed before Katie returned carrying two files and a big box.

She sat down at her desk, and opened up the files, looking through the contents and removing some HR documents and personal material.

"Here, you can have the rest, but please bring them back when you've finished, okay?"

"Thanks, Katie. "

She scooped up the box and the files and returned to her desk. She looked at the clock. It was 7 p.m. Three hours later she had just finished going through the last of the second file.

She had immediately been able to discount the first person. Rob Daines had died from cancer, an unfortunate but natural death, and he had only worked in the printing department of the newspaper. He was not a journalist.

Mat O'Brian, on the other hand, showed great potential. He had been a junior reporter on the paper, and had been with The Post for three years when he died in an unfortunate car accident in Spain. According to the file he had been trying to write an article on the founder of Trueman Enterprises, the Venture Capital Group and industrial empire founded by Buz Trueman, one of America's most secretive business leaders. No one had ever been able to interview him before, but on a reliable tip-off, Mat had followed Mr

Trueman down to Spain, where he was apparently meant to have been attending some conference or another.

The box contained the personal effects from Mat's desk, letters and folders of the stuff he had been working on when he had died. Being an only child, with both parents now dead and no recorded next of kin, the HR department hadn't known where to send his personal effects, so it looked like they had put them in storage until such time as someone claimed them. Which no one ever had.

She emptied it onto her desk and started sifting through the contents. Apart from a few photographs, and a naughty postcard sent from somewhere in Europe, the only interesting thing in the box was a large brown parcel. It had been delivered to the office but never opened. Fiona guessed that it had arrived after he had died and someone from HR or the mail room had just added it to the rest of his stuff in the box.

She ripped the parcel open. Inside was a used disposable instamatic camera and two rolls of undeveloped 35mm color film. The instructions on the outside of the camera were in Spanish, and looking at the stamps on the front of the parcel, Fiona saw that it had been posted from Spain. The post mark was from Madrid, January 8th. Fiona looked back at the file on Mat O'Brian. According to the official HR file, Mat had died on the 8th of January, in Madrid.

"Ouch…" Fiona said to herself, under her breath. A sixth sense told her that the instamatic camera and the undeveloped films were important. The rest of the parcel was empty. No note. Nothing. The address on the outside looked as if it had been written hurriedly, the handwriting almost illegible. He had probably posted it to himself just hours before his death.

She looked at her watch. It was late, but the photography department at the Washington Post worked round the clock.

Walking towards the elevator, her heart began to beat a little faster and a rush of excitement swept over her. Fiona was willing to bet her last month's pay that the camera and film held the key to why Mat had died.

Day Nineteen

It was almost 9.45 a.m., and Kerrin had been driving for over half an hour. Perhaps he was taking his new security precautions a little too far, but he wanted to be sure that no one would be able to trace him from any of the calls he made.

Most of the calls he had been making recently had been monitored. How they did it, he didn't know, but whatever precautions he had taken in the past were simply not enough.

It was time to get smart.

In future, if he needed to talk to someone, he would drive somewhere far away from the motel before making the call. That way, if they did manage to track any of his calls back to the pay phone he used, they wouldn't be able to find them staying within fifty miles of where he had made it from.

He arrived at JKF airport, parked in the short term parking-lot, and walked around the airport, trying to find a phone somewhere quiet. After ten minutes he settled on a pay-phone in one of the shopping areas, just outside a bookshop.

"Ralf? Hi, is that you? It's Kerrin here...sorry, I'm at the airport. It's a bit noisy."

"Hey Kerrin, wow, long time no speak? How are you man?" the enthusiastic young computer hacker replied. "Still working for The Post?"

"Sure thing. Listen, have you got a minute?"

Kerrin had first met Ralf Weisman while doing a story for The Post on computer hacking and network security two years before. Ralf was only nineteen at the time, but was perhaps one of the best computer wizards that Kerrin had ever met. Kerrin had tracked him down on the web via a chat-group for hackers, and although Kerrin discovered that the young university student was guilty of hacking into some very large commercial websites and wreaking havoc on their web pages, he admired his skills. Ralf saw himself as an 'urban knight, defending the people and the innocent citizens of the metropolis', and only ever hacked websites of large companies that were known environmental polluters. Kerrin sympathized with his views, and over the coming months had got to know Ralf quite well. He liked the guy, and he knew the feeling was mutual. Since then he had called him several times, and had paid to use his computer skills to 'obtain' the occasional snippet of information while researching articles for the Washington Post. Basically, Kerrin paid Ralf to hack into computer systems on his behalf and retrieve information. Slightly illegal, but very useful.

"Yeah, just studying for the college exams...nothing exciting...what can I do for you? Want another job done?"

"You could say that. For $100 could you hack into the data-systems at Washington airport, and try and get some flight details for me?"

"Would it not be simpler to just ask a travel agent?"

"It's not that sort of information."

"Sounds interesting. What do you want?"

Kerrin went on to explain about his flight to Cape Town, and how he wanted the details of the passenger in seat 2B.

"Listen, I've created an email account for myself." Kerrin read out the email address to him. "When you've got any information, can you mail me?"

"Sure thing."

176

Next, Kerrin wanted to call Fiona at the office. He was sure she would be expecting a call from him by now. He dialed Paul first of all. He picked up straight away.

"Paul, it's me. Listen, don't talk, can't explain just now. Our calls are definitely being monitored. Don't mention any names, but can you transfer me to the Wunderkind?"

"Sure thing. Hey pal, take care of yourself, okay!"

A short pause, the line went quiet a second, then Fiona picked up.

"Hey Kerrin, where are you? I've been waiting..."

"Sorry to interrupt you, but we can't talk on the office phone. Somebody could be listening. Do you know where I have lunch every day?"

"Yes...it's just..."

"Don't say it aloud. Can you please go there now...I'll call you in ten minutes on the phone inside the shop."

Kerrin hung up. Ten minutes later he called the telephone number of the pizza restaurant, where he was almost a local fixture at lunch times. He spoke to Luigi, the owner, and asked if he could see a woman fitting Fiona's description.

"She's just come in the door... hang on, I'll give the phone to her..."

"Kerrin? Is that you?"

"Yes. Sorry for all the secrecy, but I'm in a lot of shit and my phone calls are being taped."

"It's okay. I can guess why you're calling. It's about the 'C.C.' company isn't it?"

"Right first time."

"Kerrin, I need to meet you...I've got something you should see..."

Kerrin was silent for a moment. Obviously thinking.

"...Okay...Do you know where you celebrated your last birthday party?"

Fiona thought about it. Only two months ago she had reached the grand old age of twenty-eight, and a group of them had gone out to the theatre to celebrate.

"Yes."

"Right, I'll meet you there in four hours. Three o'clock on the dot. But make sure you're not followed."

The line went dead, and Fiona rushed back to the office. She needed to pick up a few things, and finish analyzing the photographs she had spent the past few hours scrutinizing.

Kerrin hung up and checked his watch. Eleven o'clock. He smiled to himself. It was time to throw his first spanner in the works.

He walked through the airport and made his way to the British Airways desk where he booked a seat in Business Class flying to London the next day.

He used his old company Amex card, knowing full well that the booking would be immediately traced.

He had no intention of flying to London tomorrow, but he wanted 'them' to think that he was. No, on the contrary, if everything went well, the next day Mark Twain would be flying to San Francisco from Washington. Hopefully, if Kerrin was lucky, he would throw their scent and be able to arrive in California unexpected.

On the way out the door, Kerrin picked up another payphone and called Ralf again.

"Hey, it's me. Call me impatient if you like, but have you got anything yet?" Kerrin asked.

"Yes, and no...I was just about to email you...I got into the flight details okay, and found your name and seat number no problem. It was definitely the right flight..."

"So, what's the problem?"

"It's interesting...I found seat 2B, but it was empty. Apparently it was never booked. According to the system no one flew on that seat to Cape Town that night. What did you say she said her first name was? Carol?"

"Yes, at least she called herself Carol."

"Well, I checked the whole flight for a Carol. The only one I found was a little girl called Carol Young. She's only twelve."

"No one else?"

"Nope. Officially, there was no one in Business Class called Carol, and that seat was unallocated and unoccupied. But..."

"But what?"

"I checked some other details. It seems that someone in seat 2B pre-booked a Vegetarian in-flight meal. And the after-flight budgetary cross-check says that it was eaten."

"So what are you saying, Ralf?" Kerrin asked.

"Just that, contrary to the official records I would say that your mystery lady did exist, but her details, well...most of them, were erased afterwards. Someone beat me to it!"

"Shit. These guys are good." Kerrin shook his head, mentally kicking himself for not having called Ralf immediately he had returned to the States.

"Ralf, thanks. I'll send you the money in the mail."

Four hours later Kerrin was sitting in his new hire car drinking a Columbian Café Latté. He had rented the dark blue Chevrolet the day before, courtesy of Mark Twain, and now he was parked about a hundred yards away from a small theatre on the outskirts of D.C., where Kerrin was patiently waiting for Fiona. Sipping the coffee slowly, he scanned everyone who went in and out of the entrance for a friendly face. He didn't have to wait long.

Fiona got off a passing bus, walked up to the theatre, looked around the street, and glanced at her watch. Kerrin flicked the ignition, and drove up to the theatre, leaning over to the passenger side and calling her name through the open window.

She bent over, and smiled at Kerrin.

"Hey stranger…"

"Quick…get in!", he said, pushing the door open towards her.

She jumped in and they drove, Kerrin keeping an eye on the rear view mirror for the first ten minutes until he was satisfied they weren't being followed.

"Don't worry Kerrin… I was careful. I even changed my bus three times. I've seen enough spy films to know when and how to lose a tail. I think we're okay."

"Better safe than sorry." He replied. "Are you hungry?"

A few minutes later they were seated at the back of a rather shabby pizza restaurant, cold beers in hand. The rest of the restaurant was empty, except for the chef who was sitting talking to the owner near the door, and smoking a cigarette. Kerrin was tempted to get up and point out to them that it was no longer legal to smoke in a public restaurant, but thought better of it. The chef didn't look like the type of man it would be wise to argue with, and Kerrin was trying to blend into the background, not end up in a fight and spend the night locked up behind bars.

"Okay, I think we can talk here. What is it that you have to show me?" Kerrin asked, after they had ordered.

"First things first…I knew you were going to want to know about the 'C.C.' company. So I did my best to find out what I could about them…" Fiona told Kerrin about her 'contact in the government' and what she learned from her about the Chymera Corporation, and then how she had come to look at Mat O'Brian's file, and about the undeveloped film which she had found in the parcel Mat had addressed to himself from Spain.

She reached into her bag, pulling out a large, thick, white envelope.

"I think you should take a look at these…" She said, passing them across to him. "I made several sets of copies. These are yours."

Kerrin opened up the envelope and slipped out three sets of developed photographs. It was immediately obvious that one set was taken from a cheap camera, the instamatic that Fiona had mentioned, but the others had been taken with an expensive camera using a powerful zoom lens.

The quality of the other two sets was very high. They were pictures of groups of people arriving at a hotel somewhere, the photographs being mainly of people getting out of cars and walking up the stairs to the hotel entrance. Close ups of people's heads and faces, and photographs of some people shaking hands as they greeted each other on the steps. Most of the people in the photographs were of people that Kerrin did not know, but there were three people in the photographs that Kerrin immediately recognized.

The first one he spotted was David Sonderheim. It was unmistakably him. Kerrin had studied Sonderheim's face on the driver's license until he could draw it blindfolded in his sleep.

One photograph was of him walking up the stairs, and another was a full portrait shot of his head just as he emerged from a car at the base of the flight of steps heading up to the hotel.

The second person was the Chairman of NCD, one of America's largest broadcasting companies.

He went through the photographs again slowly, this time managing to pick out some more familiar faces. Although he didn't know their names, he knew they were all important business men, heads of large conglomerates or national industries. Rich men, and powerful.

"What is it, some meeting of industry leaders? Do you know what hotel it was?" Kerrin asked.

"Yes, I do now, but Kerrin, don't you know who these people are? Bloody hell, the photographs read like a 'Who's Who' of Contemporary America! Look, do you know who that is...and him?" Fiona started pointing out the people in the photographs. She had obviously done her research. The names she reeled off included Senators, presidents of most of America's largest companies, and members of some of the richest and most powerful families in America. According to Fiona, the meeting had taken place at a large, luxury private hotel in the countryside on the outskirts of Madrid in Spain, eighteen months before. That so many of these people had gathered together under one roof without it headlining in every American tabloid was incredible. Which, it at last dawned on Kerrin, was precisely the reason the meeting was held abroad, ...so that it was out of the spotlight of the American press.

"And what about these photographs?" Kerrin asked almost rhetorically, as he picked up the cheaper set of photographs from the instamatic camera. This set included photographs taken at an airport, and some more taken in the town centre of Madrid, as well as others taken in a hotel room: snapshots capturing images of a person on a television set, being reported on the evening news channel.

The pictures all showed the same person.

Kendrick Hart, the President of the United States of America.

Kerrin sat back in his chair, looking up at Fiona.

"So what does this tell us? That Kendrick Hart was in Spain at the same time, and went to the same meeting?"

"Maybe. I checked it out...the President was on a tour of Europe last year, and was in Madrid in Spain last January when this meeting took place.

There are no photographs of the President at the meeting, but if he did attend, maybe Mat O'Brian wasn't able to spot him arriving or leaving the hotel."

"It's too much of a coincidence that all these people met together in a hotel in Spain at the same time that the President was there."

"Why did they meet in Spain at all, and not in the States?"

"...Because they were trying to keep the whole thing secret. Can you imagine what the press would have made of it, if they had found out...no, it makes sense...but the fact that it was a secret meeting in a foreign country far from US soil, sort of points to it being a clandestine meeting, doesn't it."

"I think so. By the way, this photograph here is Buz Trueman. The person Mat was following to Spain. The thing that puzzles me though is that my 'contact' in the government tipped me off about Mat by mentioning that someone had died at The Post while doing a story about a company called the Chymera Corporation...There was no mention of Buz...It was only his internal file that said he was abroad researching Buz Trueman. According to his notes, he had followed him to Spain to try and get an interview with him."

"And he ends up getting these photographs. Shit, are you suggesting that..."

Fiona lifted her finger to her mouth, urging Kerrin to speak quieter. His voice had been getting progressively louder.

"...Yes...Mat went to Spain following Buz Trueman hoping to get an interview with him, and ends up coming across a meeting of the most powerful industrial leaders in America..."

"...Which according to the connection made by your friend in the government tells us that these photographs are probably a record of people attending a meeting of the Chymera Corporation?" Kerrin added excitedly.

"...Of which Buz Trueman and the President of America are both members!" Fiona hypothesized.

Kerrin whistled.

"And what did you say happened to Mat?" Kerrin asked.

"He died in a car accident on his way back to the airport, the same day he posted these photographs back to himself at the paper."

"Do you believe that, or are you thinking what I'm thinking?" Kerrin looked at Fiona.

"No. I think we're pretty much on the same wavelength...Mat O'Brian took photographs of a secret meeting of the Chymera Corporation and was killed for doing so."

They both sat silently, lost in their own thoughts.

Just then, the pizza arrived.

They finished the food quickly, excitedly discussing their revelations between mouthfuls and planning what they should do next.

"Fiona, I need your help, but you have to be aware that what we're doing is obviously upsetting some very powerful people. Mat O'Brian probably got killed for what he found out, and now we're treading in his footsteps...how do you feel about that?"

"Excited, and scared, both at the same time. But this is the newspaper business, and I guess it goes with the territory." Fiona smiled back, her cheeks twitching nervously.

"Can you do something else for me then? I have a list of five companies... R.E.W, Purlington Venture Holdings, Small Holdings, Philadelphia Pharma, and Sabre Genetics Inc. Can you do some research on them? Get me any details on the owners. Photographs of the directors even. I would like to see if any of their faces appear here," he said, stabbing at the pile of photos with his forefinger.

"Do you think there is a link from these companies to Chymera?"

"It's just a hunch. Obviously there was a link from Chymera to Gen8tyx quite a long time ago, hence the photograph of David Sonderheim turning up at the conference in Spain. So I wouldn't be surprised if these companies all had something to do with the Chymera Corporation too."

"Sure thing. I'll get right on to it."

When Kerrin left the restaurant, he gave Fiona a big hug. It didn't really seem appropriate to just shake her hand. Before today there had been little connecting the two of them, just a small friendship and mutual sharing of respect from the office. But now that they were both pursuing the truth behind Gen8tyx and the Chymera Corporation, their lives were dependent upon each other for survival and an unspoken bond had been forged between them.

Fortunately, it was unlikely that those chasing Kerrin would have realized that he had recruited a helpful ally, and for as long as that was the case, they had to take full advantage of her freedom to act and move undetected.

Before they parted they had agreed that in future if Kerrin needed to speak to her, he would call her at her desk, ask her about 'the weather', and she would take it as a sign to cross the street to the pizza parlor where he would call her ten minutes later. If they needed to meet, they had agreed to meet at the entrance to the Church of Saint John, a church they both knew in Washington D.C..

Driving back to the motel on the outskirts of Philadelphia, Kerrin's mind started to wander its way through the information Fiona had brought him. There was so much to take in. Thankfully, before they had left the restaurant Fiona had mentioned that where possible she had made notes on the backs of the photographs, giving the names of the people shown, who they were and which companies they represented.

About five minutes away from his motel, another piece of the puzzle suddenly fell into place in Kerrin's mind. During the months leading up to the purchase of Gen8tyx by the other companies, Sonderheim had started to recruit other geneticists into his company. It had troubled Kerrin that Sonderheim would suddenly be able to recruit other top scientists without advertising the positions. The other scientists in Gen8tyx had not been aware of the positions being vacant or that the head count had been increased. The answer had not been obvious to Kerrin.

Two of the companies purchasing stakes in Gen8tyx were genetics companies! Philadelphia Pharma, and Sabre Genetics Inc.. Which putting two and two together, meant that Sonderheim had probably allowed staff from Philadelphia Pharma, and Sabre Genetics Inc to infiltrate his workforce, and slowly replace them during the preparations for the takeover.

It was becoming obvious that the takeover of Gen8tyx had been planned long in advance.

CHAPTER 29
Day Nineteen
Fort Dixon
NSA American Surveillance Centre

Deep in the National Security Agency bunker in Alabama, the job of processing all the telecommunications in America was handled by six hundred government agents. To an outsider the agent's work would perhaps seem like a dull job, sitting in a man-made concrete cavern four levels beneath the ground, glued to a computer screen with a pair of headphones strapped to their ears for every moment of their three, two hour shifts. The routine was strict. Two hours on, thirty minute break, then two hours back on. Lunch for one hour. Then two hours back on before handing over to the next shift.

The communications analysis was divided into three groups: phone conversations, emails and faxes. Each group was further subdivided by language, and handled by agents fluent in that tongue.

Every email, phone-conversation or fax in the United States of America passed through this system, each call being monitored and analyzed by the billion-dollar Multi-Neural Digital Array Processing grid, a massive array of parallel optical processing computers linked into each other in such a way that the processing power of the combined grid was one million times the power of the individual computers that made it up.

The latest in neural network technology had been employed to build the array, and the servers which made up the grid took up the entire fifth and sixth floors of the underground complex. The area the computers occupied was so large that technicians maintaining them ran around the twenty-five acre complex on little underground cars. On the ground above the bunker, an array of satellite dishes received signals fed to it from the various collection centers on the east coast, and fed them into the computer grid below.

'George', the unofficial name given to the 2nd Generation 'Echelon' network by the NSA agents who worked on it, had been operational for two years now, and provided the greatest computational resource known to mankind.

Its purpose?

To defend the citizens of the United States of America by listening to every single word they said. They had nicknamed the system after George Orwell, the author of '1984' and the man who inspired the phrase 'Big Brother is Watching You'.

Sector Nine Alpha of the fourth level was no different from Sector Ten Beta or Eleven Gamma, or any other sector within the base. They were all as boring as each other. The artificial lighting and the constant hum of the computer systems and the ventilation units were present wherever you sat.

It was in Sector Nine Alpha that Agent Johnson had been given the task of monitoring Washington for any conversation that Kerrin Graham may take part in. The system itself was impressive. Every phone conversation in America passed through George, who never slept and never stopped listening. Each sentence that passed through its digital ears was broken down, analyzed and scanned for individual key words. If any person in the United States held a phone conversation in which he or she mentioned three or more of these key words, the conversation was automatically recorded and then stored in a massive data bank.

Once recorded, these phone conversations were available to be retrieved and analyzed in greater detail at any time in the future. In fact, once it had been recorded, a phone conversation could be dissected and analyzed in any way that was required. New sets of keywords could be defined, and George would happily scan all the recorded conversations for any new combination of keywords, highlighting any conversation which contained them.

The system was simple. All Agent Johnson had to do was to decide what key words he wanted to listen for, and the friendly computer would do the rest.

Then, at different times of the day Agent Johnson would log-on and ask George for the progress so far, and he would listen to the conversations that had been recorded that day which involved his key words.

It was also possible to program his friend to alert him by SMS, email or pager whenever something really interesting took place.

It took a certain type of person to work in the NSA centre in Fort Dixon, and Agent Johnson was definitely that type of person. He loved his job.

Of course, Kerrin was not the only person Agent Johnson was tracking. He had well over a hundred other names on his identified target tracking list, but that morning Kerrin Graham had just jumped to the top ahead of the others. Kerrin Graham, whoever he was, had just been given a Code Green status. This meant that the NSA had to do everything they could to find him in the next twenty-four hours. He was seemingly an immediate threat to national security.

Agent Johnson was pleased to get results so soon. Within two hours of receiving the new directive, Kerrin Graham had been tracked making several phone conversations from JFK airport. Since the calls had been made at the airport, Agent Johnson had contacted a colleague in another department which monitored flight reservations, and he had not been surprised to find out that using his corporate Amex credit card, Mr Kerrin Graham had just booked a flight, which left the next day to London - England. Johnson had immediately passed on the details to his superior, who was undoubtedly happy with the speed by which first contact had been made.

By five o'clock the next day thirty agents had been deployed at the airport, discreetly monitoring the British Airways check-in desk and the various entrances to the airport. Thanks to Agent Johnson's fast work, they would be able to arrest Kerrin Graham the moment he arrived at the airport for his international flight.

Unfortunately it did little for Agent Johnson's promotion prospects when about the same time that evening Kerrin walked into Ronald Reagan National Airport outside Washington D.C., picked up the ticket he had booked over the internet and boarded his flight to San Francisco.

"Have a nice flight, Mr Twain!" the air stewardess wished him as she handed him his ticket.

"Thank you. I will," he replied with a smile.

Carmel
Day Twenty

The lightning flashed outside, lighting up the surrounding hills through the warm torrential rain and illuminating the massive waves crashing onto the beach below. Seconds later, a deafening thunderclap rolled across the valley, the wall of sound ricocheting from the cliffs onto the glass windows of the prison cell. Dana sat in her wheelchair, her hands tied by thick orange cord to the armrests, a piece of silver duct-tape stretched tightly across her mouth.

As Kerrin entered the room, she looked up and blinked, her eyes screaming a warning at him. Too late, a heavy hand fell on him from behind, crashing into his neck and driving him to the ground. He fell awkwardly, sprawling on the floor, his hand losing its grip on his gun which hit the ground with a metallic clunk before skidding across the ceramic floor tiles to the other side of the room, impossibly beyond his reach.

His senses stunned, and little flashes of light sparking around his peripheral vision, he struggled to lift himself up and turn towards the direction of the next blow. Just then another lightning bolt lit the sky and for the briefest moment in time he found himself looking up at the figure of David Sonderheim towering above him, his outstretched hand pointing a gun straight at Kerrin's chest.

Kerrin reacted instinctively, kicking out at the legs of the figure and sweeping his legs from under him with a swift sideways blow to his shins.

As Sonderheim went down, a single gunshot lit up the room, the loudness of the shot reverberating around the walls of the cell and mixing with the next peal of thunder which boomed across the valley.

Kerrin jumped to his feet, swinging a second blow from his foot at Sonderheim's head. He felt the impact through the leather in his shoes, the heavy blow being absorbed completely as Kerrin's foot smashed hard into the man's temple, killing Sonderheim instantly.

With no further thought for his victim Kerrin turned to Dana, lunging towards her wheelchair in an effort to free her and escape from the cell as soon as possible.

Another flash of lightning lit up the interior of the room. In disbelief at what he saw, Kerrin collapsed at Dana's feet, a long, low, guttural scream making its way from the pit of his stomach, up through his torso and out of his wide open mouth.

Dana's head lolled to one side, her eyes staring blankly at Kerrin's face. A large patch of red was spreading rapidly across the chest of her white blouse, the blood flowing fast and free from the large bullet wound where Sonderheim's bullet had found a target.

The lightning flashed again, and Kerrin screamed aloud. He jumped up from his bed, his eyes staring wide open, his brain racing, the dream still running in his mind's eye while he struggled to full consciousness and tried to work out where he was. For a few seconds confusion reigned, and his heart pounded furiously as the fear and adrenaline coursed throughout his body. The sweat ran off his forehead, and the sheets of his bed were cold and wet, drenched by the fever that had burned within him, ignited by the horror of the dream.

Staring around him, fighting furiously to find familiarity in his surroundings, slowly his mind began to clear. Another peal of thunder shook the air about him, and outside the hotel the storm raged unrelentingly. The rain crashed in sheets against the large windows overlooking the beach, and the air was heavy with static electricity from the storm. Jet lagged and confused, Kerrin slowly began to surface from the nightmare.

Awake now, he relaxed back on to the bed in his hotel room just outside Carmel, shaking and cold, but grateful.

Grateful that it had only been a dream. Grateful that Dana was still alive. Grateful that soon he would meet the man that had turned his life into a living hell. Grateful that his dream had shown him clearly that he had to kill Sonderheim before Sonderheim killed them.

Purlington Bay
Day Twenty

"Please come in gentlemen" David Sonderheim shouted loudly in reply to the knock at his door.

It was 3 p.m. and he was expecting both Trevor Simons and Colonel Packard for a meeting to discuss their progress so far.

Trevor opened the door and stepped inside, his stature once again strong and powerful, his commanding presence once more capable of demanding instant attention the moment he entered any room. The weak and frail man that had entered the clinic over two weeks ago was gone. In his place, a new Trevor Simons was emerging from the chrysalis of the old.

Trevor turned around, holding the door open for Colonel Packard. He walked slowly, the Zimmer frame in front of him supporting much of his weight, and the sweat rolling off his forehead as he laboriously moved his legs forward one at a time, placing each foot carefully, but solidly, one in front of the other.

Sonderheim stood up from his desk and walked around towards Trevor and Colonel Packard. He placed a hand on Trevor's shoulder and smiled at him, a gesture of familiarity and cordiality that both shocked and pleased Trevor. Simons had detested Sonderheim when he had first entered the clinic, but over the past few weeks he had realized that Sonderheim was not the man he had first taken him to be. And there was no doubt that he was one of the people to whom Trevor owed his life.

Sonderheim held out his hand to the Colonel and he took it in his own, clasping it firmly.

"Gentlemen, please sit." Sonderheim waved at the chairs around the conference table set beside the large curved windows overlooking the bay beneath. "There is much to discuss."

Sonderheim knew better than to offer to help Colonel Packard with his Zimmer frame, so he waited patiently as the Colonel walked carefully to one of the chairs at the table, and sat down slowly, moving his walking frame to the back of his chair and out of his way.

Simons took a seat on the opposite side of the table from Sonderheim, alongside the Colonel.

"I have invited you here today to congratulate you in person on your outstanding progress. I have read the full reports from your doctors, and I am both pleased and impressed by the pace of your recovery so far."

The two men in front of him sat silently, listening to his every word.

"Trevor, as your doctors have told you, your blood cell count is returning to normal, and the leukemia is in full remission. Colonel, the stem cells that you were injected with have grafted and developed well, repairing the nerve cell damage to your spine, and although the process is not yet one hundred percent complete, we expect that at this rate of progress your spine will be fully functional within a week."

Sonderheim watched the men for their reactions. He was pleased to see that in spite of their best attempts at stoicism, emotion was clearly bubbling away behind their eyes. It did not surprise him when the Colonel smiled, and then quickly wiped a tear from the corner of his eye. Sonderheim could only imagine the happiness and exhilaration these men must be feeling.

"I am happy for the both of you. I imagine it will take a while for the full impact of the success of the treatment to dawn on you both. However, I can assure you that our tests indicate that this is not a temporary respite you are experiencing. This is a genuine resolution to your problems. However, although you were both admitted to the Phase Two trials in order to demonstrate the possible effectiveness of the Gen8tyx Treatment on your particular medical conditions, the extent of the treatment will reach further than anything you can imagine..."

"...I can't overemphasize enough the importance of completing your log books every day. We need you to record the progress of your bodies as the Orlando Treatment works within you. You must record everything,... all the changes you notice within your body...anything..."

"...As you know, the decision to advance to the Phase Three trials will be made at the board meeting next week. You are both executive officers of the Chymera Corporation, and I recognize that as such you are senior to myself in rank. However, as Executive Officer in charge of the Orlando Project I have been given authority over you, temporarily of course, and therefore I must require of you, ...or should I say more politely, that I would like to invite you both ...to attend the board meeting with myself to present a summary of the results from the Phase Two program so far! Your participation in this meeting would be most appreciated. Of course, I'm sure you understand the importance of your presence and will comply with the invitation?..." Sonderheim looked from one man to the other, eyebrows raised questioningly, but before they could answer he continued.

"Good...that's settled then... I will of course brief you in a few days time on your participation in the meeting next week, and I will make all the necessary travel arrangements on your behalf. Do you have any questions, gentlemen?"

The Colonel coughed, stood up slowly from the desk, and looked down at Sonderheim.

"I would be most grateful if you would explain to me exactly what is happening within my body. The changes that are occurring within me...I do not recognize myself..."

"I too would appreciate a full explanation..." Simons added his voice to that of the Colonel's.

"...And you shall both receive one. All in good time. I promise you!" Sonderheim answered. "However for now it is important that you continue on your program of rehabilitation. As we will be leaving for New York to attend the meeting, I have personally reviewed your recovery program, and have authorized a few changes to your nutritional intake, as well as your exercise and physiotherapy programs. I would like to have you both fully independent and mobile for the board meeting...it will create a better impression that way..."

"Will we be returning to the clinic after the meeting?" Colonel Packard asked.

"Perhaps...perhaps not. A lot of progress can be made in five days...shall we reserve judgment on that question till later?"

Sonderheim smiled at both of the men before him.

"Good...that takes care of that...I would like to thank you both for your time...I will be meeting with you again in two days time...but until then, may I invite you to enjoy the facilities here at Purlington Bay as much as you wish? Thank you gentlemen."

Sonderheim stood up. Evidently the meeting was over.

When Trevor made it back to his room, he stood in front of the mirror and studied the man before him. He was hardly recognizable as the man he had lived with for the past ten years. The skin under his eyes and around his jaw had once again become tight, and the lines on his forehead and around his eyes had started to disappear. His skin was fresh and clear, and on the top of his bald head, dark black stubble had begun to appear in the middle of his scalp.

Energy coursed through his body. His muscles were growing tighter and firmer by the day, his eyesight becoming sharper.

His nurse had been right when she had told him that the fatigue would pass.

He owed a lot to her: for personally supervising his exercise program, for monitoring his body's response to the exercise she gave him, and encouraging him whenever he felt weak, or when doubts set in. Thanks to her, the results had been outstanding.

As he bent forward across the sink, leaning with both hands on the edge of the basin so that he could bring his face right up to the mirror to examine the irises of his eyes more closely, he could clearly remember how tired he had felt the first time he had walked along the corridor outside his room and then down the stairs.

Yet, only two minutes ago he had walked all the way back to his room from Sonderheim's office unaided, having just played a game of table tennis with Senator Mendes prior to the meeting. Not forgetting of course, the additional non-prescribed, extra-curricular, anaerobic exercise he had enjoyed with his nurse earlier that morning.

It was still hard to grasp, but there was no doubting the results. The leukemia was gone. The Orlando Treatment had worked. His life had been saved.

CHAPTER 30
Day Twenty-One
Pine View Hotel
Carmel

Kerrin woke late the next morning. In spite of his plans to get up bright and early, he hit the snooze button on the alarm the moment it rang, and turned over and went back to sleep. He only woke later when he heard the door to his room opening, hastily pulling up the sheets to cover himself just as the chambermaid walked in to change the bed.

Perhaps more embarrassed than he was, she retreated hastily and closed the door behind her. He glanced at the clock on the side cabinet. 11 a.m.

"Shit, its late!..."

He dragged himself out of bed, and turning the shower to cold, stepped into the spray, looking up towards the jet of cool refreshing water.

As the water ran over him he remembered the nightmare from the evening before, and shivered at the vision he recalled of Dana slumped in her wheelchair. Dead.

He called room service and ordered up some breakfast. By the time it arrived he was dressed and sitting on the balcony outside his window, reading through more of the documents Fiona had given him.

The ingenuity of the girl never failed to impress him. Her reputation in the office as a person who could find out almost anything you wanted was certainly well deserved. She wasn't just smart, she was inspirational.

Okay, so the problem was that Kerrin needed to know where the Gen8tyx Company had relocated to in California. And he desperately needed to know where he could find David Sonderheim. All the normal methods of obtaining this information had yielded negative results. On the face of it, the Gen8tyx Company and Sonderheim had disappeared. Most normal researchers would have given up. But not Fiona. What she had done was truly brilliant.

Only two months ago the Washington Post had run an article on the Ubichip, a 'scary' new computer chip, so small that it could be implanted beneath the skin of a person.. The technology section on the paper had trialed the Ubichip and published the results of its very own trial of the new technology. Apart from containing all the medical records of that individual, it could also be programmed for a myriad of different uses in a whole variety of security, emergency and healthcare applications: it could even be programmed to contain all the necessary information dealing with a user's bank accounts, so that when the Ubichip was scanned at a supermarket or in a shop, the wearer's bank account would automatically be debited for the charged amount.

More interestingly though, the Ubichip used technology which implemented the first ever combination of advanced bio-sensors and web-enabled wireless telecommunications, linking the chip to the satellite controlled Global Positioning System. The idea reviewed in the paper had been that by implanting the Ubichip underneath the skin of a child, or a convict, or even a pet, and then by monitoring the position of the Ubichip via the earth orbiting satellites, it would be possible to locate the wearer of the chip to within a yard on the planet's surface within a matter of seconds. In the future, the article announced, 'children could be chipped, and they would never get lost again!'

So what had Fiona done?

She had called the makers of the Ubichip and told them the Washington Post wanted to do another article on the technology, and to run another experiment for the story. They had sent her a few more of the microchips, and she had inserted them into the lining of two large bubble wrapped jiffy parcels. She had cheekily filled the parcels with copies of the most recent editions of the Washington Post and sent them to David Sonderheim via UPS Special DeliveryPLUS. She had sent one of the parcels to David's home address in Orlando, which she had easily got from the local telephone directory, and the other to David Sonderheim c/o Gen8tyx at the old company address in Florida.

Fiona had a hunch that although the Post Office had not been exactly forthcoming in helping her, Sonderheim would have left a secret forwarding address for personal mail arriving at his old home address, and would likewise have made arrangements for mail for the Gen8tyx Company to be redirected to the new company location in California.

UPS Special Delivery PLUS guaranteed delivery within 24 hrs inside the US, and as part of the service, as soon as the delivery was signed for upon receipt, they either called you or sent you an SMS message on your cell phone to inform you that the delivery had just been made.

As part of the so-called trial of the Ubichip, Fiona had arranged that the moment she received the message from UPS telling her the parcels had been delivered and signed for, that she would pick up the phone and call the Ubichip company, who in turn, would immediately use their satellites to trace the exact GPS location of the chip in question.

It had worked like a dream. As expected, both parcels had been forwarded by the US Post Office to the new locations in California.

Within seconds of David Sonderheim signing for the parcel at breakfast-time at his new home just outside of Carmel, and the night-watchman signing for the delivery of the parcel on behalf of Sonderheim at the new company location at Purlington Bay, Fiona had been given the exact location of both, down to the nearest yard.

"The girl's a bloody genius!" Kerrin laughed to himself, as he finished his orange juice and memorized the addresses in Fiona's report. Minutes later, he left the motel room and was driving down the road en route to Purlington Bay.

According to the map, Purlington Bay was just around the headland from Tippleton, a little coastal town not far from Carmel. Driving south along Pacific Highway No.1, he passed one fantastic view after another: stunning high cliffs plunging down to the Pacific Ocean and crashing onto the rocks and beaches below. Kerrin had read in the in-flight magazine on the plane that the drive from San Francisco down to Carmel through the area known as the Big Sur was considered to be one of the most beautiful drives in the world. Although it had been dark yesterday when Kerrin had driven down through that particular stretch of the coast, if the scenery was anything to compare with the road he was driving along now, he was not about to dispute the claim.

Kerrin was only too aware that he didn't really have a plan. The trip to California to find David Sonderheim and the new Gen8tyx Company was an attempt to do something, but what that something actually was, he didn't know. All he knew was that he and Dana were now in real danger, that time was not on their side, and that he had very little to go on. He needed to come up with something on Gen8tyx. And fast.

Apart from being caught, what worried Kerrin most of all, was being recognized or traced. The memory of him being tailed by the Mazda in Miami was still fresh in his mind. He knew that they had probably identified him from his car registration plate and the rental records at Hertz. He didn't want to make that mistake again. Now he had a new identity, he had to protect Mark Twain at all costs. He couldn't afford to be recognized and spotted with his new rental car, or there was a risk they could trace the registration plate and track down Mark Twain too.

The car he had hired was from one of the cheapest firms available, a local company which he had found on the internet. Kerrin had taken a taxi from the airport, and was dropped off at the company's garage just outside San Francisco. It was in the middle of a run down suburb north of the city, and even the local taxi-driver had problems finding it. Which was exactly the reason why Kerrin had chosen it. If he was spotted in his rental car, he wanted to make it as difficult as possible for anyone to find out where he rented it from.

It wasn't exactly 'Rent-a-Wreck' but it wasn't far off it either. The best thing about the firm was that Kerrin's experience as a policeman told him that although the car looked sound enough, it was probably stolen, and almost certainly the number plates were not properly registered. So, even if someone did try to track down the number plate, the chances were that they would not have any luck tracing it back to the rental firm and to him.

As he entered the sleepy tourist town of Tippleton, he spotted a bicycle shop and pulled up outside it. He walked in and looked around. All the latest models of bicycles were available in the shop, brightly colored, and gleaming silver and gold, tempting the boy in every man.

"Hi...can I help you?" a voice boomed from behind him. He turned round to find a young man in a cycling shirt and shorts, hands on hips and a big smile beaming from ear to ear.

"I hope so...nice bikes, but I was actually hoping just to rent one for the day. Do you do rentals?"

"Sure, what price range are you looking at? What type of frame do you want?" the young man replied, stepping towards him and resting a hand on the handlebars of one of the many bikes lined up in a row on display. "But if you're wanting to rent the bike, you'll have to secure it with a credit card."

"Oh dear," Kerrin replied. "Then we've got a problem. I only have cash!"

Since they had tracked down his true identity, Kerrin's new alias was the most precious thing he had. To use Mark Twain's credit card on the doorstep of those who were after him was inviting disaster, so he had decided that wherever possible, he would pay for everything in cash.

"Do you have any cheap second hand bikes?"

"I have a few...depends what you want..." the boy replied moving to the rear of the shop and waving his hand at a selection of second-hand bikes along the back wall.

"Oh...medium...nothing too flash, but something not too heavy..." Kerrin bluffed. He didn't have a clue what bikes were made of nowadays, or what they cost.

"Okay, let's see. We could give you a good deal on this 'Specialist' bike if you wish. It's aluminum, I'd say it's your height, and it's got twenty one gears. You'll need them if you're going cycling around here!"

"Sounds good. I'll take it."

The boy pulled out a red and white mountain bike from the row, and lent it against the counter. Stepping behind the till, the young man started to ring up the bill. $500. This was one expense that Kerrin would gratefully let The Post pay.

"Can I ask you a question? When I was a kid I used to cycle around here with my dad. We used to cycle to a place somewhere nearby beginning with P...I've forgotten its name...something like Parl..or Pirl Bay?" Kerrin knew exactly where it was, but he was fishing for any local information he could get on the place.

"Oh, that'll be Purlington Bay...it's only about forty minutes from here. Lovely place. I used to swim there too, when I was a kid. But you won't get anywhere near it now. They've closed the bay to public access."

"Purlington Bay! That's the one! But why's it closed?"

"Some big science company bought all the land down there just over a year ago. Since then they've built a big factory and lots of offices. Rumor has it that it looks incredible, but I don't know anyone who's actually been down there. They have security guards that keep the place pretty much airtight. The closest you'll get to it, is to the security gate at the top of the valley, about two minutes off the road."

"Is there any way I can get down to the beach off-road?"

"Not really..."

"That's a shame. I was really hoping to swim there again."

"I know what you mean, the locals are really angry about it. We're a friendly bunch around here, and they're too secretive for the likes of us."

"Any idea what they're called or what they do?"

"No idea what they do, but I know they're called Gen8tyx. Old Larry delivers the mail down there still, and goes down there once or twice a week...but only to the security gate...he hasn't seen the building itself. Strange, all that security. I reckon it's some government place. They certainly don't like unwelcome visitors. Can I get you anything else?"

"What about some cycling clothes...I could do with a new T-shirt and trousers..."

If Kerrin was going to cycle down to Purlington Bay, he wanted to get into character and look like a proper amateur cyclist. $200 worth of cycling gear later, and after a quick lunch at the local deli to boost his energy supply, he was on his way.

He could see what the shop assistant meant about the gears coming in handy. It had been years since Kerrin had cycled anywhere, and going up and down the winding hills along the coastal route was harder work than he had imagined it would be.

Hard work though it was, the scenery was brilliant, and a couple of times he stopped to pause and catch his breath while admiring the tall hills on his left which swept down in long, pleasant curves to the deep blue sea on his right. The sun was shining high in the sky, and there weren't any clouds to be seen. It was a perfect day.

As Kerrin cycled around the next hill he followed the road back inland as it swept along the edge of the coastal inlet. The head of the valley was narrow inland, broadening out as the mouth opened up towards the sea. Large trees covered most of the valley slopes, tall conifers reaching high into the sky and offering some well appreciated shade.

At the top of the valley a dirt road led off from the main road down the hill towards the valley mouth. A large sign announced "Private Land. Trespassers will be prosecuted. Security Dogs Patrolling." Enough of a warning to put off the average person from venturing anywhere down the path.

Kerrin switched down a gear and pointed his bike down the road. Inside the forest, the smell of spruce filled the air and pine needles crunched under the wheels of his bike. The wheels jumped and skidded off the stones on the dirt-track, and Kerrin's body jarred violently as he wished he had gone for a more expensive bike with better suspension.

About a hundred yards down the hill the road swept to the left, a security gate blocking off the road ahead, beyond which a newly tarmaced road led off through the trees. Two armed security guards in black uniforms stepped out from small security buildings on either side of the road. They stood in front of the gate, weapons brandished across their chests. Kerrin cycled up to them, taking the time to notice the electrified wire fence that extended away from the gate on either side, running into the woods and disappearing along the edges of the valley.

"Excuse me sir. This is private property. Please turn around and return to the main road." The bigger of the two men announced loudly as Kerrin slowed his bike down and came to a stop by the gate, resting his weight on his right foot and remaining seated on the bike.

"I'm sorry...I used to cycle here as a kid, right down to the bay, and then swim in the sea. Part of my training for the triathlon before we all moved to New York. So what's down there now? Can't I go down there?"

"It's private property sir. As is the track from the road down to here. You're trespassing right now, sir. I must insist you back up and leave, before I have to ask you for some ID."

"Hey, ...I'm just being friendly. No need to take that attitude...You're not from around here are you sir? If you were, you'd know we're all friendly people. No need to get so..."

The guard stepped forward, moving the barrel of his automatic rifle menacingly towards Kerrin.

"May I see some ID please sir?" he asked threateningly.

"What authority do you have to ask me for ID? Do you work for the government?" Kerrin probed.

"I have all the authority I need." He replied, gesturing with the automatic rifle. "Please do not be difficult sir. Either identify yourself or leave. Immediately."

Out of the corner of his eyes, Kerrin noticed a camera on top of one of the security gates swiveling around towards him. Kerrin couldn't afford to be identified. He swung his bike around and without engaging in any further conversation with the beefy security guard, he cycled back up the hill.

When he got to the main road, he turned right and continued along the edge of the valley rim. He wanted to try and get a view of the Gen8tyx building if it were at all possible, but disappointingly the woods ran around the whole valley, and he couldn't find any clearing where he could get a view over the tree tops to the valley below.

When the road started to turn inland again, he realized from the terrain that he had turned from one valley into the next. His best bet at getting a view of the complex would be to leave his bike somewhere and head up through the trees on foot until he came to the top of the hill. Hopefully from there he would get a clear view over the buildings below.

After thirty minutes of steep climbing he came out into a clearing, leaving the tree line behind him. The track to the top of the hill took him another thirty minutes, and he continued without resting, until sweating, overheated and incredibly thirsty, he finally emerged onto a small, stony plateau.

He sat down on a rock, gasping for breath and mopping his forehead and neck with the cycling shirt he had long since taken off his back. From where he was sitting he could see quite far out to sea, with an impressive panoramic view of the hills and cliffs running along the coastline.

Kerrin's binoculars weren't the best in the world. They were really opera glasses, one of those practical but well thought out presents that he had got from his parents as a Christmas present a few years ago. Nevertheless, they were still quite powerful and using them to scan the trees in the valley below Kerrin was able make out the shape of several buildings nestling amongst the trees.

Unfortunately he couldn't see much, only the tops of the buildings, but those he could see seemed to span quite an area.

As he watched, a helicopter came towards him from the sea and disappeared amongst the trees onto a landing site near the complex. A few minutes later it rose again from the tree line and headed back out to sea.

Still very hot, and rather tired, Kerrin conceded that there was little he was going to be able learn from the Gen8tyx Company headquarters, save from the fact that the new owners had gone to great lengths to secure its privacy and security.

Heading back down through the trees to find where he had left his mountain bike, Kerrin just hoped he would have more luck in getting information from David Sonderheim when he met him face to face. Tonight, if everything went well, Kerrin was planning to surprise him at his home address, and hopefully bring this affair to some sort of conclusion.

First of all though, he had to go back to the motel and pick up his gun.

Kerrin was nervous. Very nervous. The first thing you learn in policing is never to underestimate anyone you might be investigating or arresting. Never. Kerrin knew too many widows of colleagues who had.

Sonderheim was a powerful man. From what they'd discovered about him, he was well-connected and rich beyond his wildest dreams. His every instinct told him that Sonderheim was the man behind all the Orlando murders, the death of his brother-in-law and his friend James. As such, Kerrin had no intention of going up against the man unarmed. He needed some sort of protection.

After loading the bicycle into his rented car, he drove back to his hotel. The woman at reception was pleasant, but too talkative. She was probably bored sitting behind the desk all day long, and welcomed any opportunity for company and conversation. If Kerrin had not been in such a hurry he would have been happy to spend some time chatting with her, but it was already getting late and he had places to go.

"Hi, I'm from room 506. I was wondering if I've had any parcels delivered for me this afternoon?"

"Hello...nice day isn't it...say, are you from the East Coast? I like the accent...I've got a sister in Philadelphia...ever been to Philly? Maybe you know her?..."

Kerrin raised his eyebrows at her and smiled.

"Oh...okay. A parcel? Actually yes. UPS delivered it just an hour ago...Can I ask you to sign for it please?"

She pulled out a large heavy box and pushed it over the counter to Kerrin, along with a receipt form and a pen.

He signed for it, thanked her and made his way back to his room. Once inside, he threw the box onto the bed, and pulled out a pair of gloves from his suitcase. Opening the parcel, ripping off the brown paper and discarding it into the trash can, he took out a large metal tin full of cookies. Turning it upside down, he emptied all the biscuits onto the bed, and picked up the heavy brown envelope that fell out on top of them.

His Beretta 9mm pistol.

Opening the top of the envelope he pulled out the pistol that he had confiscated from a drug addict during a raid in Miami, along with two magazines full of bullets. He held the gun in his gloved hands, inserting one of the magazines and feeling the weight of the pistol, balancing it in his palm. It was a good gun. When he had confiscated it, he had noticed that like most crime weapons, the serial number had already been filed off. As an added precaution he had once fired a bullet from the gun and run a ballistics check on it. There were no outstanding crimes associated with the Beretta. It was clean.

When he had flown over from Washington he couldn't take the gun with him on board the aircraft or in his luggage: since 9/11 the risk of getting caught was way too high. Instead, he had posted it to himself courtesy of UPS Special Delivery to the hotel he had been staying at. That way there was almost no risk.

He flicked the safety catch on and slipped the gun into a shoulder holster. He was ready to face Sonderheim.

It was four thirty. It would take him twenty minutes to drive to the location he had been given by Fiona. He planned to park his car a few blocks away from Sonderheim's house and then to cycle the rest. When he got to his house he would wait for Sonderheim to come home, and approach him man to man.

What exactly would happen next, Kerrin didn't know.

Kerrin had never broken the law before. For years he had upheld it, and on a daily basis had put his life on the line to defend it. But when he met Sonderheim today, if he couldn't provide some very satisfactory explanations to everything that had happened, it was very likely that Kerrin would have no choice but to kill the man that threatened not only the life of his wife, but also those of his friends and family. It was either Sonderheim or him.

Sonderheim lived on a large new exclusive housing development just outside of Carmel, purpose built to attract some of the wealthiest people in the state. The term 'housing development' was perhaps not the best way to describe the collection of ten massive mansions all built along the perimeter of their own private golf course. Each mansion was set in its own small estate, and was individually designed by one of the country's leading architects.

'Millionaire's Avenue' swept around in a long, gradual curve, a broad avenue from which small roads discreetly disappeared through large security gates into private driveways beyond. It took Kerrin ten minutes to cycle along the avenue before he got to 'No. 6', the new home of David Sonderheim, and once there, he couldn't help but wonder how on earth he was going to get through the impressive entrance so that he could talk to Sonderheim.

He cycled further along the road, past the grand entry gates, before getting off his bicycle and walking slowly back towards the entrance. Standing at the gates he looked through the large wrought iron metal bars and gawked at the impressive Spanish style villa nestling pleasantly at the end of the long drive, between Palm trees and large ornate fountains.

He looked at his watch. It was six o'clock. It shouldn't be too long before Sonderheim came home.

The security guard inside the plant at Purlington Bay had not really expected to come up with a match, but he had run through the security procedure as a matter of course. When the light on top of the computer console started flashing red, he entered the computer room, switched off the alarm, and turned to the computer monitor.

There were two pictures on the screen which the computer had digitally mapped together. The one of the left was the photograph that they had scanned in from the image captured on the video cameras on top of the main security gate.

The photograph had been digitally compared to over twenty million photographs on their system, which was linked to the National Criminal Photograph Recognition Bureau in New York. Strictly speaking a large proportion of the people on the system were not criminals. Many were normal people. Law abiding citizens with no criminal record. But all of them were people that the government was, for one reason or another, very interested in keeping tabs on. According to the system, the photograph on the right of the screen belonged to a Mr Kerrin Graham from Washington. He was a reporter for the Washington Post. A note underneath his photograph indicated that his file had only just been added to the database.

The guard smiled to himself, while picking up the phone to call the 'alert number' mentioned at the bottom of the screen.

After speaking to the man at the other end of the line somewhere in New York, he called his boss in the main building of the Gen8tyx clinic.

"Perhaps we should alert Mr Sonderheim?" he suggested casually.

"No... too late...He left about ten minutes ago. What's the guy's security threat rating? Does it say what he'd done?"

"No. Nothing. It's a new file...just says to advise when found. Take precautionary measures where appropriate. Apprehend where possible."

"Should be okay then, but just in case, why don't you send a car round to Sonderheim's house, just to check everything is okay?"

A few minutes later, two security guards jumped in to one of their mobile units and set off for the Sonderheim residence.

CHAPTER 31
Day Twenty One
The Sonderheim Residence
Millionaire's Avenue
Carmel

It had been a long, hard day. The preparations for the board meeting were now in their final stages and all things going well, David would fly out in two days time to meet with some of the other Chymera Executives on the Tuesday, before presenting to the assembled board of the Chymera Corporation on the Wednesday. Although he was not invited to attend the whole of the board meeting, he had been given over three hours to make his report, signifying the importance which the Board placed on his work.

David was excited. The Orlando Treatment was proving to be more successful than they had ever thought it would or could be. This would be only the second time he had addressed the board, but hopefully with what he was about to tell them, he would impress them and exceed all their expectations.

Things were going well for him. Very well. David was now richer than his wildest dreams had ever let him believe he could be. His new house was the epitome of luxury, and the power now at his command was intoxicating.

Becoming a member of the Chymera Corporation had been the result of five years of personal hard graft, and he didn't underestimate the opportunities that such membership now opened up to him.

He loved the power.

He liked to breathe it in, to play with it, and to let it wash over him. To watch how people obeyed him, and carried out his every command.

Yet somehow that wasn't enough. One day he was determined to be promoted and become a full executive member of the Corporation. That was what he now worked towards, the beacon which lit his way.

As he drove home through the outskirts of Carmel he smiled to himself as he pulled into 'Millionaires' Avenue': what a place to live!

The sunlight caught the tops of the trees, the light slowly deepening its orange hues as dusk approached. The tall trees which lined the edges of the avenue were majestic. Things of beauty in their own right. An added touch from the designer of the development which did not go unnoticed by David.

As his Mercedes swept around the curve of the avenue he could see the entrance to his estate just ahead. For some strange reason there was a man trying to fix his bicycle on the road immediately outside his gate, preventing him from driving through onto his land beyond. He pulled up slowly in front of his house and called out to the man through the car window.

The man ignored him.

He shouted again, then opened the door to his car, and got out.

The approaching car, an imported blue Mercedes SLK, slowed down and started to turn its wheels onto the driveway leading up to the gates. The owner peeped the horn several times, then wound down the window and shouted something at Kerrin.

Ignoring everything the man said, Kerrin kept his back turned to the car and hunched over the inverted bicycle, messing around with one of the tires, pretending to try to inflate it with his hand-held pump. He heard the man get out of his car behind him, and the 'beep' of the remote control as the driver activated the large metal gates which swung open slowly in front of Kerrin.

"Excuse me please. You're on my drive way. I can't get past...will you please move!" the man bellowed.

Kerrin turned and looked straight into the face of David Sonderheim: the deep blue eyes, the cut of the jaw, the high cheek bones.

It was definitely the face of David Sonderheim, and yet... it wasn't. There was something very wrong. The man standing before him was...different. According to the date of birth on the driving license which James had given him in Miami, Sonderheim was forty eight years old, and the photographs that Fiona had given him of David Sonderheim backed that up: they had been taken while he was at the Chymera meeting in Spain, and they were of someone who looked close to fifty.

Yet the man standing before him could only be about thirty.

Kerrin was momentarily stunned, his eyes fascinated by the man before him, his brain hurriedly trying to work out the answer to a problem which simply did not compute.

"What are you doing?" the man asked him again loudly, coming towards him and standing very close beside him and bending over the bicycle.

"Oh...I'm sorry...I'm here to see David Sonderheim...but my bicycle has broken down."

Another car was coming down the street now, its driver ignoring the signs warning of a 20 mph speed limit.

"That's me. Who are you please? Do I know you?" The man replied, his face red with anger.

"I think you may have heard of me…" Kerrin started to reply. "My name…"

The first gunshot caught Sonderheim in the shoulder, flinging him sideways over the bicycle and onto the tarmaced road beyond the gates. With the experience of Alex Swinton's shooting so fresh in his mind, Kerrin reacted instantly, diving to the ground and then lunging for the protection of Sonderheim's car.

Another gun shot rang out, and Sonderheim screamed again, the second bullet catching him in the foot as he lay sprawling on the ground.

The gunman had stopped his car sixty feet from the driveway and was firing rapidly at Kerrin and Sonderheim through the open passenger door.

Lying behind Sonderheim's Mercedes, Kerrin pulled off his jacket, and ripped open the holster underneath his shoulder, unclipping the gun and whipping it out in a single movement.

With the feel of the gun in his hand, his many years of target practice and his experiences from being under fire in several drug-related shootouts on the streets of Miami, all came flooding back to him. Despite the massive adrenaline rush which Kerrin felt pumping through his veins, Old 'Deadeye' was suddenly calm and in control.

Sonderheim had already scurried for cover behind the wall on the other side of the gate, just as another round of shots landed on the ground near where he had been. Finding no target, the burst of automatic fire moved upwards and played along the top of the wall, the bullet-cases bouncing back and ricocheting off the top of the Sonderheim's Mercedes.

Kerrin judged the source of the gunfire and in a classic maneuver which would not have been out of place in any James Bond film, he rolled out from the protection of the Mercedes onto the ground on the other side of the car, appearing from behind the back tires onto the patch of grassy ground beside the road.

He came to rest with both elbows finding support on the ground and his Beretta extended horizontally in his two hands in front of his face. Kerrin sighted the assassin in the car on the street, lined up the sights on the gun and pulled the trigger. The Beretta jumped three times in quick succession, the bullets flying through the air and blowing the head of the gunman in the front passenger seat.

Kerrin rolled back into the protective cover afforded by the Mercedes, waiting patiently for the sound of a second gunman. As he listened acutely, in his mind's eye he examined the mental visual imprint of what he had just seen, searching the image for any other people that may be there. Satisfied that he could not recall any, but acting on a strong gut feel, Kerrin crawled around to the other side of the Mercedes on his belly. Coiling himself up into a jumping position, he sprung away from the car firing rapidly at the closed rear passenger doors of the red car in the middle of the road. There was another scream, the rear car door burst open, and a man ran towards Kerrin firing wildly.

There was one more bullet left in Kerrin's gun. He looked on terrified as the man charged at him, gun outstretched, bullets flying past his head.

The world seemed to slow down, and amidst the deafening loudness of the gunshots and the smell of cordite in the air, he was dimly conscious of his own right hand coming up in front of his face, his eyes calmly taking a sighting, the slight pressure from his finger on the trigger, and the body of a man falling at his feet.

Kerrin looked at the man lying face down before him, the blood pouring from his wound.

Then, almost in a dream-world, and calmly expecting the worst, his detached mind looked down at his own body, examining himself for bullet wounds.

His hands searched his body, probing his clothes and his flesh for the wounds he surely must have, but miraculously there were none.

He looked up.

With the immediate danger now gone, he breathed deeply, his body suddenly gasping for air.

It was as if he had been watching it all taking place on a darkened cinema screen, his field of vision restricted only to the movie playing in slow motion directly ahead of him. But now, with the rush of oxygen to his brain quickly bringing back all his senses, the world started to speed up again.

Once more alert, his experience shouted at him, warning him that the danger may not yet be over.

Realizing that his own gun was empty, and that stupidly he had left his spare clip of bullets in the pocket of his jacket beside the Mercedes, he crouched beside the body, replacing his empty Beretta back into his own shoulder holster and taking the gun from the dead man's clasped hand. He reached quickly into the corpse's pockets, finding and taking out a spare magazine, which he immediately loaded into the Glock his victim had been firing.

He stood up, still pointing the gun at the seemingly dead man. "Never underestimate your enemy" he heard a voice within him say. He kicked the body, flicking it over with his left foot. His bullet had taken away most of the man's chest and throat. There was no question he was dead.

Arms outstretched, the Glock clasped tightly in his hands, he moved quickly towards the red car, running around the back of the vehicle, poised to shoot instantly should there be anyone lying in wait on the far side.

He glanced inside. The back seats were empty. In the front of the car, the body of the driver who had taken the first shots lay half in, half out of the car. His head was splattered over most of the windscreen, blood and brains coating the windows and inside of the dashboard, dripping slowly onto the floor.

'Sonderheim,' Kerrin thought to himself aloud. He ran back to the gate, just as the heavy metal gates swung closed in front of him, preventing him access to the man who was slowly pulling himself up onto his feet.

"Are you okay?" Kerrin heard himself asking, not believing that the words which came out of his mouth were actually his.

"Does it look like it?" Sonderheim replied, holding his shoulder with one hand, the blood oozing out from between his fingertips, and also pouring out of the sole of his shoe, where the second bullet had caught his foot.

For a second, the two men stared at each other.

The spell was broken by the sound of another car approaching, screeching around the corner at the end of the avenue. Realizing that he was very exposed, Kerrin took a last look at Sonderheim and jumped into the driver's seat of Sonderheim's Mercedes. The key was still in the ignition, the engine purring away.

Without looking back, Kerrin kicked the car into gear, then drove forward, swerving around in a tight curve and scraping the pristine bodywork along the edge of the wall bordering Sonderheim's estate.

The other car swung up to the gate, and two security guards in black uniforms from Purlington Bay jumped out and starting firing rapidly after the disappearing Mercedes.

Accelerating away fast, Kerrin swung the car back onto the road and vanished down the avenue ahead.

The men made no attempt to follow, and as the metal gates to the estate swung open, the last Kerrin saw of them in the rear-view mirror was as they disappeared through the wall, rushing to Sonderheim's side.

A few blocks away he cut his speed in half in an effort not to draw any unnecessary attention to himself. He found the street where he had parked his own car, driving past it and parking the Mercedes a hundred yards further down the road.

The street was a normal residential area, and people were attending to their gardens and chatting to each other on their porches in the approaching dusk.

He walked casually back to his own car, climbed in and drove back to his hotel. Once inside his room he quickly showered, packed his bags and checked out. He had already paid up-front for three nights in cash, but he didn't bother wasting any time asking for a refund for the night he hadn't used the room.

It was only when he had driven a hundred miles along the route to Las Vegas that he started to relax.

It was then that he noticed that his hands were still shaking.

CHAPTER 32
Day Twenty-One
The Sonderheim Residence
Millionaire's Avenue
Carmel

The two security guards rushed in through the gates, grabbing Sonderheim just as he began to fall backwards onto the ground. Within minutes they had applied a tourniquet to his left leg, had bundled him into their car and were speeding off to the hospital in Carmel.

Sonderheim was beginning to show the first signs of shock, but it looked like they had managed to stem the blood loss just in time. He would probably survive.

As Sonderheim lay in the back of the car, drifting in and out of consciousness, he started to wonder what had just happened. It made no sense to him.

He guessed that the man who had been waiting at his gate was Kerrin Graham. He had read the file on him, and had been fully debriefed by Laura on her successful trip to South Africa.

David had expected Kerrin to try to kill him. That Kerrin had managed to track down his new, supposedly secret address, was a warning that David had completely underestimated the man. Kerrin was dangerous. Perhaps he should have ordered Laura to kill him after all.

But what David couldn't understand and was puzzling him the most was, who was it that had just tried to kill him? Had the assassins being trying to shoot at Kerrin, in order to protect himself, with him accidentally getting caught in the cross fire, or had the assassins been trying to kill him?

And if they had been trying to kill himself, why had Graham saved his life?

The most likely scenario was that they had tried to kill the Graham man, and that the assassins had been incompetent fools who had not known who David Sonderheim was.

208

The alternative, that somebody else apart from Graham was out to kill him too, was not a thought that he wanted to entertain. At least, not yet.

The Road to Las Vegas
Nevada

The drive to Las Vegas through the dark night was a long and boring one. The road was straight, and clear, but void of any landmarks or distractions to break up the journey. Exactly what he needed to let him think.

What had just happened didn't seem to make any sense to Kerrin.

Could it be that Kerrin had effectively just saved the life of the person he had come all this way to kill?

As best as he could make out, while he had been in the process of assailing David Sonderheim, potentially even about to kill him, someone else had beaten him to it.

At first, he thought that the assassins must have been trying to get him, in order to defend Sonderheim, but thinking back upon it again the events didn't bear out that conclusion.

These guys were trained killers. Professionals. They'd had two clear targets, and their first shot had been at Sonderheim, who had been behind him. When they had hit him and Sonderheim had fallen, they had repeatedly shot at him on the ground. Kerrin had not drawn any fire to himself. Only when Kerrin had killed one of them and wounded the other had the second assassin opened fire on him, in what may actually have been self-defense.

If only he had got the chance to examine the bodies for some clues as to who they were. Interestingly, Kerrin noted the fact that the Glock he had borrowed from the second dead man was one of the preferred weapons of a large number of CIA agents. Was this just coincidence, or were the dead men trained CIA assassins? If they were, why did the CIA want to kill Sonderheim?

Another traffic sign flashed past, announcing the imminent arrival of Las Vegas at his car, ...or was it the other way around...it was all relative anyway, wasn't that what Einstein had said?

Kerrin was a bundle of emotions.

His stomach was busy shouting reminders at him to eat something, and he knew that by all rights, he should be feeling really tired. Exhausted even.

Yet, in spite of the exertions of the past two days, Kerrin felt completely awake.

As he overtook a car in front that was driving far too slow for his liking, Kerrin realized just how much more vibrant he had felt in the past few weeks. He had begun to feel like his old self again. The thrill of the chase, the buzz of being involved in a real criminal investigation, the challenge of trying to find and put together the clues, flirting with danger, and the knowledge that he was now both the hunter as well as the hunted. It was him versus them. It all added up. It reminded him of his days on the force, and for the hundredth time that year, he hankered after times past.

Kerrin looked at his watch.

It was getting late.

Although Kerrin had not finished introducing himself to Sonderheim before he was shot, it was very likely that Sonderheim had recognized him, or at least, had guessed who he was. Which meant that Kerrin now couldn't fly back to the east from any of the major airports in California. He just couldn't take the risk of being stopped at the check-in.

No, his best bet was to get out of the state and make his way to one of the smaller airports, like Las Vegas, and fly back first thing in the morning. It would take a day or two for any interstate alert to go out. Chances were, that even if the security staff at Las Vegas had received a warning, it would be a while before they read the thing, let alone acted on it. Kerrin felt sure that he would be safe to board a flight to Washington the next morning without there being much risk of being identified and caught. There was even a chance that the Californians may never even get round to alerting their colleagues in Nevada at all.

Kerrin hated incompetence in anyone, but now with his life under threat, he was banking on it.

Day Twenty-One
Divisional Director of the CIA
Florida
E.S.T

Cheng Wung knew the score.

He knew that California wasn't really under his jurisdiction, and ordinarily he would never interfere on someone else's turf.

But after his team had successfully recovered Alex Swinton's hard drive with the missing copy of the 'Orlando File', Buz Trueman had called him to ask if he would be interested in another two jobs. He had accepted both.

The first had not worked out exactly according to plan. Buz had wanted someone terminated. Cheng knew not to ask too many questions. Unfortunately, the hit had not gone smoothly: the target had survived and his team had been eradicated. It was not yet clear exactly what had happened and why the mission had failed...

The second job sounded interesting.

True, the 'bonus' Buz had offered for its successful completion was substantial, but for Cheng it wasn't just the money.

The thing was, Buz Trueman was a powerful man, and the fact that Buz was trusting him to resolve the Graham issue, was the sort of trust that money couldn't buy.

$1.5m was, after all, a lot of money.

But if Buz hadn't mentioned the money first, he might even have done it for free: now, more than ever, Cheng had a reputation to uphold. Sonderheim might have survived, but Cheng would ensure that Graham would be caught and delivered as promised.

At all costs.

In this case, the road to riches and recovery would start with a call to an FBI colleague in California:

"Hey Don,...it's Cheng Wung...howyadoin? Fine?...That's excellent. And how's little Don Junior doing? How old is he now...He should be about four now, right?...Yeah, I know, it's been too long...yeah,...We should definitely get together soon...Yeah, that would be nice...Thanks...and you too...Listen, now you come to mention it, there is something that you could do for me...One of the guys we're trying to track down looks like he's scarpered over to your neck of the woods...What's he done? No firm evidence yet, but he's heading up our list for one of the guys responsible for the terrorist bombing in Disney World...Yep, that's the one...sure...even if he isn't the one, it looks mighty like he did do it, and we need to bring him in straight away...We know he was in the Carmel area yesterday, but that's all...It's pretty obvious he's using switched names again...Listen, if we send you the last photo-id we had on the guy, can you arrange for some of your guys to go around all the hotels and the motels in a hundred mile radius of Carmel and see if anyone recognizes him? Yes? Excellent...that would be great...and if we can't catch him, it would be great to at least find out what his latest alias is...great...By tomorrow? Fantastic!...Okay, got to rush too...but I like your idea of getting together soon. Give my regards to Junior and your wife. Thanks...bye Don."

One phone call. That's all it took. Cheng was pretty sure that by this time tomorrow night they would have Kerrin Graham's latest alias.

Day Twenty-One
The Road to Las Vegas
Nevada
P.S.T

With only another five miles to go to Las Vegas, Kerrin's mind turned to the other problem that was vexing him about his encounter with David Sonderheim. Something else that didn't make sense at all...

When Kerrin had first stood face to face with David Sonderheim he had been talking to a man with the appearance of someone only about thirty years old. Kerrin knew, no...Kerrin could *prove* that Sonderheim was forty eight years old. So why had the man he had met had the physique and looks of a thirty year old? How could it be possible?

An oncoming car flashed his lights at Kerrin, just in time to warn him that he was slowly straying over to the other side of the road. The car passed him by, his horn blazing, the tone of the blast becoming deeper in the classic Doppler effect you hear whenever an ambulance passes by with its horn blaring.

Kerrin returned to his thoughts, which now switched to Alex Swinton. Kerrin remembered how when he first met him on the beach, how struck he had been by how much younger Alex had looked compared to the last time they had met. He must have looked at least five years younger...

He thought hard about him, desperately trying to remember what it was that Alex had told him just before he had been killed...He thought about their meeting in the restaurant in Langebaan. He could picture him so clearly sitting opposite him at the table, he could remember the sound of his voice...and then suddenly it was there, the last words he had said before he was shot...

" Yes...but that's trivial in comparison to what we discovered next...Mike Gilbert was the one who noticed it...the one who should get the credit. It will maybe even go down as the single most important discovery in the field of genetics and medicine ever..."

But there was one more thing prodding at his memory...one more thing that Alex had said.

What was it...?

Try as he might he couldn't put his finger on it, and after a while he decided to leave it. If it was important, his subconscious would drag it to the surface in due course.

The lights of a Texaco station glowed bright red in the darkness ahead, and a few minutes later Kerrin pulled over onto the forecourt, parking beside a phone booth. He searched through his pockets and pulled out a handful of quarters.

He pushed open the doors to the phone booth and stepped inside, laying his note book on the shelf in front of him, and arranging the quarters in little pile beside the book.

The first person on the list to call was Mrs Calvert.

The phone rang six times before it was answered.

"Mrs Calvert, this is Kerrin Graham. We met a while ago when I came to ask you some questions about the death of your husband?...Yes, that's me, Martin's brother-in-law. I'm really sorry I'm calling so late, and I'm sorry if I woke you, but something's come up and I needed to ask you a question. It may sound stupid, but please bear with me on this one...Mrs Calvert, in the months or weeks leading up to his death, did you notice any changes in your husband's health? I mean, were there any indications that his health was improving or...well, did you notice any changes in his appearance at all?"

There was a silence at the other end of the phone.

"Mrs Calvert?...Are you still there?" Kerrin prodded.

"Yes. Yes...I'm still here. It's just that it's all still so fresh in my memory...Sorry." She started to cry. There was the sound of a little sniffing into a handkerchief, and then she was back.

"Actually, now that you mention it, the answer is 'yes'. In the weeks before he died he couldn't sit still! He kept talking about how he wanted to take us all up to the mountains, and do some walking and fishing in the Rockies. I didn't know where he was getting the energy from. I can't say that he was looking any younger though, well, apart from the color of his hair. The silver bits had started to turn brown again. I thought he was dying it. Maybe he wasn't?"

The next person he called was Henry Roberts' widow. She was not at all happy at being disturbed so late, but when Kerrin had managed to calm her down and persuade her that the questions he had for her were very important, she agreed to listen to him.

When she heard the questions, her anger vanished, and she answered them without hesitating, a touch of excitement even showing in her voice.

"No, I can't say that I saw any physical changes in his appearance, but he did seem to be healthier and stronger... When he was young he was quite an accomplished runner, even won a few races and awards, but he hadn't run in over twenty years. Then all of a sudden Henry started to do laps of the garden before breakfast. I thought it was his way of fighting back, coping with the stress...And then about a week before he died, he told me that he had actually sent in an application form to run in next year's New York marathon! I laughed of course. I couldn't believe it, but he was deadly serious, and if you knew Henry, you would know that once he set his mind on something, he would do it..."

Afterwards he had called Mike Gilbert's fiancée. She too had an interesting story to tell.

It turned out that when they had just bought the new house, they had both taken out new life assurance policies. The insurance companies had insisted on them both taking stringent medicals.

"But Mike got full marks for everything. Practically got a Gold Star. The doctor said Mike was one of the fittest men he'd ever seen."

And Sam Cohen?

His sister was wide awake and watching Letterman when he called, and Kerrin could tell from her voice that she was genuinely pleased to hear from him. When asked about his health, at first Sam's sister replied that she hadn't noticed anything out of the ordinary: he had always been a strong swimmer and was incredibly fit. But then she told Kerrin that she had noticed a distinct improvement in the quality of his skin, and she had even commented to her brother when he was alive that the brown freckle-like markings on his hands and forearms, the tell tale signs of ageing, had almost all but disappeared.

No doubt if Kerrin were to ask his sister about any health improvements she had noticed in her husband before he had died, she would have a few to report. Kerrin would almost bet on it.

Kerrin walked into the gas station and picked up some fresh coffee. Returning outside he stood outside in the desert night, away from all the bright lights, and looked up at the stars. Holding the coffee cup in both hands to keep warm, he sipped the brown liquid, his eyes looking up and watching the night sky above. The stars were incredibly bright, the constellations forming amazing patterns in the sky. Kerrin had learned the names of all of them as a boy, and as he finished the coffee he remembered the nights he had spent stargazing with his father all those years ago, on the coast near Baltimore where he grew up.

A shooting star blazed a fiery path across the heavens and Kerrin smiled to himself. It was a sign of luck. A good omen.

He got back in the rental and drove on, one hand on the steering wheel, the other hand pulling absentmindedly at the hair at the base of his neck.

What was it that Alex Swinton had said? He needed to remember. It was something he had mentioned about trials...What had he called it...?

The Orlando Treatment?

Yes, that was it! The Orlando Treatment. Now, that was an interesting word...Treatment...Yes, that was it! They had been discussing the Orlando Treatment...

And then suddenly Kerrin remembered what it was that Alex had said. And in one sudden, blinding moment of clarity, it all fell into place. Kerrin knew what this was all about, and the importance of what was at stake! ...

They had been talking about how the core group members were planning to get even with the Gen8tyx Company by downloading their research notes and files onto their own computers, and Alex had said...

"...... We all succeeded in getting the information we needed, and storing it off line, on our own home computers, or on servers elsewhere. Put it this way, we got what we needed. And we proved the process worked...The Phase One trials were a success."

"And what were they?" Kerrin had asked him.

"We all took the Orlando Treatment...We're walking examples of what it can do. The results were almost immediate......and every day it becomes more apparent ...better...more effective...Kerrin, it's incredible..."

That was it! It all made sense now. The Orlando Treatment went way beyond anything Kerrin, or for that matter, anybody else could possibly have imagined. Kerrin had seen for himself how effective it was. All the Orlando Team had been living, breathing proof that the process was working.

And that was the reason they had been killed. There was no way that the Chymera Corporation could afford to let them live.

They all had to die.

For while trying to find a cure for Alzheimer's and Parkinson's disease, while messing around with genetics, tampering with the fundamental building blocks of life itself, they...or rather Mike Gilbert...had made a discovery that would change the future of mankind. A discovery of such great importance, and incalculable value that the Chymera Corporation would do anything to protect its secret.

The Gen8tyx Company had found the key to eternal youth.

CHAPTER 33
Day Twenty-Two
Las Vegas

The motel on the outskirts of Las Vegas was a dump. In better days it had probably been a decent enough place, but now it was the preserve of the desperate and the bankrupt, the last stop in Las Vegas for those who had arrived with a dream and a fistful of dollars, but left with nothing more than a hangover and a handful of aspirins.

The room smelt damp and the toilet didn't flush properly. In spite of the annoying sound of water running constantly into the toilet bowl, Kerrin threw himself onto the bed and fell asleep instantly. He was tired, physically and mentally, and desperately needed to rest.

The next morning he was woken by a loud rapping on his door. Springing from his bed and pulling the Glock from the shoulder holster underneath his pillow, he stood slightly to one side of the door, and with the chain over the lock, opened it a few inches.

Yes?"

A fat teenager with long, unkempt hair stood outside. Kerrin couldn't make out whether it was a boy or a girl.

"Ma wants to know if you're staying another day. It's twelve o'clock, and you only paid for one night...it's time to check out otherwise, and someone else wants your room..."

"Okay...sorry...I slept in...I'm checking out...give me ten minutes, okay?"

"Okay."

'It' smiled, then turned and walked back to the motel office. Kerrin closed the door, tossing the Glock onto the bed. Looking around the room, he couldn't believe that anybody else would 'want the room', as 'it' had just insisted. Still, if they did, they were welcome to it.

After what loosely passed as a shower, Kerrin gathered together his stuff and drove to the nearest diner, where he ate a hearty all-day breakfast and planned his day ahead.

The first stop he had to make would be at a fancy-dress shop. He wanted to pick up a disguise, just in case somebody might be keeping an eye out for

216

him at the airport. Luckily, since Las Vegas was the biggest party town in the whole of America, finding one wasn't exactly hard.

After trying on numerous facial accessories he settled for a black beard, a pair of ridiculous heavy brown framed glasses with thick glass lenses, and a black haired wig. When he looked in the mirror he realized with horror that he looked almost believable. Totally unrecognizable, but believable. Could he really look like that?

He paid the woman behind the shop counter, took the bag containing his new identity, and left.

Next stop was the nearest ATM. He slid his credit card into the machine, nervously expecting it to instantly snap the card up and retain it. However, a few nerve-ridden moments later, the machine asked him how much money he wanted, and he borrowed the maximum amount. It was a good sign. It looked like he was still ahead of the game, and the people in Carmel either hadn't found out his alias yet, or if they had, the banks had not yet been alerted.

Kerrin knew that Mark Twain was living on borrowed time. It would not be long before they found out who Mr. Twain really was and terminated his credit card. And then he would be broke. How long could he and Dana survive without a steady stream of cash?

Realizing that the bank was still extending credit to Mark Twain, he hit upon another idea. It was important to get hold of as much cash as possible, before the well went dry.

The lady behind the counter at the large new Russian themed Casino looked up and smiled at Kerrin.

"How much would you like?" she asked as Kerrin slid the credit card over to her through the metal tray underneath the bullet proof glass.

"How much can I have?" he replied innocently.

"Let me see sir..." The lady swiped his card, and typed his name onto the computer, checking to see if he had been blacklisted by the Casinos or the banks.

"According to your bank, your limit is $10,000. But I can't give you that much. You've already got expenses of $1300 pending against that limit. I can only give you the balance."

"Fine. That sounds good."

"How would you like the money...cash or chips?"

"Cash please."

Walking out of the casino, Kerrin could imagine what it must feel like to win a small fortune on one of the roulette tables. In total he was now carrying just short of $9000 in cash. That should last them both for a couple of months at least.

Avoiding the centre of downtown Las Vegas, he drove through the side streets and headed out to the airport, parking the rental car in the long term parking lot.

Wearing his new disguise Kerrin walked into the airport and booked himself onto the next plane to Washington D.C. After a very nervous hour, constantly looking over his shoulder and expecting to be arrested at any moment, he finally made it onto the plane. At 6.20 p.m. the plane touched down in Washington D.C. and after picking up his luggage he walked out of the airport and found his other rental car in the long-term parking lot.

He had left it on the third floor, deliberately choosing a dark, almost empty area at the back of the parking lot. As he opened up the trunk, he scanned the rest of the floor. There were about thirty other cars parked around him, and he was the only person there that he could see.

Looking up at the roof he scanned the ceiling for security cameras, but noticing only one, about twenty yards away and pointing in the opposite direction, he focused his attention on the other cars parked near his own.

Dropping his stuff in the trunk of his car, he searched through his luggage and pulled out his red Swiss Army Knife. He looked at the multiple blades that the knife offered, and selected the small screwdriver.

He looked around him again. There was still no one else on his floor.

Walking past five cars parked against the wall, he selected a new looking Ford and slid into the gap between the wall and the front bumper. Working quickly, he knelt down and using his screwdriver, he removed the front registration plate from the car.

Standing up straight again, he slid along the wall until he came to another Ford which had similar plates to the one he had just taken off. Like the other car, this one was also registered in Pennsylvania. He knelt down again quickly and removed the front registration plate of the second car.

Walking back to his car, he threw both plates into the trunk, closed the lid and drove out of the parking lot.

So far so good.

He had thought about it a lot on the plane, trying to come up with another way of safeguarding his new found identity. The last thing he wanted to happen was for him to be spotted in his car, and his new alias to be tracked down from the rental records at Hertz. The best solution seemed to be to put false number plates on his car, but the question was where could he get them from?

The streets in the suburbs of Philly were littered with wrecks of cars, either stolen or abandoned, but it wouldn't be a good idea to take those plates just in case some policeman noticed the plates belonged to a stolen car and stopped him.

On the other hand, he could buy a second hand car from a wreckers yard, and take the plates from that, but he would probably need identification to buy it, and he didn't want to connect his new ID to the purchase.

After a lot of thought, he realized the best option would be to simply steal a single number plate from two different cars. It seemed a safe bet that anyone noticing that a single number plate was missing from their car would assume that it had either fallen off, or that it had been stolen by some kid who wanted to hang it on the wall in his den. It was unlikely that anyone would report it. And once he had put them both onto to his rental car, the chances of anyone spotting that his car had two different registration plates was minimal. People simply didn't notice things like that.

At least, he hoped they didn't.

Day Twenty-Two
Carmel

The FBI agent smiled. At last, after a whole day's searching, they'd found the motel the suspect had stayed at for the past few days.

"So you definitely recognize the man?" Agent Walker asked the talkative woman behind the reception desk, holding up the photograph of Kerrin in front of her face.

"Absolutely! He was a strange man. Not too friendly...Kept himself to himself...yeah, that's him! He had a parcel delivered...Yeah...I remember! What's he done...anything bad?"

The woman looked up at Agent Walker, her eyes glistening. This was the most exciting thing that had happened to her in ages. Even better than when the man in Room 302 had killed himself last month.

"I'm afraid I can't say. Tell me please, what room is he in and what is his name?"

"Oh,...he checked out yesterday...Just missed him, you did. If you'd been here yesterday you'd have got him...."

"So, what was his name?"

"A funny name...German I think...here, let me check the system..."

She turned to the computer and typed away at the keyboard, scrunching her forehead up in an act of intense concentration.

"Here it is...Room 506...there you go...told you it was a German name...Sonderheim... David Sonderheim!"

Agent Walker thanked the woman, and walked back out to the car.

His partner looked up at him expectantly, handing him back his coffee as he sat down.

"Bingo...found him. But he left yesterday..."

"So what's his name?"

"David Sonderheim."

"Are you sure?"

"Why? Of course I'm sure...I saw the computer entry myself."

"Fine... It's just that, I'm sure that that's the name of the guy our suspect tried to shoot and kill over in the big house on Millionaires' Row...I think someone's playing games with us!"

Day Twenty-Two
Sunshine Villas
Cherry Hill, New Jersey

"Who's there?" Dana asked anxiously from inside the motel room.

"It's me...I'm back!" Kerrin whispered against the doorframe, smiling at the sound of her voice.

The door opened a crack, and Kerrin pushed it slowly open. Inside, Dana moved back a few inches to let Kerrin in, balancing on the tops of her crutches. Tears were beginning to stream down her face, and a smile was fighting against the sobs which welled up from within her chest.

"Oh, Kerrin! Thank God you're back!" she cried, dropping the crutches to the floor and falling into his open arms, wrapping her hands around his neck and burying her head into his chest.

Kerrin reached down and swept her legs up, cradling her in his arms. Kicking the door closed behind him, he walked towards the bed, and turned, falling backwards onto the mattress, cushioning Dana on top of his body as they fell.

They made love, slowly and passionately, their tears intermingling with smiles and the sounds of their pleasure.

Afterwards, Dana engulfed herself in his presence, imbibing her senses in his smell, his warmth and his steady, strong heart-beat, her head lying flat and still against his chest.

They lay silently beside each other for a long while, Kerrin stroking her long hair, and caressing the side of her face, his hand sweeping over her head and down the contours of her cheek.

At last Dana spoke.

"I was so scared. I felt so alone. And if I had to spend another day in this horrible smelly motel room by myself, I think I would have gone mad!"

"I'm sorry. I hated the idea of you being here by yourself. I wanted to get back as soon as possible." He replied softly. "Did you leave the room much?"

"Only to the mall to get some food...oh, by the way...two parcels arrived for you about an hour ago. I signed for them..."

"What name did you sign?"

"Mrs Sonderheim. I didn't forget."

"Well done. Where are they?"

Dana pulled out two parcels from under the bed. Kerrin was happy to see that the Glock pistol and his own Beretta had already arrived safe and sound. It was amazing how fast UPS could deliver parcels interstate.

"Talking about Sonderheim..." Dana started to speak, then hesitated. She had to know. She had to ask him..."Kerrin...did you ...did you...?"

"Did I kill Sonderheim? Is that what you want to know?"

"Yes...did you?" she lifted herself up onto her elbow, her head inches away from his, looking deep into his eyes searching for the truth of the answer.

"No I didn't. I thought I was going to...but someone tried to kill him before I got round to it..."

He told her the whole story, about the trip to Purlington Bay, the meeting with Sonderheim, and then the trip to Las Vegas. She laughed when he showed her his new disguise, but told him to take it off immediately. She preferred the Kerrin she knew.

He told her about the discovery that the Gen8tyx Company had made, and she looked on in disbelief as the true meaning of it all sunk home.

"So what do we do now?" she asked.

Kerrin had been dreading her asking that question. He had gone to California to confront Sonderheim, and had come home empty handed.

He wished he could take her home, back to their house, back to their real life. He wished he knew how to answer her, so that she could believe that an end was in sight. But he couldn't tell her that. So he lied.

"I'm meeting Fiona tomorrow. She has something new. A new idea. Something big! Don't worry, it's all going to be fine...Just you see!"

He bent forward to kiss her, but she turned away.

"What do you think I am? A kid? Don't 'just you see' me! Kerrin, these guys are serious. If we don't come up with a plan soon, and I mean a *proper* plan...it's only a matter of time before they find us...and then, we both know what's going to happen to us!"

Kerrin looked at his wife. The smile slipped from his face and when he spoke, this time his voice was calm and determined.

"Dana, I won't let them touch you. I don't know what is going to happen, or how we're going to get out of this, but I promise you...I swear on my life, that I'll get us through!"

Looking at him as he said it made her feel a little better, but in reality, they both knew that if he didn't come up with something soon, Kerrin would soon have no life to swear on.

Sector Nine Alpha
Day Twenty-Two
Fort Dixon
NSA American Surveillance Centre

Technically Agent Johnson had not done anything wrong. The report he had given to his superiors, indicating that Kerrin Graham was going to fly to England, was based firmly upon the data he had recorded. He had made no mistake.

Yet, when Kerrin had not turned up for the flight as predicted, his boss had reprimanded him severely.

"Do you realize that we had thirty people staking out the airport, as well as people on alert in England? For fuck's sake Johnson, something went wrong. What? Why didn't he turn up?"

His boss was an asshole at the best of times. Even more so when things didn't go according to plan.

No, it had not been Agent Johnson's fault, but he had been made to take the rap, and he had not enjoyed it one bit. Whoever the man was, he hated Kerrin Graham with a passion. It was Graham's fault, and now it had become personal. No matter how much effort it took, Johnson was going to find the man and bring him in.

All he really knew about Graham that could assist in the search was that he worked at the Washington Post. His personal file gave him a lot of other information, but nothing else that would immediately help track him down. Graham had already stopped using his cell phone, and it was obvious he had gone to ground, so finding him would not be straight forward. Still, it was a challenge. Him versus Graham.

He decided that he would start by searching through all the phone conversations and emails made from or to the entire workforce of the Washington Post during the past two months, looking for any mention of his name. After a bit more thought, he realized that the search would yield up hundreds of files, each of which he would have to go through individually. Without getting other people allocated to helping him, this would take too long. No, he had to be smarter.

He needed better keywords.

If only he knew what the story was the reporter had been chasing at The Post, then it would be easy to search through all the communications for reference words relating to the subject matter of the article he was working on.

The last thing he wanted to do was to go and ask his boss for help, but if he was going to track the Graham man down, he needed more information.

In the end, the anger he felt towards Graham weighed heavier than the negative feelings to his superior.

"Okay, I'll see what I can do," was all 'the asshole' had said, when Agent Johnson had explained to his boss what he needed.

It didn't look hopeful, but an hour later he walked over to Agent Johnson's desk, and without saying a word, his boss slipped a piece of paper onto his keyboard. There were two words written on it: 'Chymera Corporation.'

It took two hours for George to run through all the emails and phone conversations made to or from the Washington Post over the past two months, searching the contents of all the communications for any mention of 'Kerrin' or 'Kerrin Graham' in combination with the other keywords 'Chymera Corporation'. Yet, when the run was complete, Johnson was no better off. No communications had been found that simultaneously combined both sets of keywords.

Frustrated and tired, Agent Johnson decided to sleep on it. It was late. Time to go home.

The next morning he returned, determined to try again and kicking himself for not having done the obvious the night before: why had he not just initiated a search on the two keywords in isolation, searching only for any voice conversations or emails that contained the words "Chymera Corporation" by themselves without the connection to Graham.

He looked at his watch. It was 8 a.m. It would take another two hours to run the search again. That would take him to ten o'clock.

If that search didn't turn anything up, then he would repeat both searches, increasing the search period from two to four months.

He edited the program to include the new keywords, pressed the return key on his keyboard executing the search program, and went to get a fresh coffee.

11.30 a.m.
Day Twenty-Three
Washington D.C.

The phone rang twice before Fiona picked it up.

"Hi. Back from holidays. How's the weather?"

"Fine. But I'm busy. We'll talk later."

Kerrin watched from across the road to make sure that Fiona wasn't being followed, checking the cars and pedestrians around her for any covert surveillance as she walked into the pizza restaurant. Everything seemed fine. Nothing unusual, and no men in long, brown leather coats following in her footsteps. Of course, these days the FBI weren't anything like their stereotypical public image, so what exactly he was looking for Kerrin couldn't say…just something different…

When he walked into the restaurant after her, he sat down in the booth next to hers and was pleasantly amused to see that Fiona hadn't recognized him in his wig, glasses and false beard.

He stared at her.

After a few moments, her head turned towards him and she looked across at him briefly, shifting uncomfortably in her seat, before turning her attention back to the phone sitting on the edge of the counter, willing it to ring.

Kerrin stood up and walked across to her booth, sitting down beside her. She looked shocked, said something and started to get up.

"Relax…it's me!" Kerrin said quietly. He turned, took the glasses of his face and winked at her.

Fiona half-turned in her seat, covering her face with her hands and laughing out loud.

"Good grief!"

"Shoosh…sorry to surprise you, but I'd thought I take a risk and come and see you…"

"Wow! It's incredible! Nobody would recognize you. Not even your mother!"

Kerrin grabbed a couple of beers from the cold-unit opposite the counter, ordered a pizza and sat down again beside Fiona. He told her all about the trip to California, about his ideas on what Gen8tyx had discovered, and then confessed that he was short on ideas on how to proceed.

Sensing a certain amount of desperation Fiona reached out and touched his hand gently.

"It's my turn now. I think I've got some good news!" she said sitting up in her seat and excitedly relating what she had got up to in the past few days.

"…So I checked out the companies who'd bought into Gen8tyx… researched their directors, got press cuttings, the works. Turns out the CEOs of Philadelphia Pharma and Sabre Genetics Inc. were both in the photographs from Spain…"

Kerrin perked up a little, looking across the top of a piece of sliced pizza at her with a fresh twinkle in his eye.

"…And totally coincidentally, yesterday's Post ran Ed Harper's latest article. It was a follow up piece of research done on the article he…sorry, you…wrote on the Utilities fraud…seems that as soon as the electricity company was exposed in the press, it went into receivership. Within hours another company had put in a bid for it, which was later accepted."

"Who's the buyer?"

"Small Holdings!"

"Interesting."

"That's not all. Ed did some research and showed that Small Holdings have bought five other power and water companies in the past two years...all at knock-down prices in interesting circumstances...And there's some nice photographs of Nigel Small, the owner, on the front page. And guess what? You can see Buz Trueman in the background, standing just behind Small!"

"So it looks like there could be a definite connection between Small Holdings and Buz Trueman and the Chymera Corporation?" Kerrin suggested.

"It's not clear cut by any means, but it's too much of a coincidence for there not to be."

"I agree. Anything else?"

"Maybe...but I'm not sure. What was the name of your sister's husband who got killed in the plane crash?"

"Martin Nicolson. Why?"

"I have a parcel from him. It was sent to you, and arrived while you were in South Africa...I didn't notice who it was from, and didn't really even give it a second look until the drawer I keep your mail in got so full I had to move some of it elsewhere. Kerrin, you've got so much mail...I've got nowhere else to store it now...every morning I empty your post before anyone else picks it up and stick it into my desk drawer or a box I keep in one of the cupboards. I put the bills and commercial trash on your desk, just to make sure people think you're still getting mail...just in case the boys in brown come back to search your desk again...but anything that looks personal or interesting I hide!"

"So how do you know it's from Martin?"

"He wrote his name on the back of the parcel. One of the guys in the mailroom signed for it, and it arrived with all your other mail. You get so many big parcels delivered that I didn't think it was anything special...what is all that other stuff you get sent to you?"

"Oh, I don't know...stuff...mostly correspondence or research material I send off for...So how big is the parcel and when was it sent?"

"It's quite big...about this size..." Fiona lifted her hands up in a classic fisherman's pose, holding her palms out about one-and-a-half feet apart. "...And it's quite thick and very heavy. It was postmarked the day after his plane crash. He probably sent it to you just before he tried to fly to the Bahamas to meet your sister."

Kerrin's heart started to beat faster. The parcel had to be important. Very important.

"Have you shown it to anyone else?"

"No. No one else knows it's there..."

"Where have you hidden it?"

"In my bottom drawer. Most of your other stuff is in the stationary cupboard in a big brown box, with my name marked on the front of it...on the shelf beside the window…But I don't think there's anything there that's worth looking at just now. At least, nothing of real importance. Were you expecting anything?"

"No, but I think you're right. From what you're saying, this parcel could be really important. Can you go and get it for me now?…"

CHAPTER 34
Day Twenty-Two
Sector Nine Alpha
NSA Headquarters
Alabama

The search program had just finished, and Agent Johnson switched out of the other application he was working on, and opened up the results of Search Pattern 192871.

The search results contained a single file.

He opened it up. It was a phone conversation. Using his mouse, he hit the play button on the search file and started to listen to the phone conversation through his headphones.

It was a conversation between two women:-

"Fiona, hi it's Sheryl. I've got something for you…it's not much, but it's all there is. Ready?"

"Go for it…what have you got?"

" 'C.C.' stands for the Chymera Corporation. There are no files on it, nothing. No list of directors, no annual reports, nothing, nada…zip. But there are a few rumors about it…best as I can make out, the company is registered in Buenos Aeries. The company funds some of the government officers down there, and basically, they can get away with murder…the whole company is shrouded in secrecy, operates as a law unto themselves…don't post results, or record their interests. The government there doesn't challenge them. I bet they don't even pay any tax there. I can't find out anything about what they do, or who runs it. Total information shut-down. It's very weird."

"Well, that's a lot more than we knew before."

"There is one thing though. About a year ago I heard that a reporter across at The Post was trying to run an article on the Chymera Corporation. Apparently he died before the article was finished. Maybe his death wasn't a coincidence?"

"Who did you hear that from?"

"Sorry, Fiona. I can't say. I shouldn't even have told you what I did!…"There was a pause at the other end of the line…"Anyway…Does that help? I have to go now…"

"Yes, it does! What can I say, you're a star! I owe you one now…see you at Thanksgiving."

"Don't mention it." There was a pause. *"I mean it Fiona, don't mention this to anyone, okay?"*

"No problems. I protect my sources too..."

While he listened to the conversation Agent Johnson made a few notes on the Word file he had opened up on the screen in front of him. After he had listened to the conversation four times, he checked the stats file that went with the call. The phone call had been made from a phone from someone in one of the government offices in Washington. The Calling Line Identification number of the call had been initially withheld by the dialing party, but as with all the telephone calls George listened to, he disregarded such trivialities and automatically provided the telephone number of the phone from which the call had been placed.

Agent Johnson ran a search on the telephone number, and within seconds he had traced the call to the desk phone of Sheryl Mather in the State Department of the United States. A few minutes later he had pulled her personal file. Agent Johnson often wondered what the average Joe on the street would do if he knew that the United States of America kept a file on each and every one of its citizens, recording and maintaining a record of almost anything they did during their life that could be of interest to the government.

Returning to the stats file, the search results also told Agent Johnson the number Sheryl Mather had dialed. A few minutes later Johnson had tracked it down to the desk phone of Fiona Cohen, who, according to her personal file, was a Junior Researcher at The Post.

Working methodically, Agent Johnson scanned Fiona's and Sheryl's files, downloading copies of the photographs in their driving licenses, and any other recent photographs which would help in making a positive I.D. on the suspects.

An hour later Agent Johnson knocked on the door of his boss and walked into his office, carrying the file he had just compiled from the information gathered from Search Pattern 192871.

Two minutes after Fiona had left the pizza restaurant, Kerrin ventured out onto the street, and keeping a respectable distance, followed her around the corner as she headed back to the office to pick up Martin's parcel.

Kerrin was excited. Whatever was in the parcel was something valuable. Why else would Martin have sent it to him, just before he was killed?

As he rounded the corner to the street of the Washington Post he looked up at the big building and wondered how long it would be before he was free to set foot in his place of work again.

It probably wouldn't be a good idea to go any closer just now, so watching Fiona cross the almost empty road in front of him, he stepped back and leant against the wall of the insurance company opposite the Washington Post.

There was the sudden loud screeching of brakes and two black Fords swept into the middle of the road from the edge of the sidewalk, effectively blocking Fiona off from the other traffic as she stood in the middle of the street.

Fiona looked up in abject terror as men in black uniforms jumped out from the cars, pointing guns at her and shouting at her to lie down on the ground.

"Down...don't move... Hands out in front of your head...!"

On each side of the two cars, the traffic screeched to a halt, and people started running away from the pistol waving uniformed men in the middle of the road.

Fearing it was another terrorist attack, the people in the road dived for cover behind parked cars, or in the doorways of the buildings along the street. A woman beside Kerrin screamed, picking up her child from a pushchair and running through the door of a nearby bank.

Fiona fell to the ground, and Kerrin watched helplessly as one of the assailants stepped onto her back with one foot, pressing the barrel of the gun against the back of her neck, while another of the armed men handcuffed her hands behind her back and ran his hands up and down her body, checking her for a weapon.

Another of the assailants started shouting something which Kerrin couldn't quite make out, and then suddenly the two men beside Fiona pulled her to her feet and dragged her into the back of one of the cars which had blocked off the road.

Just before one of the men forced her head down and pushed her through the car door onto the back seat, Fiona turned towards Kerrin and their eyes met, the look of terror on her face an image that Kerrin would find hard to forget.

The two cars swept around and drove off, one following the other. Kerrin watched in disbelief as he saw them disappear out of sight around the corner.

They had got Fiona.

Divisional Director of the CIA
Florida
1.10 p.m.
Day Twenty-Two

Cheng Wung had authorized the immediate arrest of Fiona Cohen and Sheryl Mather as soon as he had read the report that had been emailed to him by one of his agents in Washington, who had himself received it only minutes before from one of his contacts in Fort Dixon.

It was time to step up the operation. He had promised Buz results, and Cheng intended to deliver.

Fiona and Sheryl had already been picked up and within the hour they would have them both in one of their secure interrogation houses, where the business of debriefing the suspects would begin immediately. Cheng hoped they would both cooperate fully, but if they didn't, he was confident that their modern methods of information retrieval would ensure that they soon knew everything they needed to know.

Of course, the arrest of both Sheryl and Fiona would not be officially recorded. He had personally asked for all records to be sent to him for storage, and that meant that outside of the recovery team, no one else would ever hear of the event.

The police would suspect terrorist involvement, but even if they didn't, they would never be able to track it down to the CIA. Cheng had made sure of that.

Thankfully, there was at least one good thing that had come out of the botched attempt on Sonderheim's life. It gave Cheng the perfect excuse to put out an All Points Bulletin on Kerrin Graham and his wife. The fact that Kerrin had not fired any of the shots aimed at Sonderheim was beside the point. What was important was that Kerrin had been present, and as such he was now a criminal suspect in an attempted homicide. Furthermore, since Kerrin's wife was in association and hiding with him, she was now also a criminal suspect. Cheng would be entirely within his rights to bring them both in.

He had already had one of his agents prepare the bulletin, and it was scheduled to be issued within the next hour. With the entire US police force, the CIA and the FBI all looking for them, Cheng was almost certain that within the next twenty-four hours he would have both Kerrin and his wife in custody. The case would soon be closed.

The Durham Bar
George Town
Washington D.C.

Kerrin sat at the back of the bar, his head down, staring at the half-drunk beer in his hands.

He couldn't forget the look of terror on Fiona's face as she was being bundled into the car. She had trusted him, had been willing to risk her life to help him, and now the bastards had got her!

After the cars abducting Fiona had disappeared out of sight, Kerrin had made his way back to his rental and driven across town. There was little else he could do.

He had found a quiet bar in George Town and ordered a beer. He needed to think. He needed to understand what had just happened.

And he needed to stop shaking.

He was scared.

Across the room, a television set was playing loudly on a shelf above the bar, and some of the early afternoon drinkers were watching CNN, and commenting loudly about each of the news items. A fat man in a grey suit swore loudly at the recent decision to increase the interest rate, and when he had finished cursing at the government's ineptitude at being able to handle the economy better, he downed his beer and ordered another.

Kerrin turned his attention back to the TV screen, a surge of panic erupting within him.

Two photographs were being broadcast on the news bulletin.

The one on the right was a photograph of himself, and the other one was of Dana, both copies of photos they had used for their driving licenses. While the photos dominated the screen, the CNN newscaster read a news story about two suspects wanted urgently for suspected terrorist activity, and a recent attempted homicide of an important businessman in California. The picture switched back to the studio, and the camera zoomed in to the lady newsreader who read out the names of the two wanted suspects, urging the public to contact the police or the FBI if they had seen either of the two people in the past forty eight hours.

"Kerrin Graham and his wife Dana Graham, were last seen in Washington D.C.. Police are urging extreme caution in approaching the husband, who is considered to be dangerous, and have warned that although the woman is disabled and is restricted to the use of a wheelchair, they should not attempt to apprehend Dana Graham on their own. Anyone who has any information on either of the suspects should contact the following numbers as soon as possible..."

Kerrin was stunned. Instantaneously his heart rate shot up to a hundred and twenty beats a minute, and he felt dizzy.

His first reaction was to check the false beard on his chin, and fumble with the wig on his head to make sure it was still firmly in place. Lowering his head, he picked up the pair of brown spectacles, which he had taken off and dropped on to the table, and thrust them back firmly onto the bridge of his nose.

He looked around the bar, half expecting everyone to be staring at him. No one was.

The newscaster had moved on to talking about the latest baseball scores, and no one at the bar seemed to be interested in what she was saying. One of them got up to go to the toilet, and another waved at the barman, threw a ten dollar bill onto the bar and walked out.

Kerrin's hands had started to shake again.

What was happening?

What was he going to do now?

First Fiona, and now this…

Kerrin could feel the walls of the bar closing in on him. For the first time in his life he felt small, and weak. Hunted. It was only a matter of time now…

And then he thought of Dana…He had to get back to Dana!

CHAPTER 35
Sunshine Villas
Cherry Hill, New Jersey

Mrs Wanamaker, the wife of the owner of Sunshine Villas, was just finishing a late lunch in the room behind the reception desk. It had been a busy morning. One couple had tried to sneak off without paying, the cleaning company had been late in delivering yesterday's laundry, and there had been a late rush of bookings, with people trying to track down last minute accommodation for the big Travel Convention that was happening somewhere in town. If it wasn't one thing, it was another.

She picked up the remote, and flicked through the channels looking for something more interesting to watch. As she flicked onto the local news channel, she caught the tail end of a story on the upcoming Travel Convention and laughed when the newsreader mentioned how well planned it had been this year.

"If it's so well planned, why is everyone struggling to find anywhere to stay...Idiots!" she muttered to herself.

Before she had a chance to flick to the next channel, two photographs flashed onto the screen, and the newsreader started talking about two of the latest terrorist suspects the government was looking for.

Mrs Wanamaker leant forward in her chair, turned up the volume on the remote and stared intently at the TV screen...

There was something very familiar about the people in the photographs...Something very familiar indeed!

The drive from Washington back to the Cherry Hill New Jersey took over three hours and Kerrin was revved up the whole way. Each time a car came into sight in his rear-view mirror, he panicked that he was being tailed. Several times he nipped in and out of the traffic, trying to shake off cars or vans that looked just a little bit too suspicious for his liking, only to find that they blended into the other traffic easily, and made no attempt to keep up or overtake him.

The sweat was running off his forehead and the wig and the beard had begun to itch terribly. As soon as he reached the freeway he ripped them off and stuffed them into the plastic bag on the seat beside him, along with the ridiculous glasses that kept slipping off his nose.

A woman pulled in front of him from the inside lane and Kerrin swore loudly, smashing the palm of his hand onto the steering wheel horn. He looked over his shoulder and accelerated past her in the fast lane.

Sunshine Villas was set back from the main road running through Cherry Hill. The bulk of the motel rooms were accommodated in two buildings, each set out on two levels with balconies overlooking a swimming pool shared between all the rooms. The motel reception was at the front and to the side of one of the buildings, on the edge of a large paved parking area which ran along in front of the two buildings and the pool.

As Kerrin drove along the street towards the motel, he could see blue flashing lights from several blocks away. Stopping at the traffic lights one block away, his heart sank as he saw several policemen standing on the road outside Sunshine Villas waving the traffic on and past the entrance to the motel.

Suddenly a helicopter swept over the street, hovering above the motel complex. The State Troopers on the road ducked involuntarily, reaching up with a free hand to keep their hats from blowing off.

The lights changed to green.

Caught up in the flow of traffic and with no choice but to follow the policemen's instructions, Kerrin changed into the middle lane and continued driving past the motel, glancing sideways and trying to see what was happening .

Half a dozen police cars stood in the parking lot, forming a ring around the room at the bottom end of the large building on the left of the pool. State troopers and policemen stood behind the doors of their police cars, resting rifles and pistols on the roofs of their cars and pointing towards the open door of Room 302.

Kerrin's room.

Then, as he looked over his right shoulder, he saw two women police officers wheeling Dana in her wheelchair out from the room towards a police van parked by the edge of the pool. A wave of despair swept over Kerrin, and he screamed loudly at the top of his voice, slamming his fist into the dashboard and drawing blood across his knuckles.

Dana! He was too late...they had got Dana!

As Kerrin drove past the entrance to Sunshine Villas he was so shocked at the sight of Dana being whisked away from their motel room, that he failed to notice the two cameras sitting on top of large metal tripods on either side of the road, each camera carefully aligned at just the right height so that while one could see in through the front window and scan the faces of the driver and front passenger, the other recorded the registration plates of the passing vehicle.

The latest toy of the Pennsylvanian Police Department, the Automatic Digital Face Recognition System was capable of seeing into the cabs of moving cars, recording the faces of its occupants, digitizing the images and comparing them instantly with all police and state records of known criminals or suspects wanted for questioning by the police.

The system was not cheap, but in the new war on terror since 9/11, it had proved an invaluable aid for tracking down suspected terrorists and dangerous individuals who posed a threat to society. Linked by satellite to the George computer in Alabama, each street unit could process two hundred pictures a minute, and within four minutes provide a readout to a laptop computer located near the position of the cameras, in this case controlled by a state trooper sitting in a car only yards from the camera.

As Kerrin's car passed by the motel, he was not aware that his face had been digitized and processed and that even before he had driven more than two blocks from the motel, a young captain in a state police car had been alerted to his presence and was just about to raise the alarm on his radio.

As soon as Kerrin passed the motel, he reached into his hold-all on the seat beside him and pulled out the old police radio. He had bought it several years ago from one of the many dubious contacts he had met over the past five years. It was a reminder of his days on the force, and he liked to listen to what the police were saying to each other when driving around the city. Sometimes when he was working on a news story, he used it to keep tabs on what was going on, and it helped him to stay hot on the heels of the latest developments.

He switched it on and tuned it into the local police frequency, hoping to pick up some bulletins and radio discussion on what was happening. Hopefully he would be able to find out where they were taking Dana, and what was happening to her.

There were normally about three different radio bands that the State police would broadcast on. Kerrin listened to each of them in turn but although he heard lots of calls going back and forward between the various stations and their men out on patrol, none of them seemed to be dealing with the incident at Sunshine Villas. It was peculiar. Almost as if the police were not aware of what was going on...but if they weren't the State police that had just arrested Dana, who were they?

A flashing light reflected in his wing mirror caught his attention.

A glance in his rear view mirror showed that several police cars were coming towards him, making their way through the traffic behind.

"Are they chasing me, or just leaving the scene of the incident?" he thought to himself.

He pulled over quickly into one of the side streets and put his foot down. His car accelerated quickly towards the other end, but as he waited to turn right onto the main road ahead, he caught sight of one of the police cars swerving into the street behind him.

"Shit, they're tailing me." Kerrin swore under his breath.

Suddenly all thoughts of Dana were pushed out of his head and he had become the hunted again. He knew that he had to escape, at all costs. Both Dana's and Fiona's lives depended upon him evading capture, staying alive and finding out what was going on. How they had spotted him he didn't know, but he didn't have time to worry about that now. He had to escape.

A second police car appeared in the street behind him, joining the other one already heading towards him. The traffic on the main road in front was heavy and Kerrin realized he didn't have the time to wait patiently for a gap to open up and let him into the traffic. Without hesitating, Kerrin gunned the accelerator and shot into the moving traffic in front. There was the loud screeching of brakes and blaring horns as several cars came to a rapid halt on his left, the cars behind them trying furiously to avoid colliding with the now stationary cars in front of them.

Kerrin swerved onto the other side of the road, nearly colliding with a car coming directly at him, but missing the collision at the last moment by swerving across the front of the oncoming traffic and disappearing down another side street on the left.

Behind him he could hear the large crash of several cars ramming into each other, and the sound of a horn hooting protest at his shoddy driving skills.

At the end of the road, he accelerated across the junction without slowing down, praying that he would not be rammed by any cars coming from his right or left.

Luckily, he made the junction okay, and was soon hurtling down the next street unharmed.

From memory Kerrin was hoping that turning right at the next road would take him onto the freeway, and then out of the city. Using all his skill, his rental car rocketed out of the side street and swerved onto the main road ahead. This time he was not so lucky, and he clipped the back of a car as he emerged from the junction, sending the other car spinning across the street and into the path of the oncoming traffic. There was a loud crash, followed quickly by an explosion as a gas tank ruptured.

In his rear view mirror he could see the smoke and fire billowing upwards from the ruined cars, and he realized with horror that it was unlikely that anyone had survived the impact.

"Shit..." Kerrin swore loudly, fighting to maintain control of the wheel and forcing himself to concentrate on his driving and not dwell on the crash he had just caused.

Suddenly, from out of the cloud of smoke engulfing the road behind him, Kerrin caught sight of one of the police cars charging after him.

The sign for the ramp for the Freeway flashed by him, and Kerrin changed lanes, narrowly missing a large van carrying pressurized gas cylinders.

The police car behind him was gaining ground. Powered by a highly tuned engine and driven by a more experienced driver, it was making easy work of weaving in and out of the traffic and catching Kerrin up.

Accelerating as fast as he could, Kerrin drove onto the long upward ramp leading to the Freeway, just as he heard the first gun shot.

With alarm he realized that his pursuers were firing at him.

Keeping a firm hold of the steering wheel with one hand, he reached into his shoulder holster and touched his Beretta reassuringly...

Phaanngg! Suddenly the back window disintegrated behind him, and a spray of broken cubed glass covered Kerrin's head. Before a second bullet could get him through the open back window, Kerrin swerved the car hard over to the left.

The car behind him was closer now, and in his rear-view mirror he could make out the shape of one of the pursuers leaning out of an open window, firing at him.

Phaannng! Another shot, and the car lurched sharply to the right.

A bullet had blown out one of the rear tires. Kerrin fought furiously to control the car, but succeeded only in missing a collision with a large RV on the inside lane, before his car swept over the edge of the ramp, through the protective wall and down the sloping grassy bank on the other side.

Unable to control the skid, his car started to turn, at the same time bouncing into the air and spinning once in a complete sideways somersault, before thudding back into the grass bank and coming to a violent halt right-side-up.

Amazingly Kerrin was unhurt. The seat belt he had been wearing had miraculously protected him from any serious injury, but as the car rocked back and forward on its damaged suspension, Kerrin became immediately aware of the smell of leaking gasoline.

Reacting instantly, he flicked himself free of the seat-belt, grabbed the bag containing his disguise which had landed on his lap, and dived out of the side door. Without looking back, he staggered to his feet and started to run.

A large explosion and a blast of hot air caught him in the back, propelling him forward onto his face, and he fell, sprawling, onto the ground. A ball of flame from the exploding car swept over him, singeing his hair and scorching his clothes.

Coming quickly to his senses Kerrin staggered to his feet and started to run. In front of him he could see the entrance to a subway which passed underneath the ramp and the freeway and emerged somewhere on the other side.

He ran as fast as he could, taking the subway steps three at a time, then along the dark, dank, urine-stinking tunnel, until he emerged into the light at the other end onto a patch of open ground, covered in broken glass, rubbish and discarded supermarket trolleys. Jumping across an empty metal oil-drum lying in his path, he crossed the open ground quickly, and found himself running along a street, whose buildings were mostly boarded up and were obviously abandoned and in various stages of collapse. In some of the doorways, vagrants languished drunkenly, a few of them looking up to watch him as he passed.

He ran without looking back, expecting at any moment to hear the sound of pursuing gunshots or a roaring car engine chasing after him, but there was none. Not stopping to wonder why he wasn't being followed, he realized that he must be heading towards the railway line. If he was correct, he would be close to one of the commuting stops for the local trains.

Almost at the end of his strength, he crossed a couple of side streets, eventually coming out in front of the entrance to a station. He staggered inside, only able to take the steps one at a time, before just managing to summon up the strength to jump over the ticket barrier at the top of the stairs.

He came to a stop at the edge of the tracks, bending forwards and resting his hands on his knees as he gasped for air and tried to regain control of his breathing. As his head began to clear, the tracks in front of him began to sing, a high pitch whine which was soon swamped by the loud rumbling of an approaching commuter train rushing towards the platform.

The train came to a halt, and Kerrin jumped aboard, clinging to a pole and swaying unsteadily on his feet as they accelerated out of the station. His eyes swept the station on both sides, trying to catch sight of any pursuers, but there were none. The platform behind him was empty.

It didn't occur to him until later that evening, when he was safely inside a dingy motel room on the other side of town, that those who had been pursuing him had probably wrongly assumed he had been killed in the exploding car.

For now at least he had evaded capture one more time, but he knew his luck couldn't hold out much longer.

He was just one man against an unseen army, an enemy with the backing of what seemed like the entire security forces of the United States.

And yet, in spite of everything, Kerrin refused to give up hope.

He had a gut feeling that things were about to change, and that for once, things were about to start going his way.

CHAPTER 36
Day Twenty-Three
Old Creek Farm
Delaware
8 a.m. E.S.T.

Doctor Smiles opened his bag, and took out the tools of his trade, lying them in an exact order upon the clean, white, cloth that he had just spread upon the top of the metal trolley.

He like things to be ordered. He found that being meticulous in all things produced better results. It was more professional.

He liked white.

White was one of his trademarks.

He took it as a matter of personal failure if blood was spilled, little drops of red polluting the cleanliness he strived to maintain.

Blood was unnecessary. Totally unnecessary. He looked down upon his colleagues who were forced to result to more brutal methods of information extraction. They had no skill. They were amateurs.

Why did people insist that interrogation had to be brutal?

If God had meant interrogators to use force, why had He given them modern drugs and so many effective methods of hypnosis?

Interrogation was just a matter of asking the right questions in the right way. It had always been his experience, that if you used the right words, that in general, people would be happy to tell you what they knew. All you had to do was make sure that they were relaxed, and to encourage them a little to want to share their knowledge with you. It was so simple really.

And there was no blood involved.

"Hello!" Dr Smiles said warmly, turning to greet the young lady lying flat on the padded couch in the centre of the room. He estimated she was about half his age, about twenty six. She was a little overweight, but underneath her thick glasses, her face was not at all unattractive, and she had wonderful blue eyes which were actually quite pleasant to look at. She looked good in the white hospital smock. Almost virginal. Especially with her childlike, schoolgirl pigtails.

240

Fiona looked up at the man who had just come back in through the door. He was quite old, a full head of white hair, and light blue eyes that twinkled out from a round face with red cheeks.

"If he grew a beard, he would almost look like Santa Claus," Fiona thought to herself. She felt very relaxed.

For the past few hours they had been piping relaxing music into the room. It had started with a string of natural sounds from nature: first there was the sound of a river, then the rain falling in the jungle and bouncing lightly off the leaves in the trees, followed by a lightning storm during a monsoon, with thunder peals and large, heavy raindrops. Afterwards, the soft classical music playing in the room had almost lulled her into sleep. The effect of the music and the sounds of nature had been magical. She couldn't help but be relaxed.

She could guess why the man had come to see her again, but she was almost glad for his company. After he had given her the injection, she had been left in the padded white room all by herself for the past two hours, strapped down to the couch. Just her and her thoughts.

Nice thoughts.

It occurred to her now that perhaps she should be a little more scared, but try as she might she couldn't bring herself to feel anxious. Her heart beat remained a constant sixty beats per minute, and she felt calm.

"How are you?" Dr Smiles asked her. " I'm sorry I'm late coming back…I was just talking to your cousin… Nice girl…*very* helpful…She's sleeping at the moment, so I thought that perhaps now we could have a *little* chat…" He lent forward and tugged the straps binding her to the table.

"I hope these are not too tight…are they *okay*?"

The girl smiled back.

"They're not too tight, but, to tell you the truth, I would prefer if you removed them…" She replied.

"Oh, I'm sorry, but I'm not allowed to do that, …but I'm glad you're being truthful. I so much prefer the truth…don't you?"

The girl smiled and agreed.

"Good…then let's make a start then? As I understand it, you have something that you really want to *tell me*…something very interesting?…"

The Doctor pulled up one of the chairs from the corner of the room and sat down beside her. There was no need to take any notes. He knew they were being recorded by hidden microphones and video cameras.

"Why don't we introduce ourselves to each other properly...I'm Dr Smiles...there, we're almost friends already. What is your name then young lady?"

"Fiona...Fiona Cohen..."

"And where do you work Fiona?"

"At the Washington Post..."

In spite of herself Fiona couldn't stop from wanting to answer the old man's questions. Every time he asked her something, she felt an overwhelming urge, almost a compulsion, to answer him. She couldn't help but like him. She felt drawn to him. His voice was so soft, so friendly. He reminded her of her father. So kind...so patient...

She wanted to tell him everything...

"...And then after you left Kerrin in the pizza restaurant you were walking back to the office to get the parcel, when the policemen picked you up?" Dr Smiles asked, obviously very interested in her story.

"Yes...but they weren't policemen, they were not nice..."

Fiona was proving to be a most helpful subject. Far more helpful than her cousin had been. Unfortunately, from what Dr Smiles had learned from the two ladies, it seemed that they knew far too much. It was unlikely that after the interrogation he would be able to sign the release forms as he had initially hoped for. The risk would be far too great. Meanwhile, until they were sure that no one else was involved and until he heard for certain that they had brought in the last member of the group, he would have to keep them alive.

"Can you tell me where you put the parcel that you just mentioned, Fiona?"

"Yes, I would like to..." She replied, and Fiona proceeded to tell him exactly where it was.

Room 232
Day Twenty-Three
The Easy Motel
Maryland

Kerrin slept only fitfully during the night. He was tired and exhausted, both mentally and physically, but whenever he closed his eyes and started to dream, he had repeated visions of Dana being taken away in the big white van.

He could see her reaching out towards him through two open rear doors, waving and calling after him, begging for him to rescue her. Then David Sonderheim would appear in the van beside her, smile at Kerrin and then close the doors from the inside.

That's when he woke up..., but only to dream the same dream again and again whenever his eyelids closed and sleep overcame him.

He felt lost. He missed her so much. He needed her...and he knew how much fear she must be going through just now. She would be worried sick. If she was still alive...

He dismissed the thought as soon as it entered his mind, jumping from the bed and splashing cold water over his face in the bathroom. He lay on the bed again and tried to relax. He needed to be calm so that he could make plans.

By now they would have discovered that there was no body in the burnt out car, and they would have resumed the hunt for him. He would now be their No.1 priority. And as soon as they had him, it would be all over.

He knew that for as long as he was free, they would not harm Fiona or Dana. Kerrin was no fool. He knew that they would use Dana, and his love for her, as a weapon against him, but as long as they couldn't contact him, they couldn't threaten him. In the meantime they would not harm her. He was sure of that. They would not do anything as long as Kerrin was still free and posed a threat to them.

It would be hard, but he knew that he must make no contact with Dana's captors until he had something to bargain with.

At least as long as he was free, there was hope.

An hour later, as Kerrin lay on the bed staring at the ceiling, the first rays of dawn slowly beginning to creep into the room, two simple words jumped into his mind.

"The parcel!"

Kerrin suddenly remembered the parcel that Fiona had been trying to fetch for him when she was captured.

In that moment, he knew what it was that he had to do.

He had to retrieve the parcel from the Washington Post at all costs.

And he had to get to it before the others did.

Four Hours Later
Washington D.C.

It was a risk, but doing nothing was probably worse. He had no choice. He looked at himself one more time in the mirror. A stranger stared back. There was no way anyone was going to recognize him in his disguise.

Flushing the toilet for effect, he opened the door of the toilet in the pizza restaurant, and walked out past the lunchtime diners. Heartened by the fact that even Luigi, his friend and the owner of the restaurant, still hadn't recognized him in his black beard and wig, he left the restaurant, walked around the corner and down the road to the entrance to the Washington Post.

Approximately six hundred people worked in the big eight-storied office building, and the guards at the security desk at the front of the building had no way of knowing the faces of all the employees. They only ever tried to stop and question those who looked lost, or were obviously somewhere they shouldn't be. When Kerrin walked up to one of the turnstiles, inserted his security identification card, and slid through the barrier as it opened in front of him, no one took any notice or tried to stop him.

Dressed in a big black coat, to complement the beard, hair and glasses, he walked with a slight hunch, so that he appeared a few inches shorter than his true height.

He walked quickly along the marble floored entrance lobby, deciding to take the third elevator, near the back of the hall. He pressed the 'call' button.

It was twelve thirty. Lunch time. Most people on his floor would be out. There should be hardly anybody there.

The elevator doors opened and a few people stepped out, including his friend and boss, Paul. For a second Kerrin was tempted to stop him, but as he brushed past without recognizing Kerrin in his disguise, he thought better of it. He didn't want to draw any unnecessary attention to himself just now.

He rode the empty elevator up to the sixth floor, which gave him the opportunity to take off his disguise and stuff it into the pockets of his coat without drawing funny looks from anyone. The elevator bell 'dinged', and Kerrin stepped out onto his floor.

He glanced about quickly, and was pleased to see only a handful of people dotted around the large open plan office. In twenty minutes time, when people returned from lunch, there would be over one hundred people here, all shouting and screaming at each other, and tapping away on their keyboards, creating the slogans and copy which would fill tomorrow's paper. But for now, there were only thirteen or fourteen.

He walked quickly over to his desk, checking to see if there was anything of interest on it.

Nothing. Just the bills and crap that Fiona had told him about.

He made his way through the rows of desks and computers towards Fiona's desk in the corner at the back of the floor, about thirty yards away from the elevators.

A few people looked up from their desks, waved at him absentmindedly and then got back to their screens. Kerrin waved back.

"Kerrin...is that you?"

A voice behind him caught his attention.

'Oh no, it's Ed Harper!' Kerrin realized with dread. This was the last thing he needed just now.

A good looking young man with yellow braces, and a white shirt and smart yellow tie which had been loosened considerably around his neck, came bounding over to Kerrin.

"Hi there...where have you been? It's good to see...did you see our article? Wow, there's so much going on...and did you see our follow up article yesterday? So what's this big article you're working on now...need any help?"

"Woooaaahh... one question at a time!" Kerrin lifted his hands up in the air. "Why are you so excited?"

"Because you're back! I've got some good stuff for you to look at!"

"I'm sorry, kid...I'm very busy at the moment..." Kerrin tried to break off the assault from the younger generation.

The look of disappointment in the young man's eyes was almost palpable.

"Oh...oh...I'm sorry...I just thought you might want to see what I'd written on the follow up to our utilities story..."

Kerrin didn't want to start. This wasn't the time or the place, but he couldn't hold back any longer.

"What do you mean 'ours'? And come to think of it, what the hell happened to my name on the first article you wrote? That was my material..."

"Oh no...sorry...shit, that was a mistake...no, please, don't be mad...that was a mistake...look, I can show you the original article... it's got your name on it...honestly... some fool in typesetting knocked it off because it screwed up the layout...The first I heard about it was after they'd gone to print...I was out for a couple of days, and didn't get a chance to check it beforehand...! Anyway, I made up for it yesterday, look, see, here's yesterday's story, and look, I did put your name on it!"

As he was speaking Kerrin had reluctantly followed Ed back to his desk, where he had swooped up a copy of yesterday's paper and was now thrusting it out towards him. Sure enough, there was the article that Fiona had mentioned yesterday at lunch, the photograph of Nigel Small taking up the top left hand corner of the page, with the story spread over both page four and five. And there was his name right alongside Ed's.

"...But I had nothing to do with this story...it was all yours..." Kerrin stumbled.

"...What do you mean...I thought we were working on this as a team... Paul said that you would be my mentor, and that..."

Kerrin was getting a bad feeling. The man in front of him was little more than a kid in big shoes. An amazingly talented kid, but someone who was obviously looking up to Kerrin as a role model, someone he was trying to emulate, someone whom he was trying to please and win respect from. Kerrin had got it completely wrong. The kid wasn't trying to beat Kerrin: he was just trying to copy him!

"Hey, I'm sorry. I've just been so involved in something else...sorry, kid...Hey, this is great! It's great work...really good stuff!"

The young man's face beamed. The sparkle returned to his eye and he went bright red.

Kerrin was going to kill Paul. He hadn't mentioned anything to him about becoming Ed's mentor. Now it made sense. The whole time Paul had been trying to wind him up as part of yet another one of his silly pranks, trying to make him jealous of the young man...And he had succeeded. The bastard.

"Look, this is the other stuff I'm working on...what do you think?"

He reached onto his desk to get something else to show him, but Kerrin reached forward and touched him lightly on the shoulder.

"Listen, Ed...it's nothing personal, but I haven't got time for this right just now. I have to get something from the Wunderkind's desk...something important...I only have a few minutes...perhaps later, okay?"

Ed looked up from his desk at Kerrin, not knowing for a few seconds how to react.

Kerrin smiled at him. Ed smiled back.

Crossing the office, Kerrin found Fiona's desk in the corner, and ignoring the piles of unopened mail on top, he pulled at the large drawers on the side cabinet. They didn't open. He tried them all. They were locked.

"Kerrin...hey, I think you should see this, something's happening outside!"

Kerrin looked up.

Just then the elevator on the left hand side of the floor 'pinged' and the doors opened, people spilling out and beginning to return to their desks after lunch. Ed was at the other end of the office, looking out of the window and staring at the street below.

"What is it?" he shouted back.

"Come see!" Ed replied.

Kerrin ran back across the room, skirting around the desks, and narrowly avoiding someone who just stepped out of one of the glass-partitioned offices. Coming up level with Ed, he put one hand on the young man's shoulder and the other on the edge of the glass window. In the street six levels below, four large black Mercedes had swept up to the front of the building and parked hastily in front of the entrance, partially blocking off the road and causing havoc with the traffic. The inside lanes heading past the entrance to The Post were completely blocked, and the cars were already starting to back up and come to a halt. People were blaring their horns and stepping out of their cars, shouting at the car drivers in front, who in turn were shouting abuse at the men in black suits who were jumping out of the Mercedes and running in through the doors of the Washington Post.

It didn't take a genius to work out that trouble was heading his way. They were either after him, or the parcel. Since they didn't know he was there, it had to be the parcel.

Kerrin ran back to Fiona's desk, tugging at the drawers, trying to force it open.

The keys. Where did Fiona keep her keys?

Time was running out. Kerrin knew that any second now, a horde of big, ugly, powerful men in black suits were going to burst through the elevator doors and surround him with an arsenal of firepower even Superman couldn't escape from.

In frustration he grabbed hold of the edge of the desk and using all his might, lifted it up, forcing the desk onto its side, with Fiona's computer and monitor crashing to the floor in a shower of sparks. People all around him turned to stare, and a few of them started moving towards him.

"Kerrin...what the fuck are you doing?" Philip O'Hara, one of the sports editors shouted at him.

"Do you know the police are looking for you?...I saw it on CNN yesterday... Should you really even be here?"

Kerrin ignored him. He started to kick the bottom of the drawer, aiming his blows at the join in the corner. It moved a little but not much. Kerrin looked around him for something heavier, then seeing a large red fire extinguisher, picked it up and started swinging it at the base of the drawer. On the third swing the panel buckled, and on the fourth try it jumped forward and bent inward.

Kerrin reached down and managed to get his hands around the edge of the panel, and by jerking it violently back and forward, he managed to push it into the drawer space behind and rotate it at an angle so that he could pull it backwards and slip it out through the base.

He reached inside and pulled out the contents of the drawer, spilling it all over the floor, grabbing the edge of a large brown parcel and turning it over in his hand. On the back of it, in blue ink, was the name of the sender: Martin Nicolson.

He had found it.

By this time, a crowd of his colleagues had gathered around the spectacle, wondering what the hell was going on and if Kerrin had gone mad.

Suddenly the elevator behind them 'pinged', and the doors slid open, revealing seven burly, black suited men. Sizing up the situation immediately, the men jumped out and started heading towards the group hovering around Kerrin.

Kerrin's eyes darted around the office. He had to escape...he couldn't let himself be caught...

The way to the elevator was blocked. He was trapped. Like a rabbit stuck in the lights of a car's headlights, Kerrin panicked but failed to move…where should he go?

"Kerrin,…the fire escape!"

It was the voice of Ed Harper.

"Behind you…the storeroom…go, NOW! "

Kerrin looked up and saw the men running towards him, jumping over the desks, vaulting over chairs and knocking over and pushing aside anyone that got in their way.

A couple of the men were only a few feet away now. Kerrin lunged at Philip O'Hara, pushing him back into the crowd. O'Hara fell backwards, falling heavily against the oncoming attackers.

In the same movement Kerrin rebounded off O'Hara's chest and dived towards the storeroom behind him. Flinging the parcel on to the storeroom floor, he turned and swung the door shut, slamming it closed in the face of one of his pursuers just as he lunged towards him. Swinging his hand downwards, Kerrin pushed in the button in the centre of the door handle, locking the door and making it impossible for anyone outside to open it without breaking it down.

He looked around him quickly. He was surrounded by tall green metal frames forming open shelves, containing boxes full of stationery supplies and various files and back copies of the newspapers from past years. Grabbing the edge of one of the shelves, Kerrin pulled hard, managing to topple the metal frame forward slightly. He readjusted his grip and pulled again, springing back just as the shelves came crashing down in front of the door, blocking the way and making it impossible for anyone to swing the door inwards.

Ignoring the loud pounding on the doors, Kerrin picked up the parcel and ran to the back of the storeroom. Flicking the latch on the window and sliding the lower half of the frosted window upwards, he climbed through onto the fire escape beyond.

It was one of the old fashioned types that can still be found on the back of most American buildings, metal cages with stairs or ladders that slid down to the level below.

Kerrin ran down four flights of the stairs, to the second floor. His heart pounding in his chest, he stopped in front of the window leading from the building onto the fire escape and hit the lower half of it hard with the flat edge of Martin's parcel.

The glass shattered and fell in large splinters inwards into the building behind. Ignoring the flashing burglar alarm, Kerrin reached inside and flicked the catch, so that he could open the window properly and then climb in. Once inside, he found himself inside a ladies toilet. A woman came out of one of the cubicles and screamed.

Kerrin followed her out of the toilet, pushing her aside as he came out onto the floor beyond. Most of the people who worked on the paper had now returned from lunch, and there were probably about eighty people on the floor in front of him, the majority of whom worked in the Sales and Marketing group of the newspaper.

Looking rapidly around the walls, he quickly located what he was looking for, and ran over to it.

Picking up a paper weight from a nearby desk and ignoring the protests of the proud lady owner who shouted something at him, Kerrin swung it at the panel on the wall, smashing the glass and quickly pressing the Fire Alarm button inside.

Immediately the building was filled with the wail of fire alarms, and people started jumping up from their desks in consternation.

"FIRE! FIRE!...EVERYONE OUT! NOW! FIRE! HURRY! IT'S A BOMB! ..."

Kerrin shouted as loud as he could, running towards the stairs as he went. By the time he had made his way across the office to the top of the stairwell, he was caught up in a ground swell of people all panicking and trying to get out of the office as fast as possible.

Within seconds the fire exits were swarming with people, as six hundred employees all tried to leave the building at the same time. The Fire Marshals on each floor started shouting and begging for calm, doing their best to bring some order to the fleeing crowds.

As Kerrin joined the throng and made his way down the stairs, surrounded by hundreds of his work colleagues, he reached into his pockets and pulled out his wig, glasses and false beard.

By the time he made it to the ground floor and had been swept out with the masses onto the road in front of the building, Kerrin had disappeared again.

He had blended in with the others, one unknown face amongst six hundred.

The men in black suits stood on the roofs of their Mercedes, trying to spot Kerrin's face amongst the crowd as they surged past them on to the sidewalks around the building.

Yet, even if they had been able to spot him through his disguise, it would have been impossible for them to single him out from the crowd and grab him.

They had lost him. Once again Kerrin Graham had got away.

And now he had the parcel.

CHAPTER 37
Day Twenty-Four
Rohloff Tower
New York

The helicopter took off from the top of the Rohloff Tower, having disgorged the last-but-one of the Executive Officers of the Board of the Chymera Corporation.

They had been arriving all morning, either by executive limousine into the secure private car-park underneath the Tower, and catching the express elevator to the seventy eighth floor, or by air across the throbbing metropolis of New York, landing on the helipad and catching the elevator down the top three levels to join their companions below.

It was already 10 a.m. and as Rupert Rohloff and Buz Trueman greeted their colleagues, they ushered them politely into the large boardroom and encouraged them to take their seats. As they prepared for the start of the meeting, the last helicopter arrived on the helipad above, and five minutes later, the CEO and President of the Chymera Corporation walked into the boardroom to a rapturous standing ovation.

President Kendrick Hart of the United States was a tall man, and dominated the room from the moment he walked through the door. Just turned fifty-five years of age, his body was firm, his hand-shake strong, and the sparkle in his eye as charming and charismatic now as it was thirty years before. The only real significant sign of ageing was the bald dome which capped his skull, separating the otherwise healthy brown hair growing on either side of his head. His shoulders were broad, and the shirt he wore under his jacket was large enough to be comfortable, but tight enough to show off the powerful muscular frame beneath. The effect was exactly what his PR men wanted. Kendrick Hart was a powerful man, and every inch of his body exuded that power. He was in control and everyone else knew it.

"Welcome everyone. Please sit...I trust that Rupert and Buz have been making you all comfortable?" the President greeted them once the applause had subsided, waving his hands at their chairs and encouraging them to once again take their seats.

Kendrick Hart looked around the faces of those gathered around the long polished mahogany table that dominated the Executive Board Room. The fifty-two men and women before him were without doubt the most powerful people in the United States of America, and at the last audit, collectively they either owned or represented sixty-five percent of the financial assets in the United States. Like himself, over the years, each of them had been personally selected and invited to join the Corporation, based either upon the assets and wealth at their personal disposal, or because of the enormous economic, technological and industrial power they individually oversaw and controlled. Directly, or indirectly, the assembled board controlled over seventy percent of the working population of America.

As the C.E.O. of the Chymera Corporation looked around his assembled colleagues, he recognized them all individually, smiling or winking at some, nodding his head at others. The list of those assembled in the room was truly impressive: sitting before him were the owners of the largest pharmaceutical companies; the majority shareholders and C.E.O.s of the major Utilities companies controlling most of America's water, gas and oil; two heads of the largest communications companies, who between them owned most of the major TV, Cable and Radio networks in America; heads of the three largest banks; and owners or majority shareholders of motor companies, armaments, telecommunications, food, biology and chemical giants, newspapers and the media, banking and insurance. The list went on.

Kendrick Hart had known most of them personally for years.

Since their last meeting, a few new Board members had been selected and appointed, and for those fresh faces, this would be the first full Board Meeting they had attended. They were the successors of those who had died or had stepped down due to ill health, those for whom Item 12 on the Agenda today, the Orlando Treatment, had come too late. Kendrick had read and scrutinized the new members' files many times over, and had met privately with all of them on more than one occasion. As C.E.O. of the Chymera Corporation, it was Kendrick that had granted the final approval to their appointment.

Each of the Board members was worthy of the accolade which had been extended to them. They were the best in America. Forget the American Government, the Senate and the House of Representatives. Nowadays they were just figureheads, a PR exercise that appeased the people.

It was the Chymera Corporation that really governed the United States of America. In this room, the decisions that this select group of people made whenever they sat in session together, controlled the lives and future of the whole country. They were the real elected representatives of the country, elected by virtue of the power they yielded and the fact that it was they who truly owned the country; the citizens of the United States were no more than worker ants who burrowed and toiled at the coal-face under their guidance and their leadership.

Yet there was not one amongst them that did not understand and respect the position or responsibility that was theirs. The burden they carried was a heavy one, and none of them did so lightly. For to underestimate the power they wielded was a weakness. A weakness that they could not afford.

Each of them knew and understood the importance of their contribution to the group, and no one had ever failed to deliver on a promise they had made to the Board.

They ruled their land in private, an organization that had existed since before the Second World War, which had grown in power from year to year through its investments, and from the careful planning and execution of its decisions.

There were few outside of the Corporation that had ever heard of them. They were a jealous organization, ruthlessly protecting their identity, their purpose and their vision, keeping their organization hidden from all those who would seek to discover them.

Together they formed the purest of organisms. They existed for one reason only.

Power.

And they exercised that power in the pursuit of a single goal: to make the United States of America the most powerful and wealthy nation on the planet.

"Okay, to business."

Kendrick Hart sat down almost theatrically in his seat, turning his attention from his fellow board members to the documents lying in front of him. Around the table the delegates followed his lead and picked up the special portfolio that been meticulously prepared for each of them. It contained an agenda, the minutes of the last meeting and numerous reports which would assist in the decisions that had to be made that day.

As they each studied the agenda from their pack, Buz pressed a button on the control panel beside his seat, and the doors of the meeting room closed electronically. With a loud 'clunk' large metal bolts slid out from the centre of the doors into special grooves bored into the surrounding metal frames, locking the doors firmly in place. Across the windows, thin tinted glass panels containing an invisible micromesh metal gauze slid up from the lower wall; although the occupants of the meeting room could still see out, no one outside would be able to see in. Either visually, or electronically.

As part of the latest security technology, the micromesh in the windows extended throughout the walls surrounding the meeting room, wrapping the occupants in a glorified Faraday cage which, like the system deployed in

David Sonderheim's office in Purlington Bay, prevented any form of covert electronic surveillance from being able to penetrate the room.

Security officers expert in the art of electronic surveillance sat in a room close to the boardroom, continuously monitoring the airwaves for indications of any attempt to eavesdrop upon the goings-on within the meeting room, and using the latest multi-frequency filtering loops, they would be able to identify and nullify any intrusive signals, simultaneously blocking and jamming them by re-transmitting a junk signal back to the source.

Inside, electronic sensors spaced throughout the room automatically detected any form of electronic transmitting or recording devices, preventing anyone from recording anything that took place within the boardroom. In the Chymera Corporation, security was a prime concern, and nothing was left to chance.

Buz pressed another button on his panel, and the wall at the end of the office behind Kendrick slid backwards, and a large plasma screen slid down from the ceiling. The lights in the room dimmed and a bright colorful map of the Middle East appeared on the overhead screen.

"Ladies and Gentlemen, we have a busy agenda ahead of us. Items One to Three this morning are issues that demand our immediate attention. As you know, recent events in Saudi Arabia have caused a significant rise in the price of crude, and a significant drop in the value of gold. Our oil production in Kuwait has been severely affected, and the situation looks as if it's not likely to rectify itself in the near future. The question of our interests, and American interests in the Middle East..." Kendrick Hart began the business of the day, moving from one item to another.

"And now, Item Four, and a report from Mr Small on the new hydro-electric dam that he is suggesting we build in Colorado...", which was swiftly followed by a report suggesting that the Corporation acquire more stock in Microsoft, and then another proposing the acquisition of a new Satellite Broadcasting company that had just announced a joint venture with Europe's largest news and media empire.

And so it went on. Hour after hour. Topic after topic. Decision after decision.

At 2 p.m. the agenda allowed them time for lunch, and Buz pressed one of the little buttons on his magic panel. There was a buzzing sound and the bolts clicked loudly, before sliding back into the centre of the doors, which opened automatically to let them outside.

In the reception area beside the boardroom, a buffet had been laid on. The lunch was small, so as not to encourage drowsiness when they returned to the meeting, and alcohol was strictly forbidden. Fruit juices, coffee and water were the order of the day.

At 2.30 p.m. sharp they filed back into the boardroom, and excitedly awaited the next item on the agenda. Item Twelve was to be a report on the Phase Two trials of the Orlando Treatment, followed by a decision on whether or not to proceed to the next stage and to the wider and long hoped for Phase Three trials.

Without further encouragement, the assembled group took their places and turned their attention to their chairman.

Kendrick turned to Buz and nodded, and the doors closed automatically.

Kendrick slowly stood up and faced the Board. He stood there silent before the group.

They looked back at him expectantly.

Kendrick had long ago learned to use the power of silence to emphasize and underline the importance of something just about to be said. For a few moments he said nothing.

The expectation that hung in the air was so heavy that Kendrick could almost reach out and touch it.

It was time.

"Gentlemen," and he turned and smiled at a few of the more attractive members of the board, "...and of course, ladies...now we come to what I am sure we all agree is perhaps the most interesting item on the agenda." He paused. There was a round of nodding heads around the table, and several people nervously adjusted the position of their portfolios on the table before them.

"At this point I would like to invite Rupert to report to us on the progress of the Orlando Project. After all, Orlando was his idea..."

Kendrick clapped his hands together a few times and Rupert Rohloff stepped to the front of the room. He spoke slowly and clearly, his voice authoritative and powerful, his German accent barely discernible.

"A number of years ago, the Chymera Corporation became aware of the work of the Gen8tyx Company, a fledging biotech and genetics company, with a revolutionary entrepreneurial spirit and a new approach to some of the major problems facing our increasingly ageing society. Over the years we have kept a keen eye on their progress, and have seen them turn into a billion-dollar company with some truly market-leading products. However, as you will all remember, a few years ago when we learned of their most recent field of research, we realized we were shortly to be faced with some interesting questions. Putting aside the profit motive, we knew we would soon have to decide whether or not we could allow their research to continue unchecked. Then, and I am sure you will remember as I do, Harry West from Sabre Genetics addressed the board and gave us a most memorable presentation." Rupert waved his hand at Harry who was sitting towards the back of the room. Harry turned slightly red and nodded his head in response to the praise.

"As a result of Harry's recommendation, the Board recognized that this research did indeed pose a threat to society. But we also realized that it simultaneously presented us with a golden opportunity which we could not pass over... the opportunity to re-engineer and correct the decay that affects all our bodies as we live our lives from year to year, ...the opportunity to halt and prevent the onset of old age. No, not just an opportunity,...an obligation! An obligation to build a society where the leaders of mankind would be able to extend their active life spans, giving them the opportunity to retain the precious experience that they had built up over the decades of their existence and to exercise that experience for longer, to the benefit of a much needing society..."

"Gone will be the days when the wisest men in the world will forget the wisdom they have learned, and when the greatest intellects in our society will be reduced to cabbages as senility sets in and robs them of everything that makes them who they are..."

He paused in mid-sentence, his words hanging in the air...

"I'm sorry, I do not intend to redo the speech that Harry gave us last year. You have all read the files...You all know the value of the Orlando Treatment, and its potential..." Rupert paused.

"...At a previous board meeting we made the decision to acquire the Gen8tyx Company, based in Orlando, Florida. This has been done. The company has now completed the move to its new, more secure headquarters in Purlington Bay, California and the second phase of the trials of their revolutionary treatment has just been completed. In a few moments I will invite David Sonderheim, the CEO of Gen8tyx to come and present their findings to us. Before I do so however, I wish to impart to you the importance of this research. At the end of the meeting I will ask for a vote. I will ask the Board for its support in agreeing to fund Phase Three of the project."

There was absolute silence in the room. The average age of the assembled group was sixty three years old. The eldest person in the room was seventy one. There was not one person on the board that had not privately already signed up for the Phase Three Trials.

Rupert Rohloff spoke again.

"First of all, you may have noticed two empty places at the table. As many of you know, Trevor Simons has been fighting advanced Leukemia for several months now. Unable to find a suitable bone marrow donor, it was estimated that he only had a few weeks to live. The other seat belongs to Colonel Packard. I'm afraid that due to their deteriorating medical conditions both have had to seek urgent medical care...and could not make the meeting as we expected."

There was a hasty flurry of glances and murmurings around the table. Many of the Board members looked in sympathy at the two empty seats.

"At this point I would like to hand over to the Chief Executive Officer of the Gen8tyx Company...Ladies and gentlemen, please welcome David Sonderheim..." Rupert stepped backwards towards the wall and swung out his arm towards the door, which opened automatically under Buz's command.

David Sonderheim walked through, a little surprised by the applause and the warm reception he was receiving. He walked with a slight limp, but the wounds in his foot were healing at an incredible rate and in the excitement of the day it was easy to forget the pain.

He stepped up to the front of the table, and behind him a large logo of the Gen8tyx Company appeared on the plasma screen.

"Thank you. I'm truly honored to be given the opportunity to talk to you all today about our most recent work...But before I begin...I think we should welcome two more of our friends who have been sitting outside waiting patiently to join us..."

All eyes turned to the door. No one else had been expected. There were few people on the planet who knew of the existence of the Chymera Corporation, let alone had seen them. The Board Members guarded their identities with the tightest of security...A number of the Board members shifted uncomfortably in their seats, and several rose as if to make a protest. Guests were not only an absolute breach of protocol, they were a threat...

A man came through the door into the room, walked around the table and sat down in one of the empty seats. There was a chorus of gasps of surprise and disbelief from all those present.

"What's this...some sort of trick? Who are you? What's going on?" A man at the back of the room asked loudly. He was the owner of one of the largest multi-media broadcasting corporations in the world, and did not appreciate surprises.

"It can't be...surely not..." one of the ladies gasped, standing up from her chair and moving towards the intruder to get a closer look.

Just then, the second person walked through the open door. The Board members turned around, and this time their surprise was a wave which swept over them all. One by one they stood up from their seats, and gasped aloud. Some clapped their hands involuntarily, others smiled and laughed. There was no mistaking the second person who had walked into the room. One of the most powerful of the board members, and perhaps the longest serving of them all.

And yet...it was impossible...

Colonel Packard had just walked into the room unaided.

No wheelchair.

No crutches.

No assistance whatsoever.

But that was not all.

As Colonel Packard walked around the table and took his seat beside Trevor Simons, the assembled board members stared in disbelief at the youthful men who had taken the seats previously occupied by men at least twenty years older.

"You...you're so young..." Maria Wiesenbaum, owner of the Wiesenbaum Bank and Chairwoman of Wiesenbaum Industries, exclaimed. Unable to stop herself, she walked around the table to Trevor and stroked the soft skin on his face.

There were tears running down her cheeks.

CHAPTER 38
Rohloff Tower
New York

Kendrick Hart and Rupert Rohloff looked around the room at the reactions of those assembled before them. They were pleased by what they saw. Rupert turned to Sonderheim and nodded. David recognized his cue.

"Ladies and gentlemen..." he paused for a few moments to allow everyone time to return to their seats and compose themselves. As he began to talk the air was filled with excitement, every eye turned towards him, the most powerful men and women in America putty in his hands.

"Ladies and gentlemen, as legend would have it, thousands of years ago in Greece, the daughters of the god Zeus and his wife Themis were given an extraordinary task. Perhaps you have heard of them? We often refer to them as the three Fates, three beautiful daughters...Atropos, Clotho and Lachesis, who according to mythology oversaw the fates of us lesser mortals. Each of the Fates had a special job. Atropos was given the task of cutting the thread or web of life. Her sister Clotho was given the task of spinning the thread of life, and it was Lachesis who measured the length of each thread, the length of which determined a person's lifespan. It would appear that of the three, Lachesis was the one who had most power over us mortals, for it was she who determined how long our lives would be..."

"...An interesting story, I think you will agree. But one to which we can all identify. As each of us nears the end of the thread of life that has been allotted to us, we all begin to wonder at the course our lives have taken, at the web of mortal experiences we have built around us, and at the strength of the threads that bind us to our lives. And while we wonder at all of this, we see for the first time how painfully thin each of these threads really are...As we stare our own mortality in the face, how many of us would be prepared to give everything we had to extend or thicken the thread of our life...how many would be prepared to embrace Lachesis and offer her any price that she demanded in order to extend our lifespan."

"...And if Lachesis was to hear your plea, and she were to turn to you and offer you a life extension, a new 'thread' to add to your existing life span...what price would she demand? This price which each of you would gratefully pay in order to live longer, fitter, and healthier?"

David Sonderheim was in his element. This was the moment he had looked forward to for the last three years.

As he walked from one side of the table to the other, gesturing slowly with his hands as he spoke, the eyes of the Board followed, glued to him, unable to look away.

"The natural barrier which seems to be the upper end of the human life span is 120 years of age. Yet, the average life span in the world today is only about 77 years of age...if we are lucky we, ...you and I... can hope to live to between 75 and 80! But the older we get, the greater the chance we have of being struck down by neurodegenerative diseases such as Parkinson's and Alzheimer's. And if we survive over 85 years of age? Did you know, that over the age of 85 Parkinson's affects about ten percent of all people, and Alzheimer's over fifty percent?..."

"What use is extending the span of our lives, if the life extension we are granted is only a ticket to senility and a life without meaning and purpose, a life without memory. That is no life at all..."

"At the Gen8tyx Company we have never seen the sense in extending our life spans unless we can do so meaningfully. When I started the company eight years ago, it was my dream to find a cure for the most common neurodegenerative diseases which rid us of the quality of our lives as we grow older."

"Our research has not been directed at increasing our life spans, but rather to extending the effective life spans within our given lives, by extending the health span each individual enjoys. To each person I wanted to add years of health, productivity and vigor, not years of decline..."

"Only later, after we have solved the problems we face within our existing life spans, will we allow ourselves to dream of actually pushing back the barrier which limits the number of years a human may live on this earth. Perhaps, if time permits, I will address this question again later..." As he spoke, Sonderheim lifted up a finger in the air, and raised his eyebrows questioningly.

The audience were puppets on the end of his string. They danced before him, following the top of his fingertip.

Now, now..Not later!...tell us now...

"For the first few years we looked at the processes which caused Parkinson's and Alzheimer's. The motive behind this, you will be pleased to here, was not entirely philanthropic. With more and more people living longer, the number of people being affected by these conditions is steadily increasing...If we could come up with a treatment, an effective treatment, we could charge almost anything we wanted for it…imagine…fifty percent of all 85 year olds…and also a significant percentage of all those younger than that…the potential market is vast! And growing every day…"

He could see them all licking their lips. They could taste the money.

"As you all know, we have already released many products into the market place which effectively treat the symptoms, and keep the condition at bay…and hence our market capitalization has shot to over $1.6 billion dollars…"

"…But over the past two years we have made great strides…vast leaps over our competitors…we've begun to penetrate the veil which has shrouded the mystery of how and why these diseases begin to develop in the first place …what actually causes them…and once we were able to discover that, we were able to start thinking about how to prevent them in the first place…"

A big burly businessman in the back row shifted uneasily in his seat. He was Lars Pederson, CEO and majority shareholder of one of America's largest insurance conglomerates. He owned a third of all the major insurance companies in the US.

"Of course, there is also a great incentive to do this from a socio-economic perspective…remember that we are not talking about extending people's lives…we are talking about eliminating or reducing the decrepitude that eats away at our society from within. People will still die when they get old, but during the latter part of their lives they will be vital and productive…our new discoveries will wipe out the astronomic medical costs incurred by people who 'exist' as sickly, pathetic, shadows of their former selves, a burden to society. A burden that costs insurance companies billions every year…"

Lars smiled, and settled back into his seat, comfortable once again.

"Yes… ladies and gentlemen, we have made many amazing discoveries! While we were looking at the causes of degenerative diseases we stumbled across many wondrous things…*wondrous* things…and in our awe we looked hard at what we saw. Yes, it is true that at Gen8tyx, we have found out many of nature's secrets…But what is a secret if everyone is told of it…?"

David stopped in his tracks. He looked out of the window, gazing out towards the Statue of Liberty, his mouth half-open. To those in the meeting room, it appeared as if he were trying to make a decision, trying to decide if he should tell them something…whether or not he should share with them the secrets he had discovered…

Share with us…you must…you have to…we own you…the secret is ours…tell us…tell us… please, tell us!

As if he had come to a decision, David walked back to the centre of the room, and turned once more to face his audience.

"How many of you have ever heard of mitochondria?"

Like two school children the heads of Philadelphia Pharma and Sabre Genetics both put up their hands, then realizing what they were doing, immediately came to their senses and pulled them down again, but not before they had exchanged glances with each other and turned bright red with embarrassment.

"A few...well, if I may, I would like you to meet a little friend of mine. He is the basis of what I will later introduce to you as the Orlando Treatment..." David turned to the screen and pointed the portable mouse at it. The Gen8tyx logo disappeared and was replaced by an image of a human cell.

"...The human cell is made up of many smaller parts, called 'organelles'...but there is one type of organelle in particular which concerns us, which we call mitochondria...this is a picture of it..."

The image on the screen changed, and was replaced by a picture that looked rather like a balloon with a slice of walnut inside it.

"These mitochondria are tiny...there can be several thousand mitochondria in any one cell...the mitochondria have quite simple structures...there is an outer membrane and an inner membrane. The outer membrane covers the mitochondria and the inner membrane wraps over itself many times...it's like a table cloth that is folded over and over ...the more folds you get in, the more surface area of the table cloth that you can fit into the cell. Which is important, because it's across the surface area of the inner membrane where the chemical reactions take place within the mitochondria...and these chemical reactions are vital to us all. You see, it is these chemical reactions that give us energy, that give us our life. The larger the surface area covering each mitochondrion...the more energy it can produce for us..."

David stopped for a second. It was very important not to lose his audience.

"Let's step back a second...So when I say that the mitochondria give us our energy...what do I mean? Let me ask you all a second question...Who has heard of respiration?"

Everyone put their hands up.

Kendrick Hart laughed. David Sonderheim had reduced the most powerful people in America to a room full of children.

"Good...for it is respiration that keeps us alive...we breathe, we live...we don't breathe, we die. But what does that really mean...? "

"When we breathe...air enters our lungs, and respiration floods our bodies with oxygen. Without oxygen we die. Yet there is another thing that we need in order to survive. Yes...that's right...food!...without food we die too!"

"I suppose a better explanation, a more correct explanation, would be to say that respiration is the process by which organisms within our cells combine the food we eat with the oxygen we breathe, in such a way as to extract chemical energy which fuels life-sustaining processes within our body…"

"…So for those of you who have ever wondered what happens to the food we eat, this is it. Nature has given the mitochondria the task of converting the foodstuffs we eat into the energy which keeps us alive. They do this by extracting energy from the food and turning it into an energy rich compound called *ATP* or *Adenosine Triphosphate*…Now, looking back to the picture of the mitochondria on the plasma screen again, as I just mentioned, try to imagine that the surface of the inner membrane of the mitochondrion cell is like a big table cloth and that the larger the surface area of the inner membrane of the mitochondrion then the more foodstuffs you are able to put on that table cloth,…or in other words, the larger the table cloth, the more food that can be digested and the more energy each cell can produce…"

There was a round of smiles. They all understood that.

So far, so good.

"Great…I think we can all see that so long as we have food, oxygen and zillions of mitochondria dotted around our bodies, we can have lots of ATP, lots of energy, and lots of healthy cells…"

It was a statement framed as a question, and everyone nodded in response.

"…So long as we have lots of healthy mitochondria, we're all fine. That's what we call being young…it's what we define as 'youth'."

"So what happens as the mitochondria stop making so much ATP? I'll hazard a guess that you're all thinking the same thing as I am…and you'd be correct!…When the mitochondria stop making ATP, we run out of energy…"

"And without enough energy, our cells can't function properly, or they starve and die. And when cells die, in general that's not good for us…"

A few people laughed.

"When we're young that's not so much of a problem…when we are growing up there are plenty of cells about which are all full of mitochondria,…plenty of ATP…plenty of energy…and if a cell dies, another living cell just divides, turns into two cells, then four, then eight…you get the picture…We don't miss the dying cells so much because more are always being produced to replace them. But as we grow older, we start to lose our mitochondria and we can't create new cells fast enough to replace the ones that have died."

"So, without sufficient mitochondria around to produce enough ATP, we start to die. And that is what we call growing old. Our physical strength, our stamina, even our consciousness…it all depends upon there being enough of the ATP around to keep us going. Even subtle deficits in the ATP can cause us to feel weak, or tired, or unable to think…"

"Quite significantly, we also discovered that when cells do not receive enough ATP from their mitochondria, they do not function optimally. We noticed that as we get older, a significant proportion of mitochondria start to function wrongly. So we started to ask questions like, 'Why do the mitochondria die?' and 'when the mitochondria do malfunction, what effect does it have on the rest of the body? ' These questions were fundamental to the discoveries we went on to make..."

Day Twenty-Four
Burgess Hill
Pennsylvania

It was a nice hotel. Quiet. Small. And in the middle of nowhere. Exactly what Kerrin had been looking for.

After escaping the mayhem at The Post, Kerrin had made his way to the nearest train station and caught the first commuter train heading north. He didn't care where it was going, so long as it was as far away from the city as possible. Preferably a small town in the country where people probably didn't watch the news so much, and he was unlikely to be recognized from the news bulletins.

He rode the train for an hour and a half, until he got to the last station, a small town out in the sticks, one main road, a few shops, and a lot of nothing. Exactly what he was looking for. Outside the train station he had found a taxi and asked the driver to take him to a good hotel, somewhere where he could take a break from the city.

The taxi-driver, an ex-New Yorker, knew exactly where to go.

"My sister-in-law runs a lovely place not far from here. It's quiet...but very plush...and surrounded by fields, and nature. It's very restful, if you like that sort of stuff..." He said, looking over his shoulder at Kerrin as he drove and not paying enough attention to the road ahead.

Kerrin checked in, took a room at the back of the hotel, and showered. Only after he was refreshed did he sit down on the bed with the parcel in front of him. He sat staring at it for ages, until the exhaustion overtook him and he fell into a deep sleep.

When the late morning light woke him the next day, the parcel was still where he had left it.

He looked at it nervously, scared to pick it up and open it.

It didn't look much, but everything rested on the brown parcel and its contents. The lives of Dana, Fiona and himself. What would he do if he opened it, and found that it contained nothing important?

He had slept fitfully for over ten hours, but Kerrin was still tired: his hands were shaking, and one of his eyelids had started to twitch uncontrollably, and for a second he worried that he was on the verge of some sort of breakdown. His stomach was a tight knot, and he couldn't think clearly.

He looked in the mirror on the wall in his room. His face was tired and drawn. The man who looked back at him was desperate. A pathetic figure whom he didn't recognize. Kerrin was fed up of running. He had come to the end of the line. The parcel was his last chance.

Swallowing hard, he picked the parcel up, ripped off the end, and spilled the contents onto the bed in front of him.

Rohloff Tower
New York

Sonderheim coughed.

"Please excuse me..." He leant forward and picked up a glass of water from the table and took a few sips.

"That's better..." he continued. "Now, in trying to understand the ageing process, we began to look more closely at the role of mitochondria, and to understanding the chemical reactions that take place within in the cells..."

"...As we get older, more and more mitochondria are destroyed throughout the daily course of our lives, which leads to an overall drop in energy production. Some parts of the body get weaker, some parts of the body die ...and the body ages..."

"As we saw earlier, it is the mitochondria that produce energy for the cells in the respiration process. In the course of these vigorous chemical reactions, many electrons are observed to 'leak' away from the mitochondrial cell structure. These 'leaking' electrons also interact with the oxygen which is present, to produce imbalanced chemicals which we call superoxide radicals...or 'free radicals'..."

"...'Free radicals' are really best described as molecules that possess one or more unshared available electrons as part of their structural configurations. The unshared electrons in their chemical make-up makes them unstable and highly destructive compounds, which try desperately to find another electron in order to achieve stability."

"In their hunt for electrons, these free radicals act like little bombs, which destroy or damage other cells and molecules. Unfortunately, some of the free radicals which the mitochondria produce actually kill or damage other mitochondria..."

"Now, although in the normal course of respiration, mitochondria do create many free radicals, the situation is made far worse when the mitochondria get damaged...as this causes more and more electrons to leak from the reactions which fuel the respiration process, which in turn leads to an ever increasing number of free radicals being spewed out of the cells into the body. etc, etc. The whole process increases exponentially as we get older."

"...When too many of these free radicals are produced, the normal repair mechanisms of the cells in the body are not able to cope, and are unable to repair all the damage being incurred by the free radicals ...So the cells start to get permanently damaged, or die...or start behaving badly...and when the cells of our body start to behave badly and start reproducing in the wrong way, this could lead to cancer, diabetes, heart disease, Parkinson's, Alzheimer's, etc."

Sonderheim walked around the table speaking slowly as he went. As he paced the room, the eyes of the audience stayed glued to him. They were absorbing every word he said.

"Before I come on to describing the Orlando Treatment...I want to add one more thing...I have mentioned to you that free radicals are produced during the respiration process, when mitochondria react with the oxygen and the foodstuffs we eat...Well, a natural conclusion from this is that the more we eat, the more reactions take place in the respiration process and hence the more free radicals are produced, which as we have seen is bad, bad, bad!"

"In other words, the more we eat...the faster we die...!"

There were a few murmurings around the table, particularly amongst the more overweight of the group.

"In fact, it has been well documented by many independent groups, that if you cut down the calorific intake of many creatures, these creatures live longer. There's no question in fact, that by reducing the amount of food, and hence the number of calories, by 30% to 70% it is possible to extend the life span by up to 40% in a number of different animals or creatures. In the laboratory, we ourselves have shown that by reducing the calorific intake of mice by 40%, they will live almost twice as long as their fatter siblings... Now, that gives us some food for thought...doesn't it?"

There were a few quiet laughs around the table.

Day Twenty-Four
Burgess Hill
Pennsylvania

Kerrin stared at the pile of documents lying on the bed. There were a number of folders, several files in brown dividers, a box of CDs, a single high density DVD, and several USB memory sticks. Kerrin picked up one of the brown folders, flicked through its contents and realized immediately what he had in his possession. The folder contained pages and pages of documents, copies of laboratory tests, reports on the research the group had been conducting, with drawings, schematics, chemical formulae. The works! There were documents

265

on 'therapeutic cloning', folders containing details on the "Treatment of Mitochondrial Dysfunction", another on "The Role of Ziatimine Beta 6 in the Reduction of Oxidative Stress". And more. Much, much more. Report after report, of which he couldn't even understand the titles, let alone the contents.

He didn't know what the reports said, but in a way he didn't need to. It was obvious what Martin had sent him. He had just struck gold. This was exactly what he needed in order to save Dana, Fiona, and himself, and he suddenly felt an immense gratitude to Martin, for helping them from beyond the grave.

Calming himself down, Kerrin searched slowly through the files and the documents, trying to put them in some sort of order. He would need to look carefully at everything, and as best he could, he would have to try and understand the scope of the information he had.

It took him several hours to go through the documentation and the files, and it was late afternoon before he came round to the problem of trying to find out what was on the DVD, CDs and the memory sticks. Perhaps the manager of the hotel would have a laptop he could borrow...

The lobby of the hotel was empty, but the smell of a wood-burning fire drifted gently on the air, wafting its way into the hall from the main part of the hotel.

As Kerrin opened the door to the guest's lounge, a roly-poly lady in her early sixties with white hair and an apron stretched around her large waist looked up from the fire, where she was busy putting a few new logs onto the glowing embers beneath.

"Mr Graham," she said with a warm smile. "How are you? Is your room okay?"

Mrs Doyle was the hotel manager, the sister-in-law of the taxi-driver who had checked him into the hotel the previous day. Unlike the taxi driver whose accent had been one hundred percent New York, Mrs Doyle spoke with a lilting Irish accent. It sounded like she had just arrived off a steamship from Dublin, but Kerrin could guess that she had probably been living in America for years.

"It's excellent, thank you. And I love the view."

Mrs Doyle stood up, putting both hands on her hips and stretching her back up straight.

"Aye, that's a fine view, that is...that's why I bought the hotel in the first place. Fell in love with it straight away I did. Just what I wanted. Glad you like it."

"Mrs Doyle, I was wondering if I could ask for your help?" Kerrin asked politely.

"Certainly my boy, I'll be glad to help out if I can. What can I do for you?" she replied, moving over to an armchair by the fire and resting a hand on the top of it.

"I was wondering if you had a computer in the hotel that I could borrow, maybe a laptop, if you're not using it?"

"So it's a computer you'll be wanting is it? Aye, no problem. My nephew put one in for me last year, but I can't tell you how to work it...I hope you know how to switch it on? ...Good...I don't touch the thing myself...I just let the accountant use it when he comes by every month. He says it's a good one, though...even got a connection to the Wide World Web, or whatever it is you call it!"

"The World Wide Web...Excellent. Thank you very much...and could you maybe tell me where I might be able to make a few photocopies in town?"

"Oh, that I can show you myself. I've got one of them in the office. Couldn't exist without the thing. Everybody always wants me to copy something. I'm always having to send off copies of receipts and invoices...always having to prove everything to them nosy IRS people..."

CHAPTER 39
Rohloff Tower
New York

David Sonderheim stood before them. He could feel the power.

To each and every person in the room he could offer health and long lasting youth. They were the elite of American society, and soon they would be flooding from all over the country to his clinic in Purlington Bay.

His clinic.

Soon they would agree to provide him with the funding for the next phase of his research.

$1 billion dollars.

Enough money to help him smash through the final barriers to understanding why cells die.

Enough money to find the holy grail of genetics.

Enough money to make him a veritable god.

To find the secret of eternal life.

The power to choose who would live life everlasting, and who would die, young and diseased.

His eyes glazed over. He was so close.

"Okay..." David continued. "...So now we know a bit about why the body ages, what can we do to stop it? This is the area a lot of our research has concentrated upon for the past few years. It's an incredibly exciting field of research and every day we come across new things. Every day we push back the frontiers of known science..."

"Our research followed several different paths. First of all it was pretty clear to us all, that the big enemy of our body seems to be the free-radical. In effect, they are nature's terrorists...they go around blowing up our bodies' utilities in a random fashion, hitting us hard and fast, and we never know exactly where they'll attack next..."

"What we needed to do was to find some way of getting rid of them. A way of attacking the free radicals, before they attack us!...Our research led us to two discoveries. First of all we realized that the body has its own inbuilt missiles, a type of enzyme called Superoxide Dismutase or S.O.D. for short. S.O.D. enzymes hunt out the free radicals and destroy them. What we have done is to develop an synthetic enzyme mimetic which mimics the process of this natural enzyme. We inject this into a patient, and the mimetic circulates throughout the body and systematically reduces the number of free radicals in the body. We have also developed a mimetic filtering mechanism using the synthetic enzyme, which enables us to put a patient on dialysis, pass his blood through a special filter, and remove the free radicals directly from his blood."

"...It sounds simple, but let's not underestimate the effect this can have on the body. Without it, as the number of free radicals in the body increases, the cells are put under an increasing stress load just trying to keep track of the cellular damage as it occurs, and then to repair it as fast as possible. We call it oxidative stress. The body wastes a lot of time and energy doing this...Now, if we can subsequently reduce the oxidative stress, even eliminate it, the body can spend this time and energy doing more constructive things, and we should observe the body's natural repair mechanisms kicking in with a powerful rejuvenating effect...resulting in a healing of the damaged tissue caused by ageing... "

"In other words...the combinative effect of healing residual damage and preventing further cellular damage may be to either halt the ageing process or even reverse it... as the old cells are replaced by new fresh ones, an older man may begin to look younger...the years would literally begin to drop off him, and it may be possible for him to regain the physical appearance of himself when he was ten, maybe even twenty years younger...And if we start this process in say, a twenty-three year old female...well, she could potentially remain twenty-three for an indefinite period..."

Suddenly all eyes were on Colonel Packard and Trevor Simons.

"Gentlemen, perhaps you would both like to stand up and take a bow?"

The excitement in the room was electric. Emotions were running high as the two men stood, and theatrically waved their arms in front of themselves, and bowed to the other board members, who burst into spontaneous applause.

Every man and woman in the room was thinking the same thing: "*if it can work for them...it can work for me!* "

Sonderheim let the applause subside and then continued.

"...So you can see that we have made at least one step in the right direction. Another approach is to try and stop the mitochondria being damaged by the free radicals in the first place... Some of our scientists have undertaken some really quite revolutionary work! By reaching deep inside the DNA of the mitochondria, they have found a very exciting way of switching on a natural defense mechanism within the mitochondria themselves. So now, we are able to chemically induce the mitochondria in a patient's body to start defending themselves against any attack from free radicals. The effect of this is two-fold: fewer mitochondria now die, and hence energy levels within the cells and within the body are now maintained at more constant levels...and secondly, because fewer mitochondria are damaged, less of them become 'dysfunctional'...which means we get fewer damaged mitochondria spewing out free radicals as they go haywire..."

"In one stroke we have cut down the number of free radicals being produced, and stopped the mitochondria from dying so fast."

"We were all very proud of what we had achieved so far, but then one day, one of our scientists had another idea...a really clever one..."

"About a year ago, our company decided that instead of just focusing on preventing the mitochondria from dying, we would also look at the mechanism by which they were created in the first place. After all, every time a new cell is created, thousands of new mitochondria are generated inside it..."

"After quite a few false starts, we eventually realized that when a cell divides, a certain chemical button is pushed, which causes the mitochondria to make thousands of copies of themselves, and when the cell splits and divides into two new cells, these new mitochondria are shared between the two new cells which are created..."

"So what we have done is to find out how to chemically trigger the replication process in the cells within our body, which automatically starts reproducing new mitochondria within existing cells so as to replace the mitochondria which have become damaged or are now dead."

"So what does this mean? Well, actually it's quite startling...using this new treatment we are able to reverse the years of damage that have been done to the cells, and are able to restore the energy production levels within them to the same level as they were when we were adolescents..."

He hesitated for a second, the words he had just spoken left hanging in the air, their meaning being soaked up by the eager-eyed disciples before him.

"...Wow...that's a hell of a lot of information to take in all at once.."...he said, stepping forward to the edge of the table, and resting his hands on it, leaning forward and raising his eyebrows. "...Are you all still with me?" David asked.

Yes...yes...we're all still here...tell us more...tell us more...

"Can you manage a little more? There are two more aspects to the Orlando Treatment that I would like to cover briefly with you all!"

Yes...yes...tell us more...

"Good, then unless there any objections, I'll proceed..."

"...This is the unpopular bit, the part of the program that we find we get most resistance from...It's the one part of the program that although we recommend, is not obligatory. We can't force you to do it, but if you're serious about possible life extension or wanting to maximize the years God has given you on this planet, then you'll all be wise to take it seriously..."

"Diet. The simple way to stay young. As I mentioned before, it's already been well-proven that by cutting down on the number of calories you eat, you reduce the amount of oxidative stress you put on your system...Diet, and you will live longer and more effectively..."

"So...if you sign up for the Orlando Treatment, the first thing we'll do is put you on a detox diet, analyze your eating patterns, change the way you think about food, and replace your old diet with a new, nutritional, low calorie diet...which, incidentally, will also increase your energy levels and your libido. Now that can't be bad, can it?"

Smiles all round.

"Fine...and now for the last part of the program..." He turned and walked back to stand beside the screen.

"...When we started looking at Parkinson's disease, some of our scientists turned their attention to a growing area of new scientific interest...cloning. There was a lot of excitement about the possibility of using the latest therapeutic cloning techniques to repair the damage that disease or old age had done to our bodies. What excited our scientists was the possibility that by understanding how cells grew and multiplied within our bodies in the first few days after our parents conceived us in our mother's womb...by understanding how our bodies created our livers, our hearts or our kidneys in the first place...perhaps we would be able to repeat the process, one bit at a time, repairing or replacing parts of our bodies that had become diseased or worn out..."

"...What we realized was that during the growth period, there is a stage in the cell's development when the cell does not yet know exactly what type of cell it is going to become...it looks to the other cells around it for instructions, and it learns from them how it should develop, for example whether it should become a brain cell, or a kidney or a heart muscle cell, etc. ...We call these special cells 'stem cells', and we realized that if we could manufacture them by cloning them in the laboratory, then we could introduce these special stem cells into the damaged parts of a body, where they could become an army of cells that would rebuild the damaged tissue around it, repairing blood cells or bone marrow that wasn't working before...or even replacing the neurons in the brain that have withered away or died..."

Sonderheim walked around the table to where Colonel Packard was sitting.

"I know what I'm talking about may seem all a little far-fetched or difficult to understand, so let me give you a living example of what we have done...Colonel can you please stand for me?"

The Colonel pushed back his chair and stood up.

"Colonel Packard first came to us a few months ago. He arrived at the door of the clinic in a wheelchair...a wheelchair in which he has sat for over thirty years, since a bullet in the Vietnam war damaged his spinal cord. What we did was take some of his cells, clone them, extract the special stem cells that we were looking for and injected them back into his spine around the area of the damage. Because we used cells from his own body, his body's immune system didn't reject them...in fact, they welcomed them. After that we didn't need to do anything else. Colonel Packard's body did the rest. In effect, the other nerve cells in his spine told the new stem cells exactly what type of cells were damaged and needed to be replaced, and the stem cells then started to grow and multiply around the area of damage. Within weeks the damaged nerve tissue had been restored, and Colonel Packard's spine began to function normally. Well, you all saw him walk into the room, unaided...that was no trick...his spinal cord had been rebuilt, and now he can walk again...So you see, the Orlando Treatment does work!"

Sonderheim turned quickly to Trevor Simons.

"When Trevor came to us, he was in the advanced stages of leukemia. To be quite honest, we didn't know if we would be able to treat him. We knew that we may be able to prompt Trevor's cloned stem cells into differentiating themselves into healthy blood cells or healthy bone marrow cells...but we didn't know how effective it would be. Well, now we do!"

Trevor, in a rather uncharacteristic and unexpected show of public emotion, found himself turning to Sonderheim, and offering his hand to the man who had saved him. Sonderheim took it in his own, shaking it proudly, while patting Trevor gently on the shoulder with his other free hand.

Sonderheim walked back to the front of the room and turned to face his rapt audience, smiling at the President of the United States, whom he noticed was now as much in awe of every word that he said as everyone else in the room.

"I have one more example for you..." Sonderheim turned to Buz and nodded.

The plasma screen came alive with the image of Sam Novak, the Texan senator who had consistently beat Trevor at table tennis in Purlington Bay.

"Hi there Sam. How are you feeling today?"

The image on the screen smiled. Sam Novak was on a video link and was standing outside on what looked like a fleet of white marble steps leading into a large building.

"Couldn't be better..." He replied in his Texan drawl.

Another murmuring of surprise swept around the meeting room.

"So where are you now, Sam?" Sonderheim asked.

"I'm just outside the Senate office in Texas...just about to go in and put some of these young guys straight, give them a surprise they didn't quite expect...Listen, y'all. I'm sorry I couldn't be there, but I hope you're all listening to this young man...he's a miracle worker...!"

"You're too kind. Anyway Sam, thanks for joining us..."

The screen went dead, and Sonderheim turned back to the group.

"I know that Senator Novak is well known to you all...and that you are all well aware that he was removed from the board of the Chymera Executive because he was deemed mentally unfit to continue in his duties. His Parkinson's condition had reached an advanced level, and most people had quite frankly given up hope on him. Now, in Parkinson's disease, the death of brain cells that normally produce a chemical called dopamine, leads to uncontrollable tremors and paralysis...By introducing cloned stem cells from Senator Novak's body into the affected areas of his brain, he was able to re-grow the cells which had died, and restore his brain to normal. You'll have noticed that he wasn't shaking at all."

"...Of course, as well as the stem cell treatment, Sam Novak underwent the full Orlando Treatment, and as in all the others who took part in the Phase Two trials, we also have observed the rejuvenating effect kicking in...that's why Sam appears about ten or twenty years younger than the last time you saw him!"

Sonderheim nodded to Buz, and the plasma screen slid away, leaving him standing alone.

David Sonderheim stood before them in silence. He looked around the room at the faces of the Chymera Executive. One day he would be one of them. He hoped that he had impressed them here today...his future would depend upon it.

"Ladies and gentlemen, The Phase Two trials of the Orlando Treatment have now been concluded. I am pleased to report to you that they have, in my opinion, been a complete success. In Phase Two of the program we have concentrated upon understanding the processes which seek to attack and degenerate the condition of the body during the natural lifespan of a human. By understanding these processes and how they work, we have been able to combat them and to alleviate many of the conditions caused by ageing. Thanks to the Orlando Treatment, we believe that our bodies will now be able to reach and maintain their true potential. Consequently, I see no reason why many of us around this table today should not be able to reach the maximum natural life-span of one hundred and twenty years, but doing this with the full functionality of our youth and unimpaired capability of our brains..."

"...I mentioned to you at the start of my presentation that later I would perhaps address the issue of what could possibly be achieved once we begin to look at extending our life-spans, by pushing back the natural barrier of one hundred and twenty years so that we can start to live to two hundred, or five hundred years of age...As I stand before you today, I cannot guarantee you anything, BUT, it is our hope and intention that in Phase Three of the Orlando Project, we will be able to address this area. We have already begun the research, and we are all excited by our initial progress, but in order to continue our existing work and commence the new program properly we need you to approve the $1bn funding that we have requested. The details are all in the business plan, of which you each have a copy in front of you…"

"Ladies and gentlemen,…In summary, I have great pleasure in recommending to you, the board of Chymera, that we progress to Phase Three of the Orlando Project. I hope you will agree with me and approve the motion in the vote that I know will follow this presentation. "

"And for those of you that have signed up for the Phase Three Trials, I look forward to soon welcoming you to Purlington Bay."

Spontaneous applause erupted around the table, and almost as one, the Executive Board of the Chymera Corporation rose to their feet.

Kendrick Hart looked across to Rupert Rohloff and smiled. Rupert knew the vote would go in his favor. In spite of his intense dislike for the man, Rohloff had to agree that Sonderheim had done a good job.

CHAPTER 40
Day Twenty-Four
Burgess Hill
Pennsylvania

There didn't seem to be many other guests in the hotel that night. According to Mrs Doyle they had twenty rooms, but Kerrin guessed that now the summer was over, not many people made it out this far into the country.

After Mrs Doyle insisted on bringing him a cup of fresh coffee and some large, home-made chocolate brownies, Kerrin sat down in the small hotel office and started photocopying the entire contents of the envelope Martin had sent him. Luckily, he was able to find a whole box of new photocopying paper, and in one of the desk drawers he found a box of rewriteable DVD's, with nine unused disks inside.

Under normal circumstances he would have asked permission to borrow the paper and the DVDs, but deciding that it would be easier to get forgiveness than permission, he helped himself to what he needed.

It took him until 8 p.m. that evening to copy nine complete sets of the material he had been sent. He also burnt nine new DVDs, each an identical copy of the original, which turned out to contain a myriad of comprehensive files on the Orlando Treatment, which he would never have enough paper to print out and copy; all the additional materials he found on the memory sticks and the CDs he added to the DVDs.

Not surprisingly, Mrs Doyle also had a box of large oversized envelopes on one of the shelves. It seemed that Mrs Doyle had one of the best equipped offices in town, although Kerrin guessed that she probably didn't know what half the stuff was there for.

"I just want the accountant to have everything he needs whenever he comes around," she told Kerrin later when he offered to pay for all the material he had used.

"Now, if you're finished your work, I've made you a little Irish stew for your evening meal. My guests don't go hungry. So, please, come along!"

Mrs Doyle reminded him of one of his mad aunts, although Kerrin realized she was probably more lonely than mad. She seemed like a good soul that just liked to have company. That's why she probably ran the hotel. Kerrin followed her down a corridor to the guest dining room, and nodded a greeting to a few of the guests that looked up at him as he walked in behind Mrs Doyle.

He sat at a table beside a large window, looking out in to the dark night and thinking about Dana. There wasn't any way to properly describe the feelings he was going through. His emotions were so mixed. Once again David Sonderheim became a central focus for the hate he felt towards all those who had taken it upon themselves to attack his family and his life. He should have killed him when he had had the chance. If he had, then none of this would have happened.

Kerrin felt guilty, sitting in the comfort of a lovely country hotel, eating a hearty meal and washing it down with a large cold Guinness, while out there somewhere in the dark, cold night, his wife and colleague were locked up and probably being threatened or interrogated.

It took all his effort to steel himself against the pain and the worry. He forced himself not to think of Dana. He knew he couldn't afford to let himself get upset. Instead he had to channel his hatred and anger into his determination to complete the tasks he had to carry out in the next few days.

He had a new plan.

A good plan. One which had every possibility of working.

All he needed now was a little luck, and by the end of the week they would all be free, and the whole ghastly affair would be behind them.

Day Twenty-Five

The next day he left the hotel early. He told the manager he would probably be back in a few days, and asked her if she could look after a few of his things for him, along with one of the parcels he had made up containing a copy of everything that Martin had sent him, including the original DVD with all the files stored on it.

Mrs Doyle's brother-in-law gave him a ride into the small town and he caught the train into a suburb of Washington. He had spent a fitful night dreaming about Dana, the same nightmare of him entering a room and finding her tied to her wheelchair and him then struggling with and eventually killing Sonderheim. The dream tormented him every time he closed his eyes. Drenched in sweat, he always woke up when he came to the point where he realized Dana was dead, the bright red blood blossoming against the pure white of her blouse.

While lying awake between the nightmares he had run through the plan again, over and over, making a timetable in his mind against which he would drive himself until he completed everything that had to be done.

The sooner it was all finished, the sooner he would be able to go to rescue Dana.

After a day spent in Washington, making phone calls and meeting the few people left in whom he believed he could place any trust, he caught the train up to New York where he checked into a sleazy, low-budget hotel in one of the red-light districts of the city. Here nobody asked any questions. No one looked each other in the eye, no one cared who you were or what you were doing. So long as you didn't disturb anyone else.

It took Kerrin two days to do what he had to do in New York: to post the parcels to the people he had contacted so carefully from a myriad of different payphones, and opening new accounts with several international banks with strict instructions on what to do with the contents of his safety deposit boxes should he not service the accounts regularly every three months.

Only on the third night in his downtown hotel, was he able to sleep throughout the night for the first time in ages. He fell into a deep sleep as soon as his head hit the musky pillow, in spite of the police sirens blaring on the street outside and the sound of people coming and going all night long along the corridor outside his hotel door.

Day Twenty-Eight

When he woke up the next morning, he washed himself in the broken sink which somehow magically managed to stay attached to the wall, even though the plaster around it was broken, and the tiles had started to fall off. He shaved without looking at himself properly, scared to see what his reflection would tell him, and then left the hotel room before anyone else in the building seemed to have woken up.

It had been a long time since he had last been to visit Dr. Zinfadel. When he had called him on the phone yesterday afternoon, he half expected to be told that he no longer practiced in New York, or that he had died. Instead, the Israeli born hypnotherapist had picked up the phone himself, a sense of relaxation and calm welling up inside Kerrin just at the mere sound of hearing his voice again.

His office was a dingy room on the affluent Upper East side. It hadn't changed much in eight years, and Kerrin could have sworn that some of the piles of magazines and papers which were stacked up against the walls and in every corner of the apartment were the same magazines and papers that were there on his last visit.

Organized chaos. That's how Kerrin could best describe it. He had no doubt that the good Doctor knew exactly what was in each pile, and could locate any article or document easily. Only to the uninitiated did it look like a complete mess.

"Come in, come in..." Dr Zinfadel welcomed him at the door to the apartment.

At the ripe old age of seventy two, his hair and his long beard had more grey in it now than before, but apart from that he looked quite the same.

In another age Dr. Zinfadel would have made a good wizard, and it wouldn't have surprised Kerrin if one of the many piles of books and magazines contained a collection of spells, or if somewhere hidden in one of the corners Kerrin would have found a bubbling cauldron.

In a way, Dr. Zinfadel was a wizard. He was a wizard of the human mind. He could look deep into a person's brain and weave incredible spells on a person's subconscious. In a few moments of time, he could make a person who had smoked all his life, give up smoking without going through any withdrawal symptoms. He could take a man who was scared of spiders, and make him love them. He could steal a person's phobia and replace it with a fascination or an indifference to whatever it was they had feared. A person could walk into his apartment timid and scared of life, and walk out a new person, to whom every second was a precious moment which must be savored and enjoyed to the max.

And being a wizard, Dr. Zinfadel could probably have turned dross into gold if he had put his mind to it. But instead, this thin, wiry looking Jewish man from a small town outside of Bethlehem in Israel, spent his life helping other people for relatively little or no personal gain. Whereas other hypnotists in Central Manhattan charged hundreds, even thousands of dollars an hour for their time, when you walked out of Dr. Zinfadel's apartment you were only expected to cross his palm with $35 for every hour you spent with him. That and a smile, and perhaps a little postcard a few months later to thank him again and let him know how you were.

Instead of wallpaper, his walls were covered with these postcards, sent from every corner of the globe. Sent from people whose lives he had changed, and who had perhaps found happiness and peace for the first time in years. Rich and poor people alike came to see Dr. Zinfadel, but the price was always the same. $35 an hour. It had been for the past eight years, and Kerrin was not surprised to hear that it hadn't changed. Dr. Zinfadel must be deaf, because he had obviously not heard of inflation.

"Ah...Graham, Mr Graham is it not? Come in...sit down...over there please...make yourself comfortable...Ah...it eez good to see you ma boy. How is your life? And your dreams...are they still with you, or did they go away as I told them to?" He greeted Kerrin with his strong, confused New York, Hebrew accent.

It had taken a while for Kerrin to get used to his mannerisms and his directness, but once Kerrin had realized that this was simply his way, and that there was not a single malicious bone in the doctor's body, he had come to trust him and begun to tell him about the darkest secrets of his life.

Dana had never known of Dr. Zinfadel, or the visits that Kerrin had paid to him.

After years of guilt ridden sleep, Kerrin could stand the nightmares no longer. He had never been able to forgive himself for the accident, and for his part in Dana being forced to spend the rest of her life in a wheelchair. He had tried tranquillizers, but they had not helped, and after three months on the tablets, Kerrin's doctor had scribbled a telephone number and address on a tiny piece of paper, and slipped it over the table to Kerrin during one of his many visits to the doctor's surgery.

"Call him if you wish...officially I can't recommend him to you, and for insurance purposes I never gave you this, okay?... but Kerrin...if I were having your dreams, and if I were you...I'd throw the pills in the bucket and give this man a call..."

To this day, Kerrin didn't know what the wizard had done, or what he had said to him, but when Kerrin had left the dingy apartment on his third visit, the dreams had all but stopped, and the guilt, although still present, never returned in anything like the same degree as it had been previously.

He had walked out of there a different person, and had begun to live a normal life again.

"So...vhat eez eet that I can do for you, ma boy?" Dr. Zinfadel asked him warmly, picking up a notebook from a corner table and adjusting a pair of old fashioned horn-rimmed glasses on his nose.

Kerrin, still quite surprised that the old wizard could remember him so well, sat down in the corner of the room, and began to tell him exactly what he wanted the hypnotist to do.

"I see,...and why not? Perhaps, for you, it is the right thing to do...why not indeed...you are a brave, young man...a brave man...for you, I will do this thing you ask..."

"...But first, if you please, you will listen to this music, and also to the sound of my voice,...and notice, that just like the sound of the music, my voice gets louder...and softer...and then louder again...and now, s-o-f-t-e-r, and as you hear the rise and f-a-l-l of my voice, you will close your eyes and r-e-l-a-x..."

When Kerrin left the apartment an hour later, he walked out and down the solid stone stairs from the front of the building to the street below, and in spite of himself, with every step he took, he felt better and better. Almost jubilant. The wizard's medicine was powerful medicine indeed. Kerrin felt ready and confident for the next phase of his plan.

"Right, Mr David Fucking Sonderheim...now I'm coming after you!"

Out of the corner of his eye he caught a flash of yellow, and without thinking he stepped off the sidewalk and into the road, raising his right arm high in the air.

The New York taxi cab screeched to a halt and Kerrin got in.

"Take me to JFK please." Kerrin said to the driver, before settling back in his seat, and planning what he was going to do when he once again came face to face with the man that he hated more than any other person alive.

CHAPTER 41
Old Creek Farm
Delaware

Dana was scared. She knew exactly what Dr. Smiles was trying to do. She knew she had to try and resist him as much as she could.

She wasn't scared for herself. No, she was scared for Kerrin, and she knew that his life depended upon her.

Dr Smiles rolled back her sleeve, then tapping the vein in the crook of her arm a few times, he lifted the needle and injected her with a clear liquid.

A few minutes later he got up and left. It was a good hour before he returned, but when he did, she was not nearly so apprehensive about everything as she had been before. Someone had started to play some soft, soothing classical music from the loudspeakers in their padded white room, and she was beginning to realize that perhaps the best thing to do would be just to tell the doctor everything.

He seemed kind, and gentle.

Perhaps he could help her.

Dr. Smiles liked Dana. Genuinely, he did. She was kind and considerate. When the time came, as a mark of respect and of kindness to her, he would kill her quickly. There would be no pain.

An hour later he left Dana in the room, the door sliding shut and locking electronically behind him. He walked along the hall and took the elevator down three floors to the fifth level in the subterranean underground bunker. His office was in the far corner, bright and cheerful. A small oil painting, a copy of his favorite Matisse hung on the wall across from his desk, and as he picked up the phone and dialed Cheng Wung's number, he admired it as he did every day. He never tired of it.

"Cheng, good to speak to you again. Yes...I've made some good progress. I think I've got everything I'm going to need from his wife...Fine...Thank you, that's very kind of you...Yes, well, that's the reason I'm calling you. You see, I've been able to establish the identity of his current alias...quite clever really...yes...well, I would suggest that you tell your guys to start looking for a man called Mark Twain. Yes, like the writer...Thank you...oh, by the way, what do you want me to do with the other two? The woman from the state department and the journalist...? Kill them now or hang on a bit longer?...Excellent, I think that's the right decision..."

Day Twenty-Eight
John F. Kennedy Airport
New York

Kerrin jumped out of the taxi and walked across the main hall of the airport. He strolled up to the American Airlines desk, and asked when the next flight would be to Washington D.C..

"Good, that'll be great. I would like a single ticket, and I want to pay for it by credit card."

He pulled out his Amex card and passed it across to the pretty young sales assistant behind the counter.

Above her head a security camera was recording the transaction, and as Kerrin watched he noticed the lens turning and focusing on him.

He smiled back.

The woman behind the desk looked up at Kerrin and apologized.

"I'm sorry sir, my computer has just crashed...I'm sorry to delay you, but I'll have to reboot it and start again."

"No problem. I'll wait."

Kerrin knew the girl was bluffing. She didn't have a computer: she was using a terminal, connected via a hub to a central server. There was nothing wrong with her screen. More probably the truth was that as she had swiped his card to pay for the transaction, a warning message had flashed on her screen telling her that the passenger was wanted by the police, and that security personnel were on their way.

Good. Things were going to plan.

Just as Kerrin had hoped for, Dana must have told them his new name.

He would only have to wait a few moments now, and then the fun would begin.

The security guards took up their positions within minutes. The team leader had a clear visual on the suspect, and was pleased to see that he was still standing by the ticket desk, oblivious to the trap that was being set around him.

The young sales assistant was doing her job well, asking new customers to move to another kiosk where they would be served quicker.

The team leader ordered three of his plain-clothed officers to approach the desk slowly, feigning being customers. Two other officers were already crawling slowly along the floor behind the row of ticket desks and would be in position within seconds, ready to spring up at his command beside the sales assistant.

Three more armed officers in full protective uniforms would charge in from the front entrance to the ticket hall, and he himself would enter through a service door quite close to the ticket booth.

His radio clicked twice. The signal that the last of his men were in place. He pushed the broadcast button and spoke quickly into his microphone. "Go. Go. Go!"

Even though Kerrin had been standing and waiting for them, he was still surprised and very impressed when out of nowhere, what seemed like an army of security guards charged at him from all angles and overpowered him.

He offered no resistance, but he doubted that he would have been able to, even if he had wanted to. After years of anti-terrorist training, the security men were thorough and proficient in the execution of their duties.

Within three seconds, Kerrin was lying face down on the cold, polished floor of the terminal, his hands cuffed tightly behind his back, the weight of three security officers pressing down on him hard. Out of the corner of his eye, he could see the sales assistant screaming behind the desk, a security officer standing beside her, his weapon pointing straight at Kerrin. He couldn't see the others, but he reckoned that there were at least eight of them.

Within minutes he was being forcibly lifted and taken from the ticketing hall out to a waiting car. As he was bundled into the back seat, a guard inside the car reached across towards him. Kerrin felt a prick and some pain in his arm, then the world around him went black.

Day Twenty-Eight
Old Creek Farm
Delaware

Cheng Wung arrived in a cavalcade of three cars. He had flown up on a private jet as soon as he had heard the good news that they had Kerrin Graham in custody.

There had been no problems in taking charge of the prisoner and transferring him from the airport security into their hands. Once they'd had Kerrin's new alias, it had literally only been a matter of hours before he had been located and seized.

Frankly, he was a little surprised how easy it had been. He was surprised that the Graham man had not anticipated how simply they could extract his alias from his wife, and that he had not taken suitable precautionary measures.

No matter. They had him now, and that was all that counted.

Cheng stepped out of the bullet-proof limousine and looked around. He wiped his forehead with his handkerchief. Even though it was late, it was still hot and surprisingly humid for this time of year.

He had never actually been to this location before and was curious to find out if it compared to his regional office down in Miami. He looked at his watch. It was six thirty in the evening. He had not yet contacted Buz to tell him about their success. He would leave that a little longer. First, he wanted to talk to the prisoner himself. He was eager to meet the man who had managed to elude him at every twist and turn.

Behind him, his new assistant, Agent Laura Samuels stepped out of the car and followed in his footsteps. She had recently transferred to his department in the CIA after several exceptional years of service in the FBI. Cheng was renowned for surrounding himself with exceptional talent, and Laura's work in South Africa had impressed him. Normally, such a transfer would have been difficult to organize, but Buz Trueman had owed him a favor and he had arranged it all very quickly.

Several other agents jumped out from the other two cars and formed a cordon around them as they walked to the entrance to the farm house. Inside they were welcomed by the farm owner, a strong young man in military uniform, who checked their ID and then asked them to move into a room in the centre of the building.

Both Cheng and Agent Samuels stepped up in turn to the retina scanner, and then allowed their finger prints to be scanned. Satisfied that they were both whom they claimed to be, the man in uniform pressed a button underneath his desk and the far wall of the room slid aside, revealing the entry to an elevator.

They stepped inside, pressed the button for number three, and rode the elevator down to the third subterranean level. As the door slid open they stepped out into the chilled, air-conditioned moisture free atmosphere.

"Aah...at last...somewhere cool!" Cheng exclaimed.

They were standing in a small reception area. In front of them a large glass wall, on the other side of which they could see a corridor leading away from them into the bunker complex beyond. A young man walked towards them from a desk beside the wall on their right, and after greeting them, asked them once more for their ID, and to comply with another compulsory retina and finger print scan.

Again, their credentials were in order, and as the system recognized them officially, the young agent turned a light shade of red.

"Oh, Director Wung, I am sorry. No one told me you were coming. I did not know to expect you...I hope you understand, the security checks are necessary!"

"Don't apologize. I'm pleased to see that you're doing your job. Carry on, Agent...?"

"Agent Weisenbaum, sir!"

"Carry on Agent Weisenbaum."

The young officer stepped up to the glass partition, looked into the camera above the door and nodded. The door opened before them, sliding automatically to the side, and the three of them stepped into the corridor beyond. Director Wung explained the purpose of his visit, and they then followed Agent Weisenbaum to the second last room at the end of the corridor, where he knocked lightly on one of the doors, opened it, and then ushered them into the room beyond.

Kerrin looked up from the seat he was tied to, and recognized the woman immediately. It was the mystery woman from seat 2B who had killed Alex Swinton in South Africa.

Laura smiled back. She turned to her boss and nodded.

"Yes, that's him. There's no doubt."

"Excellent." Cheng said, patting her lightly on the shoulder, but letting his hand linger for just a second longer than would be normal. They both walked into the room and stood in front of Kerrin.

The room was bare and completely empty apart from the single chair upon which Kerrin sat. The walls and the floor of the interrogation room were white, and the bright lights overhead bounced strongly off the shiny gloss walls, making it difficult to see the edges of the room clearly, where the floor ended and the walls or the ceiling began.

Cheng could easily imagine that after several hours in the room, a person would begin to lose their sense of reality.

The door behind them opened once again, and a strong, powerful man in a blue suit walked in. He was carrying a large brown envelope which appeared to be bursting at its seams.

"Cheng Wung. It is a pleasure to have you here in Delaware...I am Agent Daniels. I run this facility. We have the other three ladies in other rooms on this floor, should you wish to talk with them."

Kerrin sat bolt upright in his chair.

Three other ladies? They would almost certainly be Dana and Fiona, although who the third was he couldn't think.

"When Mr Graham was apprehended at the airport, he was carrying this parcel. He didn't have any luggage with him...just this..."Agent Daniels said, handing over the parcel to Cheng.

"Thank you. Listen, Agent Daniels...could you do something about this lighting, turn it down a bit perhaps, and could you bring us some chairs and a table...and some coffee?"

A few minutes later several security guards marched in, carrying the furniture.

"Excellent, now...Mr Graham...boy, am I pleased to meet you! You've led us all a merry dance..."

Kerrin had been silent till now.

When he had woken up in the chair in the white room, he had been interrogated briefly by a series of progressively more senior people. He had refused to speak to any of them, except to insist that he be allowed to meet with and speak to David Sonderheim.

"I am a journalist for the Washington Post, and if I am not allowed to call my editor by 10 p.m. this evening, in tomorrow's edition of The Post we will publish the truth behind what is happening at the Gen8tyx Company. Now let me speak to David Sonderheim, he's the man I've come to see..."

From the way Agent Daniels had greeted Cheng Wung, Kerrin guessed that he was one of the top men in charge. He wasn't Sonderheim, but for now he was probably the best he was going to get.

It was time to go to work.

Kerrin looked up at the Oriental-American standing in front of him. The man did not scare him, even though from the presence of Alex Swinton's assassin, Kerrin knew these people were ruthless to the core and would think nothing of killing him. He didn't know who they were but for the moment that was unimportant. What was important, was that it was now up to him to save Dana's life.

"My name is Kerrin Graham. I work for the Washington Post. I would like to speak to David Sonderheim."

"Oh, we know exactly who you are, Mr Graham. We know all about you, and what you do. Your wife has explained a lot that is of interest to us...She was most helpful..."

He emphasized the word 'was'. Kerrin ignored it. He knew they were trying to put him on edge.

"I repeat, I would like to meet and speak with David Sonderheim. Unless you arrange this immediately there will be severe repercussions." Kerrin threatened.

"Mr Graham. You are in no position to threaten us..."

"Oh, but I think you will find that I am. The parcel you have in your hand contains a complete copy of the Orlando Treatment. Are you familiar with what that is? Are you familiar with the Chymera Corporation? Well, if you are not, I suggest you do exactly what I tell you to do. I demand that I be allowed to meet with my wife, and see that she is well and unharmed, and I demand that your friend David Sonderheim shows his cute little face here in the next couple of hours. If you know all about me as you claim, then you will be well aware that I work for the Washington Post, and I must reiterate that unless I am allowed to call my editor by 10 p.m., which I would guess is in less than two hours from now, he will print my story on the Orlando Project and Chymera and release the entire contents of the Orlando Treatment to the public...and I'm sure that you don't want to be personally responsible for causing the fall of a second US President at the hands of the Washington Post."

Laura stepped forward and was about to speak, but Cheng immediately grabbed her by the arm and motioned for her to stay quiet.

Cheng looked at Kerrin, and saw that there was no fear in the man's eyes. He looked at the parcel in his hands and thought about Kerrin's threat.

He made a decision. This was not a time to act rashly.

Perhaps it was time to call Buz Trueman after all.

Realizing there was nothing more to say, Cheng turned and walked out of the room.

Laura cast a blank look at Kerrin, then followed him out.

CHAPTER 42
Day Twenty-Eight
Four Seasons Hotel
New York

David Sonderheim took the call just as he got back to his hotel suite overlooking Central Park. Four days ago he had been on one of the biggest highs of his life, but the past few days had rapidly disintegrated into a nightmare.

The meeting with the Board of the Chymera Corporation had gone better than he could have hoped for. His presentation had captured all of their imaginations and the board had loved him.

There was only one small problem.

In the discussion that took place after he had left the room, there had been an embarrassing question from one of the board, -he suspected it was the CEO of Sabre Genetics-, asking for clarification on the rumors circulating about a possible exposé that would soon be published by the Washington Post.

How it had got out, David couldn't prove exactly, but he was pretty sure that the rumor had been cleverly started by the one person who had seemed most concerned about it: Sabre's CEO, Calvin Mead. Ever since Gen8tyx had joined Chymera, Calvin had made it no secret that he was after David's job.

In the end, Rupert had reassured those in the board room by promising that the situation would be cleared up immediately. He pointed out that Buz Trueman had already been handed the case, and that Buz had promised the issue would be dealt with within the next few days.

Everyone trusted Buz.

Rupert had called for a vote for the necessary funding, and the decision had been unanimous to proceed, with one billion dollars to be provided as requested. The news should have been excellent, except there was one small caveat: the approval was conditional upon the potential problem with the Washington Post being resolved within the week.

The subtlety of the public shift of responsibility to Buz to resolve the issue was at first lost on David, but it soon dawned on him that it made his handling of the problem look bad and unprofessional.

When he first realized this, he had initially hoped that he could save face by still resolving the issue himself. He had called his two main contacts in the FBI, John in New York and Laura in Miami, only to find out that John was out of the country somewhere and that Laura had left the FBI to join the CIA. Rumor had it that she had met one of the Divisional Directors, had spent the night with him, and within a few days had been transferred and promoted to his personal assistant! Wherever she was now, she was no longer returning his calls.

Sonderheim was mad. His anger and hatred towards Kerrin Graham had multiplied ten-fold. If he disliked the man before, now he was ready to rip him apart with his bare hands. David was close, so close, to being elected to the Board. And Phase Three of the Orlando Trials represented the dream he had been working towards all of his life.

There was no way that a stupid, meddling, bastard of a reporter from The Washington Post was going to stop him!

When the phone rang, Sonderheim picked it up, already in a bad mood.

"David, hi! It's Buz Trueman. Just thought I'd let you know, we've got Graham. He's being kept in one of our safe houses for questioning. He's demanding to see you...Ordinarily I wouldn't get you involved, but I don't think I've got any choice in this one. Graham is blackmailing us. And I believe he has the capability to back up his threats. We would be foolish not to take him seriously. "

David gripped the phone with both hands, rage seething through his body.

"How the hell can that fucking idiot blackmail us? What's he got?" Sonderheim demanded.

"We can't talk on the phone. I'm sending a car over for you now. Be ready in five minutes."

The line went dead and Sonderheim slammed the phone down onto the cradle. He sat down hard on the edge of the plush bed. For a few seconds he stared into space, then he turned towards the pillow, slid his hand underneath it and pulled out a gun. He slid the magazine out, checked the bullets, then pushed it back home with the base of his palm.

Perhaps it wasn't too late to resolve the Graham issue after all.

Day Twenty-Eight

It was 11.15 p.m. when Sonderheim arrived at the farm house. As best as David could make out, it was somewhere south of Wilmington in Delaware, but more than that he couldn't tell. They had left I-95 long ago, and had travelled cross country through the dark.

When he stepped out of the car in the middle of the countryside, David couldn't quite figure out why they had stopped in a field in front of a farmhouse. It was tiny, only a single square building with a porch running all the way around it, and a large barn at the back.

When they walked inside, he was surprised when they were stopped and met by an armed soldier. It was then that he realized they were probably standing above some sort of bunker, with the main building somewhere below them.

After numerous security checks he was taken down to a floor three levels beneath the ground. Sonderheim followed his escort to a room towards the end of a long corridor, and after being ushered inside, the door was closed quietly behind him. Surprised, Sonderheim turned and tried to open it again.

He reached out and tugged the handle.

It didn't budge and he realized with alarm that he couldn't turn the handle from the inside.

The room itself was quite dark, and strange noises which sounded like the beginnings of a thunderstorm were being piped into the room via loudspeakers.

His eyes adjusted quickly to the reduced lighting, and he realized that he was not alone. Although otherwise empty, there was a woman sitting in a wheelchair in the centre of the room. Her arms were bound to the sides of the chair, and she was obviously asleep.

Sonderheim stepped up to her side.

The woman's eyes opened and looked at him directly in the face.

Sonderheim had never seen the woman before in his life, but from the fear that he saw in her eyes, it was obvious that the woman knew him.

Suddenly a peal of thunder roared through the loudspeakers and it sounded like it had begun to pour with rain.

The helicopter touched down a hundred yards from the farm house. As the rotary blades began to slow down, Buz Trueman jumped from the open door and almost stumbled on the hard gravel-strewn ground below. His personal aide, jumping from the helicopter behind him, immediately offered him his arm, but Buz shrugged it off and quickly recovered his composure.

Together they walked towards the farm house, and after being greeted at the entrance by Agent Daniels, the base commander, they caught the elevator down to the fifth level.

He followed Agent Daniels to Dr Smile's office, where he was met by the doctor, Cheng Wung and his new assistant. Buz couldn't help but smile when he shook her hand. She was obviously a woman of many 'talents'. No wonder Cheng had been so keen to have her transferred under his command. Though, from what Buz had read and heard about her, he wondered if Cheng realized just exactly what he was getting himself into, or onto, as the case may be. If everything he had heard about her was true, Cheng had better watch his back.

"Agent Samuels? It's a pleasure to meet you. Agent Wung has spoken very highly of you..."

He felt her hand linger slightly in his as he released her grip, and as he studied her pretty face he caught the flicker of interest in her eyes.

Yes, Cheng Wung better keep an eye on this one. Buz doubted she would waste much time with him. She had already made her plans for promotion quite clear.

Pouring himself a glass of cold water from the glass jug on Dr. Smile's desk, he listened carefully as Cheng briefed him on everything they had learned from Kerrin. When he had heard it all, Buz turned to one of the agents standing by the door.

"Bring Graham here now. I would like to meet him..." And turning to Cheng, he asked to see the infamous parcel that Kerrin had been threatening them with.

The uniformed CIA officer opened the door and stepped into Kerrin's cell. He crossed the room with his gun trained on the suspect and spoke aloud to an invisible security officer who was sitting in another room, surveying Kerrin remotely by hidden cameras.

"Undo the armbands!" the officer shouted curtly.

Immediately the two orange bandings holding Kerrin's arms tightly to the sides of the chair were electronically released.

Kerrin was fully aware that a guard was standing beside him, but from the moment he had entered the room, Kerrin had feigned sleep, his eyes remaining tightly shut.

The guard spoke loudly, his gun still pointing towards him.

"Please stand, Mr Graham."

Kerrin remained slumped in his chair showing no obvious signs of life.

"Mr Graham, if you would please come with me?"

Kerrin waited.

"Mr Graham..."

His every sense was straining, his muscles tensed and ready to react, his reactions primed and ready to go. He knew there was only one person who had entered the room. He had listened carefully.

He could hear the guard breathing. He could sense the guard's proximity and uncertainty as to what to do next. Kerrin knew he had to time it right.

As the guard spoke his name again, he could hear the slight change in tone as he turned his head away from Kerrin to look questioningly at the hidden camera and the other guard watching them from the other room.

Sensing the moment and the guard's distracted attention, Kerrin opened his eyes and kicked upwards with his legs, knocking the threatening gun upwards and out of the guard's hand. At the same moment, he pushed backwards on the arms of his chair, propelling himself up and at the chest of the guard in front of him.

They sprawled backwards together, knocking over one of the two chairs and falling hard against the metal edge of the table that had been carried into the room only an hour before.

The edge of the table crashed into the base of the guard's skull, and as Kerrin's momentum propelled them hard against it, the agents neck bent quickly at an awkward angle. There was an audible 'crack' and the table was pushed aside as Kerrin and the agent hurtled clumsily towards the floor. Even before they had hit the ground, the body of the agent had gone limp underneath him, and as Kerrin struggled to pick himself up as fast as he could, he realized with shock that the agent was dead, his neck broken during the fall.

There was no time to think. Kerrin knew that even as he was moving towards the door the guard in the other room would be raising the alarm.

Picking up the dead agent's gun from the floor, he raced out of the cell and into the corridor beyond.

According to what he'd overheard Agent Daniels say to Cheng Wung earlier, Dana and Fiona were somewhere in the rooms on this floor. He had to find them.

He looked quickly around him. There were five rooms on his right towards the back of the corridor, and six doors on his left, leading towards the elevator.

Choosing to move away from the obvious source of trouble, he ran to the last door at the end of the corridor.

He turned the handle. The door was locked.

Shit.

He turned and tried the handle of the door behind him. It didn't budge.

His heart racing, and the sound of an alarm now ringing in the corridor about him, he reached quickly for the next door handle in sight.

The handle turned, and the door opened inwards.

Kerrin stepped into the room beyond.

The room was quite dark, and as he entered his senses were accosted by the sound of a loud thunderstorm, the rumble of thunder, and the sound of torrential rain.

In the centre of the room his attention was immediately drawn to the sight of a hospital wheelchair.

There was a woman sitting in it, her arms bound tightly to the arm rests, but before his eyes could adjust to the darkness so that he make out the features on her face, Kerrin realized with a sickening sense of panic that he had seen this scene before. Many times.

This was his worst nightmare come true.

The memory of the dreams came flooding back.

He knew exactly what was going to happen next.

He started to turn towards the blow that he knew must surely come from behind him, but he was too late.

From the dark shadows, an arm swung down, a heavy metal object smashing into the base of his neck.

Kerrin went down with the force of the blow. He sprawled on the ground, the gun in his hand flying away from him and skidding heavily across the floor.

Impossibly beyond his reach...

Without waiting for any brilliant flash of lightning, Kerrin kicked out at the legs which he saw silhouetted against the brightness coming from the open door, sweeping his assailant's legs out from under him with a swift sideways blow to his shins.

As the stranger fell, a single gunshot lit up the room, the loudness of the shot reverberating around the walls of the cell and mixing with the next peal of thunder which boomed out from the overhead speakers hidden in the walls of the room.

Kerrin screamed...this couldn't be happening.

He jumped to his feet, swinging a second blow from his foot at the stranger's head, which lay clearly before him in the light of the door... He felt the impact through the leather in his shoes...

Déjà vu. Déjà vu...

He turned towards the woman at the centre of the room, lunging towards her wheelchair in an effort to free her and bring the nightmare to an end.

But even as he fell helplessly at the foot of the wheelchair, he could see the dark stain of the blood already blossoming on the white blouse...

He started to scream, the same long guttural scream that he had dreamt a hundred times before. He wept, not able to bring himself to look up at the face of the dead woman, not able to look at the face of his dead wife…not able to grasp that after all this, Dana, his wife, was dead.

CHAPTER 43

All of a sudden, the lights in the cell were turned up bright. People poured into the room, and rough arms grabbed hold of him in an unnecessary attempt to restrain him.

Kerrin blinked at the bright lights, and made no effort to resist as he was pulled to his feet.

Behind him he heard the voices of people in conversation, people shouting, more people rushing into the room.

Then abruptly, the awful thunderstorm stopped and the loudspeakers went quiet.

Kerrin opened his eyes wide, and as the men behind him started to drag him out of the room, he turned to look at the face of his dead wife.

"Dana...I'm sorry...Dana..."

He stopped in mid-sentence, not able to understand what he was seeing.

He blinked quickly, trying to clear the tears from his eyes.

The woman's head lolled awkwardly to one side but he could see her face clearly now.

It was not Dana.

Instead, Fiona looked back at him with unseeing eyes, blood oozing slowly from the corners of her mouth.

The two guards holding his arms lifted him and dragged him around the body on the floor. Kerrin looked down at the man, and with a pang of shock realized that he was looking straight back at him.

His eyes were blurred, but he was not dead. Kerrin had not killed him after all.

On the contrary, David Sonderheim was very much alive.

The sight of Fiona's lifeless body stirred a strange mixed reaction within Kerrin. The immediate rush of relief and emotion that hit him like a rushing train as he realized that it was not Dana, was quickly replaced by a sense of incredible guilt and loss.

Guilt that his first reaction upon seeing Fiona's dead body was that he had been relieved. Guilt that he had brought her into this whole fucked up mess, and guilt that she was now dead because of him.

And then guilt again, as it slowly hit him that if he had killed Sonderheim when he'd had the chance in California, she would still be alive today.

They dragged him back to the room where he had been incarcerated only minutes before. His feeble attempt at finding Dana had resulted in the unnecessary deaths of two people, and now he was back where he had started with nothing to show for the passing of their lives.

While a policemen in Miami he had often been involved in shoot-outs on the street. More than once he had witnessed the death of a close colleague, and he had learned through painful firsthand experience that at these times the worst that a man could do was to dwell upon the tragedy that had just occurred. There would be plenty of time for that later. To think too much was to be weak.

For now, more than ever, Kerrin had to be strong.

Dana.

He had to think of Dana. Her life depended upon him and how he reacted in the next few minutes.

A few people he hadn't seen before came and went from the room. Then a large man arrived along with an entourage of others, including the Chinese-American Kerrin had met earlier. Kerrin had seen the large man before…in the photographs that Fiona had given him.

Buz Trueman.

The man came close to Kerrin, and bent over him, his eyes only inches away. He didn't speak.

Kerrin could smell the aroma of expensive cigars and high-class cologne.

His clothes were handmade, his shoes polished and gleaming, the watch on his wrist a limited edition from Switzerland. He smelt of money.

Yet, there was one more thing. The man oozed power.

Confident. Relaxed. In charge.

Buz pointed to the table beside Kerrin's chair and one of the men behind him put down a telephone, taking the lead and plugging it into a small, almost invisible phone socket on the wall.

At the same moment, one of the hand restraints loosened automatically and Kerrin was able to lift his arm.

"Mr Graham. I am sorry for the experience you have just been through, and I deeply regret the death of your colleague. I trust you will appreciate it was an accident. It was not planned or intended…in the same way that the death of one of our guards a few minutes before was also not planned or intended. It was an accident. Nothing more, nothing less... Now, I would be very grateful if you would call your editor and tell him that you are okay, and that there is no need for him to print the story he was intending to. It is now 9.57 p.m."

Kerrin looked up at the man. He was impressed. Buz was taking the initiative. He was taking Kerrin very seriously indeed.

"I will, but before I do, I have to know that my wife is alive and well. You have nine minutes to bring her here and let me talk to her."

Buz looked back at him without speaking. Behind his eyes Kerrin could see that he was thinking fast. Then he saw the change in luster of the irises which showed that Buz had made a decision.

He turned to one of his men.

"Bring his wife. And treat her gently."

"Thank you, Mr Trueman." Kerrin said, addressing him by name.

For the slightest instant in time, Kerrin saw a flicker of surprise in the man's eyes. He obviously hadn't reckoned with the fact that Kerrin would know who he was. But then it was gone, and the man's face was a mask again.

Buz drew up one of the two chairs and sat down.

Just then David Sonderheim walked into the room, looking disheveled and dazed. He was rubbing the side of his head with one hand, the place where Kerrin had kicked him. His other hand dangled by his side, the gun which had killed Fiona hanging loosely in his grip.

Kerrin reacted instantly.

"Get that man out of my sight. Keep him away from me, or swear to God, I will kill him with my bare hands..." The venom behind his words surprised not only himself but Buz too.

Buz simply waved one of his hands without looking around, and instantly two men grabbed Sonderheim and dragged him out of the room, his protests echoing down the hall.

"I'm sorry about that," Buz said.

Kerrin found it interesting that Buz had apologized for one of his own team. That was definitely curious. It struck Kerrin that this was a man he could do business with. And from what had just happened, it was obvious that he was higher in the chain of command than Sonderheim. This was the man he needed to talk to.

Kerrin looked at Buz's watch. It was 9.54 p.m.

The seconds ticked by slowly. Then the sound of footsteps and suddenly she was there.

Buz nodded at the security guard watching them covertly from the other room, and the other wrist band restraining Kerrin popped open.

Kerrin jumped up and ran to his wife as she was wheeled into the room. He kissed her, looked closely at her face, and held her hands. There were no signs of violence on her body, but he noticed a small piece of surgical tape on the inside of her elbow, the tell-tale sign of an injection. She had been drugged. Probably given a truth serum to get her to talk.

"Are you okay? Have they harmed you at all?"

She looked back at him, tears brimming in her eyes.

"No...I'm fine...I'm sorry, Kerrin. I tried not to tell them anything..."

"It's okay. It wasn't your fault. They didn't catch me. I gave myself up. Don't worry it's going to be okay now. I promise you..."

Kerrin stood up and walked over to Buz. He picked up the phone and while looking at Buz straight in the eyes, he dialed the number for Paul, his boss at the Washington Post.

The phone was picked up after one ring.

"Kerrin...is that you? Are you okay pal?"

"Hi. Paul, I'm fine. I don't want to talk just now, but don't print the story tonight. But we'll have the same arrangement for tomorrow and the next day, and each day after that unless I say different, okay? If I don't call you before 10 p.m. each night...print, and damn them to hell!"

He had always wanted to say that.

"Thank you Mr Graham," Buz said, taking the handset out of his hands and handing the telephone to one of the guards, who promptly took it away. "Now gentlemen," he said to the remaining guards, "if you don't mind, I would appreciate it if you would escort us topside, and out of this little establishment. I would like to speak to Mr Graham and his wife in private, and where we will not be overheard." Buz announced, referring obviously to the electronic surveillance gear embedded in the walls of each of the rooms.

"But sir...do you think that's wise?" one of Cheng Wung's agents began to object.

Buz looked at the man sternly, and he immediately shrank away.

"I can see no reason why I should not trust Mr Graham. Contrary to what Mr Wung believes, it's obvious to me that Mr Graham chose to give himself up...he wanted to meet us as much as we wanted to meet him...and if they were to try to escape where would they go? We're in the middle of nowhere, and there's no way he could carry his wife across the countryside to the nearest city, which is hours away...No, I get the feeling that Mr Graham will not be going anywhere in a hurry."

With Kerrin pushing Dana in her wheelchair, the group made their way to the surface, and then out onto the porch. One of the guards helped Kerrin with the wheelchair down the few stairs to the ground below and they made their way across the hard ground out into the field away from the house.

When they were out of earshot of the farm, the guards left Kerrin and Dana alone with Buz Trueman.

Buz pulled out two Kohiba cigars from his breast pocket. Kerrin immediately recognized the yellow and black boxing and the branding of the Cuban cigar. It was the same type he liked to play with when he tried to write.

"Join me?" Buz asked, raising his eyebrows.

"Don't mind if I do!" Kerrin replied, taking it and the matches from Buz.

Copying Buz, he snipped the end of the cigar off with his fingers, and then wafted it back and forward in the flame of one of the matches. Then he popped the cigar in his mouth and puffed on it slowly, rotating it in the flame to light the tobacco evenly.

The aroma drifted over his tongue and he savored the flavor. This was the first time he had ever really tried to smoke one.

He coughed loudly, then smiled.

"My favorite brand..." He joked.

For a moment they stood in silence. A full moon hung high in the cloudless sky and lit the fields brightly all around them. The air was warm, but thankfully cooler and less humid now than earlier that evening. In the distance they could hear the sound of an animal crying to its mate.

"It's a fine night..." Buz said silently.

"That it is," Kerrin agreed, his eyes cast upwards, looking at the craters depicted so clearly on the surface of the moon.

Another moment of silence.

"Well, Mr Graham, we've both come a long way to speak to each other. Given the circumstances, I think we should be entirely frank. If I may start, I think I should say that I know all about you, and I know that you know all about us. The question is what are we going to do about it?"

"I appreciate your candor, Mr Trueman. I think at this point all I want to say to you is that I know all about the Chymera Corporation, your involvement, and exactly what happened at Gen8tyx. I know everything about the Orlando Treatment. The parcel that I brought with me is one of many identical copies that I have in my possession. It turns out that on the evening Martin Nicolson, one of the founding members of Gen8tyx, was shot down and murdered by a US fighter jet,...earlier that evening, before he took off in his Lear Jet, he took some precautions and mailed a complete dossier to me containing complete, comprehensive details about Gen8tyx and its discoveries. Enough for anyone who has the dossier to start a new company and replicate the research and the discoveries that Gen8tyx made." He paused.

"...And I also have an extensive dossier on those who are involved in the Chymera Corporation. I won't pretend to know exactly what the Chymera Corporation is about, but I know enough. I have photographs of you, and most of the members attending a meeting in Spain, including the Chief Executive Officer, President Kendrick Hart."

Kerrin was guessing about Kendrick Hart being the CEO, but from the way Buz's face muscles twitched when he mentioned it, he knew that he was on the mark. He waited to see if Buz wanted to say something in reply. It wasn't long before he did.

"Mr Graham. I think that perhaps the Corporation made the mistake of underestimating you. That is not a mistake I intend to make again. I presume that before you marched so freely into the airport and expected to be picked up, that you took concrete measures to ensure the safety of yourselves and those you love…"

"Are you threatening me?"

"No. I am merely stating the obvious. Unless you have taken some additional precautions, now we have you, it will be a simple enough matter to find out where you have hidden those parcels…"

Kerrin smiled.

"And you would be right to presume I have taken precautions. I served my time as a policeman on the streets of Miami, for years the drug capital of the world. I've seen truth drugs being used before and I know that ordinarily it wouldn't take long for you to extract that information from me. I guess that's how you got Dana to tell you my new alias in the first place? Now, I'm not about to tell you how many parcels I made up, or where they are…that would be stupid. Suffice it to say, that I have many contacts, in the press, in the world's media…in pharmaceutical companies and the financial markets and other industries…as well as a number of politicians who would dearly love to see the end of Kendrick Hart. I think I should make it clear that I have placed a large number of parcels with these trusted 'holders'…some of these are newspapers, some are banks, some are acquaintances…some are just people I can trust…as well as the obvious, my own newspaper the Washington Post, for example, who I think you are very familiar with. They are not scared to tell the truth, even if it does bring down the President. The thing is, unless I report in regularly to these people, the parcels will be released or dropped into the post and sent to a variety of interested parties, who would just *love* to get their hands on the information they contain. For example, if I don't turn up at work next Monday, the Post will print everything. And if I should stop turning up for work one day without warning…even if it's in two years or ten years…they'll print. Newspapers have long memories…we can wait. So, it wouldn't be a good idea to arrange to have me killed some time in the future…just when I think everything is cool… As for your truth drug, I have taken precautions against that. Are you familiar with the workings of the mind, Mr Trueman?"

"I would like to think I am, but I am sure you know more about it than I do, Mr Graham. Please elaborate."

"The mind is an interesting thing. It would seem that we are all a little schizophrenic after all. We operate on two levels…our conscious, and our subconscious. I suppose you could compare the subconscious with the operating system in a computer. It runs the thousands of sub-programs that keep our bodies alive…they tell us when to eat, or how to move a hand…they assemble and store the knowledge in our brains so that whenever we want to, we can access it, can recall past experiences, or remember a list of names or telephone numbers...that sort of thing. None of us are really conscious of our subconscious. Are you?"

"I can't say that I am,...and your point is?" Buz asked, looking at Kerrin and slowly exhaling a mouth full of cigar smoke.

"Well, there are a group of people who are very familiar with this concept. They are called 'hypnotists'. I am sure you are familiar with them. In fact, I am sure you use them yourself to extract information from people. Everyone else does...Anyway, I was faced with a small problem. I had to be able to come and visit you here today, but I knew that I also had to protect the identities and locations of where the parcels and dossiers have been stored...I like to think of them as little time-bombs that will go off if anything should happen to me...I'm sure you understand...So I came up with a little plan. I went to see a hypnotist, and together we hid that information in my subconscious. Oh, don't worry, I can access it freely whenever I want...but should anyone try to tamper with my brain, *should anyone hypnotize or drug me* and ask me to retrieve that information, my subconscious has been programmed to erase it...to forget it completely. Think of it, if you will, like a little mental key...only my consciousness has the key...if anyone else tries to force me to access it, even if you made me 'want' to access it...then, phufff,...it'll all just go up in some imaginary mental smoke. Quite clever really, isn't it...in fact, I think it's the same technique that the CIA and FBI use on their own agents to protect and prevent confidential information being extracted from their people when they are captured or tortured... Of course, if anyone did try something on me, at any time in the future... the problem for us would be that even if I wanted to, I couldn't tell you anything: my hypnotic programming would ensure that the important memories would be erased. I would forget everything and then unfortunately I wouldn't be able to make the calls...to visit the people I had to be seen by,...to do the things I had to do in order to stop the parcels from being sent out and the Orlando Treatment from being exposed to the world..."

"I suppose it's all just a rather long winded way of saying...'*if you fuck with me, you're fucked*'...Do you get my drift?"

Buz walked away from him, his back turned. He looked up and cast his eyes over the fields surrounding them, seemingly lost in his thoughts. "So, Mr Graham, it would seem you have positioned yourself very carefully...what then, may I ask, is it that you want from us?"

"Oh, it's quite simple really. But I will only tell you in the presence of another man."

"And who, pray tell, would that be?" Buz asked, turning towards him, the end of the cigar in his hand glowing bright red against the dark night.

"The CEO of the Chymera Corporation, the President of the United States,...Kendrick Hart, And one thing more...I want to see him tomorrow afternoon!"

Buz was thinking fast. Kerrin Graham was smart. Very smart. He had them by the balls. But his timing was good. The President was due to fly to Camp David on Saturday, the day after tomorrow. Buz had promised the Board that he would deal with the Graham issue before the end of the week. A meeting tomorrow would satisfy both his and Kerrin's agenda. Either way, the issue would be resolved by the time the President took off on Air Force One on Saturday morning.

He dropped the cigar and squashed it into the ground with the base of one of his expensive shoes.

"Okay, Mr Graham. I'll make the arrangements."

"...Just one more thing..." Kerrin asked as they turned to walk back into the house.

"Yes..."

"Make sure you bring David Sonderheim along too. I want him to be there when I tell the President what it is that I want in return for my silence."

Day Twenty-Nine

Late the next morning, after a good breakfast, and the chance to clean themselves up, Kerrin and Dana joined Buz and several security guards and boarded a helicopter bound for Washington.

David Sonderheim had left earlier that morning in the private limousine. He had cheered up considerably since the events the previous evening, the change in his humor being on the most part due to Buz Trueman telling him that now the Graham affair had been dealt with, he had arranged a private interview with the President later that afternoon.

Sonderheim could guess what the meeting would be about. He was sure it was to discuss his promotion to the Board.

CHAPTER 44
Day Twenty-Nine
Oval Office
The White House
Washington D.C.

It was 1 p.m.

The President of the United States of America nodded to his assistant who walked over to the door, and after letting the guests in, discreetly stepped out of the room and closed the door behind her.

Kendrick Hart stood up from his desk of office and walked around it to welcome his guests. In real life the President was even taller and more imposing than the impression he gave on the television. As he came towards them, Kerrin couldn't help but feel slightly in awe of the man.

The President bent forward and took one of Dana's hands in both of his and smiled one of his best diplomatic, charismatic, 'I-want-you-to-like-me' smiles. Next he extended his arm to Kerrin and shook Kerrin's hand warmly, a gesture which both surprised and stunned him. Then, in quick recognition he reached out and grabbed Buz's hand.

"Welcome to the Oval Office. It is a pleasure to meet you Mr Graham. I have heard a lot of things about you...Now please,...come. Make yourselves comfortable...May I?"

The President gestured to Kerrin, indicating that he would like to push Dana's wheelchair the remaining few feet into the room, and Kerrin stood aside to let him.

"Here, Mrs Graham, let me put you right beside me..."

"Please sit..." The President waved Kerrin and Buz to several leather arm chairs grouped around a large coffee table in the centre of the room. The President sat opposite them, with Dana in her wheelchair on the left of his chair.

The Oval Office was a truly impressive room, an institution in itself. The President's desk looked exactly like it did in any of the many TV broadcasts that Kerrin and Dana had seen coming from this room. In the corner, the flag of the United States hung loosely from the pole, the symbol of their great nation, and the truth that would set any man free...

Kerrin and Dana were unprepared for the royal treatment, and were fervently trying to work out the tactics that were being played. Yet it was hard not to enjoy the honor of being in the Oval Office of the White House, with the President of the United States...

Which was, Kerrin realized, probably the whole purpose of the red carpet treatment. To overawe them and throw them off balance... No, Kerrin had to snap out of it. This wasn't a pleasure meeting, this was a matter of life or death...theirs!

"Tea, coffee? Some cookies?...I trust you have had lunch already?" the President asked.

"No thank you, Mr President. I am afraid we didn't come here for that..."

"Well, Mr Graham, perhaps you would like to explain what you have come here for?"

"In good time, but first, I requested that David Sonderheim be present. May I ask where he is?"

"Ah, yes...He's waiting just outside. Shall I ask him to come in now?" The President asked.

"Please..."

The President walked to his desk and pressed a button on his phone, and spoke to his secretary outside.

"Could you please ask Mr Sonderheim to come in now?"

A door to the side of the room opened, and David Sonderheim walked briskly through the doorway into the Oval Office. Kerrin watched him, noting how the broad smile and look of excitement that lit up his face quickly vanished and was replaced by a blank, almost fearful expression the moment he caught sight of the others.

The President made no attempt to greet Sonderheim as warmly as he had done with Kerrin and Dana. Instead, he simply said,

"Thank you for coming Mr Sonderheim. Would you like to join us and take a seat, please...", pointing to the one free chair which was shielded from Kerrin by the presence of Buz in-between them. Sonderheim sat down, his demeanor quiet and apprehensive.

"Well, Mr Graham, now we have everyone present, I think the ball is in your court...Please feel free to speak candidly...and don't worry...our conversation is not being overheard or taped in anyway..."

It was a subtle attempt at humor, the meaning of which was not lost on Kerrin. He smiled back weakly, the reference to the Watergate tapes being deliberate, openly acknowledging that Kerrin worked for the Washington Post.

"Perhaps Mr Graham, you would now like to start by answering me the question that Buz asked you yesterday, namely...what is it that you want from us? Buz has briefed me on your conversation yesterday, and I fully understand the precautions you have taken, and the potential you have to embarrass us, and to destroy one of the most important scientific programs ever undertaken by mankind..."

Kerrin straightened up in his chair.

"As I said yesterday, what I want is very simple. I think you will know that for many years I was an officer of the law in Miami...I served my time on the streets. I suppose it takes a peculiar type of person to want to put his life at risk from one day to another, in the pursuit of one thing..."

"And what would that one thing be, Mr Graham?" The President asked, foolishly walking into the trap that Kerrin had laid for him.

"Justice, Mr President. Justice." Kerrin answered. "You see, Mr President, to coin a phrase, once a cop, always a cop, and perhaps even more so now that I'm a journalist and a voice of the people...But putting that aside for a second, this is more personal than that...Someone messed with my family, someone killed the husband of my sister, and took away the father of my nephew and niece...that same person killed my colleague and friend, Fiona Cohen, and authorized the deaths of a string of other people...Okay, so you're the head of the Chymera Corporation, but we're sitting in the Oval Office, the centre of the American empire...based upon liberty and freedom...and justice. And that's what I'm here for today...just one thing. Justice."

The President was silent. He looked at Kerrin, and then at Dana. He was thinking fast.

"I am aware of your personal pain. I am aware of the events in Orlando. I am also aware of your trip to South Africa, and the events that occurred there..." The President did not look at David Sonderheim, but the tension in the room was growing and everyone could sense his presence.

"...But Mr Graham, are you saying that after all this, and even though you are now in possession of some, shall we say, very privileged knowledge, and even though you are a journalist...and the desire to 'print and be damned' must be high indeed, that in spite of all this, all you are seeking is 'justice' ? "

"Yes!"

"And if you get your 'justice', Mr Graham, what is it that you can give us in return?" the President asked.

"The question is not what I will do if you do give me what I want, but rather what I will do if you do not. I'm sure that if Buz has briefed you fully on our conversation last night, that you know I am in a position to destroy the Orlando Project, to expose it to the public, along with the existence and membership of the Chymera Corporation, and of course yourself...Personally, I like your politics, I even voted for you at the last election, so I think it would be a shame if I had to expose you and you were to subsequently go down in history as the second President of the United States of America to be kicked out of office by the Washington Post..."

The President stood up slowly. Buz shifted uneasily in his seat.

"No Buz, it's okay..." The President waved at Buz, gesturing to him to stay seated.

"So...this whole thing hinges around one thing...the pursuit of justice...the great American ideal?"

"Yes, it does."

The President stepped away from the chairs and walked back towards his desk, easing himself slowly into his seat of office.

"And all you want is for justice to be seen to be done..."

"Yes Sir, that's all I want..."Kerrin replied.

As Kerrin spoke the President sank back in to his chair, at the same time reaching out with his right hand and slowly sliding open a drawer. He reached inside, and in a swift fluid motion, the President pulled out a gun, raising it clear above his desk and pointing it at the chest of David Sonderheim, only feet away.

Phutt...Phutt.

The gun in his hand jumped twice, the silencer on the end of the muzzle spitting two bullets into the air.

David Sonderheim jerked violently, his chest jumping twice, and his arms flaying wildly through the air as the bullets ripped into his chest. The momentum of the bullets pushed his body backwards, and his chair toppled over, crashing onto the ground with David Sonderheim sprawled awkwardly on top of it.

Dana screamed and Kerrin and Buz both jumped to their feet. Sonderheim looked up from the ground, his eyes glazed and his mouth wide open, the expression on his face one of complete surprise...

"As you said, all you wanted is for justice to be seen to be done. I think you both just saw it being administered," the President of the United States said as they all stared at the body on the floor.

Kendrick stood up, and while Kerrin and Dana watched, he put the gun back into the drawer and closed it slowly. He walked around to the front of the desk and sat back down beside Dana.

"I'm sorry Mrs Graham, but your brother-in-law was one of those whom Mr Sonderheim killed. You had every right to witness justice being done..." He turned to Kerrin, and indicated for him to sit again.

"Please, I have complied with your wishes, and now I must tell you mine. But first, if you don't mind..." he nodded to Buz and waved at the body.

Buz stood, and picking up the back of the chair in which Sonderheim was lying, his legs dangling loosely over the edge of the seat, he dragged it backwards to the edge of the Oval Office, opened a side door, and took the body out of the room. That was the last Kerrin saw of David Sonderheim.

Kerrin and Dana stared after the body as it was dragged away, speechless and in shock. It had all happened so quickly.

It was hard to believe what had just taken place. Kerrin had spent the past month chasing after the man who had killed his brother-in-law, determined to see 'justice' be done, determined to exact revenge on the person responsible for the deaths of all those who had died at Gen8tyx. He had appealed to the highest power in the land for 'justice' to be done...and his plea had been heard. He had got what he wanted.

It was just that it had all happened so fast.

And now what?

A minute passed then Buz returned.

"Thank you Buz...now Mr Graham...may I call you Kerrin...and Dana? Before I tell you what I want from you...I want to tell you a bit about us, and what it is that you have the power to destroy...the mark of any true hunter is that they fear and respect the prey they kill...and I would like to think that you know enough about us to respect us, if indeed you later decide to kill and destroy everything we have achieved."

The President stood up and walked slowly around the room, one hand in his pocket, the other gesturing passionately in the air.

"Kerrin, do you believe in America?...no truly...*do you*? Regardless of your politics, at the end of the day, are you a patriot? Let me assure you, that there is nothing, nothing, I would not do for our country. I am its servant, and it is my master...The Chymera Corporation is a group of like-minded people...but not just ordinary people. They are powerful people. Rich people. Influential people, people who have dedicated their lives to the service of their dreams, and having achieved them are now dedicating their lives and their power to their country..."

"...We all share one goal, namely that America stays 'the' best and 'the' most powerful country in the world, and that other countries where freedom and liberty have no meaning, come to embrace our philosophy and our constitution...and that slowly, the world will become as one with us..."

"There will come a time, when this will happen. When injustice will disappear and every man shall be free..."

"...But I cannot stand here and in a few minutes tell you how an organization that is over sixty years old was born and grew, and became what it is today...The history of the Chymera Corporation is long and deserves more than to be summarized in just a few short minutes...perhaps one day I will be able to tell you more...I would like you to understand us..."

"...Being part of Chymera is a privilege that only very few ever experience...few are invited to join...You are right to guess that I am their C.E.O.. It is an office I hold with honor and with pride!"

Kendrick's eyes were almost glazed, such was the reverence with which he spoke his words.

IAN C.P. IRVINE

"...But for now, I want to talk to you about the Gen8tyx Company, and the Orlando Treatment. You've read the dossiers and the files and you know what they have achieved..."

"Excuse me, please. Before you go on..." Kerrin spoke up, wanting desperately to interrupt the tirade he was being subjected to.

"Yes?"

"I don't understand. This is all about the Orlando Treatment...keeping it secret...protecting the organization...but you just killed the founder and architect of the whole project! What will you do now?"

"Kerrin, to be frank, Sonderheim had become an embarrassment. His handling of the Gen8tyx takeover was a disaster. We couldn't believe what he did to the founding members...Cold blooded murder is not something the Chymera endorses! Frankly, the man had become a liability. Steps had already been taken to curtail his actions...steps, which ironically, you prevented being fully implemented!...But enough of that. Justice has been served...Yes, Sonderheim was the founder of the project, and yes, he was a genius. But there are *many* geniuses in Chymera...Have you heard of Sabre Genetics? Yes? Well, their staff, Chymera staff, now run Gen8tyx...and as from tomorrow I will appoint the CEO of Sabre into a new role as the head of Gen8tyx. I know he wants the job, and he's a good man. His hand-picked staff have already been running the Gen8tyx organization for the past two months..."

"We first became aware of Gen8tyx several years ago. We gave them some venture capital, helped them on their way...all done very discreetly at arm's length, you understand...but we kept a keen eye on them..."

"...Their progress was remarkable. We soon got our initial investment back, and more...then one day, we realized that things were going just a little too well. We realized that the scientists at Gen8tyx were beginning to push back the frontiers of science just a little too far. Things were becoming dangerous...Can you understand me when I tell you that the discoveries that they were making were beginning to threaten the very existence of our society?..."

"I can't say that I do...Please elaborate..." Kerrin replied.

"Society is based upon death. Everything we do is based upon the basic fact that life is limited, that one day we will die...The economics of our society are based squarely upon the fact that we grow old, that we stop working, that we get ill, that we retire, we become frail...and then we die...That's why we have children...to replace the dead and the dying..."

"...Gen8tyx was starting to tinker with the fundamental laws of nature...starting to make discoveries which would let people live longer, healthier, fitter lives..."

308

"But surely that's good. If people live longer, healthier lives, our productivity would go up, and the cost of healthcare would go down!" Kerrin interrupted.

"Yes,...in the short term there are some positive advantages...but with people remaining fitter and healthier for longer, fewer people would want to retire...the population would rise dramatically, there wouldn't be enough jobs to go around...which would lead to unemployment and depression, a cancer that would eat away at our society, and which, as history quite clearly shows, would ultimately lead to war..."

"Rubbish! We would just create more jobs, increase our output...more people buy more, sell more...the cycle of money would simply expand..." Kerrin argued back.

"Kerrin...more people means more pollution, more raw materials required for washing machines, more metal for cars, more power for all the new homes...where is all that going to come from...? Believe me, our scientists have gone over it a thousand times, for every benefit you can think of, for every positive aspect you can find to it, our guys came up with a thousand negatives. A thousand reasons why things will ultimately get worse..."

"This planet is not capable of continuing to support the rate at which the human population is growing. And if the truth were to be known, it's probably already too late to stop the pollution, the destruction of our forests, our atmosphere...What we need right now is for the population to decrease, dramatically, not to grow indefinitely..."

The President suddenly looked tired, and drawn.

"So, if you think it's so wrong and dangerous, why did the Chymera Corporation buy Gen8tyx?" Dana asked, speaking for the first time.

"Quite simply to control it...*and* to protect it... At the moment they are light years ahead of anybody else... and now we own Gen8tyx we own and can control all their patents. The knowledge base is ours...and if anyone else duplicates the work they've done in the years to come, we can prevent them from doing anything with any discoveries they make...we own the copyrights...and our lawyers will do anything to protect them...We will prevent the Orlando Treatment becoming publicly available. We will never release the news of our scientific progress or provide details of our discoveries. Can't you see?...We mustn't. We have no other choice. It is our moral duty to do so. We have to be cruel to be kind...If we let this knowledge get out, ultimately it will lead to the end of us all!"

Kerrin listened. Stunned.

He wanted to object to what the CEO of Chymera was saying...he wanted to shout his protest and disagree, but in spite of himself, he could see that there was sense behind what he was being told.

"So what do you do, simply disregard all that you have discovered?" Kerrin asked eventually.

"Of course not. In fact, we will continue the research to its natural conclusion. There is much to be learned that will benefit mankind, even though it can't be released to them! In fact, we are just about to start the next phase of the research..."

The President stood in front of Kerrin, looking down into his eyes as he spoke.

"Although we can't apply this knowledge to everyone we would like to, imagine what good we can do with it...Society is led by its leaders...if you have good leaders, you have, hopefully, a good society..."

"...Of course, we all make mistakes, but most of us learn from them...Unfortunately, one of the cruel aspects of nature is that as we grow older, the wisdom we learn from our experiences is taken away from us by senility or decrepitude, or death...Imagine what it would be like if our leaders, the people who control the destiny and lives of millions of people...if *they* were given the opportunity to exercise their life-long gained experience for longer. That instead of dying, or having to retire, just when they had accumulated the real wisdom that would enable them to govern properly and wisely, that they were allowed to continue to lead their people to even greater heights of success...imagine what it would be like if the wisdom of society could be kept and maintained, nurtured and allowed to flourish yet further...Imagine what it would be like if we could help the greatest artists and writers and musicians to continue to give their gift to mankind for many years longer than they currently can...take Ludwig Van Beethoven for example...how many more pieces of beautiful music would he have been able to compose if he had not gone so profoundly deaf,...or think about what other wonders of literature William Shakespeare would have been able to produce if he had lived another twenty or thirty or fifty years?...Think about it...and then imagine what would the world would be like now!"

Kerrin stood up from his seat, looking across at Dana. She was white faced, yet caught up in the words of the President.

"You're talking about giving the Orlando Treatment to the leaders of society?...In other words, you are suggesting that we create a new class of people...a semi-immortal race of humans that govern and dominate the rest of the world?"

"That's not exactly what I'm saying...the way you put it, it sounds cruel and sinister. That's not what this is about. We want to..."

"...And what buys the right to be given the Orlando Treatment? Money? Power?" Kerrin interrupted him.

"Perhaps, but also artistic ability, or outstanding service to humanity...Think Kerrin, *think*...And so what if money and power form part of the criteria for selection? Take Buz here: he runs a multinational industry employing tens of thousands of people...he built it from scratch...*he* did... Buz is the driving force and inspiration for all that's been achieved...and thanks to him tens of thousands of parents go home every night to a table full of food, and a family where the children sleep under a solid roof and have wonderful toys to play with. Buz doesn't just create money, he generates happiness and security for his employees. He's good at it. Successful. Now what happens to all those people when he dies or steps down? I'll tell you what, ...the chances are that the companies he owns will not prosper as well as they once did under his leadership. And that means that thousands of families could lose their jobs and their way of life...If we have the ability to protect their happiness and security by extending the ability of Buz to lead them into the future, and ensuring his ability to carry on making the right corporate decisions with continued vitality and intelligence, is that not something that we have a duty to do? I say it is! And if Buz is seen to benefit from it by being rewarded with long life and an expanded span of natural health, so what? I would think that that's the least form of reward that we can offer him for offering so much to so many others!"

"Kerrin...in war, everyone knows that the worst thing that can happen is to lose our leaders...without leaders the people cannot be led...In peacetime it is exactly the same. We owe it as a duty to our society to protect our leaders, to nurture them and give them long life....and if that is what the Orlando Treatment can do, then so be it!"

The President sat down in his chair, and put his face in his hands. He sighed heavily, then looked up at Kerrin.

"Please sit with me Kerrin. I have something to ask you..."

Kerrin looked at Dana, then returned to his seat, facing the President.

"Kerrin, you've seen the documents, and you've read the dossier on the Orlando Treatment. You know the potential of this research...we could sit here and discuss this for years, but we can't. A few days ago the board of the Chymera Corporation met and were appraised of the success of the project so far. The Board agreed to proceed with the research and to start the next phase, which we are calling Phase Three. The threat you pose to the project was also discussed at the Board meeting, and it was a condition of the agreement for further funding that action was taken to ensure that the Washington Post is not able to expose the work that is being done, or the existence of the Chymera Corporation..."

"What are you saying, Mr President? Are you threatening me?"

Kendrick looked across at Dana, his eyes resting long enough on her legs and her wheelchair for Kerrin and Dana to notice it.

"No, not at all. On the contrary...I look at the both of you now and I am, quite honestly, impressed by the fire and the passion with which you have fought to get here today. That you have strived through so much to fight for 'justice', speaks highly of you both as individuals. And it touches me that such bright young lives were destroyed by the accident that you both had... Imagine what fantastic lives you could have led together if you hadn't both been crippled? Yes...It's not just Dana that's in that wheelchair...you both are! The car accident robbed you both of the future that you had planned together. One stupid moment in time that took away all your dreams..."

"...You've both suffered...and I would bet that you Kerrin, have suffered as much up here as Dana has suffered down there..." The President said, pointing to Kerrin's brain and to Dana's legs..."

"What would you both say, if I told you that I could offer you both back your dreams...that I could take away your pain, that I could remove the guilt you still suffer from, Kerrin, every time you look at your beautiful wife...and that I can give Dana back the ability to walk? And what if I were to offer you both back your youth...to return to both of you the years that you have lost, that were stolen from you by one tragic, unplanned moment in time?"

Kerrin and Dana looked at each other in confusion.

"What are you suggesting, Mr President?"

"I am asking you to join us. To become part of the Chymera Corporation! The Orlando Treatment is not a dream...It works! ...Join us! Take part in the next round of clinical trials, with myself and other leaders from the Chymera Corporation, and become part of the new elite...Our doctors have already looked at Dana's medical files and have assured me that the therapeutic cloning techniques that have been pioneered in the Orlando Treatment using stem cell technology, will be able to successfully re-grow the areas that were damaged in Dana's spine. If she takes part in the trials I can promise you that within months, maybe weeks, Dana will walk again...And I think that you have already witnessed for yourself that one of the major benefits of the treatment is the ability to stop and partially reverse the ageing process...We can take ten or twenty years off your biological age! We can make you both twenty-eight again, and hopefully we can help you to maintain that age for the rest of your life..."

"...Just think! You can both be young again...you can travel the world, laugh and run together, swim in the ocean, climb mountains...whatever it is that you always wanted to do together...it's yours for the taking!"

"And in return, what do we give you?" Kerrin asked, holding Dana's hand tightly.

"Nothing...you just promise that you will never betray the brotherhood of which you become a part...It works two ways...We keep you alive, healthy and fit, to make sure that you are able to make the phone calls to your boss and whoever else has the documents...and in return, you make sure that the documents are never released to the world."

Kerrin stood up, and walked away from his chair towards the window of the Oval Office. He looked out over the grounds of the White House, not seeing how green the grass was or the beautiful deep blue of the sky above. His mind was awash with emotion.

He felt dizzy, and faint, and his heart was racing.

They had lived through hell this past month. People they knew had been murdered. Friends, relatives and acquaintances. They had all gone. And the suffering of the bereaved relatives would still go on for year after year, for longer than Kerrin would dare to guess. Death is always harder on those left behind.

He turned to look at Dana, and for the first time in years he saw how old she had become, how the years had begun to add lines to her face and how the skin had slowly begun to lose its elasticity and luster. He looked at her wheelchair, and for a fleeting second he could feel the jarring impact of two cars colliding on a remote country road, and the sight of Dana's bloodied and torn body in the wreckage of the accident so many years before.

And then he could see two people running along a beach, splashing through the waves, before they both plunged headlong into the surf and swam out to sea, swimming hard and fast, ...together.

"So Kerrin," the President asked the Washington reporter. "What will it be? Will you join us ...or destroy us?"

Kerrin glanced across at Buz who had been silent throughout, but who now watched Kerrin expectantly, his attention not leaving him for a second.

Kerrin walked up to Dana, and looked down into her eyes. She reached up her hand towards him and he took it in hers. Tears were streaming down her face, and it was only then that he realized that he too was crying.

Kerrin looked back at the President, and began to form the answer with his lips. He knew that there may be times in the years to come that he would hate himself for the answer he was about to give.

Yet really, in spite of it all, there was only one answer he could give...

It was one word.

CHAPTER 45
Epilogue
January
Chapters Bookshop
Washington D.C.

The young couple walked into the bookshop, as they so often did these days. They split up at the door, and each went their own way. He to the thrillers and crime sections, and she to cooking, travel or world geography.

They liked to travel a lot, and she wanted to get the latest edition of the Lonely Planet Guide to Southern Africa.

The young man, probably somewhere in his middle-to-late twenties, passed by a display of the latest hardbacks in the centre of the shop, and stopped in his tracks.

The podium was covered by six different piles of books, each belonging to a different up-and-coming author. Above each pile there was an upright plastic card with the writer's name on it and a picture of the author smiling proudly at his achievement.

The young man picked up one of the books and flicked it open to the inside cover to read the summary of the plot. His hands were shaking.

Normally he would never buy a hardback, preferring to wait until it came out in the cheaper paperback form, but without hesitation the young man walked across to the cashier and handed the young assistant the book and his credit card.

"Good choice," she replied. " 'The Untamed Gene' has become one of the fastest selling books this month...if only the author were still alive, he'd be a very happy and wealthy man by now."

The young man took the book and his receipt and hurried over to find his wife in the travel section. A mixture of emotions swept through him as he searched for her amongst the rows of bookshelves. Excitement and fear mixing together to produce a curious blend of emotions.

According to the synopsis on the back cover, the book was a fictional thriller based on the real work and actual discoveries of the author, the now world-famous scientist called Mike Gilbert.

Published after the author was mysteriously killed, according to the author's surviving fiancée, the thriller was an exposé of the secret work conducted at the genetics company the author used to work at, ... before he died in such strange circumstances...

Book in hand, the young man found his wife who was lost in adventures in foreign lands in a corner at the back of the book store. She looked up and smiled.

"Anything interesting?"

"Yeah, look at this..."

She took the book from his outstretched hands, and read the cover. Her eyes lit up as she read the summary on the inside cover.

"But...?"

"That's not the worst of it...look at the first chapter!"

She turned quickly to the first page of the book, read the first line, and then laughed.

"I'm sorry, darling...he's stolen your thunder!"

"Talk about coincidence! The bastard stole my line!" he said, looking over his wife's shoulder.

As far as first lines for a new novel go, it was a cracker. Two words. Simple, but effective:

"...So what?..."

THE END

ABOUT THE AUTHOR

Ian Irvine was brought up in Scotland, and studied Physics for far too many years, before travelling the world working for high-technology companies. Ian has spent a career helping build the internet and delivering its benefits to users throughout the world,...as well as helping to bring up a family. Ian enjoys writing, painting and composing in his spare time. His particular joy is found in taking scientific fact and creating a thrilling story around it in such a way that readers learn science whilst enjoying the thrill of the ride. It is Ian's hope that everyone who reads an Ian C.P. Irvine novel will come away learning something interesting that they would never otherwise have found an interest in. Never Science fiction. Always science fact. With a twist.

Other Books by Ian C.P. Irvine

The Crown of Thorns explores the power of genetics, explores the questions that the potential to clone humans will raise, and asks the ultimate question...what would happen if a scientist found a way to clone Jesus Christ?

London 2012 : What If? departs from the world of genetics and explores an interesting theory in Quantum Physics that raises the possibility for parallel worlds to exist alongside each other...and what would happen if a man who wondered what other types of lives he could be living had he made other choices, where unexpectedly to step from one world into another parallel world. "What If?" is also an interesting voyage through human emotions, and many readers will find themselves asking themselves similar questions that the lead character does as they read the book. As with both 'The Crown of Thorns' and 'The Orlando File', at the end of the book the reader is left thinking...and different readers may take away different views on how the novels did, or should have ended... It is hoped that in this way, the novels will make themselves ideal subjects for reading clubs or book clubs.

'The Sleeping Truth' is a romantic thriller that takes place in London, UK in the year 2005. Marrying Slovakia is a story about relationships, and how without trust, love cannot survive. Perhaps one of the first novels to tell this story from the eyes of a man, it will make you laugh, cry, and stop and think.

For men and women alike, it is a tale of the heart, set in the form of a romantic thriller that is set against the backdrop of the terrorist attacks in London in 2005. It is a tale of our time. A tale of love between West and East. Unlike the other very fast paced thrillers Ian has written, Marrying Slovakia starts more slowly, builds steadily, then speeds on to an unexpected conclusion.

'Haunted From Within' is a murder, mystery detective novel that deals with the sensitive area of Organ Donation and Transplantation. It is a fast paced contemporary medical thriller, based upon a true medical mystery that scientists and doctors do not yet understand, a medical phenomena that few understand and most are unaware of! The Story: When Peter Nicolson, a reporter with the Edinburgh Evening News, is almost killed by a gang leader out to make his mark, the only way to save his life is through a double kidney transplant. One of the first people in the world to be treated with the new genetic wonder drug 'SP-X4', Peter makes a remarkable recovery. Yet as he recovers, his personality begins to change, and he discovers that he can see visions of unsolved killings committed by a murderer that no one has ever caught. Peter sets out to solve the murders, to track down the killer, and find out the truth behind the visions that he sees. As time progresses, and as Peter uncovers a trail of death that stretches across the United Kingdom and Europe, the makers of 'SP-X4' watch his actions from afar, anxious that he will uncover the incredible truth behind their new drug treatment, and conspiring to make sure he does not succeed in revealing it to the world. 'Haunted From Within' is also the story of seven separate lives: readers will follow each character as the plot develops and their lives intersect, culminating in a surprise ending that few will predict.

'Alexis Meets Wiziwam the Wizard' : Ian's latest novel is his first attempt at writing a 'thriller' for children learning to read, and who are just discovering the joy of reading by themselves. 'Alexis Meets Wiziwam the Wizard' is a bit of fun, and hopefully your children will enjoy it too, if they are aged between 6-9 years old.

Ian hopes that if you honour him by spending the time reading one his novels, that you will find it a positive experience, and enjoy it. He also invites you to email him and let him know if you did or did not enjoy the novel. And if you did, what were your favourite parts?

iancpirvine@hotmail.co.uk

www.iancpirvine.com.

24553695R00180

Printed in Great Britain
by Amazon